Ace Books by Alan Dean Foster

INTERLOPERS

Alan Dean Foster

ACE BOOKS, NEW YORK

This is a work of fiction. Name, characters, places, and incidents either are the product of the author's imagination or are used fictitiously, and any resemblance to actual persons, living or dead, business establishments, events, or locales is entirely coincidental.

INTERLOPERS

An Ace Book / published by arrangement with
Thranx, Inc.

PRINTING HISTORY
Ace mass-market edition / May 2001

Copyright © 2001 by Thranx, Inc.
Cover art by Jerry Vanderstelt

All rights reserved.
This book, or parts thereof, may not be reproduced in any form
without permission.
For information address: The Berkley Publishing Group,
a division of Penguin Putnam Inc.,
375 Hudson Street, New York, New York 10014.

Visit our website at
www.penguinputnam.com

Check out the ACE Science Fiction & Fantasy newsletter!

ISBN: 0-441-00847-X

ACE®
Ace Books are published by The Berkley Publishing Group,
a division of Penguin Putnam Inc.,
375 Hudson Street, New York, New York 10014.
ACE and the "A" design
are trademarks belonging to Penguin Putnam Inc.

PRINTED IN THE UNITED STATES OF AMERICA

10 9 8 7 6 5 4 3 2

One

Khuatupec was hungry.

He stirred within the stone. As solid and impermeable as it was beautifully carved, it stood upright alongside its unformed and uninhabited basaltic kin. No light penetrated the ancient temple where the stones reposed. None had entered for hundreds of years. The absence of illumination did not matter to Khuatupec. Light meant nothing to him. He and his kind utilized means and methods of perception that did not require its presence.

Within him boiled The Hunger; a sere, seething whirlpool of dissatisfaction and emptiness. Considering how long it had been since last he had fed, it was surprising the discomfort was not worse. Yet he contented himself. For the first time in living memory, food was at hand. Something to eat. Something to suck at.

He divined its presence nearby, had been aware of it for some time now. Some days would see it draw tantalizingly close, others would find it moving maddeningly away. There was nothing Khuatupec could do but wait. In order for him to be able to feed, physical contact with the food was necessary. Because of his nature, his *situ,* that contact had to be initiated by the food itself. He envied others of his kind who could move about more freely in search of sustenance. Most of them were much smaller than he, however, and needed less feeding. His kin were multitudinous and diverse, but there was only one Khuatupec. He. Him.

Having been patient for so many centuries, he would perforce have to be patient a while longer. But it was frustrating to have so much fresh food so close at hand yet be unable to taste any of it.

Khuatupec waited within the carved stone, and brooded, and contemplated the ecstasy that was eating. Soon, he persuaded himself. Soon enough the taste, the pleasure, the exhilaration of feeding would once more be his. He wondered which of the food would be the first to make contact.

The condor descended in a lazy spiral, great hooked beak and immense black wings inclining in the direction of something unseen and dead. It reminded Cody of the much smaller turkey vultures that haunted the skies above the family ranch back home. Wiping perspiration from his forehead, he crouched down and resumed gently blowing dust from the punctured skull in the center of square N-23.

The hole in the hoary cranium was large enough to admit his little finger. Working carefully within the delimitating grid of white cord that was suspended above the soil, he finished cleaning the skull before gently depositing it in a waiting box padded with bubble paper. Unlike the Incas, for whom considerable evidence of the primitive surgical procedure existed, there was no record of the Chachapoyans practicing trepanning. If detailed study of the skull turned out to prove that they had employed the procedure, the results might serve as the basis for a formal paper. "Evidence of cranial medical practices among the Chachapoyans circa A.D.1100-1400—Apachetarimac site, Amazonas Province, northern Peru." An effort suitable for *Archaeological Review*, certainly, with a slightly more sensationalized version made available for *Discover* magazine or *Popular Science*.

Pictures—he needed pictures. Straightening, he turned and reached for the rucksack that was lying on the higher level nearby. On the far side of the excavation, Langois and Kovia were working on their knees on opposite sides of a cracked monochrome pot. It displayed several of the same designs that decorated the tawny limestone walls that formed the ancient citadel. Unlike the Incas, whose dark stonework tended to be smooth and featureless, the Chachapoyans had incorporated an assortment of patterns into the foundations of their round stone houses and rectangular temples. So far, diamonds, waves, and undulating figures that suggested serpents had been discovered.

Pots were rare. Apachetarimac was not Tucume or Pacatnamu, ancient cities that had hardly been touched by archaeologists or tourists. Around their weathering adobe pyramids lay millions upon millions of potsherds, relics of a thousand years of pottery-making by cultures with magical names: Chimu, Moche, Lambayeque. The Chachapoyans had not left behind nearly as many clay vessels depicting their lives and beliefs. Nor were the Calla Calla Mountains as conducive to the preservation of pottery as was the dry coastal desert. The cracked pot was a fine discovery. Even so, Cody did not envy Langois and Kovia. He was content with his punctured skull.

After taking several close-ups of the skull as it rested In its box, he removed it and set it on the chest-high dirt ledge nearby. Checking the position of the sun, he tried to establish what he thought was the most dramatic angle for another photo. He could shoot up against the sky, but finally decided to use the distant mountains as background. Wearing their blankets of green and soaring to heights of fourteen thousand feet and more, they would make a colorful backdrop for the dark brown bone.

Apachetarimac, he mused as he clicked off shots on the digital camera and then checked them in the viewscreen. Having conquered and absorbed the Chachapoyans as they had the majority of cultures in western South America, the Incas had rechristened many of the cities inhabited by their new subjects. They had left behind few clues as to the reasons for some of their choices. Some, like Machu Picchu and Ollyantaytambo, were obvious. Apachetarimac, which translated from the Quechua as "sacred talking spot," was not. If his skull were capable of speech, it probably could have provided some answers. But the brain that had once inhabited the weathered, dark brown ovoid had long since become food for worms.

Where it might have made another person queasy to think of it in such a setting, the prospect of the evening meal set off a mild chain reaction in Cody's stomach. Though tall and lanky of build, he was no more immune to the pangs of hunger than were his smaller colleagues. A steady diet of physical labor in the thin air at nearly ten thousand feet worked up ravenous appetites. Frowning slightly, he placed the skull back in its padded box and wondered if today dinner might be any different from what was expected. He doubted it. Vizcaria, the camp cook, was nothing if not predictable. Cody would gladly have handed over ten bucks for a decent chicken-fried steak.

He would have to be satisfied with the thought and the memory. Here in the heights of the Calla Calla Mountains there were no roads and no restaurants. Choctamal, the nearest town, was three days' hard ride to the north on the back of a plodding, crotch-splitting mule. The nearest real restaurant was in the provincial capital of Chachapoyas, another four hours' frightening ride down a narrow, single-lane road boasting some of the longest, steepest drop-offs Cody had ever seen. Coming as he did from the relatively flat hill country of south-central Texas, he had a harder time than some of his friends with the thousand-foot precipices that seemed to lie beneath every bend in the lonely dirt track. Frankly, he preferred the mules to the brake-pad-deprived minibuses and pickups.

"Looking good, Mr. Westcott!" a voice boomed from above. Langois and Kovia glanced up briefly before returning to their own work. Dr. Harbos would query them in due time.

Martin Harbos, Ph.D., was director of the excavations at Apachetarimac. Five-ten or so, he was half a foot shorter than the senior graduate student laboring beneath him. A candle or two shy of sixty, he still had more hair than anyone else on the project, though every strand had long ago turned a startling silvery-white, the blatant hue of a cheap Santa Claus wig. Rather than being a consequence of normal aging, the network of deep lines that crevassed his face was inherited from his ancestors. His skin was burned brown from years of field work, and beneath his shirt and shorts small, corded muscles exploded like caramel popcorn. He had the bluest eyes Cody had ever seen, a ready sense of humor, and the ability to flay a student naked with a casual, sometimes off-hand comment.

Today he chose to be complimentary. "Trepanning?" He was crouching at the edge of the excavation, peering down at the skull in the box.

"I'd like to think so, Dr. Harbos." Though friendly, even jovial, the professor insisted on the honorific. Fraternizing between officers and enlisted men was limited on Harbos's shift, Cody thought with a hidden smile. "It'll take lab studies to confirm or deny." He indicated the packaged skull. "The edges of the cavity are pretty regular, but it could have been made by a weapon."

Harbos nodded. "Or something else." His expression was sympathetic. "It's always frustrating when you find something potentially exciting in the field and know that it won't be properly identified for months." Straightening, he moved on, keeping clear of the rim of the straight-sided excavation so as not to knock dirt or pebbles into the hole.

Pleased with this mildest of compliments, Cody carefully began to fold the lid of the box closed, bending the corners of the cardboard so the top would stay shut until it could be reopened in the field lab. Somewhere, a bird chirped. The paucity of birds in the semi-cloud forest was striking. Unlike elsewhere in the Andes, here they kept to themselves, as if their boisterous warbling might disturb the sleeping mountains.

Except for the condors and the buzzards, of course. Ever on the lookout for harbingers of death, they had a job to do that required constant patrolling of the translucent blue sky. Their occasional appearances provoked admiring comment from those of his fellow students who hailed from the city, which he ignored. Back home, such aerial visions were common as dirt.

He wondered how many other intact skulls might lie buried and waiting to be found nearby. By the standards of the remarkable but little-known Chachapoyan culture, Apachetarimac was not a big site, no more than four hundred meters long by ninety wide. Gran Vilaya, for one, boasted far more individual structures, and Cuelap was more physically imposing. But Apachetarimac remained one of the most impressive, occupying the top of a forest-clad mountain whose sides fell away sheer on three sides. Walls of cut limestone over a hundred and twenty feet high formed the basis of the citadel, with the interior structures rising higher still. Combined with dense overgrowth, its inaccessibility had kept it hidden from the outside world for the last five hundred years.

Locals whose farms clung with the tenacity of dirty spider webs to the sides of nearby mountains knew of its existence but had no reason to speak of it to the outside world. While they had made it plain they didn't care for the busy visitors who delighted in digging in the dirt, neither did they attempt to interfere with the excavation. The presence of a pair of Peruvian federal policemen, camped on site to prevent looting and ward off any wandering *narcotráficos*, also served to keep the superstitious locals from causing any trouble.

"Well, does inspiration strike, have you been bitten by a fer-de-lance, or is this paralysis due to an inability to decide whether to go forward, back, or simply wait for instructions?"

He turned sharply. The only time Alwydd could look down on him was when he was standing in a hole. Not that she was particularly short, but he was the tallest person in camp. For that matter, he was the tallest person in this immediate region of Peru, height not being a notable characteristic of the local indios and mestizos.

Embarrassed, he fumbled for a witty response and, as always, came up with nothing. She was much too quick for him. Harbos could keep up with her, giving as good as he got, but no one else in camp had her lightning wit. She was also brilliant, and beautiful, about a year away from her doctorate, and convinced that she and not Cody ought to be Harbos's first assistant in the field. If not wit, however, Coschocton Westcott possessed endless reservoirs of patience. In an archaeologist, that was the far more valued commodity. Brilliance was cheap.

He had never met so attractive a girl so indifferent to

her appearance. From the dirt-streaked baggy bush pants to the equally frumpy beige-toned field shirt, she looked every inch a bad copy of a silent screen clown after a particularly rough car chase. The limp-brimmed hat that slumped down around her ears sat atop her head like broccoli on a stalk, rising to unnatural heights in order to accommodate the long hair wound up beneath. A mussed pixie drifting through a khaki wilderness, he mused. For all that, a most erotic pixie.

Forget it, he told himself firmly. Though he had never asked, and she had not volunteered the information, he would bet that she wrote regularly to several captivated males back in the States. Dazzling young doctors or up-and-coming investment bankers, no doubt. Gangly half-breed dirt-grubbers from West Hicksville were not likely to fit neatly into her definition of potential mate material.

Everyone had tried, he knew. He'd even seen the temptation in Harbos's face. You had to give the good doctor credit, though. He might brush up against his students every now and then, but he was quick to voice apologies—even if he didn't feel apologetic. It struck Cody abruptly that she was still standing there, looking down and waiting for some kind of response.

"I'm just packing Curly here for the trip to the lab." He indicated the skull.

With the agility of a gymnast she hopped down to the mid-level shelf, careful not to kick any dirt into the excavation. Kneeling while pushing back the brim of her rumpled hat, she scrutinized the vacant-eyed skull thoughtfully.

"Not exactly the second coming of the Lord of Sipán," she quipped tartly.

"What is?" The great, unlooted tomb of the Moche chieftain that had been discovered near the coast was unparalleled in the history of South American archaeology.

Its gold, silver, and lapidary treasures were the stuff of every field worker's dreams.

"Nothing, I suppose. If this is Curly, where are Manny and Moe?"

"Show a little respect for the dead." He nodded toward the silent skull. "That's a cousin of mine. Distant, but still a relation."

Straightening, she grinned down at him, enjoying the temporary and entirely artificial adjustment to their respective height. "Don't try that politically correct guilt crap on me, Cody Westcott." She tapped the box with a booted foot. "This dude's about as much your relative as Mary Queen of Scots is mine. It *is* a dude?"

"I believe so. Kimiko will make the final determination." Kimiko Samms was the group's forensic anthropologist, a specialty that required her to live in even closer proximity to the long dead than her colleagues. "I can feel a kinship across the centuries to whoever this person was."

"Funny." Reaching back, she scratched the arch of her behind through the soft bush poplin of her pants. "All I can feel are chigger bites."

"Salar should have something for that. If he doesn't, I do." Turning away, Cody started toward the steps that had been cut into the dirt above a nonsensitive corner of the site. Sweat poured down his face, mixing with accumulated dirt and dust—archaeologist's rouge. Time was passing and he wanted to get the skull to the field lab and return in time to do some more digging before the daylight shrank too far below the undulating green horizon. The sweat did not bother him. At Apachetarlmac's altitude the air began to cool rapidly once the sun had passed its zenith.

"What's that?"

He almost didn't turn. In addition to her beauty, wit,

and intelligence, Kelli Alwydd was renowned in camp for her jokes, not all of them practical. At least, he mused, she hadn't shouted "snake!" or something equally juvenile. As he paused, he wondered why he was reacting at all, giving her what she wanted. Maybe, he decided, he was a sucker for clever women. Or maybe he was just a sucker. Irrespective of the reason, he turned.

She was in the pit, having jumped down from midlevel so softly that he hadn't heard her land. Crouching, she squinted in the receding light at a portion of grid square V-9. Only slightly uncomfortable at finding the pose as pretty as it was professional, he ambled over to join her, affecting an air of studied disinterest.

"Let me guess." He fought to keep a lid on his trademark sarcasm. "A solid gold peanut, like those in the necklace from Sipán? Or is it just silver? Silver-and-turquoise ear ornaments, with articulated figures?"

She did not look up. "No. I think it's another skull." Reaching into one of her many shirt pockets, she brought out a pair of brushes: one bold, the other fine-haired sable, and began methodically flicking at the dirt in front of her feet.

He could have knelt to peer over her shoulder, stealing a small pleasure from the proximity. Instead, he walked around to crouch down in front of her, careful to step cleanly over the white cord that sliced the excavation into neat, easily labeled squares. Her brushwork was rapid and precise, like the rest of her.

Reminiscent of scorched polystyrene, the smooth curve of a human cranium began to emerge from the soil of ages in which it lay entombed. It was large, but not outrageously so. Like the rest of their South American brethren, the Chachapoyans were a people of modest stature.

With a sigh, Cody straightened. The sun was going

down fast now. It would be dark soon, no time to be bumbling around in the area of active excavation. Aside from the danger of stumbling into an open pit, a misplaced foot could do irreparable damage to half-seen, half-exposed relics. Dr. Harbos was an easygoing individual, but not where the work of serious archeology was concerned. One of his rules required everyone to be back in camp by the scheduled dinnertime. In addition to preventing damage to the sites by overzealous diggers, this was also a safety measure. Snakes and uncomfortably large spiders emerged soon after sundown, and in a land of precipitous cliffs and hillsides, wandering about after dark was not a good idea anyway.

"It's another skull, all right," she murmured. Busy appraising the sunset, he did not look down. "But this one's weird."

That drew his attention back to his companion. With the sun setting, it was already dark in the bottom of the pit. "What do you mean, 'weird'? That's not acceptable scientific terminology."

Bending over the spot, she blocked his view of the emerging bone. "It's got a hole in it, like the one you're taking to the lab—but not like the one you're taking to the lab."

"Is that anything like the sense you're not making?" He knelt to have a look for himself, frowning slightly. His flashlights reposed on the compact field desk back in his tent. At the same time, repressed excitement surged through him. A second trepanned skull lying close to the first would be a good indication that they had stumbled on an important ceremonial or medicinal center, perhaps the nearest thing that existed to a Chachapoyan infirmary.

Sitting back, she continued to work with the two brushes, using the larger to sweep away clumps of earth and the smaller for cleaning the depressions in the skull.

Immediately, he saw what had inspired her comment. There was indeed a cavity in the new skull, but it was considerably larger than the one marring the specimen he was going to deliver to the field lab. No only was it larger, but irregularly shaped, with ragged edges. Even the clumsiest shaman-surgeon could not possibly have expected to cure any patient by opening such a grievous lesion. Furthermore, it was—weird.

Without waiting for her to finish exposing the base of the skull, he reached down and cupped his long fingers around it, ignoring her protests as he pulled it from the earth. For the first time in centuries, it was fully exposed to the air.

"Hey!" she objected, "I haven't finished cleaning that!"

"Look at this," he said, holding the osseous discovery out to her, his right index finger tracing paths across the bone as he spoke. "This isn't weird—it's impossible."

Around the rim of the opening in the roof of the skull, a jagged ridge of bone the diameter of a silver dollar rose upward, like water rising around a pebble dropped in still water. It stood frozen in time, testament to some unimaginable cerebral convulsion.

Kelli stared. "That's pretty extreme. It looks like the inside of his head blew up. Some kind of pressure buildup in the cerebral fluid?" Her tone had turned serious.

"I don't know. I didn't have that much physiology." Straightening, he held the second skull up to the rapidly fading light. "It sure doesn't look like the result of some intentional medical procedure, no matter how primitive. What could cause the bone to rise up and solidify in this kind of position?" Carefully, he ran one finger along the thin, sharp edge of the cranial crater.

She shook her head. "You got me. It's ugly. Samms is going to go crazy when she sees this."

Gently, he knelt once more to replace the skull in the

slight depression from which it had been removed. "I haven't got another suitable box or any more bubble wrap here, and it's getting dark. We'll come back for it tomorrow."

Her eyebrows rose slightly. "We? This is your dig." She nodded briskly to her left. "Mine's over there, with Marie-Therese, at the base of the serpent wall."

He protested. "You found this. It's unusual, and you're entitled to the credit."

Her head turned slightly to one side as she gazed up at him, carefully placing her brushes back in her shirt pocket. "Okay, then. 'We' it is. I'll come over early and we can pack it up together."

"Good. That's fair." Her acquiescence pleased him for reasons that he did not elucidate to himself. "Walk back to camp?"

"We'd better." She scanned the darkening sky speculatively. "Harbos won't wait five minutes before sending someone to look for us if we're late. Then we'll get chewed out for wasting camp resources, et cetera."

"Give him credit." Cody's long legs made easy work of earthen steps his companion had to negotiate with care. "We haven't lost anybody on this dig yet."

"Sometimes I'd like to get lost."

Joining him on the surface, she studied the surrounding mountains. In the distance, smoke rose from the cooking fires of small, vertically challenged farms. No contrails marred the pristine purpling sky. Northern Peru did not lie at the intersection of any major transcontinental jet routes, and there was virtually no local air traffic. A silence that was largely extinct elsewhere in the world stalked the immense mountain valleys like some vast, nebulous, prehistoric visitant.

"Me too." Together they followed the trail through the grass that led toward camp, dodging around the huge trees that grew out of the citadel's soil-cloaked foundation. Around them, the circular walls of empty buildings turned single doorways to the sun, and the rectangular pyramid of the recently identified royal quarters cast its long, broad shadow on their progress.

The narrow defile, barely wide enough for one person at a time to squeeze through, cut steeply downward through the hundred-foot-high wall. Where it opened onto the rocky, grass-covered slope it was still just wide enough for two men to enter abreast. Eminently defensible against an attacking enemy, it made the immense stone walls that flanked the opening seem even higher and more impressive than they were.

Turning to their right, they followed the trail that had been etched into the slope along the base of the wall, careful to keep it close at hand. Wander too far away and a thousand-foot drop waited to greet the indifferent. Ahead, the flicker of lanterns coming to life began to dance within the intensifying darkness. There were more than twenty tents for the field team, plus additional lean-tos and makeshift shelters for the native help. By far the largest canopy, a substantial, well-anchored sweep of tough jungle-resistant weave, served as dining room, lecture hall, library, and recreation area. Another, slightly smaller, housed the field lab.

"Hungry?" he asked her.

"I'm always hungry, Cody."

He tripped over the compliment before he realized it. "I've seen you eat, and I wonder where you put it."

"Up here." She tapped the side of her head. "Mental exertion burns a lot of calories." In the twilight, her smile shimmered like one of the approaching lanterns. "You don't exactly starve yourself."

"When you grow up always hungry, you get in the habit of eating anything and everything that's offered to you." Espying a long, twisting shape on the trail ahead of them, he hesitated only an instant before resuming his stride. In this part of the world, a smart hiker was wary even of fallen branches. Anything with multiple curves demanded a second look.

Her smile faded away and her eyes locked on his as best they could in the gathering darkness. "I don't know much about you, Cody. You're friendly, you'll stop work to chat with anyone, but you never talk about yourself." In the creeping shadows her slight shrug was barely perceptible. "This is only my second dig. Maybe that's the normal condition for more advanced field associates like yourself. I don't know. Or maybe it's just this place." A casual sweep of one hand encompassed mountains, valleys, and the citadel wall that towered skyward on their right. "Up here, everyone tends to focus on dead people."

"There's not much to know," he began, and for the next hour proceeded to give the lie to his own claim of conciseness. Considering how fast her mind and mouth worked, he was astonished in retrospect at how intently she listened.

Khuatupec was beside himself, literally as well as figuratively. The food was moving away! There was nothing he could do but fume silently, exactly as he had for hundreds of years.

Nor was he alone. Amnu writhed inside her tree as the food almost, but not quite, brushed against one of its branches. Tsemak twitched below the ground, inexorably wedded to his slice of subsurface stratum. Chakasx hummed within the stream that served as both home and prison. Throughout the citadel, the mountain, and the fortresslike slopes that had protected the Chachapoyans of Apachetarimac for centuries, They stirred. Moved about and were active as they had not been for more than five hundred years.

In that time, other food had come close, though none had been so tasty as this promised to be. Its sheer virgin delectability was unprecedented in Khuatupec's long experience. To have it pass so close, on so many occasions, was maddening. There was nothing he or any of the others could do. In order to eat, it was the food that would have to make proper contact with them. They could not leave their *situs* to initiate feeding. It was an infuriating, horrific existence, mitigated only by the fact that Khuatupec's kind were almost impossible to kill. Yet, he thought furiously, to suffer near immortality in a state of perpetual craving was as much curse as good fortune.

Even worse than not being able to feed on such delectables was the thought that contact might be made with another of his kind instead of him. Watching another feed in his place would be almost as intolerable as not being able to feed himself. Should that occur, there would remain only the hope of snatching up some carelessly discarded leftovers from the main feeding.

It might not come to that. He could still be the first. Thus far, none had managed to feed on the newly arrived food, although a week ago Sachuetet had come close. She had been too quick, however, from an eagerness to eat born of hundreds of years of abstinence. Sensing that something was not right, the food had freed itself before Sachuetet had been able to begin feeding fully. Her agonized cry of frustration and loss had resounded throughout the mountain.

From the others she drew no solace. Khuatupec and his kind knew nothing of compassion. They knew only how to wait, and to eat. The light was vanishing from the mountain as if sucked up by the ground. Light or dark, day or night, it was all the same to Khuatupec and the others. They never slept, not in the thousands of years of their existence. As a concept, sleep was known to them. Food, for example, slept. Trees and rocks and water did not. Khuatupec and Anmu and Tsemak and the others did not. Even if they had known how to go about initiating the process, it was something they would have avoided assiduously. Self-evidently, sleeping was dangerous. Sleeping was risky.

Sleep, and you might miss a feeding.

Two

As Coschocton Westcott and Kelli Alwydd had suspected it would, the second skull did indeed drive Kimiko Samms crazy. Struggling with her laptop, supplementing the information stored on her hard drive with disc after disc of data, the expedition's forensics expert could find no medical condition compatible with a culture as ancient as that of the Chachapoyans that might account for the spectacular and unsettling hole in the cloven skull. Such an extensive, presumably violent perforation should have driven the cranial bone inward, or shattered the surface into small fragments. Due to the age of the subject material, she could not even determine if whatever had caused the inexplicable calcareous formation was the cause of its owner's death.

"C'mon," Kelli asked her one day, "surely somebody couldn't walk around with a cranial deformation like that!"

The diminutive Samms was noncommittal. "People with far worse deformities have survived. The Elephant Man, lepers, Asian and African peoples suffering from severe elephantiasis, ancient dwarves and hunchbacks—you'd be surprised."

"It's not the circular bone ridge that makes me wonder, extreme as it is." Standing alongside the anthropologist, Kelli examined the skull and its inscrutable rupture. "It's the exposure of the brain."

"People can live with that, too." With the delicacy of a surgeon, Samms was using a fine brush to coat the interior of the skull with a stabilizing preservative. "Maybe not for long, but they can live."

Kelli's gaze drifted to the ingress to the big tent, the outside masked by the protective insect mesh that was all that presently restricted entry. "Whatever the cause of the initial trauma, it must have been hellishly painful. The mother of all migraines."

Samms concentrated on her work. "We don't know that. There are people with cranial deficiencies who, though they have to wear protective headgear all the time, live normal and productive lives." Sitting back, she rubbed at her eyes, swatted away a mosquito that had slalomed the mesh screen, and smiled speculatively up at her visitor. In front of her, the laptop glowed insistently.

"Speaking of productive lives, I haven't seen much of your tall, silent-type, warrior chieftain lately."

They shared a mutual chuckle. His ethnic origins notwithstanding, the owlish, workaholic Westcott was about as far from either woman's image of a warrior chieftain as could be imagined. Or as Samms had put it on a previous occasion, definitely not romance-novel cover material.

"He's not my warrior chieftain, or anything else." Alwydd's prompt reply was convincing. "But he is the senior student on site, so everybody has to spend time with him." She fiddled with a can of fixative. "That is, they do if they want answers to questions. Harbos is always busy."

"So's Westcott, from what I'm told." The anthropologist indicated the overflowing folding table that had to serve as lab bench, research facility, and office. "I wouldn't know, myself." She grinned, a misplaced elf with short black hair, dirt-streaked face, and impressively elevated IQ. "I don't get out much. People bring me bits of dead folk and from that I'm expected to explicate entire civilizations."

"Easier than trying to explicate Coschocton Westcott." Alwydd started for the mesh that separated the sterile, white interior of the tent from the green and brown world of bites and stings that lay in wait outside. "And he isn't even dead."

"Good luck trying to understand him." Samms snapped her high-powered, self-illuminating magnifying glasses back down over her eyes. "Me, I'll stick with dead people. Dead men might be full of contradictions, but at least they're soft-spoken. And more predictable in their habits."

"Cody's predictable." Alwydd drew the mesh aside and stepped out into the stark mountain sunshine. "He just doesn't know how to relax."

Hunched over instruments and skull, Samms replied without looking up. "Sure you want him to relax?"

Standing outside the tent, her expression scrimmed by the mesh, Alwydd stuck her tongue out at her seated, preoccupied colleague. "Funny lady. Stick to your bones."

Despite her studied indifference, Alwydd found herself spending more time in Westcott's company than could simply be justified by the need to know. Perhaps she was intrigued by his failure to fall all over her, as every other student on the site had already done. She loved a challenge, be it scientific or social. Or maybe it was because, despite his denials to the contrary, he *was* different. Or possibly it was nothing more than the ease with which they worked together. He was one bright guy, with a genuine insight and intelligence that did not arise solely from the study and memorization of standard texts. Or maybe she was just bored.

Not with her work. That was more than sufficiently fascinating in its own right. But aside from her studies, working on her paper, and keeping records, there wasn't much to do at Apachetarimac. Not with the nearest town days away by mule, and the only city of any consequence another half-day's jarring journey via minibus or jeep.

So she shadowed him when she could spare the time, admiring his skill with the tools of archaeology, his persistence and patience with something as insignificant as an unsculpted potsherd. And then one morning, when she awoke well before dawn, she decided to go and see if he wanted to join her in watching the sun come up over the east end of the citadel. That was when she found his tent empty, lights out, sleeping bag neatly zipped and stretched out on its cot. His predawn absence bemused her. Even workaholics at the site, of which Coschocton Westcott was not the only one, needed their sleep after a hard day of laboring in the cloud forest. Harbos insisted everyone be back in camp by a certain hour, but there was no monitoring of those who might want to arise and begin work before breakfast.

She ought to go right back to bed, she knew. But—where the hell was he? Making allowance for a possible call of nature, she waited outside the tent. Fifteen minutes later he still had not returned. A check of her watch showed the time: 3:20 A.M.. Even the Peruvian support staff, including those charged with preparing the morning meal, were not stirring yet.

Where in the name of Atahualpa's ghost had he gone? She had put fresh batteries in her flashlight just a week before. Thus armed against the night, with light and firm knowledge of the citadel's layout, she still hesitated. Stumbling around the site in the dark was not a good idea, even for someone like herself who knew the location of every pit and preliminary excavation. Curiosity finally overcoming caution, she started out of camp and up the main trail that led to the citadel.

There was no moon that morning, and the stars were far away and little comfort. The beam of illumination that her flashlight cut through the darkness seemed spare and constricted. Twisting trees heavy with orchids and other epiphytes pressed close around her. Soft-footed creatures and things with no feet at all rustled in the brush on either side of the narrow path. Snakes hunted at night, she knew, and wolf spiders as big as tarantulas, with half-inch-long brown fangs and multiple eyes that gleamed like black mabe pearls. She did her best to avoid brushing against the suffocating vegetation lest she spook something small and hungry that might be living among the leaves.

The improbable wall loomed above her, a familiar if not entirely comforting presence she kept on her left as she made her way to the slender defile that was the main entrance. As she climbed up and into the citadel proper, the ancient stonework shut out the starlight around her. A quick sideways turn and then she was through the keyhole and standing atop the artificial stone plateau of the city.

Of Coshocton Westcott, or anyone else, there was no sign. Only muted whispers in the grass and the sleepily moaning branches of trees indicated that there was anything else alive within the ruins. *This is stupid*, she told herself. Really stupid. It would be more stupid still if in the darkness she tripped and hurt a leg, or worse, stumbled into one of the excavated pits. Picking her way carefully along the cleared trails, she made her way toward the site where she and Westcott had found the two skulls.

It was empty, a dark, brooding maw among the encircling stones. That did it. Turning on one heel, she began to retrace her steps. It had been a ridiculous idea from the start. Wherever Westcott went wandering before dawn, it was evidently not among the ruins of the citadel.

Descending back through the narrow entrance, she emerged at the base of the wall and started to turn back toward camp, when something flickering in the distance caught her attention. It came, not from the vicinity of the tents nor from within the citadel, but partway down the steep, grass-covered slope of the mountain. Frowning, she watched it for a long moment before she was sure it was a flashlight. It might still be a local farmer, hunting for a lost sheep or pig or steer. Domesticated animals occasionally wandered up to the top of the mountain in search of fresh forage, trailing tired, fussing locals in their wake. But the poor farmers who populated the slopes and valleys of the Calla Calla could not usually afford flashlights, much less batteries. Switching off her own light, she stood motionless and alone in the darkness, the massive limestone wall towering into the night sky behind her, and waited.

Eventually a figure appeared, a dark silhouette advancing through the night. When it grew near enough for her to be certain of its identity, she called out softly. "Little early for aerobics, isn't it?"

Startled, Westcott's light came up, shining into her face. She put up a hand to shield her eyes. "Do you mind?" The beam was lowered immediately, and she switched her own on.

"Sorry. I didn't see you standing there, Kelli."

"No kidding. I thought you could see in the dark."

His expression was typically noncommittal. "I was preoccupied."

She nodded slowly. Neither of them moved in the direction of the camp. Overhead, a cavalry of clouds was advancing westward from the jungle, threatening to attack with warm, driving rain.

"Preoccupied with what?" In the absence of moonlight it was hard to make out his face.

"Nothing much," he replied evasively. "Just looking around."

"Down there?" She pointed down the slope. "Why? Is the view any better? It must be, for you to lose sleep over it. Funny thing, though: It's been my experience that sweeping panoramas lose some of their aesthetic impact when viewed in the middle of the night." She stepped past him. "If it's that striking, maybe I ought to have a look for myself."

Reaching out quickly, he caught her upper arm with one hand and held her back. The gesture was as uncharacteristic as it was unexpected, and her surprise was evident in the slight uncertainty in her tone. "*Excuse* me?" she said, slowly and deliberately.

He let go of her arm. She could feel him studying her, there in the darkness. "Okay." His reluctance was obvious. "I'll show you. But you have to promise to keep it a secret."

"Oho! Dug up something special, have we?" She was relaxed now, having found him out. "When did this happen? Yesterday? Last week?"

He was shaking his head as he turned to lead the way downward. "I've been coming here, early every morning, for weeks."

She paralleled his descent, careful where she put her feet. The grass was damp and slippery, and the grade dangerously steep. "That's not very sociable of you. I thought you were the ultimate team player." She made clucking noises with her tongue. "Dr. Harbos will not be pleased."

He was not as defensive as she expected. "I wanted

to make sure of what I had before I told anyone else. I found it. It's my discovery."

He was more emphatic than she had ever seen him. Then he *did* have emotions. "Well, I won't give you away." Looking downslope, she could see nothing but grass and the occasional tree. The ground cover began to give way to bare, loose rock. Despite her caution and her good hiking boots, she slipped once or twice. Westcott had no such difficulty. But then, she reminded herself, he was familiar with the terrain they were covering.

Featureless darkness loomed ahead. She felt a strong, upward welling breeze on her face, signifying the proximity of an unclimbable sheer drop. No wonder no one else had explored this way, she thought. Another twenty meters and they would need climbing gear; ropes and pitons and harnesses. Just when she was afraid he was going to lead her over an unscalable cliff, he stopped and turned abruptly to his left. A short walk brought them to an uncomfortably narrow ledge below which the mountain fell away to farms thousands of feet below. Raising her own light, she looked for him.

He had disappeared.

She experienced a brief but intense moment of genuine panic before she heard his voice. "Keep coming, Kelli. This way." The beam of his flashlight suddenly emerged from the side of the mountain.

The ceiling of the tunnel was low, in keeping with the modest stature of the Chachapoyans, and she had to bend slightly to keep from banging her head on the rock overhead. In front of her, Westcott was in worse shape, forced to bend almost double as he walked. Revealed by her light, telltale marks on the walls showed that the sides of the tunnel had been hewn out of the solid rock with simple hand tools.

The passageway emerged into a natural limestone cav-

ern. Stalactites were still in evidence, hanging like frozen
draperies from the roof, but there were no stalagmites.
These had all been cut away to leave behind a floor as
flat and smooth as any in the citadel. A portion of that
fortress, she realized, must now lie directly above them.
Raising her light, she searched for Westcott. Inadvertently
and unavoidably, her questing beam fell on one of the
enclosing walls. She let out an audible gasp.

As her light swept the wall, it revealed row upon row
of finely chiseled designs and pictographs, the most
eroded of which was infinitely better preserved than anything in the citadel overhead. For the first time, the neatly
etched abstract decorations of the Chachapoyans were
complemented by bas-reliefs of people, animals, and their
surroundings. It was an unprecedented record of
Chachapoyan life before the Incan conquest, perfectly preserved from damaging rain and wind in the confines of
the cavern.

"This is the greatest archaeological discovery in this
part of the world since Cuelap." Her awed words fell like
raindrops in the still air of the cave.

"I know." His guileless reply was matter-of-fact. "Even
the local people don't know about it. It's lain here, hidden away from the outside world, for at least five hundred years. Until I found it."

Utterly spellbound by the wondrous carvings, she let
her light trail along the wall, its beam revealing one marvel after another. "The farmers have been all over these
mountains. Maybe they kept this place a secret, but they
must know about it."

He shook his head. "The entrance was sealed and, as
far as I could determine, untouched."

She blinked and looked toward him. "Sealed? With
what?"

"Stones. Not Chachapoyan." In the darkness, his face

was hidden from her. "Incan. The Incas who conquered Apachetarimac and gave it its name closed this place up. I can show you a couple of the stones. The style is unmistakable: right angles on the inside, inclined on the outward-facing edge. Unfortunately, most of them rolled over the cliff below the entrance when I removed the first few." His voice fell slightly. "I was lucky I didn't get swept over with them."

"Why would the Incas seal this place up and leave the rest of the citadel exposed?" Her flashlight winked off, leaving her momentarily without illumination. She slapped the plastic tube hard, several times, and the light came back on. If they lost both lights in this place . . .

Not to worry, she told herself. There seemed to be only the one passage, and it ran in a straight line back to the outside. A check of her watch showed that dawn was approaching. Surrounded by something rather more exciting than newly exposed bones or a couple of broken pots, she was reluctant to leave, and said so.

He was already moving toward the passageway. "Come on. We don't want to be missed at breakfast."

"I'm not hungry," she replied truthfully, having stumbled across nourishment of another kind. "If you've been coming here for weeks, you must have formed at least a few preliminary hypotheses about this place. Why is it separate from the rest of the citadel? What about its function in Chachapoyan culture? What was all this for?" She swept her light around the sizable chamber. "And why did the Incas seal it up? I know you've been thinking about it, Cody. Yours is not an idle mind."

He coughed slightly. "Persistent little bird, aren't you? Sure, I've been formulating theory. But I am hungry." Bending low, he started back up the tunnel. "I'll share everything I know, I think, and what I suspect, if you'll just keep this quiet and not tell Harbos or any of the others."

"Sure thing." She followed behind him as he led the way out. "If you'll let me work with you."

He stopped so suddenly, she almost ran into him. For the second time, accidentally, his light flashed blindingly in her face. "I guess I don't have much choice, do I?"

"No, you don't." She enjoyed the feeling of control. "Not unless you toss me over the nearest cliff." His response was to go silent. "Don't be funny," she finally ordered him. "I'll keep your secret, and when you think the time is right to reveal all this to the rest of the group, I'll be there to support and confirm you as the discoverer. Also, you'll benefit from my expertise, which is different from yours."

She thought she could see him nodding to himself. "I could sure use some help. Not to mention the company."

"Then it's settled." Reaching out, she prodded him with her flashlight. "Maybe I lied. Maybe I'm getting a little hungry, too."

He ventured a hesitant smile. "You'll find that putting in three or four hours of work before anyone else is up does wonders for the appetite." Pivoting once more, he resumed following the tunnel outward.

True to her word, she uttered not a whisper about the passageway, the cavern, or their astonishing contents. Every morning she arose in pitch darkness, smothered the alarm, dressed silently and efficiently, and joined Westcott. Following the trail that had been cut to the citadel, they moved quickly and in silence, not talking or switching their lights on until it was time to begin the mildly treacherous descent to the tunnel entrance.

The first several days they were underground together Cody spent showing her the rest of the exposed reliefs and pictographs. Much more, he felt, lay concealed behind a collapsed wall of crumbled rock.

"Look at this," he instructed her, pointing upward. She expected to see more pictographs and reliefs. Instead, there was a noticeable dimpling in the ceiling, filled with broken stone. "I believe that to be the bottom of a shaft leading up to the citadel. Somewhere above us there must be an unexcavated chamber that holds the surface opening to this cavern."

She eyed the collapsed stone uneasily. "I don't think I want to spend a lot of time standing underneath that. What if our work here loosens the fill and it all comes crashing down?"

"I don't think that will happen. It's apparently been stable for centuries. Besides, I don't think it's a natural collapse. I think the shaft was plugged by the Incas, just like the entrance to the tunnel."

She frowned. "Why would they do that?"

He was kneeling beside his collection of tools for digging and cleaning. "When we find that out, we'll know why they sealed the entrance to this cave."

Bending, she knelt to work alongside him with dental pick and whiskbroom. "Couldn't have been much of a seal if you were able to take it apart all by yourself."

He gently brushed debris from a relief showing men and women working in a field. "Maybe something else kept people away. A taboo, priestly warnings, royal edict from Cuzco—sooner or later, we'll find out." His confidence was infectious.

Two weeks passed before they stumbled across the second tunnel. Narrower than the first, it proved a difficult passage even for Alwydd. She was amazed at how lithely her much taller companion wriggled wormlike through the cramped corridor.

They emerged into a second, smaller chamber. Unlike

the one that now lay behind them, the new discovery bore all the hallmarks of artificiality. No broken speleotherms presented themselves for examination. This was a room that had been hollowed out by hand, the result of back-breaking physical effort on the part of hundreds of hands working over many dozens of years. No shaft, blocked or otherwise, marred the polychromed ceiling.

Disappointment followed discovery. No one had ever found a Chachapoyan royal tomb, and the room seemed a perfect candidate. Their lights did not flash off gold or silver, turquoise or lapis lazuli. They did, however, reveal a large round stone situated in the center of the room. Unlike the surrounding limestone, it was dark granite. Somehow, it had been carried or dragged from elsewhere to this improbable site.

Very dark granite, Cody thought. Closer inspection of the stone showed why.

"Bloodstains." Raising his light, he played it around the intricately decorated walls. If anything, the carving here was even more refined than that which filled the larger chamber behind them. "This was a place of sacrifice."

"Sure was." The unflappable Alwydd was already checking her camera preparatory to methodically record-ing the succession of exquisite if bloodthirsty reliefs that lined the circular walls. "Let's get to work. We've only got an hour before we have to be back in camp."

As they began, they sensed nothing. The atmosphere did not grow heavy, the darkness did not press any closer, trying to strangle their lights. But around them, beneath them, above them, an ancient unwholesomeness stirred. It existed in a silent frenzy of expectation. As they toiled, Westcott and Alwydd occasionally made contact with a relief or ran speculating fingers over stones and stains. But never the right stone, or the right stain. Millimeters away from havoc and ruin and ultimate despair, they worked on unaware, their living, breathing, human presence driving an unseen host to fevered distraction. To the two who worked largely in silence, side by side, nothing was amiss in the archaic chamber. Nothing disturbed their work or interfered with their efforts. The only things that pressed close around them were their thoughts, the cool, damp mountain air, and the mold of ages.

So when old Elvar Ariola, one of the mule wranglers and camp assistants, went mad, they did not make the connection.

The food was very near. Nearer than it had been in a long, long time. Utchatuk trembled with anticipation, while all the others of her kind looked on with a mixture of envy and hope. If they could not feed, they could at least try to imagine the satisfaction and satiation of another. There had been *so* many missed opportunities, so many close chances.

Bending, Ariola reached for the dead, broken limb preparatory to tossing it aside, making a clearer path for the mule he was leading. Braying and bucking, the pack animal was resisting the reins for no apparent reason. The stream of barnyard Spanish the elderly wrangler spat at the animal had even less effect than usual. Muttering under his breath, he wrapped leathery, toughened fingers around the fallen piece of insect-gnawed wood.

He never felt a thing.

A vast, inaudible, imperceivable sigh swept over the mountaintop and rushed down into the deep valleys. *Another* had fed. And would continue to feed, for a long and satisfying while. The psychic ripple in the ether was not felt by any of the humans working at the site; not by the researchers, their superiors, or the locals who took care of the mundane details of camp life. But four hundred feet below, a farm dog began howling for no apparent reason, and in the cloud forest across the ridge, a flock of startled blue-headed parrots exploded from the tree in which they had been roosting. Otherwise, all was silent, normal, unchanged.

Except—the one who had been fortunate enough to feed was greedy. Having entered into and penetrated the food, Utchatuk should have settled down to a long and comfortable residence, in the manner of any successful parasite. Instead, she began to feed continuously, upsetting the natural balance of her unknowing host, undermining its stability. The others of her kind could do nothing with her. They could only remonstrate as best they were able, but were powerless to affect her directly. She continued to feed without pause, engorging herself on her host, shivering with delight at the sensations of satiation that coursed through her.

The result, of course, was that in a very short while she succeeded in severely damaging the host. Gravely unbalanced, it went mad. Only a few days had passed from the time Utchatuk had begun to feed until, clutching its head and rolling its eyes, the host flung itself screaming over the side of a sheer cliff in spite of the startled, last-second effort of other food to stop it. The result was tragic. For a little while the food congregated all in one place, confused and out of reach of any of those who would feed. Worse, in her haste to gorge herself, Utchatuk had failed to reproduce. She would leave none behind to follow her.

Tragic, yes—but hardly a crisis. There were many of the others, healthy and eager but at the same time patient and calculating. In the coming weeks, it developed that several more of them were granted the opportunity to dine. More sensible of their good fortune, they were tolerant of their hosts, and did not overfeed. Resisting gluttony, they sated their craving gradually, only damaging their chosen, unknowing organisms a little at a time, preserving them so they would continue to be able to provide unwitting nourishment well in the future. One of Utchatuk's kind even succeeded in reproducing successfully, drawing admiring, undetectable hosannas from the others.

In this one place alone, there were dozens of them. Close at hand, hundreds more. And in the larger world—in the larger world beyond the green mountains and lush valleys, there were many millions. Their presence unseen, undetected, unsuspected by the multitude of oblivious, unaware, cattlelike food. It had always been so, always would be so. Millions of them.

Each one ever hungry, and ready to be fed.

Three

The extensive, thoroughly researched and documented paper that was eventually submitted jointly by Coschocton Westcott and Kelli Alwydd resulted in both of them receiving their doctorates from disparate but equally admiring faculties. Moreover, the weeks of stolen early morning hours spent together in the close confines of the secret Chachapoyan ceremonial chamber (for such they had determined it to be) eventuated in a joint undertaking of another kind. Before leaving Peru, the two new Doctors of Science became engaged. Within a month of returning to the States, they were married. Eschewing any professional jealousy at their success, a proud Martin Harbos presented them with a double-spouted, unbroken Chimu pot in the shape of a llama.

Subsequent to the publication of their scholarly and influential paper, there followed a certain amount of spirited competition for their academic services. A delighted archaeology department at Arizona State University in Tempe accepted them jointly as instructors, with promises of tenure, professional approbation, and full professorships to follow. The newly appointed, diplomated, and happily married couple settled easily into a comfortable suburban home in east Scottsdale.

They had returned from Peru with quite a lot of baggage. Nearly a ton, to be exact, consisting of fragments of bas-relief, pottery, remarkably well-preserved weavings, and other material from the Apachetarimac site. Between teaching assignments, every bit of it had to be identified, photographed, dated, catalogued, and labeled. Though it occupied much of their spare time, the work gave rise to few complaints because each was doing what they loved, in the company of the one they loved. What more could one ask of life?

One bas-relief occupied Cody's attention particularly, so much so that he devoted an inordinate amount of time in attempting to decipher its meaning. The majority of the Chachapoyan reliefs and pictographs they had found depicted scenes from everyday life, or were representations of myths and legends. This one was different. Deep in the secondary, sacrificial chamber he and Kelli had discovered, they had encountered an anomaly: a flat, carved panel set among all the traditional curved surfaces. It struck Cody as standing apart from its surroundings, not only because of its shape but its contents. Kelli was less enamored of the object, and when it had been shown to him, Harbos had in fact been mildly dismissive, but Cody had seen to it that the panel was among those pieces conscripted for shipment back to the States. Now, much to Kelli's quiet amusement, he devoted all the time he could spare trying to comprehend a significance that seemed apparent only to him.

"You're going to drive yourself crazy trying to extract specifics from that stone." Across the lab tables, she smiled affectionately at her hard-working but sometimes obstinate new husband. Beneath her practiced fingers, a complex polychromed pot was slowly regaining its shape, like a bottle whose shattering was being filmed in reverse. "You know how generalized, and often abstract, the Chachapoyans were in their work." She indicated the basement lab in which they were toiling. Behind her, ranks of neatly labeled shelves and boxes full of the human sediment of several dozen ancient Amerindian cultures rose all the way to the ceiling. Tools, dirt, dust, and specimens speckled the tables.

"Until you found the tunnel and the chambers, there was even less to go on." Bending her head, she stared intently down through an oversized, illuminated magnifying lens, reaching out to change its supportive arm slightly to adjust the focus.

"That's why I think this particular relief is so important," he replied evenly.

Delicately, she slipped a dollar-sized piece of pottery into an open break in the pot she was restoring, holding it immobile to allow the glue she had smeared on one edge to set. One more piece of an endless puzzle done. "It's a fine panel, a good piece of work," she admitted, "but a Mayan stele it's not. There may or may not be something like a Chachapoyan Rosetta stone—but that relief's not it."

"I know that." His tone was sharper than he had intended.

His finger traced a small portion of the panel. This figure here, he thought doggedly—what did it mean? Was it supposed to represent a man, a god, a monkey, or a goat? The multiplicity of figures on the relief combined with the intricacy of the overlying abstract design made for maddeningly contradictory possible interpretations. All he could do was persevere.

The scrape of chair on concrete floor made him look up from his work. Kelli was slipping into her sweater. The Valley of the Sun could turn surprisingly cold in winter, especially at night—a fact the chamber of commerce did not trumpet in the glossy brochures it distributed nationally during the time of trolling for tourists.

"Leaving?" he asked.

She checked her watch. "It's almost eleven-thirty, Cody. I've got a ten o'clock seminar tomorrow and a little sleep would be nice. You coming?"

He hesitated. "You take the car. The last bus is at one. I really want to finish this section. I think I'm close."

"Close to what?" She favored him with a wry but affectionate smile.

Hunched over the relief, he glanced up just long enough to reply. "Understanding."

"Hey, I understand already." She wagged a finger at him. "I understand that you'd better be on that last bus." She gestured at the workbench, strewn with fine tools that would have looked equally at home in a surgery as they did in the lab. "You keep falling asleep in here and one night your head's going to land on a pick instead of the table. And I'm not going to be the one to pull it out of your obsessed brain."

"You mean, like here?" Reaching up and smiling, he tapped the top of his head.

Taking her cue, she came around the table and kissed him on the indicated spot. He drew her down and their lips met rather more firmly. When they finally parted, he whispered, "I won't miss the bus. I promise."

"I'll hold you to that. I'm sure as hell not climbing out of a warm bed to come back here and fetch you at three A.M. or some other ungodly hour." With a last kiss, she rose and exited the lab, heading for the elevator and leaving him with a clear view of a distinctly unprofessorial posterior twitch.

The calculated manner of her exit distracted him, as it was designed to, but only for a little while. Within minutes he was furiously entering notes on the laptop that rested, open and glowing insistently, on the workbench to his right.

If this was not a goat but simply a distorted man, and this was smoke instead of background cloud, then it followed that the center section, whose meaning had been eluding him for frustrating weeks, had to be . . .

Not being the demonstrative type, he did not shout "Eureka." Besides, he was not yet positive of his interpretation of the small section of relief. When considering the meaning, the abstract overlay still had to be taken into account and could not contradict his latest reading of certain shapes and silhouettes. If it did, he would have to start anew, proceeding from yet another set of suppositions and assumptions. But for the first time in nearly a hundred tries, the preliminaries looked promising. Very promising. Wiping at aching eyes, he made sure to back up his computer notes before shuttering the lab and taking his leave.

He decided not to tell Kelli. Not right away. Not until he was absolutely sure of his findings. They would demand peer review, he knew, preferably carried out in tandem with experimental corroboration. As he rode home on the bus, alone except for two grad students locked in the throes of oblivious passion in the back seat, he wondered who he might inveigle into performing the latter. He needed not another archaeologist, nor an anthropologist, but a chemist. One with time enough to spare to do some *pro bono* lab work. He would also have to contact the zoology department. If he *had* finally succeeded in deciphering the relief correctly, ultimate authentication of his interpretation was going to be very much an interdisciplinary exercise.

A fey smile lightened his otherwise self-absorbed, solemn expression. Not that anyone on the bus noticed, or cared. Harry Keeler would be perfect. This was just the sort of sufficiently fanciful, off-the-wall procedure that would appeal to him. He knew Keeler only slightly, from a couple of university social functions. But his reputation was sound, and insofar as Cody knew, he was the only faculty member out of several hundred who had appeared on the evening news during the past three months—not as a consequence of his academic work, but for participating in a record-setting multiple sky-diving jump in California. As a senior chemist, his professional credentials were impeccable. The only question was, would he be interested in a diversionary bit of interdepartmental experimentation?

Not only was Keeler interested, to Cody's relief and gratification the senior professor proved downright enthusiastic.

"I remember the announcement when you and your wife accepted your appointments here. As I recall, there was a bit of actual excitement among the old fossils in charge of your department." Blue eyes twinkled mirthfully. "What kind of experiment, exactly, is it that you want me to run for you, Mr. Westcott?"

"I've been studying Chachapoyan bas-reliefs. The Chachapoyans were a mysterious, pre-Inca people who lived . . ."

The chemist put up a hand to forestall the rest of Cody's explanation. "Some of us do read outside our fields, young fella. I feel confident that I know the minimum necessary about our extinct southern cousins. So you've been reading the elder books, have you?"

Cody smiled. "The elder stones, anyway. I'm taken with one in particular. Exceptional piece of work. Clear and unambiguous. At least," he qualified himself, "it looks unambiguous to me. It was removed from a very important place in what we now believe to be the spiritual center of Chachapoyan civilization. I've been doing a lot of work with it these past couple of months. Too much, my wife would say. But I think I've found something interesting. I need somebody like yourself to see if it adds up to anything. And I'd like," he concluded apologetically, "to do this as soon as possible."

"Why the rush?" Keeler smiled and waved at a group of students as he and his younger, taller colleague continued walking toward the Hayden Library.

"Because the panel has to go back to Peru next week. Everything we brought back with us is only on study loan and is destined to go into a new wing of the National Museum devoted to the Chachapoyan culture. I'll still have excellent photographs, but I much prefer being able to check the original material. It's a touchy-feely kind of thing, if that's not too unscientific an explanation."

Keeler stepped over a sprinkler head that was protruding slightly from the grass. On the cool winter morning, both men wore sweaters. "I quite understand. I much prefer dealing with actual chemicals instead of formulas. Wet versus dry, you might say. You still haven't told me what you want me to do."

Cody was gesturing continuously as he spoke. "I believe the panel shows various carefully configured ingredients being combined into a liquid that is intended to be swallowed. There's no mistaking the importance the Chachapoyans attached to it. Everything on the panel is exquisitely rendered and colored, almost as fine as what you would find in an undisturbed Egyptian tomb." He stopped waving his hands about. "It's not another Lord of Sipán, but we know absolutely nothing about Chachapoyan medical techniques. As near as I've been able to decipher, this brew, or potion, or whatever it is, has something to do with vision."

Keeler was suddenly uncertain. "You really want to

play around with some five-century-old pharmaceutical? I expect that could be dangerous."

Cody responded vigorously. "The reliefs clearly show that the potion is supposed to improve one's vision, not damage it. I think the prescription is too elaborate to be some form of liquid punishment."

"I see." The chemist was still hesitant. "Improve your vision how?"

"I haven't figured that out yet. It's a little confusing. Not the relief itself: That's clear enough. But there are several possible readings of the final interpretation."

They rounded the corner of the Social Sciences building. The library loomed ahead, white concrete and dark glass intended to shield the precious contents against the brutal summer sun.

"You wouldn't be reading me a riddle here, would you, Professor Westcott? Academic freedom notwithstanding, I could get into trouble if somebody thinks we're playing around with ancient Peruvian hallucinogens."

For an instant, Cody wasn't sure if the senior chemist was being serious or not. When he decided that he was, he hastened to reassure him. "I promise you, Professor Keeler, this is serious science. I'm not interested in becoming another Carlos Castenada."

"Coschocton Westcott, the Don Juan of Tempe?" Keeler chuckled at the thought. "Wasn't he was supposed to be a Mexican shaman?"

Cody held the door aside so the senior professor could enter first. "The Peruvians say Castenada stole all of Don Juan's teachings from their own shamanistic traditions, that much of what's in the books is clearly Peruvian and not Mexican. I've participated in some casual debates on the matter myself. But we're not dealing with quasi-contemporary Indian mysticism here. The reliefs on the panel are real. Real enough to interpret."

"And you intend to try this potion yourself?" Comfortable inside the perfectly climate-controlled library, Keeler was doffing his sweater.

"I'll sign any necessary releases. I'll absolve you of any responsibility." The archaeologist smiled encouragingly. "The potion may not do anything."

Keeler was not smiling back. "Or it may induce hallucinations. I believe that is typical of South American shamanistic practices. Or convulsions, or worse." He eyed his younger colleague sharply. "What does your lovely wife think about all this?"

Cody didn't hesitate. "She thinks I'm slightly obsessed."

Keeler nodded slowly as they headed for the elevators that would take them up to the stacks. "Does she also know you intend to personally sample some half-millennia-old mystic Amerindian distillation of unknown provenance and dubious taste?"

Cody looked away. "I haven't told her yet."

The older man clearly was not pleased. Cody was afraid that the senior academic was going to withdraw his expertise, but he had chosen the right chemist for the task. A thoughtful Keeler was too intrigued to back out. When he murmured on the elevator, "How complex is this ancient brew you want me to take a shot at concocting?", Cody knew he had the partner he needed.

Even so, he was instinctively reluctant to surrender the material he had spent long weeks painstakingly assembling from a myriad of sources. Among other items, these included strips of *Acacia spindida* bark from the university's botanical collection, choros beetle larvae from a professor of entomology at Florida State, sap from the gnarled omata tree that grew atop Apachetarimac itself, leaves from a handful of carefully delineated epiphytes, the flowers of two different kinds of wild orchid, and a droplet of epidermal venom from the skin of *Dendrobates joanna*, one of the most toxic of all the poison-arrow frogs. Ultimately, the only holdup came when he put in his request for the most common of all the necessary ingredients. Fortunately, Harry Keeler's standing not only at the university but within his profession was sufficient to overcome the initial uncertainty of their eventual supplier. He was chortling softly as he related the tale to his younger colleague.

"You should've seen Dr. Vinaprath's face when I spoke to him via video mail." They were in the university's organic chemistry lab. Outside, the sun was finally setting through the disgusting winter smog that tended to envelope the greater Phoenix basin on warm winter days. " 'You are not going to do anything funny with these coca leaves, are you, Harry?' " By way of punctuation, the chemist set a handful of unprepossessing green leaves down on the workbench, close to the compact blender and centrifuge. They looked like leaves from a common elm.

Cody nodded in their direction. "There aren't enough leaves there to make more than a couple of cups of tea. I can recommend it myself. It's particularly good for combating *soroche*."

"Excuse me?" Keeler was busy preparing the leaves for the blender, carefully measuring out the necessary volume of water to accompany them.

"Altitude sickness." Trying to restrain his excitement, the archaeologist scanned the length and breadth of the workbench. "Where are the other ingredients?"

Keeler looked up from his work just long enough to point. "See that small beaker over there? According to the instructions you supplied me, and very precise they were, too, the coca extract is the last component of your Chachapoyan oblation." After adding the indicated num-

ber of leaves to the specified volume of water, he switched
on the blender and checked his watch. Three minutes
thirty should do it, he decided.

"None of this is difficult to make up, provided you're
not squeamish about puréeing bugs."

Cody picked up the beaker. It contained maybe half a
pint of dark, viscous fluid. Cautiously, he sniffed the contents, his nose wrinkling in response. The odor was pretty
foul, but not intolerable. He doubted the addition of the
coca leaf extract would alter the potion's palatability very
much one way or the other.

"You still haven't told your wife, have you?" Keeler's
tone as he shut off the blender and transferred its contents to the centrifuge was mildly accusing.

"I didn't want to worry her. In case anything should
go wrong. Which I don't think it will." It was dark outside now, the lights of the campus starkly illuminating
walkways and entrances. Occasionally, a hard-working
student or two would materialize out of the blackness and
pass through the light, only to be swallowed up by the
next patch of gathering night. "Besides," Cody finished,
"if she knew, she'd kick my butt."

"I'm not so sure that wouldn't be the proper course of
action." His mouth set, Keeler switched off the centrifuge
and removed the outer container.

As Cody looked on expectantly, the older man added
its contents to the oily liquid in the beaker, then placed
the Pyrex container over a burner and activated the flame
beneath.

"I hope this doesn't ruin everything," he murmured.
"You said you didn't think it was necessary to use a wood
fire, in the manner of the Chachapoyans."

The archaeologist shook his head, his attention fas-
tened on the soft roar of blue flame beneath the beaker.

"I'm convinced it's the heat that's important, not the source."

Keeler nodded once. "How will you be able to tell when it's 'done'?"

"Color. When it comes to a boil it should be a dark green."

"How dark?" The chemist was nothing if not precise.

Cody studied one of the last photographs in the small album he held. "We'll just have to guess. The age of the original paint on the relief makes it impossible to tell exactly. But then, the artists may not have had the necessary pigments to depict the colors exactly, either."

He chose to let the odorous concoction boil for several minutes before directing Keeler to remove it from the flame. Refrigeration would have made it drinkable sooner, but Cody was anxious not to employ any processes unavailable to the Chachapoyans. The gas flame had been a necessary evil, but he felt that utilizing refrigeration simply to improve the taste would have been pushing matters too far. So he and Keeler sat and chatted and did their best to ignore the beaker of liquid that sat slowly cooling on a stone slab atop the workbench.

When the fluid had been reduced to the temperature and consistency of warm cocoa, Cody hefted the beaker. Keeler stood nearby, cell phone in hand. His younger associate eyed the device uncertainly.

"Who are you going to call?"

"Nobody, I hope." Keeler was all business now, his expression dead serious. "Emergency medical if I have to. You're sure you don't want to try this potion on a lab rat first?"

Having had weeks to think the matter through, Cody shook his head sharply. "The results would not necessarily be applicable to a human. I decided a long time ago that I'd have to be the lab rat." He raised the mouth of the beaker to his lips. "Besides, why inflict something that smells like this on some poor, unsuspecting rodent." He laughed nervously. Now that the experiment had proceeded beyond speculation to actual execution, he found himself hesitating. The longer he pondered what he was about to do, the stronger the urge became to set it aside for further study.

"You don't look in the least Frankensteinish." Despite the seriousness of the moment, Keeler was ultimately unable to suppress his natural good humor for more than a few moments.

It was the slight boost to his confidence Cody needed. Tipping back the beaker, he drank, swallowing hard and fast lest the taste linger too long in his mouth. It was less vile than he anticipated, but he didn't think he'd be seeing the concoction on supermarket shelves anytime soon, squinched in between six-packs of Pepsi and Seven-Up— or even next to bright yellow bottles of citrus-flavored Inca Cola.

The bitter liquid settled in his stomach. After forcing himself to drain the contents of the beaker to the last, acrid drop, he set it carefully aside and sat down. Holding his cell phone tightly, Keeler stared across at his tall colleague, searching the younger man's face for signs of distress.

"How do you feel?"

"Fine," Cody replied after a moment's deliberation.

"What do you feel?"

The archaeologist paused for another long moment before replying. "Not a damn thing." It was too soon to tell if he was more relieved than disappointed. "Nothing. Nothing at all."

Five minutes passed in comparative silence, interrupted only by the chemist's occasional soft-voiced inquiries as to his associate's state of health. Other than acknowledging a slight queasiness, an obvious and unavoidable consequence of ingesting so unsavory a libation, Cody felt nothing whatsoever. The longer he went without experiencing some sort of harmful reaction, the angrier the archaeologist became.

Finally he'd had enough. He rose from his seat. "Kelli was right. I've been wasting my time." Quietly furious at himself, he searched the room. "Where's my sweater? I'm out of here."

"Not a proper scientific summation," Keeler admonished him.

Though he appreciated the older man's attempt to cheer him, Cody was in no mood to engage in strained, uplifting banter. Locating his neatly folded sweater where he had left it in a corner, he pulled it angrily down over his head, thrusting his arms through the sleeves as though taking a couple of punches at an unseen opponent.

"I appreciate your help, Harry. I really do. It's just a damn shame it didn't lead to anything."

"You're sure?" Keeler followed him to the door. "Your vision has not changed in any way? You don't see clearly now that the rain is gone?"

In spite of the sour mood into which he was rapidly sinking, Cody had to grin. "I see clearly that I've spent the equivalent of more than three solid weeks of lab time obsessing on a blind alley. Maybe you have to be a Chachapoyan shaman to get the full effect of the potion. Unfortunately, the last one died about five hundred years ago, and I don't think my pharmacist at Walgreen's is going to be able to help me much with this." Turning in the doorway, he shook the senior chemist's hand. "Thank you, Professor, for your help. Not to mention your tolerance of an overeager younger colleague's fevered imaginings."

Keeler responded understandingly. "Hey, it might have

led to something. You never know. You don't carry out the experiment, you never find out if you can blow something up. Or cure a disease, or vulcanize rubber, or whatever else it might be that you're after. You and your lady—Kelli, right?—must come to dinner at my house some evening. Marlis is one helluva good cook, and I know she'd like to meet you both. Call me."

"I will." Feeling a little better, Cody gripped the older man's hand firmly one more time before letting go. No great discoveries had been made, no revelations had been forthcoming as the result of his hard work, but he had made a friend—no small achievement in the tempestuous world of academic social life. Kelli would like Harry Keeler too, he felt.

There was no one in the elevator, no one in the hallway, and no one loitering outside the chemistry building when he let himself out. A short walk would take him to his car, parked on one of the interior campus streets. When he told her everything that had transpired, Kelli would share his disappointment. Privately, he knew she would be relieved to hear that his preoccupation with the single panel of reliefs was at an end, and they could resume a normal life with normal office hours. He tugged at the hem of his sweater, the cool night air invigorating his stride. Even if nothing had come of his work and the resulting experiment, the procedure had been instructive. In good science, nothing was ever wasted, including a lack of results.

He was halfway to the car, striding nimbly through the west-side sculpture garden, when his traitorous stomach mercilessly and viciously ambushed him.

The sharp pain did more than snap him double: It short-circuited his legs and brought him to his knees. Eyes wide, he clutched ineffectually at his stomach with both hands. Breathing hard, he looked around, staring through shocked eyes that were rapidly blurring with tears. The pain was intense, as if he had swallowed a bucket of acupuncture needles that suddenly hit bottom. Weak as a kitten, he fell over on his side, his legs drawing up into a fetal position, his arms locked against his belly. His guts were on fire. No students, no groundskeepers, no patrolling security personnel saw him lying there among the mostly abstract and overpriced sculptures, a long drink of professor writhing spasmodically on the neatly clipped grass.

The timer-controlled sprinklers came on without warning. Lying in the damp turf, soaked through, he did battle with his own insides, uncertain as to the ultimate outcome. After what felt like hours but in reality was no more than ten minutes, the pain began to subside. He found he could breathe normally again. The irrigating water, falling like rain, aided his attitude if not his digestion.

Coca leaves, arrow frog toxin, and bug guts, he told himself as he struggled to his knees. *Serves you right. Serves you damn well right.* He hacked up the residue at the back of his lungs, and something black and thick spewed from his mouth. Rising slowly, he wiped his lips with the back of his wrist, not caring if he stained the sweater. Keeler would be delighted to hear that their little clandestine experiment had produced some results after all, even if their nature was such that Cody could have done without them. He felt that the same consequences could have been induced much more simply and cheaply by drinking from the carton of milk that had been sitting in the back of the small refrigerator in his office for two weeks too long.

As shaky as if he had been puking for hours, he straightened and took a hesitant step. Encouragingly, the movement did not induce the pain to return. Advancing carefully, one step at a time, he resumed walking toward the car, ready to collapse anew if his belly should try to waylay him again. It did not, but the queasiness remained, as if the ground itself had suddenly become infirm. He had never been seasick in his life, but from first-hand experiences described by others, he supposed the sensations must be very much akin to what he was presently feeling. Glancing furtively around the gently rolling, grassy sculpture garden, he was relieved there had been no one around to witness his embarrassing little nocturnal episode. As he staggered toward the street where his car was parked, his thoughts focused on home, on Kelli's waiting embrace, on bed, but truth be told, not more than a very little on the supper that she would have waiting for him.

Food! Azahoht sensed its approach. He had come close to feeding and reproducing several times in the past month, only to be thwarted on each occasion by last-minute changes in the paths of his intended quarry. But this one was very near, and moving unsteadily. It might well need to rest against something solid for support, to steady itself, and Azahoht's dwelling was as solid as any object in the vicinity. Let the food make but casual contact, and feeding could begin immediately. Azaholt waited expectantly as he monitored the erratic course of the food. *Come closer*, he thought hungrily. *That's right. This way, not that. Just a little closer. There, that left hand! Stretch it out, reach for my abode, touch it. Make contact.* Eagerly, he extended a portion of himself in the direction of the food.

Something happened then that was so extraordinary, Azahoht could scarce believe it. It was unprecedented in his experience, in the entire long course of his existence. He knew that such a thing was possible from contact with others of his kind, but he had never actually observed the phenomenon himself. Now that it happened, involving him directly, he was too stunned to know how to react. He could only draw back into his dwelling in shock. It was impossible, it was astounding, it defied anything and everything in his far-ranging experience. It was as if the very fabric of existence had been suddenly turned inside out. Inconceivable though it might be, there was no mistaking what happened. None whatsoever.

The food *saw* him.

four

Still woozy from the gastrointestinal tremor that had knocked him to his knees, Cody was less than fifty feet from the street and his car when he reached out to steady himself against the nearest sculpture. It was a sinuous, free-form needle of bolted-together pink and black granite boulders that aspired to inspiration but fell more than a little short of the artist's lofty intent. It would be cool to the touch and, if necessary, would support his weight easily, providing a convenient backrest with which to ease his disturbed equilibrium for a few precious moments. His left hand fumbled in the direction of a stone protrusion.

And quickly drew back without making contact. Blinking hard, he gawked at the smooth, polished stone. At the approach of his hand, something had begun to emerge from within. It looked like a triplet of intertwined tentacles. Each tip terminated in a dime-sized sucker, and a handful of small, glowering eyes were scattered like black marbles along the slick, writhing surfaces.

Uttering soft guttural sounds that only resembled words, Cody staggered away from this hazy apparition.

Still clearly visible and making no attempt to conceal themselves, the tentacles fluttered in the still night air, rampant eyes goggling at him, before finally withdrawing back into the hard granitic body of the sculpture.

His breathing rapid, heart pounding, stomach still threatening possible eruption, Cody forced himself to stand motionless as he contemplated the beguiling but deceitful work of art. It loomed before him in the darkness, belabored with sharply defined shadows cast by the overhead lights that illuminated pathway and street, no longer the innocent expression of an unknown artist's aspirations. Bending slowly, never taking his eyes off the twisted, spiraling shape, he reached down to pick up a handful of white gravel from the decorative border that lined a flower bed. At the last instant he happened to look down, only to have his questing fingers recoil in horror.

Each thumb-sized chunk of river rock was twitching a tiny, ethereal filament in his direction.

Emitting a soft, startled cry, he lurched backward—and fell. The thick grass helped to cushion his fall. He lay there, panting like an overheated dog, and stared at the gravel. It lay like a frozen white river behind the boundaries of its decorative border, innocent and unmoving. Rolling onto his side, he let his gaze flick between gravel and sculpture. The ground was comforting beneath him, almost cushiony. Almost—massaging. Uncertainly, he turned his face to the earth.

Inches below his nose, miniscule, almost invisible threads were reaching for him, one for every single blade of grass.

With an inarticulate cry he scrambled to his feet, pulling free of the almost microscopic tendrils, and ran for his car, pursued by nightmares. Exhausted by fear and tension, he reached it without incident, though as he ran he thought he had felt the blades of grass clutching with individual, infinitesimal force at his shod feet. Afraid to look down, scared to touch anything, he was relieved to see that nothing sprang at him from the body of his little four-door, and that the surface of the sidewalk on which he was presently standing remained flat, white, and inanimate.

God, he thought wildly, *oh God—what's going on? What's happening to me?*

Slowly, he turned, believing he was prepared for anything. The carpet of questing filaments had vanished back into the lawn. The granite sculpture stabbed virtuously skyward. Smooth-surfaced river rock gravel shielded its bed of pansies and petunias. The sculpture garden sat silent, motionless, and sane beneath powerful overhead lights.

Espying an empty beer can, he bent to pick it up, his fingers halting less than an inch from the crumpled metal. Nothing coiled forth from the shiny, garishly decorated aluminum cylinder to fumble for his fingertips. Tentatively, he plucked it from the ground. It lay in his hand; inanimate, immobile, unmoving, wholly synthetic.

Artificial. His car was a complex aggregate of manufactured materials. The sidewalk on which he stood was made of concrete, another composite material. The beer can was refined aluminum covered with paint. These manufactured articles put forth no tentacles, writhed no filaments beneath his eyes. Those had emerged from the unhomogenized rock of the gravel bed, from individual blades of growing grass, and from facilely carved but otherwise naked granite. Or possibly just from his potion-addled brain. He needed desperately to find out.

Drawing back his arm, he threw the can. It ricocheted off the sculpture with a muted but clearly audible clang. The sculpture did not react to the impact. Nothing creepy or crawly thrust in protest from its smooth surfaces. Where the can landed in the grass, the grass did not react.

Someone else did, however. "Hey! What d'you think you're doing?"

In the midst of his rounds, the security guard accelerated his pace. As the man approached, Cody made an effort to straighten himself and regain a little composure. He was aware that he was still young enough to pass for a graduate student.

The guard gestured meaningfully in the direction of the sculpture before looking back at Cody. "That's university property, friend." Small, intense eyes narrowed accusingly. "Lemme see your ID."

Cody surprised himself by finding his wallet on the first try. The guard didn't notice the slight trembling in the fingers that flipped it open. "Coschocton Westcott, Department of Archeology." Realizing he was not dealing with a mischievous or destructive student, the guard metamorphosed from accusatory to concerned. "Are you all right, Professor?"

"I'm fine." Cody did not sound so to himself, but the guard was satisfied. "I was trying for that trash can over there."

The other man's gaze swerved. The receptacle in question stood more than ten feet to the right of the granite monolith. "Not real close, were you?" The stocky guard was relaxed now, realizing he was not dealing with some nocturnal vandal. "Better stick to your digging, Professor Westcott."

Cody nodded thankfully. "I intend to."

The guard was now positively jovial. "You can't really hurt those things, anyway." He made a face. "They call 'em art, but to me it's all garbage that's been given a high polish. Steel and stone. Even though they're supposed to keep off, I've seen students crawling all over 'em. Never seen one damaged yet, though after we beat U of A last year some kids did get drunk enough to tip a couple of 'em over. The art department wasn't pleased."

"No," mumbled the archaeologist, "I imagine they weren't. I'm afraid I don't remember the incident. I was out of the country at the time."

The guard turned wistful as he remembered. "Two touchdowns in the last ten minutes. What a game." As if aware that he had lingered too long and that he had checkpoints to pass, the guard was already moving away. "Next time hold off until you pass a trash container and drop your garbage in." As he sauntered down the sidewalk and prepared to turn the corner that led back into the silent depths of the campus, he ducked just enough to pass beneath the nearest branch of a lightly leaved palo verde tree.

Something dwelling within the tree reached for him.

It had a face, maybe, with little tooth-lined slits that passed for multiple mouths, and unidentifiable unwholesome protuberances that resembled rotten fungi, and a single vertically pupiled, brilliantly glowing golden eye.

"Look out!" Cody took a step in the guard's direction.

Startled, the older man whirled, bringing his heavy flashlight up defensively. His eyes darted from side to side. The monstrosity that was living within the tree withdrew in silence. Part of the guard's arm passed within millimeters of the branch from which the horrific vision had emerged—but never made contact.

"What, what is it!" The sentry turned a quick circle, searching the darkness.

"You didn't see it?"

"See it? See what?" All friendliness fled, the older man was eyeing Cody suspiciously again. "Say, Professor— how many of those beers did you say you've had tonight?"

"None. I mean, just one. Only the one." Denying own-

ership of the can he had thrown would only confuse the
guard further, Cody felt. Better to acknowledge the con-
sumption of one beer he hadn't imbibed and get out of
there before he found himself hauled off to the campus
police station on suspicion of being drunk and disorderly.

Would he be safe from his nightmares in jail? he found
himself wondering wildly. What did he have to look forward to in lockup? Steel bars, concrete floors and walls,
manufactured bedding, ceramic john: Based on the hypothesis slowly forming in his mind, it should be a safe
place. But then, so should his car. Hands shaking, aware
that the guard was still watching him, he was relieved
that he did not have to struggle with the simple business
of inserting key into lock. The car's remote entry system
allowed him to press a button to access the door.

Slipping behind the wheel, he managed to get the en-
gine started. Forcing a smile, he waved at the guard, who
was still staring in his direction. Thank God, he thought
as he pulled out, the campus was virtually deserted at this
hour. The only traffic jam he had to deal with was in his
head, where thoughts were slamming into each other one
after another.

Turning left, then left again, he headed for the University Avenue exit, keeping his speed down lest he draw
unwanted attention from someone else on patrol. He
gripped the wheel so tightly that his fingers began to
whiten, but at least it kept them from trembling. He had
finally succeeded in calming himself a little when the explosion shattered his carefully nurtured complacency.

Swerving madly, the car jumped the curb and came to
a halt with its front right wheel high on a sidewalk. Only
the fact that he had been travelling less than ten miles an
hour prevented more serious consequences. It took him
three tries to get the door open. By the time he stumbled
out and stood there, leaning back against the roof of the

sedan, the central portion of the third floor of the building opposite was fully engulfed in flames. Those few students and late-working instructors who happened to be in the area were already congregating noisily in the street, their upturned faces strobed by the yellow-red glow of the fire. Responding with admirable speed, the aural burr of a distant siren was screaming its way toward the site. Shielding his eyes against the intense glow and heat, Cody gaped at the localized conflagration. Despite the rising temperature, a sudden and intense shiver shot right through him, icing him from head to feet. Preoccupied and slightly dazed, it had taken him a minute to identify the structure, especially since he was not used to seeing it from this side.

It was the chemistry building.

Kelli would be quietly frantic by now, or furious, or both, but he wouldn't worry about that, couldn't spare the couple of minutes it would take to find a phone and call to tell her he was all right. Stunned, he stood among students and colleagues and watched while the campus fire unit, soon reinforced by an efficient and better-equipped squadron from the city of Tempe, fought to bring the ferocious blaze under control. Operating with admirable efficiency, they quickly contained the flames, isolating them on the third floor and saving the rest of the building. Helicopters thrummed overhead as news teams from one after another of the metro area's major stations arrived, each maneuvering for the most spectacular nighttime shots. At least if his wife happened to be watching the late-evening news, Cody reflected, the live pictures from the campus would allow her to infer a reason for his late-night absence.

The flames thoroughly devoured several of the third-floor labs and their contents. No one was hurt battling the conflagration, but come the following morning university authorities would be forced to make the sad announcement that Harry Keeler, senior professor of organic chemistry, had been working late and had perished in the blaze. He would be remembered fondly by his friends and colleagues, who would extend their sympathy to his stunned and devastated family.

A no less bewildered assistant professor of archaeology turned north on Hayden, keeping well below the speed limit while resolutely hugging the slow lane. Hayden was a busy north-south route and despite the lateness of the hour, heavily traveled. Ignoring the occasional irritated horn that loudly chided him for his snail-like pace, he crept homeward.

Harry was dead. He knew it as surely as he knew he had seen vaporous, intangible horrors emerge from rock and grass, gravel and tree on the campus he thought he knew so well. Unable to reach Cody, they had killed his partner in experimentation. Or caused him to kill himself. Cody didn't know the details of what had happened in room 3447 on the third floor of the chemistry building and was sure he never would. Nor would anyone else. Certainly not the fire or police department's forensics experts. How could they identify killers who were not even remotely human, when only he, Cody Westcott, could see them?

He *could* see them, and they knew he could see them, and they didn't like it. They didn't like it one bit.

How had they traced Harry's participation, made the link to the luckless chemist? It had to be the potion, Cody knew. They'd smelled the residue in his lab, or sensed it, or in some other unimaginable way managed to trace it from its imbiber back to its maker. Then they had dealt with the poor, unwary professor. They would deal with him, too, Cody was certain as he gazed unblinkingly over the wheel, tracking the progress of his car lights through the night. Harry had touched, had made contact with, something containing one of them. Something natural and not manufactured. The thing living within had initiated the proceedings that had led to the chemist's death.

Cody didn't care about the potion. He did care about how long it would last. If it wore off and he could no longer see the creatures, would they be able to sense that and leave him alone? And if they did, how could he ever resume a normal life? How could he wade in a river and feel the rocks beneath his toes, or climb a tree, or play touch football on a clean, seemingly innocuous lawn? How could he explain any of what had happened to the empirically minded, no-nonsense, obstinate woman who was his wife? Fuliginous tentacles and tendrils extruding menacingly from inanimate objects were the stuff of cheap fiction, not science. If the night guard hadn't seen the indistinct, inimical shapes reaching out for him from the tree even though they'd been fluttering eagerly mere inches from his face, how could Cody point them out to his wife and fellow scientists?

Point them out? Hell, he didn't have a clue what they were! If partaking of the ancient potion was what had enabled him to see them, then perhaps the bas-reliefs located within the underground Chachapoyan temple might speak to their identity. Back in his office he had photographs of every carving, every pictograph to be found within those remarkable curving walls that had been shut away from the sight of man for hundreds of years. Like virtually everything else about the Chachapoyan culture, their meaning remained poorly understood.

Well, he now had a new perspective from which to examine them. But not tonight, no, not tonight. Dizzy and debilitated, all he wanted now was to make it home safely, to fall into Kelli's arms, to stand for half an hour beneath a hot, cleansing shower, and to sleep. He would deal with all this tomorrow, in the bright light of a desert morning.

Among those who were now conscious of his new perception, however, the alarm had been raised. From the unsettled center of the uncommon disturbance, the awareness spread rapidly. Cody's fervent desire to be left alone was not to be indulged.

The desert landscaping that fronted the junior high school he was passing boasted mature palo verde and ocotillo interspersed with barrel cacti and juvenile saguaros. Not every one of these trees and plants had been parasitized by the unknown, ominous creatures Cody could now see clearly, but enough of them were to cause him to jerk sharply on the wheel and send the car screeching away from the greenbelt bordering the school and over into the fast lane. Fortunately, traffic had now thinned out, and he crashed his vehicle only into empty air. The serpentine, misshapen, frightful shapes he saw coiling within tree and succulent unnerved him afresh. The effects of the potion he had ingested were as potent as ever. When a particularly long branch struck and scraped the roof of his car, he screamed out loud in spite of himself.

The car forged onward. He felt nothing. The branch had only made contact with the metal roof and not with him. Was intimate physical contact always required? he wondered furiously. In the sculpture garden he had aroused nothing until he had touched something; the sculpture, the gravel, the grass. What happened when that kind of contact was made and sustained instead of being quickly terminated? What did the questing, probing tendrils do to a person? Was it something that could be studied, evaluated, and measured, or would conjecture have to suffice?

A partial answer of sorts presented itself to him as he turned down the side street that led to his home. On either side of the road, neat one- and two-story homes painted or stuccoed in desert hues slumbered on in the darkness, oblivious to the abundance of horrid indistinct life that lingered all around. Trees and rocks and bushes, not every one but many, sprouted ghastly shapes that were visible only to the sole occupant of an innocuous Ford driving slowly and cautiously down the exact center of the street. From several houses the muted babble of families watching television or engaging in late-night household tasks filtered out onto the street, their occupants as oblivious as the rest of mankind to the supernal terror that stalked their neighborhood, their world.

Crawling eastward, Cody encountered only one other human. The man was walking his dog, a nondescript but well-groomed terrier. As a nervous, uneasy Cody passed, the dog tugged sharply on its leash. Without thinking, its owner allowed the animal to lead. While the dog did its business at the base of a mesquite tree, its idling owner reached out with a hand.

"Don't!" Cody screamed, forgetting that his windows were rolled all the way up and the car's heater was automatically warming the interior. The dog's owner never heard him.

As the man casually fingered the leaves on the mesquite, a miasmic glob of pale mist emerged. It had eyespots devoid of pupils and two long, slender hooks like insubstantial hypodermics. These penetrated the back of the man's hand—and began to suck. A shocked Cody could see them swelling with—with what? To all outward appearances the man felt nothing. The flesh of his hand, the color of his skin—nothing changed. Nothing at all.

Except his demeanor.

His face contorting, he suddenly glared down at the terrier and kicked it. Hard. The startled dog yelped and a light came on in the driveway of the nearest house. His expression still deformed, growled obscenities spilling from his lips, the man lengthened his stride, dragging the poor animal after him and half choking it in the process. Cody followed their progress in his sideview mirror.

Something significant had just occurred. His brain overloaded with more conundrums and inexplicable information than any one person should have to deal with in the course of a single night, he was still mulling over what he'd just witnessed as he pulled into the driveway of his own home and automatically activated the remote garage-door opener.

Kelli was awake and waiting for him in the den. The domestic fury she'd been keeping bottled up ever since nine o'clock had come and gone, vanished the instant she caught sight of the expression on her husband's face. Tossing the heavy scientific tome she'd been reading onto the couch, she rose and rushed to his side.

"Jeezus, Cody! What happened to you?"

He allowed himself to be led into the comfortable, welcoming room. It was filled with pots and paintings, framed photographs of their travels and Indian artifacts: memorabilia of their time spent in the southern half of the hemisphere. The feel, the touch, the warmth against him of the person he loved more than anything else in the world calmed him more than any sedative or potion he might have taken.

Potion. Angrily, he fought to think of anything but potions.

It struck him that he was sitting down. He had not remembered dropping onto the couch, had been too preoccupied to wonder at Kelli's momentary absence. But she was back now, with a glass of iced tea, sitting on the cushion next to his while gazing at him speculatively and with open concern.

"What's wrong, Cody? What happened tonight?"

Raising the glass, he examined it as carefully as he

would have a newly unearthed Moche earring. Tea, after all, was a natural substance, and in every instance, the frightful apparitions he had encountered had oozed forth from natural sites. But the processed, golden-hued liquid in the glass did not thrust out tiny tea-colored tentacles to clutch at his face. The clinking cubes of ice likewise seemed benign. The glass itself, being an artificial composite, did not worry him. He drank gratefully, feeling the cold fluid slide easily down his throat. By itself, unaccompanied by unwanted travelers.

Kelli had not stopped staring at him. "Something wrong with the tea?"

"No." He slumped against the padded back of the couch. "The tea's fine." Was the couch safe? he wondered with a start. It had a wood frame, and cotton cushions. As an increasingly anxious Kelli watched him, Cody looked anxiously to left and right. Nothing vomited upward from the solid piece of furniture.

Maybe the process of manufacture and blending and combining with other materials and products reduced the purity of the nebulous horrors he had been seeing. Not every tree and rock provided a home for the abnormalities. Still ignorant of what he was dealing with, he found himself compelled to examine and discard one mad hypothesis after another.

Perhaps the effects of the potion had worn off. He wasn't sure which was worse: to be able to see and detect the subtle frights whose unsuspected existence the foul-smelling liquid had revealed to him, or to be obliged forever after to wander the world cognizant of their existence, but unable to see them. In an environment awash in shadowy horrors, was it better to dwell in blindness? Having been, even momentarily, granted the gift of seeing what was invisible to everyone else, could he survive and maintain his sanity once forced to relinquish it?

All of the notes on the potion—its ingredients, their proportions, and the exact method of preparation—had been in Professor Keeler's lab. But the Chachapoyan panel that revealed the recipe was still intact, as were numerous photos of the relevant reliefs and carvings. It would take time to assemble the necessary constituents anew, as well as to find another chemist to prepare and combine them—but it could be done. Did he want to do it? Was it the wise course? Looking to Kelli, seeing the concern writ large in her face, he wondered how she would react to the revelation. Would she even believe him, without demonstrable proof of his claims? If he told her exactly what had happened, she would want proof. She was as much a scientist as he, and he knew her well enough to be certain that in this instance, love would not be sufficient to obviate the need for proof.

"Harry's dead."

Her eyes widened slightly. "Professor Keeler? The one you've been working with these past weeks?" He nodded. "How . . . ?"

"There was a fire. His lab blew up. That's why I'm so late. The building was burning as I was leaving the campus, and I stopped to—watch."

"There was nothing you could do?" It was as much a statement as question.

"The fire department got there as fast as they could. With all those chemicals, the blaze was very intense. You could feel the heat of it across the street."

"Damn." As she leaned back against the opposite arm of the couch, he found himself staring intently at the rolled and padded armrest. Had he seen a flicker of movement there? What synapses ruled the fine line between reality and imagination, between observation and hallucination? He would have to be careful not to see what was not there. What was there, was horrifying enough. "He was a good guy," Kelli added.

"Yeah, he was, and a first-rate chemist, too."

Rising, she leaned forward to kiss him gently. Folding her arms around his shoulders, she gave him a loving, tender hug before straightening. "It's too late to cook." She smiled. "You know I have to go slow with anything that involves activating the stove. But I could nuke a lasagna for you."

"You're not going to eat anything?" He rose, darting a glance behind her. The house was silent, unmoving, a bulwark of familiarity against a suddenly hostile outside world.

"When you didn't show at the expected time I had a couple of tuna sandwiches." Rising and pirouetting coquettishly, she pranced off in the direction of the kitchen. "I love you, honey, but I ain't gonna starve for you."

"Wouldn't want you to." Holding his iced tea, he followed her into the other room.

The attached dinette area was mostly wood, laminated and varnished. Did such treatment render natural materials like lumber uninhabitable by the organisms he had seen? If the potion's effects had worn off, how would he know? While she busied herself with the freezer, he slid reluctantly onto a bench. It was cool and unmoving beneath him. Outside, desert landscaping surrounded the small plunge pool, both chilled by the winter night. A reassuring electronic hum filled the kitchen—microwave Muzak.

Seventeen minutes and thirty-three seconds passed. The instructions on frozen-food packaging were designed to serve as benchmarks only, to be customized by consumers. Pulling a plate from a cabinet and a fork from a drawer, Kelli moved to join him as he dug at the plastic container. He took another sip from his nearly empty glass.

And dropped it as he sprang from behind the table. Sweet tea and melting ice slid oil-like across the tabletop. The heavy glass bounced and rolled on the tile floor but did not break.

As he charged his startled mate, one hand swept up a long steel spatula from a wall rack. She screamed softly as he swung in her direction—not at her, but at the bonsai she had been about to caress. Because, trailing upward and out from the branches of the shrunken tree like the tendrils of a jellyfish were a handful of silvery filaments lined with barbed hooks, waiting to sink into the naked flesh of her hand.

The spatula struck the bonsai and sent it skidding sideways across the countertop, where it slammed up against the toaster, strewing dirt and decorative pebbles in its wake. Nothing emerged from this detritus, but filmy, questing fronds continued to wave in energetic frustration from the bole of the bonsai. Staring at it, breathing hard and clutching the spatula like a broadsword, Cody found himself wondering what to do next. From the bonsai came a faint, disappointed keening.

Interesting, he thought wildly. He could hear as well as see them.

Mouth agape, Kelli Westcott was leaning back against the butcher-block island that dominated the center of the kitchen, both hands gripping the uninhabited (as near as he could tell) laminated wood.

"*Are you crazy*? What's the matter with you?"

"You don't see it? You don't hear it?"

Slowly she followed his gaze to the upended bonsai before looking back at him uncertainly. "Don't see what? Don't hear what?"

Ignoring her, he made a rapid search of the kitchen drawers until he found what he was looking for: a pair of oven mitts that were not made from cotton. Slipping on the oversized gloves, he approached the decorative houseplant with determined caution. The barbed tentacles writhed impotently as he picked up the bonsai and carried it purposefully toward the back door. The pot that was the plant's home was a composite faux-stone material and ought to be safe to touch, but he wasn't taking any chances.

A bewildered Kelli followed. "What are you doing?"

"Fumigating," he snapped at her without turning around.

There were three trash cans out back, all gray plastic. He had never been especially fond of plastic before, but the past few hours found him developing a new fondness for any synthetic material. Removing a lid, he dumped the bonsai in the half-filled can before replacing the cover. Silvery tentacles twisted helplessly as they tumbled among the rest of the garbage.

Replacing the cover, he strode back to the house, his significant other trailing behind. "Have you lost your mind, Cody Westcott? That was one of my favorite houseplants!"

"It's bad for you." He pushed the door wide so she could follow easily. "Allergies."

Her expression twisted. "Allergies? What the hell are you talking about, allergies?" She gestured behind her as they reentered the den. "We've had that bonsai almost a year. I've watered it and fed it without suffering so much as a sneeze!"

Dropping back onto the couch, he buried his head in his hands. "How about headaches?" he prompted her. "Or cramps, or dizziness. Any symptoms at all?"

This time she chose to sit in a chair opposite, with the glass-topped coffee table between them. "You've had a rough night," she responded slowly. "You've lost a friend and colleague and you're upset. You need to throw out a perfectly innocent little plant to make yourself feel more secure, okay. But it stops with that. The next unprovoked attack you make on my décor, I'm calling a therapist."

Dropping his hands, he dug his fingers into his palm. "There was something in the bonsai, Kelli. Something dangerous."

Her attitude changed immediately, though she was still wary. "What—a bug? A scorpion?" Since moving into the house they had killed several scorpions in the bathroom. The enterprising arachnids came up through the tub and shower drains.

"No, not a scorpion. It had—tendrils, or tentacles. It was going for you. I—I had to stop it."

"Well, you sure stopped it, all right." She glanced briefly in the direction of the back porch and the distant garbage cans. "Attack of the Killer Bonsai. I love you truly, Cody, but you're going to have to do better than that."

Slowly, patiently, he explained in detail the nature of the research he had been conducting in concert with the chemist Harry Keeler. Told of taking the potion and what he had seen earlier that night while walking from the chemistry building back to his car. Related the encounter with the patrolling security guard. Finished with the explosion and fire that had destroyed Harry Keeler's office and lab—and Harry Keeler.

Kelli Alwydd Westcott was nothing if not systematic. She listened, waiting until her husband was finished. Her initial reaction was to categorize everything he had told her as the biggest piece of fanciful crap it had ever been her misfortune to hear and to reinforce her previous belief that he needed therapy. Understandable as it might be, such a response did not constitute good science. Given the intensity with which he had propounded his inanity, she would grant him the opportunity to provide substantiation. *Then* she would tell him he was full of crap, and suggest he seek professional help.

In the manner of one discussing a particularly controversial passage destined for inclusion in a soon-to-be published scientific paper, she responded calmly and rationally. "I didn't see anything in the bonsai but dirt, pebbles, and fallen needles. You saw barbed tendrils." He nodded. "To the best of my admittedly limited botanical knowledge, bonsai trees don't put forth barbed tendrils, or tendrils of any kind. So you're saying that there was something else in that pot."

"Not in the pot," he corrected her. "Living in the tree itself."

She nodded slowly. "Something with barbed tendrils. And what might that have been?"

"I don't know," he confessed helplessly. "I only know what I saw."

"And what you saw earlier tonight, in the sculpture garden: They were different?"

"That's right." He found himself wishing that he smoked. "These things must have different species. They only seem to inhabit natural objects. Trees and rocks. The sculpture was worked stone, but the original granite was still mostly intact. Turning a tree into lumber might reduce the habitability factor of anything residing in the original growth. I'm not sure about that yet. Remember, I haven't had time to study these things, and I've only been aware of them since I drank that potion."

"Which leads to my next, inevitable question." She didn't even have to ask it.

"I'm not suffering from hallucinations!" he replied tersely. "I know what I saw."

"Everyone who sees things knows what they saw," she countered. "What do these things do if you make contact with them?"

"I don't know that either, but it can't be good." He thought of the man and his dog: one minute strolling and relaxed, the next violent and ranting.

She smiled thinly. "On what hard evidence do you base that conclusion, my love?"

"On the way they look, the manner in which they try to snag people. The gestures, the movements—they aren't benign. And I think, somehow, they started that fire and killed Harry."

"Now you're really starting to worry me. Wouldn't you call that reaction a little paranoid, Cody?" She said it gently, to minimize his reaction. "Couldn't this fanciful story you're weaving be a means of trying to rationalize his unexpected and tragic death?"

"It could," he admitted, "except that I started seeing these creatures before the fire. What's worse, I think they know now that I can see them." His eyes scanned the walls, the floor, the innocent-seeming furniture. "They're aware of me."

"And obviously, these will-o'-the-wisps that live in trees and rocks and God knows what else murdered Harry Keeler to silence him, and to destroy his records of the formula."

"Makes sense to me." He ignored her sarcastic tone.

"Only to you, I think." Laughing, she rose and settled herself forcefully in his lap. "Okay, Cody. It's a great story, very imaginative. But for it to be anything more than that to me I'm afraid I'm going to have to ask to see a little teensy-weensy itsy-bit of *proof*." Inclining her head to peer up into his downcast face, she smiled encouragingly. "That's not too much to ask, is it? You know how it goes: Extraordinary claims demand extraordinary proof."

"Yeah, yeah." Despite the seriousness of the situation, with her squirming around on his lap he found it hard to concentrate. "How can I provide proof of something only I can see? I'd let you try the potion yourself, except that everything went up in flames in Harry's lab. It can be re-created, but I need to find another chemist as adept as Harry, and as willing."

"I'm sure you will, Cody." She kissed him on the fore-head. "Maybe tomorrow morning everything will look different and you won't have to. You've had a difficult evening, and I'm really sorry to hear about your friend. That's one advantage that archaeology as a field of study has over chemistry. Our subject matter tends not to blow up." Rising, she headed for the bedroom. "It's late, and I've got to teach a two-hundred-level class tomorrow. Adobe construction techniques as exemplified by Lambayeque transitional period architecture." She made a face. "I get to talk about mud-brick pyramids to mud-faced sophomores and juniors. And I believe you have an assignment or two yourself, Professor Westcott."

"I'm not a full professor yet." Suddenly very tired, he rose from the couch.

"You are to me." Blowing him a kiss, she disappeared into the bathroom.

While he listened to the water run in the shower, he sat on the edge of the bed and weighed everything she had said. Could she be right? Was he hallucinating it all? Drinking an ancient shamanistic potion could be expected to provoke such a response. Viewing and interpreting hallucinogen-inspired visions was an important part of every South American shamanistic tradition. *Dendrobates* toxin was powerful stuff, even in tiny quantities.

Startled, he realized that he was sitting on a bed with a wooden frame. But he was fine, nothing had happened, nothing had materialized from beneath the sheets and blankets to assault him. He was almost convinced that re-ducing a tree to lumber expunged whatever might be abiding within when he saw the long, hooked tongue emerge from the wall behind the bed. It was the only wall in the bedroom that boasted natural, unpainted paneling. He stared at the wormlike protrusion for several minutes before it withdrew back into the wall. While visible, it had mewled softly.

Nothing made of wood could be trusted, then. Not a chair, not a desk, not even a pencil. Not until it had been inspected and pronounced clean. By him, since he was the only one who could see that which dwelt within.

Emerging from the shower, Kelli felt relaxed and in a better mood. Cody strove mightily to be his usual cheerful, contented self until and after they retired. Apparently he was successful, because among other things, Kelli did not notice that he'd dragged the bed a full inch away from the paneled wall, so that headboard and paneling did not make contact.

Five

To all outward appearances Cody was his normal self again the next morning. He did not bring up the events of the night before, and Kelli, clearly relieved, chose not to either. Perhaps she thought he would forget all about the inanity of inimical forces that resided in innocuous bonsai trees. Perhaps she thought he had done so already, now that some of the shock of his colleague's unexpected passing had faded a little. In any event, she spoke only of ordinary, everyday inconsequentialties as they joined the flow of traffic that led toward the university.

She was delighted that he no longer would be working late, though out of consideration for the deceased chemist she concealed that much of her feelings. Not unexpectedly, the campus paper headlined the incident. Watching her husband surreptitiously for any hint of retrogression as he perused the article over coffee and Danish in the faculty cafeteria, she was gratified to see that he hardly reacted at all. They parted with smiles.

Cody watched her go. Smiling he was, but also worried to death. He, and only he, knew that unimaginable horrors lurked throughout the campus as well as in the world outside. If he brought the subject up again without having incontrovertible proof of what he had seen, she would surely follow through on her threat to demand professional therapy for him. Her good and loving intentions would only cause him more distress. He had to find another chemist to work with, preferably off-campus. The potion had to be remade so that she could sample it for herself. It was the only way he knew to incontestably prove to her the truth of his assertions.

It meant that he could not yell at her to take care. Insist that she avoid touching any tree, or bush, or flower, that she keep to the concrete walkways and avoid the grass, that she not make contact with wood or stone, and she might be tempted, out of love of course, to send more than verbal therapy winging his way. Sedated, he would not be able to pursue his studies. Worse, it would make him an easy target for the same forces that had destroyed Harry Keeler.

He headed for his first class, careful to avoid touching anything growing, taking an extra couple of minutes so he could avoid the decorative flagstone walkway that led to the building's main entrance. Concrete was safe, evidently too extensively blended an amalgam of ingredients to provide a comfortable home for the repulsive beings he had seen.

It was a bright, beautiful winter morning, comfortably cool while most of the rest of the country was freezing. He would have relished it, luxuriated in it, acknowledging the smiles and waves of students and faculty he knew, if not for one thing. He could still see that which he could not put a name to.

They were not everywhere, but neither were they uncommon. As he proceeded toward his teaching assignment like a scout making his way through enemy territory, he observed the creatures as closely as he dared, studying and learning. There was nothing else he could do. And while he beheld them, he was acutely conscious of the fact that they, in turn, were watching him. With malice in mind. Well, let them glower, whatever they were. He had yet to encounter one that was capable of leaving its lair, and he would be careful not to give the least of them any opportunity to slip a hook, sucker, tentacle, or probe into his flesh.

Others, strolling blind and innocent on a clear, cool desert morning, were not so fortunate.

It was agony to be able to witness their activities and not do anything about them. Were they immortal, with their twisting, curling little malevolent probes? Or after penetrating and entering a human host, did they perish when the human died? If they were not everlasting, then unless they were a recently arrived phenomena, that meant they had to reproduce and multiply somehow. Unless they were incredibly long-lived, the latter must be the case, because their history stretched back at least as far as the Chachapoyan culture.

What must have been the reaction, he wondered, of the Chachapoyan shaman who had first concocted and then partaken of the potion that enabled a human to see otherwise invisible, undetectable monstrosities? He must have been an astonishing individual indeed not to have gone mad on the spot. Or perhaps it was not so very remarkable. Ancient peoples were closer to the inexplicable, to the spirit world, to phenomena that contemporary man dismissed as imaginary when he was unable to reduce to the coldness of a mathematical formula what he had experienced but could not explain. Cody wished he could have known that long-dead, perceptive, and incalculably brave avatar.

Now the knowledge had been passed down to him,

and a large part of him wished circumstances had decreed otherwise.

Would the effects of the potion ever wear off, or had ingesting it permanently altered his perception? Certainly his new vision was, if anything, sharper than ever today. Drifting restlessly toward his first lecture, he watched tendrils and tentacles, appendages and creepers sprout from landscaping boulders and barrel cacti, from small shade trees and the granite-faced walls of the physics building. Tenacious pebbles put forth tiny feelers while dozens of identical small stones remained unpolluted by inimical protrusions. The same was true of growing things. A cluster of dangerous-looking prickly-pear thrust only flat green, thorn-laden pads sunward, while a shaded rose bush lush with pink blossoms was lined with small, snapping gray mouths like fanged oysters. Even the little stream that ran through the campus pushed questing, intangible stingers upward, ethereal snags that weaved lazily back and forth in the current of a raging incorporeal river.

Much as he might want to, if only for sanity's sake, he could not keep from making observations and drawing conclusions. His scientific training would not let him do otherwise, would not let him conveniently ignore the inimical phenomena all around him. The preliminary theory that had been percolating in his brain ever since he'd perceived the first of the apparitions drew supporting evidence from each new, unsettling encounter.

The creatures abided only in natural objects. That much was clear. Decorative rocks regardless of size, composition, or shape; plants ranging from small old-woman cacti to bordering oleander to tall shade trees; the stream that ran into the nearby Salt River, and any insignificantly altered derivatives thereof seemed to provide suitable shelter for them. Not one synthetic or rigorously blended material put forth questing, probing feelers. Anything made of refined metal or plastic was notably sterile. A wooden beam or panel might harbor its clandestine anomaly, but a pile of sawdust would not. He still wasn't comfortable with wallboard or pressboard, or even plywood with its multiple laminated layers.

Could the creatures travel from one habitation to another? So far he had seen no evidence of that. He felt a little better. If they were restricted to their own exclusive stone or tree or watercourse, it suggested that uncorrupted objects such as furniture that did not already harbor something malicious within their wooden superstructure would be safe to sit or lie upon.

As he walked, he passed a sea of translucent, worm-like creepers writhing and convulsing from beneath a lawn in the strengthening light of morning. Having always thought that nightmares properly belonged to the night, it was stomach-churning to see them active and alert by day. None of the sightless, insouciant students, workers, or teachers he encountered reacted when they passed within reach of and through the ocean of unfriendly probes. But if actual, physical contact was made . . .

A girl of about twenty sat down on a flat-topped whitish boulder in the shade of the library annex. When he saw what was about to happen, Cody prepared to give a warning shout. What he would have shouted, what words he could possibly have employed, remained a matter for personal conjecture, since he was too late.

What looked like a pair of greenish, disembodied, broken-jointed hands emerged from either side of the boulder, grasped the girl around the waist, and vanished into her flanks. Simultaneously aghast and fascinated, Cody stopped to observe. For several moments following the incursion, nothing happened. The student set her books down next to the rock, opened a large, hand-embroidered bag that hailed from somewhere in Central America, and pulled out a text. Opening it on her lap, she began to read. Aware that he had halted and was now blocking the intermittent flow of student traffic, Cody moved off to one side—careful to remain on the concrete sidewalk and avoid the nearby lawn.

Several minutes more passed. Abruptly, the expression on the girl's face warped. Putting one hand to her belly, she just managed to turn away from where she had set down her purse before she threw up in a succession of violent heaves. Several other students rushed to see if they could help.

Was that the end of it? Cody wondered. What would happen now? Would she continue to throw up all day, or all week? As her friends steadied her next to the rock, something crawled out of her left thigh. None of them saw it, none reacted to its emergence. Only Coshocton Westcott was so cursed.

Looking like a wad of discarded, colorless jelly, the lump lay quivering on the ground. One anxious, oblivious student stepped directly on and through it. The imperceptible obscenity continued to lie where it had burst forth into the world. And then it came apart, splitting into half a dozen smaller redactions of itself. Humping off in different directions, one by one they vanished into, and presumably took up residence within, an equal number of untenanted rocks. The concerned students continued to attend to the sick girl, who was recovering rapidly.

Despite the intensifying heat of the sun, Cody felt a deep chill. The answer to one of the innumerable questions that had begun to torment him had just been answered: The creatures were indeed capable of, and probably reliant upon, a form of reproduction.

But what did they get from their human hosts? The girl was smiling now, albeit wanly. She had not lost weight and was suffering no further visible ill effects. All of the

discomfort, however fleeting, had been internal. Even if
Cody had enjoyed access to the training and equipment
necessary to begin testing her, or any other victim of the
unnamed organisms, he would hardly have known where
to begin. He resumed walking toward the General Sciences building and the lecture hall he would be using for
his first class.

Rather than being an isolated incident, the encounter
with the girl was only one of many he observed that day.
A young couple, married graduate students from the look
of them, were leaning up against a rock wall when a
dozen or more thin, glistening ropes emerged from the
bare stone. One by one they slithered into various parts
of both unsuspecting, unreacting young bodies, entering
via ear and arm, buttock or ankle. As soon as the last of
them had taken up residence within the host pair, the man
and woman fell to arguing. Softly at first, then with vehemence. Soon both were gesticulating angrily. The
woman slapped her partner, hard, catching him square
across the face. Responding, he reached out and grabbed
her by the shoulders and began to shake her violently.
Noticing that others were now turning in the direction of
the altercation, they stepped back from one another and
strode off, still arguing furiously, spewing insults and im-
precations they were likely to regret later—when it would
be too late to take them back.

From their shoulders and ribs, thighs and feet, intangible tentacles coiled outward. They were swelling, even
as a horrified, stunned Cody watched, engorging themselves with whatever it was they were taking from their
combative, belligerent, abstracted hosts. The louder and
more public the argument became, the greater the bloat
of the invisible parasites.

What were they feeding on? Cody brooded. Not blood,
not flesh. That much was apparent. What then? Some

sort of invisible fluid that humans were entirely unaware of? Violent psychic emanations? A soupçon of the electrical impulses that raced through specific portions of the brain when it was adversely stimulated? What was the connection between the unfortunate girl who had suddenly and violently heaved her guts and this abruptly bellicose couple? Were chosen, unwary hosts only temporarily impaired or did some kind of imperceptible permanent damage result? If he had any hope of descrying the answers to such questions, in addition to a chemist he would now need the help of a physiologist, a couple of doctors, and maybe a psychic or two. For the moment, though, every gathering mystery devolved solely upon him. He was the one, the only one among thousands, perhaps millions, who could See.

Sitting on a lawn, indifferent to the tiny malicious cilia that were probing his backside and legs, a gardener on break was eating an apple. Suddenly he threw down the half-eaten fruit and climbed to his feet. Hands jammed in pockets, he stomped off toward the main maintenance area, his expression drawn, his lips working as he spoke only to himself. Like glistening grains of rice, a handful of lawn cilia had penetrated his clothing. What would be their effect on their new host? Cody mused. A snappish attitude toward friends and co-workers, a long-term headache, or worse?

How deeply could the rarefied organisms affect people? Could they induce road rage in susceptible drivers? What about inspiring someone to commit robbery, or persist in child-beating, or attempt suicide? Was there a particular variety of the parasitoids potent enough to persuade one human to murder another? Or conversely, to offer up a victim? If a host died, did the parasite within derive pleasure, or some perverse kind of nourishment from the experience? He could see, but he was observing the organisms from a state of near-total ignorance, and the subjects of his scrutiny did not lend themselves to detailed examination under controlled laboratory conditions. From the standpoint of a would-be researcher into the vicious, malevolent phenomena, he was virtually helpless.

If he could not manipulate his surroundings for purposes of study, could he perhaps affect events? That, at least, was something he could test. He was determined to do so, even if it exposed him to additional danger. Standing idly by, watching quietly and doing nothing while knowing he was the only sighted individual in the country of the blind, was driving him crazy. If he could not dissect, could not measure, could not record, then maybe he could at least interfere.

The opportunity to do so presented itself following his last afternoon class, as he was on his way to the library to check out a tome needed for the paper he was ostensibly preparing to submit to *Archaeology News and Reviews*. He did not have to meet Kelli for the drive home for another couple of hours yet. She still had an undergraduate class and a follow-up seminar to teach.

The man with the van was unloading cases of canned soda, undoubtedly to stock one of the ubiquitous, coin-operated vending machines that populated the campus. Wheeling his hand truck like a skilled dancer leading his partner, he paused a moment outside a building to wipe sweat from his brow. Standing behind the hand truck, handkerchief in hand, he noticed the bed of blooming pansies nestled up against the walkway, and bent to examine them. Maybe he was drawn by their fragrance, or maybe he just liked flowers. He could not see and had no way of knowing that something brooding deep within the colorful blossoms was about to take a malicious liking to him.

Divining what was about to happen, Cody changed course and rushed toward the delivery man, shouting as he ran. Fingertips pausing a few inches from the pansies, the campus visitor looked up and straightened. Beneath his hands, a pellucid set of multiple jaws strained impotently.

"Something I can do for you?" The almost-victim's tone was curious, but not agitated.

Breathing hard, Cody slowed to a halt, careful to keep his feet away from the flower bed. "Ummm-no, nothing. I thought you were someone else. Sorry." He indicated the building. "Delivering's easier this time of year, isn't it?"

"Yeah, summer's a bitch." Flowers forgotten, the visitor gripped the handles of the hand truck, pressed them down to a comfortable angle for walking, then pushed up the access ramp and into the building.

Had he saved the man a headache? Cody wondered. Or perhaps prevented a fatal auto accident later in the day? How much of common human misery could be attributed to the chancre of invisible, malignant, ever hungry, invisible monstrosities that only he could see? The responsibility for thwarting them, for interfering with their infectious activities, was overwhelming. It was far too much for one individual, especially one as ignorant as Cody felt himself to be. And no one would believe him, would understand what he was doing or why. No one, except perhaps, one day soon, his wife. *If* he was fortunate, and if he could somehow come up with proof of what he was seeing.

It would take time, he knew. Kelli was not the kind of person to be easily persuaded of the unthinkable. But he would convince her, somehow. He would have to. Otherwise, as witness to his eccentric behavior, she might from the best of intentions have him locked up. He could

not allow that to happen. Not when he was the only one
who could See. Not when he was the only one who could
help.

It felt *good* to have saved the nameless delivery man
from infection. With luck, before the day was done he
would be able to perform the same good deed for a few
others. None would ever know that their lives had been
affected. None would realize that a stranger had saved
them from physical or mental distress, or worse. But *he*
would know. He would know, and that would be satisfaction enough.

The creatures would know, too, he realized. Could
they do anything about it? He had yet to encounter any
evidence that they could affect or influence a human
without benefit of direct physical contact. So he would
be very careful where he stepped and what he touched,
and gauge his life according to his new knowledge. He
would continue to study them, and learn about them, and
with luck, he would find a way to frustrate them on an
ever-increasing scale. The weight of his new obligation
was one he accepted without real enthusiasm, and then
only because morally he felt he had no choice.

The remainder of the afternoon was spent in effect-
ing minor salvations. He was convinced he personally
prevented at least two auto accidents; one minor, the other
with the potential to result in serious injury or even death.
In both instances an assortment of spectacularly hideous
alien apparitions visible and audible only to his chemi-
cally altered perception fumed powerlessly at him, threatening with tentacles and teeth, with razor-edged suckers
and wet, unclean fumy lips. He found that he could swing
a hand through them with little effect, as if he were swat-
ting at soap bubbles, so long as he did not make contact
with their assorted abodes. At such moments disgusting
protuberances beckoned him closer, inviting the contact

he prudently refused. Even at a distance of half an inch, they were powerless to affect him. Make contact with their stable habitats, however, and he knew he would be instantly infected.

Unlike Kelli, he had no classes scheduled that afternoon. Instead of retiring to his cramped, paper-filled office to peruse student assignments or work on his professional papers, curiosity took him off-campus. Even though the fall semester was in full cry, the main drag of Mill Avenue was aswarm with students and wannabes. The used bookstores were busy, the multitude of trendy coffee shops and juice bars and small restaurants frenetic, the theme stores alive with shoppers, browsers, and unobtrusive security staff.

Many of the larger stores, both new and old, were made of brick, with concrete or carpeted floors that lay flush against cement sidewalks. Visitors to such establishments were safe from the depredations of the creatures. One small bagel and coffee shop whose floor was laid with decorative slate was not so secure. Blurred cilia and indistinct spikes thrust upward, probing for visiting victims. For the endemic monstrosities it was a veritable feeding ground.

Most of the decorative trees that lined the street were uninhabited, but some put forth branches and shoots that were not part of the tree itself. Everywhere across the country, Cody mused, one city after another was adding the same kind of elaborate landscaping to otherwise sterile downtown areas. He found himself wondering how much of that was due to an honest human desire to be surrounded by greenery, and how much might have been influenced by the creatures in order to provide themselves with places to live in the middle of an otherwise inhospitable artificial urban environment.

A fresh-faced young girl, probably no more than a

sophomore, was preparing to chain her bike to a small sidewalk tree. From within its trunk, long, thin ropelike structures glimmering with slime emerged to reach for her. Hurrying forward, Cody put a hand on her shoulder just in time to prevent her from wrapping the chain around and making contact with the slender trunk.

"Hey, watch it!" Startled, she swung her own arm, casting off his grip. Invisible to her but all too tangible to the archaeologist, anxious threads thrashed the still air.

"Sorry." Cody raised both palms toward her in a pacifying gesture. "I'm Professor Westcott, from the archaeology department." He nodded in the direction of the steel grate that was bolted to the sidewalk outside the nearest store. "You're supposed to use the bike racks."

"Yeah, okay." Irritated, she swung the bike around and wheeled it toward the rack. "You don't have to get touchy-feely about it."

What had he saved her from? he wondered as he watched her padlock the security chain to bike and rack. A bad menstrual period? Temporary mental breakdown? Riding her bike into the path of an oncoming bus? Taking a knife to some baffled boyfriend? Turning back to the tree, he felt nothing as furious streamers of resentful, malignant plasm flailed at his face. Unless he touched the tree, they could do nothing. A pair of tiny, pupilless eyes popped out of the trunk and slid along the length of one pseudopod until they hung from the very end, gazing at him. Feeling quite invulnerable, he met the malevolent stare evenly.

"You can't touch me, can you? You can't do a damn thing unless I make contact. For all your ability to influence others, you can't lay a single one of your repulsive little tendrils on me. You can't—"

Something struck him in the back, between his shoulders. As he lurched forward, the bundle of ropelike structures emanating from the tree parted to receive him. Only by twisting violently and throwing himself to the side did he just barely succeed in stumbling past the tree instead of slamming into it, and into that which dwelled within.

Eyes wide, fear accelerating his heartbeat, he regained his footing and turned, to find himself gazing into the face of an equally frightened young man. He wore thick-lensed glasses and shouldered a book-laden backpack.

"Oh, jeez, I'm sorry, mister! You okay?"

"Yeah." Regaining his composure, Cody ignored the straining, imperceptible appendages that were ineffectively stroking his shirt.

"I wasn't watching where I was going." Smiling hesitantly, uncertain if his apology was sufficient, the student hurried off up the street and disappeared into the crowd.

Cody stepped away from the possessed tree. He had been standing there, too close really, contemplating the awfulness of the would-be parasite within the wood, and the preoccupied kid had walked into him. An accident. Or—was it? He wanted to confront the young man, to ask him some pointed questions, but he was already lost to sight, swallowed up by the milling throng on Mill Avenue. Sure it was an accident. It had to be.

He took his revenge for the near disaster by traversing the busiest portion of the street several times. By four-thirty he had lost track of how many minor and major brutal incursions he had prevented. More than he expected, less than he had feared. In every instance the creatures railed furiously at his interference. In addition to his immunity to their influence, he began to feel a sense of real accomplishment, that he was doing something tangible to help people. His intervention constituted a kind of temporary inoculation against the effects of the unnamed depravities. He was acutely aware that the creatures were conscious of his hindering, but the more often he interposed himself between them and their intended victims without suffering any untoward consequences himself, the more secure in his activities he became. It was clear that they could do nothing, and he was careful not to allow anyone else close enough to nudge or bump him into a host tree or rock.

Cody Westcott had discovered the secret of why bad things happen to good people—and the ancient instigators of those bad things were not at all happy about it.

Was it that same knowledge that had allowed the mysterious Chachapoyans to maintain their little civilization against the depredations of far more militant empires like the Chimu and the Moche? If that was the case, then how had they allowed themselves to be overcome by the Incas? Chachapoyan ruins such as Apachetarimac and Cuelap, Gran Vilaya and others showed no signs of military devastation. Instead of overwhelming the Chachapoyans' seemingly impregnable fortresses, had the Incas simply outsmarted them? Had they somehow made use of the same secret knowledge Cody was now privy to in order to conquer not only the Chachapoyans, but every other civilization that lay between Colombia and Tierra del Fuego? If they had utilized the creatures, or been utilized by them, it would explain a great deal.

If that was the case, he ruminated as he wandered back toward the campus to rendezvous with Kelli for the ride home, then how had they eventually been overcome by Pizarro and his small party of conquistadors? Perhaps the creatures had grown bored with their contented Indian hosts and their stable empire. If they thrived in the presence of human grief, what more amenable to their dark, esoteric condition than a nice, massacre-filled war with its aftermath of slavery and oppression?

In his mind's eye Cody saw the Spanish Inquisition pronouncing judgment on generations of poor Andean Indios as well as their own kind, serpentine tendrils and teeth and ichorous suckers fluttering from the foreheads of parasitized judges and prosecutors. He began to feel that there was more, much more, at stake in his discovery than the realization that something inimical and invisible to the mass of mankind might be responsible for migraine headaches, upset stomachs, and the occasional inexplicable auto accident.

So engrossed was he in this rapidly expanding exegesis that he almost started across the decomposed granite landscaping that fronted the main administration building by using the stepping stones arranged there. These were fashioned from natural flagstone, not a composite material, and they were waiting for him. At the last instant he moved his right leg sideways instead of forward, bringing it down on the crushed rock. It crunched harmlessly underfoot. A ten-inch wide, fanged mouth surmounted by a single feral, catlike eye appeared in the center of the stepping stone where he had nearly placed his foot. It snapped impotently at his ankles as he strode carefully past. Perhaps a fifth of the stepping stones harbored similar sinister orifices.

Too close, he told himself. *Cogitate all you want, but never, ever, lose sight of the world around you lest you bump into an object that is home to something hungry and unforgiving.* Once the least of the now alerted horrors got its hooks, or whatever, into him, he knew it would never let go. Gifted with a singular perception that was denied to the rest of humankind, he had become a threat to every previously ignored and discounted being that fed off the raw, ragged emotions of the planet's dominant species. The reality of that dominance, he reflected as he made his way toward the central quad, was now something very much in doubt. If it ever had been a reality.

With a start, he realized he did not even have a name for what he was fighting.

Two weeks and a day later, he had visitors.

Six

The middle-aged Asian male who strolled into the Baja Naja outdoor restaurant just off Mill did not draw a second glance from the late-lunch crowd of students, teachers, office workers, retirees, and tourists. In no way did his physique, posture, or expression impact on the bustling dynamic of the outdoor congregation. No one noticed that his stride was more confident than was typical of his age and demeanor, or that the slight upward curl of his lips might indicate a general contempt for the more youthful, more attractive people gathered in the popular hangout.

He took a table by himself, in the back, away from the street, and ordered quietly and without fuss, barely taking the time to glance at the menu. Cody didn't even know he existed until the man rose, picked up his glass of ice water, and approached him.

"Good morning, Professor Westcott." The visitor glanced at his watch. "It is still morning, I suppose. I see that you are alone. Mind if I join you?"

Cody considered the stranger, struggling to place the polite enigma who was blocking his view of the street.

"Do I know you?" His smile was instinctive, automatic, and unfounded.

"No sir, but you will." Without waiting for Cody's answer, the man slipped into the vacant chair on the other side of the round, glass-topped table. "You may call me Uthu."

Not, "my name is . . ." or "Hi, I'm . . .", but "You may call me . . ." Much bigger than his visitor, and younger, Cody felt no immediate unease in the midst of the busy restaurant. The man did not act hostile. Like any large American university, ASU was visited by its share of nut cases, each claiming to represent the righteous while indifferently trampling on the rights of others. So far, he saw no reason to think ill of this quiet little fellow, other than that he was a trifle forward. His immediate concern was to finish the remainder of the club sandwich on his plate.

"I don't think I've ever met anyone named Uthu before."

"Distinctive people should have distinctive names." The man smiled, his appearance anything but distinctive. He was nothing if not assured, Cody reflected. "You, for example, have a distinctive name."

"Westcott?" Cody's response was muffled by his mouthful of sandwich.

"You are being humorous. Coshocton, of course. That is Amerindian, is it not?"

Cody chewed. "Commanche/Cherokee. What's Uthu?"

Again the unnervingly confident half smile. "Say, Asian. No need to be specific. To us such things are a relic of another existence, before we became venues."

Now his visitor was starting to make nut noises, Cody decided. Glancing around casually as he wiped his hands with a linen napkin, he scanned the street for signs of a passing cop. None were in sight. He also paid attention to the man's hands. At the moment they rested on the table, in plain sight. If one slid toward a pocket, Cody felt he might have to react. Still, the Department of Archaeology was not typically a destination of deranged individuals. They tended to favor the animal research center, or the student newspaper, or the science labs that did work for the military. Research on bones and pots did not engender the kind of primeval passion that normally led to physical assault.

"I see," he replied carefully. Waving a bit too energetically in the direction of the waiter, he called for his check. It was time to go. "And what, if you don't mind my asking, are you a venue for?"

"This." Leaning forward, the man went slack as half-a-dozen tendrils erupted from his eye sockets. Each one terminated in a single, smaller eye that was a venomous and sickly yellow. Thicker tentacles tinged with green burst forth from his stomach, while from the vicinity of his crotch emerged a set of black jaws lined with multiple rows of small, sharp teeth.

Cody flailed wildly and nearly fell off his chair. His fluttering fingers swept through reaching eyes and tentacles and blackness. A cold dampness enveloped his hands, as if they had been plunged into a pool of liquid death. Tiny, vicious mouths snapped spitefully at his flesh but did no damage. Several diners glanced in his direction, only to return indifferently to their half-eaten meals and half-finished conversations. No one saw anything more than a lanky young man who had momentarily slipped out of his chair.

The eyeballs on stalks withdrew, the tendrils contracted, and the vile ebon maw sank back out of sight between the man's legs. He blinked once, as if he had momentarily been asleep, or comatose. No smile accompanied his revived consciousness.

Cody wanted to run away, as he had run from a nest of baby rattlers when at the age of seven he slipped and became trapped in a narrow arroyo on his uncle's ranch. It was a beautiful day. He was surrounded by happy, active people content in their work and leisure. Outside, beyond the iron fence that marked the limits of the outdoor restaurant, ubiquitous English sparrows hopped energetically to and fro, scavenging for table crumbs. A pair of rocks protruded from landscaping gravel. From each rock a saw-edged shaft projected vertically, weaving slowly back and forth like a lethal yucca. The sparrows ignored it. So did the people using the sidewalk beyond. They could not see it. Only Cody could see it. He—and Uthu.

"What are you?" Cody spoke slowly as he straightened his chair beneath him. The monstrosities abiding within the smaller man could not molest him or they would certainly already have done so. Evidently they were restricted to one host at a time. It was instructive, the cool scientific part of his mind noted automatically, to have confirmed the supposition that a single person could play host to more than one of the disquieting parasites.

"A man, like yourself. Human, but one who has given himself over to the Interlopers."

"So that's what they're called." It felt unreasonably good to be able to finally give a name to the diverse miscellany of malevolent nightmares.

"It is what we who are given over have chosen to call them. They have no name for their collective selves. We who are given over do not 'talk' to them in the accepted sense, nor do we share anything like a recognizable telepathy. We must rely on feelings, sensations, certain urges."

They had moved into territory wholly new to Cody, a place where he had not even ventured to speculate. "You mean, you *voluntarily* serve as a host to these things?"

"Not at first. No one becomes a host intentionally. The

great majority of humans who are called upon have no awareness of their altered state. They are blessed by a sustained ignorance of their condition."

Around them, the sun was shining, pretty girls were laughing, young men posturing energetically. Food and drink were being affably consumed, and traffic flowed smoothly on Mill. And he was sitting outdoors at the Baja Naja, toying with the remains of a perfectly agreeable if unspectacular lunch while discussing a kind of previously unsuspected diabolic state of being with an extensively parasitized visitor from another continent. He needed a drink, but the restaurant did not serve liquor until after five o'clock. Iced tea would have to do.

"You say they are blessed by their ignorance." Cody continued to watch the man's hands, which remained in plain view. "Doesn't sound to me like being 'given over' is a condition to be desired."

"It is not," the man assured him somberly. "One leads a life of unending misery and despair, of physical pain and mental torment. But there are compensations."

"Yeah, it sounds like it."

"Sarcasm is misplaced in a scientist." Uthu continued without missing a beat. "Sometimes when I think I cannot stand the suffering, when my brain will tear itself to pieces from the sheer unrelenting anguish of serving as a host, I console myself with the knowledge that I will live longer than all but a very few of my fellow humans. It is not immortality, not by any means, but it is something. A crumb of a gift, but a gift nonetheless."

"So these Interlopers, they can extend a life?" Cody prompted him.

A slow nod provided an answer. "Once comfortably settled within a cooperative venue, they have that ability, yes."

"That's no gift." Cody was at once fascinated and horrified by the parasitized man sitting across the table from him. "No parasite wants its host to die. If that happens, it has to go through the trouble of finding another." He frowned in remembrance. "I've passed my hands through a number of them without suffering more than a quick chill. Yet you say that once inside, they cause pain and torment."

Uthu nodded somberly. "That is what they want. They do not, cannot, induce cerebral discomfort directly. It follows as a consequence of mental anguish."

"Yet in spite of that you serve as a venue," the archaeologist murmured.

"Yes, we serve. What choice do we have? Once infected, it is not possible to be made clean again. For that to happen, an Interloper must leave of its own accord."

"Do they ever do that? Abandon a host, I mean?"

"No." The Asian's face was drawn but resigned. "Never. Not until the host dies."

"Or turns psychotic." Cody speculated pensively.

"Not at all." Uthu was quick to correct him. "Interlopers prosper amidst insanity. They thrive on the milk of madness."

"I've seen people become infected. None of them showed any awareness of what was happening to them. Why are you different?"

"Some of us, a very few, have within our minds the ability to sense that we have been contaminated. This makes us valuable to the Interlopers. They exist on a plane adjacent to our own. The many points of congruence are subtler than you think. While they can move freely within rock and solid wood, physically the Interlopers cannot affect our world. But they can affect those few like myself, and we in turn can affect *our* plane of existence. Like so."

Cody flinched, but the man's hand was not reaching

for him. Instead, it swept aside the water glass that had been set before him. Cold water and ice went flying, just missing the couple seated at the table nearest to them. The girl rose sharply, wiping at where her thigh lay bare beneath the short skirt. Her male companion looked irritated.

"Sorry—we're sorry. It was an accident," Cody apologized hastily. Sufficiently mollified, the young couple returned to their meal. Sitting back down, the archaeologist glared across the table. "There was no call for that."

"On the contrary, there is always call for that," Uthu assured him quietly. "And for—other things."

Cody's eyes widened. "*You* killed Harry Keeler!"

The Asian smiled ever so thinly. Was he by nature this calm and cavalier, the archaeologist wondered, or was he being wholly controlled by outside influences? Or in his case, inside ones. How much of what he was saying, how many of his words, were his own, and how much and how many the province of something else? Was he an independent human being working in concert with the horrors that now possessed him, body and soul, or was he nothing more than a slave, a puppet, responding to the pestilent strings that now penetrated his brain as well as his body? His was clearly a case of extreme parasitism. Had his Interlopers left him any individuality at all, or was he little more than a shell of the human being he had once been? The answers, Cody decided, were a matter for biologists to determine. Or a psychic, or possibly an exorcist, though there was nothing Catholic about the suave Uthu's possession.

"No. It was not I."

"I've seen enough of these creatures to know that they can't physically strike out at a person. You have to make contact with their habitation for them to be able to affect you. Or they can make contact by having an infected individual impact on another, just like they're making you talk to me, right now."

Uthu nodded. "A good scientist is a trained observer. You perceive, note, and draw inferences. They would like you to be like me." Seeing that Cody was watching his hands closely, the visitor smiled. "Don't worry, I'm not going to grab you. They can only pass from a natural habitation to a human, not from one human to another. Otherwise it would not have been necessary to annul the man you call Harry Keeler. He could simply have been co-opted."

"Are you going to try and kill me?" Cody was amazed at his own degree of calm, sitting outside in the shade, surrounded by laughing, conversing, debating people, discussing his own demise with a stranger whose actions were being directed by invisible, hitherto unknown parasites inimical in nature and composition. It beggared belief in ways that would have given pause to a theoretical physicist.

How many dimensions did they now claim made up the universe? Eleven, wasn't it? Or ten? Or was the matter still up for debate? Were these Interlopers intruders from one of those five dimensions kept neatly "rolled up" by physicists? Were humans their point of contact with this dimension? And what, exactly did they get out of invading and influencing and residing within humans themselves?

Despite Uthu's flattering remark, Cody was well aware that he did not know nearly enough yet to draw conclusions; not about the Interlopers, nor about the individuals they infected.

"If necessary." Uthu replied calmly to the archaeologist's question. "Keeler was abolished because he was in possession of the written formula for the elixir that enables humans to see Interlopers. That was a very dangerous thing. If humans could see the Interlopers, they would avoid them. Then no Interloper would be able to feed."

" 'Feed'?" The revelation conjured a storm of images in Cody's brain, each more repellent than the one before.

The Asian did not elaborate. "Naturally, the Interlopers wish to prevent such a calamity from happening. Since the dawn of mankind they have usually managed to do so. The Chachapoyan shamans were an exception, and their rising civilization a concern, until they were conquered and absorbed by the Incas."

"So these Interlopers influenced the Incas to overthrow the Chachapoyans?"

"Yes." Uthu smiled thoughtfully. "Though the Incas would have done it eventually anyway, just as they subjugated every other Andean civilization. The Interlopers simply assisted where possible—and of course, enjoyed the fruits of their labors: war, famine, despair. Once the Incas had conquered all their neighbors and absorbed them, their Empire of the Sun grew too content to support many Interlopers. That was when the Spanish arrived. So few in number, they could never have vanquished the Inca Empire without some—assistance.

"It became imperative that the Empire be destroyed, because when the Chachapoyan cities were incorporated into the Inca kingdom, so was their knowledge of the Interlopers, and other things. There was a great danger that the Incas would disseminate this new knowledge."

While Cody the individual feared for his life, Cody the archaeologist was fascinated by his visitor's tale. "So, after helping the Incas defeat the Chachapoyans and others, they turned on them and helped Pizarro and his conquistadors to conquer the Empire?"

"Not exactly. They helped the Incas to *lose* to the conquistadors. There is a difference." The smile widened unpleasantly. "Remember the reactions of the Incas to the arrival of the Spanish. While they could see many of the Interlopers, they could not keep track of them all. It was the Interlopers who started the fight between Atahualpa and his brother, thus splitting and weakening a previously united Empire at its most vulnerable moment. It was an Interloper who influenced the Inca to stupidly permit himself to be taken captive by the Spaniards. After that, it was Interlopers who spread divisiveness and fear among those Incas who were still determined to resist the invaders." Sitting back in his chair, Uthu sipped at his glass of water.

"You know how the Incas were terrified of Spaniards on horseback, how they thought they were a frightful combination of man and beast? They suffered from no such fears until the Interlopers spread those weaknesses among them. Why should they think such things, when they had always had around them four-legged beasts of burden such as llamas and alpacas and vicuñas, unless they had been encouraged and inflamed to think differently? Why do you think the vast reinforcements they could call upon did not come to the aid of their rulers until it was too late, allowing the Spaniards to carve up the Empire piece by piece? One of the Interlopers' great strengths is their ability to work in subtle ways."

"They influenced and weakened the whole Empire in that fashion?" Cody was nonplused. Like all of his colleagues, he had always admired the Incas and marveled at the ease with which a ruthless but pitifully small band of invading Spaniards had destroyed an Empire that reached from Colombia to Chile.

"No. It was not possible to taint every Inca. Only those in power, the nobles and the generals and their immediate subordinates, were affected. And only a few of them, at that." This time, the visitor's smile was entirely ruthless, contorted by something utterly inhuman. "The Incas, fortunately, loved to be around rock and stone. Selective infestation could be carried out in a prompt and efficient manner. Occasionally, for various reasons, it could not be accomplished appropriately or in time. Ollyantaytambo was the most glaring example."

Cody started. "The Incas beat the Spaniards there. Twice."

The Asian nodded. "Until the commanding general and his staff could be visited, and persuaded to do the necessary thing. Only then did the Sacred Valley of the Urubamba fall to the Spaniards." Gazing off into the distance, the man who was no longer unconditionally human wore a look of bliss. "Soon after that, the Inquisition arrived."

"Yes, and the consequences for—" Cody broke off, his train of thought interrupted by yet another repellent revelation. "More work of these Interlopers?"

Uthu's smile was positively feral. "You do draw conclusions well." He pushed back from the table. "We're not going to kill you. For now. Not because we can't. Your ability to see those whom we abide does not protect you from we who have been blessed." Even as Uthu spoke the words, Cody thought he could see something still human, something chained and suffering in the throes of ultimate unending torment, screaming to get out from behind the Asian's too-bright eyes. "We are the arms, the appendages of Those Who Abide. We can work physically what they cannot. This we do for them.

"We will not kill you because it is widely known that you were working with Harry Keeler. Coming so close to his, your unexpected demise would arouse suspicions. It has therefore been decided to let you live." A different sort of smile, warm and ingratiating, creased the Asian's visage. It was as faux as the wood painted to look like marble that lined much of the main reading room of the library. "All you have to do is give up any research on the Chachapoyan shamanic codex, destroy your existing notes on it, and have nothing further to do with the subject. Oh yes," he added pleasantly, "and stop interfering with the established activities of the Interlopers in this part of the world. You may observe them all you wish. It is only asked that you not intervene."

Cody had listened without comment. "Anything else?"

"Your wife will no doubt question your abrupt termination of this particular line of research. You must convince her that you have legitimate and innocuous reasons for doing so. Perhaps heightened interest in other aspects of your specialty. The rationale you concoct is of no importance to us. And of course you must also see to it that she does not pursue the work that you are to abandon. Should she do so, there could be—consequences." Uthu hesitated only briefly. "She is very pretty, your mate."

Cody's expression darkened. "How the hell would you know? What have you been doing? *Where have you been?*" Conscious that several diners had turned to look in his direction, he forced himself to lower his voice. "You keep away from Kelli. She has nothing to do with this. In fact, she thinks I was crazy for spending all the time on it that I did, especially working with Harry."

"Then that will make it easy for her to accept your change of focus." The visitor rose from his chair. "Despite what you may think, we who serve Those Who Abide are still human. We still have human desires, and needs. Remember that, lest you are tempted to ignore this warning. Defy Those Who Abide, and you will find yourself envying the man Harry Keeler." Perhaps aware that he might be erring on the side of challenge, he reached down to pick up the check for Cody's lunch.

"Why should you care, Coschocton Westcott? Humankind has survived and prospered in the presence of the Interlopers. It will continue to do so even in the presence of your silence. Leave the world as you found it a year ago. You know something of people, alive as well as dead. Are they not better off not knowing? Reveal all to them, and there would be panic, hysteria, and a reign of terror and death."

"Just as there has always been," Cody replied tersely. "The question is: How much of that is due to natural, guileless human activity, how much to enduring species immaturity, and how much to the presence of and interference by Interlopers? We don't seem to have done too well, to have acted very intelligently, while they have been active among us, influencing and persuading and 'feeding.' Maybe we'd be a lot better off without them. Maybe we would even grow up a little." Fearful but determined, he leaned forward across the table.

"I'm no biologist, but I have yet to encounter an instance of an animal that's not better off in the absence of parasites."

Uthu did not withdraw from the younger, bigger man's presence. "It is not for you to decide. Not for you, or me, or any other person." Within his visitor, Cody continued to sense the shrunken remnants of a real individual human being howling to emerge from a very private and particularly loathsome prison. There was nothing he could do for this Uthu, he knew. He found himself wondering: Could he do anything for anyone else?

They seemed to know everything. About him, his work, even Kelli. He could not make any decisions without considering her. It would be easier if she believed him. Or maybe, just maybe, it was better that she did not.

Was it so very much that Uthu was asking on behalf of the repulsiveness that abided in the world? One empire would always conquer another, with or without the outside intervention of Interlopers. People would always fight, argue, bicker and disagree, whether influenced by abiding Interlopers or not. Or—would they? Exactly how much of human misery and despair was a natural consequence of sheer existence, and how much due to the interference of this vast panoply of unearthly parasitic beings? If he could alter that equation of suffering, even a little, did he not have a duty to do so?

His research had given him the gift of sight in a world where blindness to a widespread, specific evil reigned unchallenged. Did he not owe it to his fellow man to utilize that talent to the best of his ability, and for the greater good? It was a measure of the Interlopers' concern that they had gone to the trouble of murdering one individual and threatening another to keep knowledge of their existence, and their influence on human affairs, covert. Perhaps they were not so omnipotent as the hapless Uthu insinuated.

If their intention was to frighten him, they could have chosen a more intimidating figure than the comparatively diminutive Asian. Maybe they exerted complete control over only a very few humans. Of course, he reminded himself as he sat at the table and ignored what remained of his lunch, it did not take a very large or powerful person to pull the trigger of a pistol. But they did not want him dead. Not if they could avoid it. Hadn't Uthu just said so? Coming so close to Harry Keeler's death, it would prompt inquiries more extensive than usual, give rise to questions they would rather not have asked.

For a little while then, for an indeterminate amount of time, he felt he could count on a modicum of safety. That was fortunate, because he had no intention whatsoever of complying with Uthu's demands. Once the turmoil caused by Professor Keeler's violent death had passed beyond the point of evening television newsworthiness, someone

would come for him in the night. Him, and doubtless
Kelli as well. Or they would be accosted on the street by
an armed mugger, who would "panic" and shoot them
both. Despite the Asian's reassuring speech, Cody had no
illusions about what lay in store for him. Unless he could
find a means of acquiring more positive protection than
the knowledge he now possessed and could not forswear,
he was a man without a future. The Interlopers would not
let anyone who knew of their existence live. Why should
they, when humans were so easy to kill?

They would tolerate his survival until they felt the time
was right and that it was safe for another member of the
university's faculty to depart this plane of existence without incurring a host of unanswerable questions. Even
though Kelli did not believe his stories of otherworldly
apparitions entering and somehow feeding on unwary
human beings, they would kill her, too. His wife was a
loose end who subsequent to his unexpected demise might
turn into a loose cannon. He strongly suspected that Those
Who Abide could be counted on not to leave a mess.

But what could he do? What he had managed to decipher so far of the Chachapoyan codex said nothing about
a means for protecting oneself from the influence of the
Interlopers. Was there, could there be, such a thing? And
if it existed, how was he to go about finding it? There
had to be something. If not, then the Chachapoyans could
not have raised up the remarkable mountain civilization
that eventually fell to the rapacious Incas.

There remained a trove of photographs of glyphs and
carvings that awaited explication. Far from abandoning
his work, he would throw himself back into it with a
vengeance. He had no idea how much time remained to
him, how long the Interlopers and their human vassals
would wait before deciding it was more hazardous to their

activities to leave him alive than render him dead. Meanwhile, he would trust no one, and would watch his back.

They had not been blatant in their execution of poor Harry Keeler. No one had walked up to the chemist and stuck a gun in his face. And Harry had been given no warning, had had no idea what was coming. He, Cody Westcott, was forewarned. He could keep watch.

His decision was made. Aside from his own welfare, there was too much potential for the general good riding on his continued research for him to quit now.

Which was undoubtedly why the Interlopers were so anxious to put a stop to it.

Seven

For several months, nothing happened. Though he put every minute he could spare from teaching, academic concerns, and his home and social life into his research, Cody was not disturbed. No one interrupted him, no one tried to put a stop to what he was doing. For a while, every time someone tapped him on the shoulder or grunted at him from behind, he would whirl sharply, expecting to confront the zealous, vaguely portentous shape of his menacing Asian visitor, Uthu. He never saw him again.

He had two papers published. One, a joint piece with Kelli on Chachapoyan glyphs and carvings, was widely reviewed. Kudos and commendations trickled into their respective offices. Jan Buchinski, their department head, was sufficiently pleased by the collateral academic celebrity and its attendant professional publicity to recommend both Westcotts for accelerated advancement to full professor status. Cody's solo paper on the origins of Chachapoyan shamanism, which was more narrowly focused and thus less widely disseminated, nonetheless marked him as an important young man in the field to watch. Kelli's work on Apachetarimac's architecture was likewise garnering considerable critical praise. Though they received better offers from half-a-dozen minor colleges and two major universities noted for the excellence of their archaeology departments, they elected, for the time being, to remain at ASU. Buchinski's recommendation that they both be promoted and given tenure had proved timely.

Cody was halfway through the rough draft of a follow-up paper, containing his views on certain aspects of Chachapoyan medicinal procedures both confirmed and hypothesized, when minor inscrutables began to intrude on his life.

At first they barely grazed his consciousness. For months he had been avoiding the conventional attentions of the local Interlopers. After a while it became automatic. He simply avoided making contact with unadulterated natural materials without even bothering to ascertain if they were home to one or more of the invasive creatures. Kelli still did not believe him, but when they were together he was able to steer her away from potential trouble. The rest of the time she was either at work or at home, both comparatively safe venues. Not every rock harbored a resident Interloper. Not every tree was a source of potential infection.

She had argued with him when he replaced the couch, one chair, the paneling behind their bed, and had the decorative stone in their backyard removed, but her irritation passed quickly. It was not as if he had insisted on redoing the entire house. When she pushed him for reasons he did not try to convince her yet again of the Interlopers' presence, but instead insisted he merely wanted a few minor aesthetic changes. By way of asserting her own independence in the matter, she promptly had the kitchen redone. He raised no objections. There were no Interlopers in the kitchen, and by bringing in new tile, paint, and paper she ran no risk of importing any.

So adept had he become at ferreting them out, so unthinking the process of perception, that he did not even glance anymore at the glistening greenish pseudopod that thrust forth every morning from the large decorative boulder that sat at the corner of Mill and Third Avenue. He was on his way to meet a couple of graduate students from his advanced seminar who were about to go south for the summer to work on the Peruvian site at San Jose de Moro. They wanted his advice on what to take with them. When the pseudopod groped in his direction, he simply walked right through it. So long as he made no contact with the boulder that served as its home, it could not affect him. He left it writhing furiously in his wake.

And then he slipped.

He did not see the oil on the street because it was covered with loose sheets of newspaper that had blown onto the spot and become stuck. The crumpled pages concealed a thick patch of the slick, gooey stuff, and as soon as he put his weight on it, his left leg went out from under him. The slip sent him careening sideways. A man walking nearby put down the bag he was carrying and rushed to help, but he was too far away and too late arriving. Cody went down hard, the shock of striking the solid concrete jarring his right arm and shoulder.

Odorless green effluvia clawed at his side, seeking a way in. In falling, he had just missed making firm contact with the boulder.

Shakily, he scrambled clear, eyeing the unwholesome inhabitant of the boulder as if it were a rabid anaconda tethered to a tree. It could not break loose, and he had not quite made contact. But it had been a near thing. The pseudopod represented an Interloper of considerable size. He had barely avoided a potentially severe infection.

Though late in arriving, the man with the bag was so-licitous. "You all right, friend? That was a pretty hard fall you just took."

"Yeah. Yeah, I'm okay." Still shaken, Cody was brush-ing street grime off his shirt. His shoulder throbbed where it had smashed into the sidewalk and his shirt now boasted a small rip that would cause the always money-conscious Kelli to sigh when she saw it. "Thanks for asking."

"No problem." Hefting his bag, the man resumed his own interrupted itinerary. "Better watch where you're stepping next time."

Cody looked away. "Damn papers covering the oil. I didn't see . . ." But wasn't he able to See, now?

Oil, papers, rock, Interloper. Surely just a coincidence, if nearly a lethal one. Whirling, he sought the would-be Samaritan, straining to see over the heads of wandering pedestrians. The man had vanished; into the crowds, into his car, or perhaps into a store. Cody started to go in search of him, then hesitated. What if the guy had been nothing more than what he appeared to be: a concerned bystander. In that event, Cody would come off looking pretty asinine if he challenged him, not to mention un-grateful.

With a last glance at the hungrily writhing Interloper, he resumed his walk, careful to step around any news-papers that were lying in the street whether they appeared to be hiding oil slicks or not. Safely reaching the juice bar where he was to meet the two students, he finally al-lowed himself to relax.

Nevertheless, the thought of how close he'd come to disaster stayed with him all the rest of the morning. By the time he and his students parted, he had come to the conclusion that the close encounter had been an isolated incident. While uniquely sensible of the singular dangers abroad in the world to which nearly everyone else was oblivious, he had to remember always that though he could perceive them, he was not immune to them. Awareness had made him imprudent. The incident was a warning for him to be more alert.

Disconcertingly, there were more warnings to come.

Two days later, for the first time, he witnessed an Interloper in the process of leaving its host. While walking down the hall toward an idling pair of university employees, Cody overheard one janitor complaining to the other that he had been suffering from a serious stomachache for days. As the archaeologist prepared to walk on by, he was startled to see a very small Interloper slither from the man's hand to enter the pumice stone he was holding. It looked like a bloated eel, fat from feeding on its host. How the Interlopers 'fed' was still a mystery to Cody, though his persevering work on the Chachapoyan codex was beginning to yield hints that pointed toward a possible answer.

He halted as close to the two men as he dared without being obvious about it, and stood there on the pretext of reading one of the magazines he was carrying. Ignoring him, the pair continued their conversation. One thing the eavesdropping archaeologist picked up on immediately: The first speaker's relieved declaration that his bellyache had left him.

Of all the people wandering in the hall, only Coschocton Westcott knew just how literal was the janitor's judgment. Refolding the magazine, he resumed his course, having garnered another valuable insight into Interloper behavior. At the same time, the two janitors started toward him. As they did so, their legs became entangled. Mops and buckets went flying, accompanied by startled oaths.

An alert Cody leaped straight up. The soapy contents of one bucket rushed past beneath his feet, the miniature flash flood carrying with it a pair of yellowed sponges and one sodden pumice stone. As it floated speedily by, the stone put forth a small, engorged, but still hungry Interloper. It missed the front end of the archaeologist's open-toed Tevas by inches.

Both men apologized profusely for the near-drenching. While they were doing so, Cody searched their faces, but could find nothing inimical, nothing sly, lurking within. Perhaps the men were innocent, perhaps they were dupes, or maybe it had just been an accident. Another accident.

Today being Kelli's day off, he had the car to himself. He was walking toward the parking facility when he saw an Interloper flow from the decorative tree against which a bicycle was leaning into the bike's owner. Too late to prevent the infestation from taking place, he could only look on with regret as the newly infected, unaware female undergrad began to pedal off.

That was when he saw the second student, swinging around the far corner of the red brick building on her larger, heavier, mountain bike. They ought to miss each other, he knew. There was plenty of room for them to cleanly pass one another in the paved serviceway between the two buildings, plenty of time for each cyclist to see the other one coming. But having coolly observed what had just taken place, Cody sensed that something less sanguine was about to happen. The infected girl was attractive and lightly dressed for the season, as was her onrushing opposite number. In misplaced deference to the brutal afternoon heat of a desert summer, and for the usual reasons of unjustifiable fashion, neither woman wore protective gear. The sidewalk was searingly hot, rough-surfaced, and unyielding. Raising one hand and waving, he rushed forward.

"Look out, both of you, look out!"

Either they didn't hear him, or chose to ignore a warn-

ing neither realized was being directed at them. The girl
on the bigger bike was steering with one hand while holding the booklet she was reading in the other. The one who
had moments ago become unwitting host to an Interloper
had her head down as if lost in unhappy thought, not realizing that the reason for her nonobservance of the route
ahead was a consequence of influences beyond her control. Both were moving too fast.

There was no one else around to second Cody's warning. Racing toward them while waving wildly, he shouted
a second time—too late. An instant before collision the
student on the mountain bike looked up to see the other
girl bearing down on her, legs churning fluidly, young
muscles working at peak efficiency. Dropping the booklet she'd been reading, she attempted to swerve to the
right. Her last-minute attempt to avert a collision only
worsened the impact.

Proximity led to realization on the part of the infected
woman. As she finally raised her head, her eyes widened
and she emitted a soft, startled yelp. Her bike struck the
mountain bike broadside, sending both of them crashing
to the hot pavement in a lacerating tangle of spokes, han-
dlebars, seats, wheels, and bruised flesh. Cody was at the
spot in seconds, reaching down into the moaning confusion as he worked to extricate both injured women from
the jigsaw of twisted aluminum and unyielding composite materials.

The contaminated girl was crying. Her blouse and
shorts were torn and streaks of blood showed through.
Since she appeared to be in worse shape, he knelt to as-
sist her first. From previous experience he knew that Interlopers could not flow from person to person; Intostion
could arise only from contact with their natural habitat.
So he was not worried as he put one hand on her shoulder and offered reassurance.

"It's okay. I'm going to get you out of here." He eyed her left leg hesitantly. It lay at an awkward angle, bent beneath her. "Do you think you can stand up?"

"I—Owww!" Looking down at herself, she wiped roughly at her eyes, trying to clear the tears that were obstructing her vision. "I think my leg is broken."

"Okay, okay," he admonished her softly. "Just stay like that. Don't move." Raising his gaze, he searched the far end of the passageway between the two buildings. Where was everybody? "I'm going to go call the Health Department. They'll have someone out here right away."

"Not right away. They're always slow." Sniffling, the girl suddenly looked up at him—and grinned savagely. "Besides, what's your hurry?"

"That's right. No need to rush off."

It was the other girl who spoke. Since she was less seriously injured, he had momentarily forgotten her. He remembered her now, as she threw herself against his back. At the same time, the young woman beneath him reached up with both arms and pulled him downward. As she shifted, he thought he could hear the osseous components of the compound fracture in her left leg grinding against one another. He could see the pain race across her face, but otherwise she ignored it.

Interloper influence, he surmised. But the girl on his back . . .

Fighting to throw her off, but not too roughly lest the action exacerbate her injuries, he wrenched around in the grasp of the girl on the ground. Only a great deal of self-control allowed him to kill the scream that threatened to explode in his throat.

Where the young woman's eyes should have been were a pair of battered bluish stalks that terminated in sickly yellow eyeballs. They dipped and bobbed, weaving back and forth as they hovered less than a foot from his face.

Turning away reflexively, he saw that the beautiful, innocent eyes of the girl on the ground had been replaced by a writhing mass of worms, each boasting a single bulging, oversized eye of their own. Not one, but *both* of the cyclists were hosts to Interlopers. So intent had he been on observing the newly infected girl that he had neglected to look hard at the other.

He had been set up.

But for what? Without a natural habitat to serve as vector, neither Interloper could transfer from one of the female hosts into him. The snarl of bikes and bodies lay sprawled on a pathway of neutral concrete that lapped up against a pair of inert brick structures. The nearest rocks and growing things that could possibly serve as hosts to additional communicable monstrosities lay some distance away.

"You were told to stop your research." The girl on his back clung to him with a feral tenacity that belied her appearance.

"You haven't," added the smaller figure beneath him.

He struggled in their binary hold, wanting to free himself from their grasp but not willing to hurt either of them in the process. After all, neither student was directly responsible for her actions. They were afflicted, suffering from the overriding influence of the malevolent parasites within. Though bigger and stronger, he was having trouble breaking free. Both young women were exerting themselves beyond what could normally be expected of their unremarkable physiques, their bodies driven to their natural limits by those who were presently inhabiting them. The girl beneath him should have been screaming in pain as the broken bones in her left leg grated and ground against one another. Instead, she continued to smile wolfishly at him from beneath the writhing worms that had replaced her eyes.

"I'm an archaeologist," he protested. "My research is my life."

"None among us could have put it better." Leaning forward, the corrupted young woman clinging to his back whispered into his ear. "Find other subject matter. Begin a different line of study. And stop interfering with—the feeding." In a tone so inhumanly chilling he found it difficult to believe it came from so innocent and smooth a throat, the young woman added, "This is your last warning."

"You see how easily you can be deceived, despite your irksome ability to See," declared the figure beneath him. "Ignore this warning at your peril, and sooner or later you will make a mistake. Touch a stone, lean up against a tree, caress the flower that you're smelling. Eventually you will touch, or lean against, or caress a habitat of occupation, and then you will become one of us." The glaring worm-face rippled like pustulent grass. "Continue to defy the wishes of Those Who Abide, and your eventual, inevitable hosting will not be pleasant."

"From everything I've been able to see and learn, none of them are." With one arm, he swept the girl off his back. She clung ferociously to his left arm, like a leech waving in the wind, reluctant to let him go.

The empyemic worm-things vanished, sinking back into the smooth-skinned face of the injured girl beneath him. The savage smile remained.

"It is not necessary to attend you directly, Coschocton Westcott. You may think yourself secure so long as you remain unvisited, but such is not necessarily the case. Your deviant society affords innumerable opportunities for contrivance." Glancing down at herself, she used her eyes to draw his attention to the tattered state of her clothing. "For example . . ."

Sudden, artfully constructed fear transformed her expression. Her lips parted wide and she yelled, modestly and not too loudly, *"Rape!"*

A stunned Cody started to put a hand over her mouth, stopping when he realized how the gesture might be interpreted by someone newly arrived on the scene. Her perverted grin taunted him.

"I could yell louder. Much louder."

"So could I," declared the other young woman, whom he had finally shrugged off. Rising, she straightened her clothing. As she did so, the girl lying bent and broken beneath the archaeologist finally released him from her grasp. He stumbled away from her as hastily as if she had suddenly turned into a cobra.

The girl who had leapt on his back helped her companion to get up. How the one who had lain beneath him was able to stand on her fractured leg Cody could not imagine. The pain ought to overcome even the strongest individual.

Noting the direction of his stare, the other girl elucidated. "Yes, she is in pain. Severe pain. A good thing, such pain. What is desired is to bring about suffering but not unconsciousness, anguish but not death. A deceased host is no source of nourishment."

"'Nourishment'?" Still dazed by the rapid course of events, Cody was not sure he was hearing correctly. "What kind of sick, diseased relationship is this?"

"The same kind that you will one day enjoy, Coshocton Westcott. Only it will be the worse for you, if you do not cease."

With that, the two girls turned. Perhaps they were aware of the two male students who had come upon the scene and were now rushing forward to offer their assistance. Or maybe the demonstration had coincidentally reached its end. Cody stood staring as the two young men took the suddenly weeping, openly bewildered girls in hand.

Now that the Interloper parasites had chosen to slip into the mental and physical background, all the pain and distress of the collision that had heretofore been repressed surged to the fore. The girl who had suffered the broken leg collapsed and had to be lifted and carried. As she crumpled at last onto her ruined leg, the archaeologist thought he could hear laughter. Aberrant, pitiless, demonic laughter.

There was nothing he could do. Both blameless young women were beyond his help. Grinding his teeth, he turned away and resumed his interrupted march toward the parking facility and his car.

Devious, they were. He saw now that the danger was even greater than he had supposed. They did not have to infect him with one of their own to affect his course of action or his life. Those they had already contaminated could be malevolently steered into performing actions they would never have contemplated on their own.

For now, he could see them coming. But as the incident involving the two girls demonstrated, his attention could be distracted, his perception compromised, his judgment hurried. Make one mistake, one wrong move at a critical moment, and he could easily find himself in jail, or worse.

The consequences of the cycling demonstration were not what the Interlopers intended. All his life, whenever he had been threatened or challenged, it had been Cody Westcott's nature to fight back with redoubled effort. They had just made a fool of him. He vowed it would not happen again, and not because he intended to comply with their demands or bow to their intimidation. It made him more determined than ever to find a way to disseminate the incalculably valuable knowledge he had acquired.

He would find someone to help him reproduce the results of Harry Keeler's work. More of the sacred elixir

that had been devised by the Chachapoyan shamans would
be brewed. Others would drink of it, if only to disabuse
him of his crazy notions of a scourge of invisible Interlopers that were plaguing mankind. With every new con-
vert, each new believer, the ability to resist the malicious
organisms would grow.

Could they be killed? Could one who was "abiding"
be destroyed without harming its host? Such vital, unan-
swered questions only reinforced his determination to continue with and even expand upon his research. Harry
Keeler had not known what he faced. Cody did. As he
slipped behind the wheel of his car his face was set in a
grimace of determination. Let them threaten him.

Each time they demonstrated a new way of impacting
on his life, they exposed more of their abilities. There
seemed to be only two: the ability to infect him directly,
and the capacity to induce others who were already unwilling hosts to alter their normal behavior. They could
draw no lightning bolts down from the sky to incinerate
him, spawn no toxic gases to blow into his face to poison him, and could not induce the earth to open beneath
his feet to swallow him. He was not invulnerable, but neither did he continue to exist only at their mercy. They
were insidious and clever, but they were not omnipotent.

There had to be a way to kill them. They were fearful of more than his ability to perceive them and to interfere with their activities. Otherwise, they would simply
have ignored him. What did it matter if another thousand,
or ten thousand, or a million human beings became able
to detect their presence, if they could do nothing to alter
that presence?

No, they were afraid of something. That was why they
were so anxious to stop him now, before he could un-
cover whatever it was that they feared. Something must

pose a greater peril to them than mere recognition. He, Cody Westcott, was going to find out what that was.

And then he was going to make use of it.

In the weeks that followed his confrontation with the pair of possessed cyclists, the Abiders tried to make good on their threat. He prepared as best he could. Though she looked at him askance, Kelli agreed not to touch any bare rocks or trees or plants unless he was present. An experiment, he called it, pleading with her until she consented. Shaking her head and smiling dolefully, she avowed that if her husband was going to be laboring under a continuing delusion, at least it was one that seemed comparatively benign.

They had the advantage of living in a large city. Too many natural objects, too many potential Interloper habitats existed in the countryside. Native peoples like the Chachapoyans would have been hard pressed to find refuge from the Interlopers. Perhaps that was why city dwellers were more immune than their country cousins to legends and fables of inimical spirits. That supposition alone offered material enough for another entire thesis. It would have to wait. He was too busy staying alive.

In that respect it was possible he was overreacting. With the exception of Harry Keeler, who posed a direct threat to the Abiders, he had yet to see or hear of an Interloper killing a human being. On the contrary, it would make sense for them to work at keeping their human hosts alive. A parasite without a home might starve to death.

What, exactly, did happen to an abiding Interloper when its human host passed on? Since they could not translocate directly from one person to another, did that mean the Interloper perished simultaneously? Or did they linger on within the corpse in hopes of coming in contact with stone or wood, of using one or the other as a vector to once more infect someone new? There was so little he knew about them, and he doubted even a comprehensive search of the library's extensive resources would yield very much in the way of hard information on the biology of imaginary creatures.

Not that he didn't have the opportunity to learn from observation. It was frightening to see just how many of the horrors were abroad in the world. His fellow humans went about their daily business unaware of the writhing swarm of nebulous monstrosities that shared their existence. Like some very minor-league superhero cursed with a single unassuming power, he intervened on behalf of his unseeing fellow humans whenever he could. His efforts were not always appreciated by those he saved from infestation, who had no idea of the danger they were in at such moments or the closeness of their respective calls.

The Interlopers knew, however. They screamed silently at him but were unable to forestall his interference. Time and again at work, on the streets, in a mall, outside a supermarket, and once at a football game, he saved one or more heedless innocents from being infected. Sometimes his efforts drew bemused stares, sometimes indifference, and once in a while, outright uncomprehending hostility. Irrespective of the almost-victims' reactions, he persevered, knowing that he was doing a good thing, realizing that in his own singular, small way he was helping to keep a tiny portion of mankind healthier and saner than it would have been without his intervention.

Strolling down the street either by himself or in the company of his wife or friends, seeking shelter from the desert sun, he kept a wary but inconspicuous eye on the raging horde of Interlopers that seemed to populate every third rock, every fourth tree, every tenth bush or planter full of flowers. He watched his fellow pedestrians as well, alert for indications that any might be inhabited by rancorous otherworldly things that danced grotesquely in a light that only he could discern.

They kept trying. They were persistent, and determined—but so was he. And the more aware of them he became through experience, the faster and easier it was for him to detect and avoid them. His only fear was that the effects of the potion might wear off, leaving him once more as blind to their presence as the rest of an incognizant humankind. As days and then weeks passed, however, his perception remained as clear as ever. If anything, it was sharpened by each new encounter.

They tried to deceive him with a bouquet of flowers delivered anonymously to his office. Among the roses were small arching horrors that would have pricked his soul instead of his skin. The vase they arrived in was made from cut and polished marble, but it fooled him no more than did its contents, for the vase was likewise inhabited, by an entirely different strain of Interloper. As the creatures could not inhabit or pass through any artificial material, he donned plastic gloves before picking up the lethal bouquet and carrying it carefully to the nearest dumpster. The virulent inhabitants of vase and flowers flailed ineffectively at him as he tossed them both into the big steel rubbish receptacle.

They might have got him on the morning he drove to work tired and preoccupied, but he saw the truck coming in time and instead of stopping, accelerated before it could turn into his path. It jumped the curb in his wake and bounced across half a parking lot before smashing into the side of a furniture store. In his rearview mirror, Cody could see the driver stagger out of the truck's cab and collapse to the pavement. From his spine emerged a particularly large and vicious-looking perversion that waved half a dozen eyestalks and claw-tipped tendrils in the direction of the archaeologist's fleeing car.

For every accident the Interlopers caused, Cody prevented a dozen. For every moment of misery they induced, he helped the ignorant and unknowing to avoid many more. They seethed and fumed at him but could not touch him. In spite of Kelli's chastising but tolerant tongue, he succeeded in rendering their own home virtually Interloper-proof. Meanwhile, he spent every free moment digging ever deeper into the Chachapoyan codex, searching for a means that would enable one not only to see the malignancies, but to destroy them.

There had to be a way, he was convinced. Otherwise mankind would have long since been overrun by the horrors that dwelled within, or gone collectively mad. It was not enough to be able to avoid the Interlopers. There had to exist a means for confronting them directly, and for eradicating them.

By the time the midafternoon heat had fallen from boiling to merely simmering, when the temperature in the Valley of the Sun could be read in less than triple-digits Fahrenheit and a whiff of approaching fall manifested itself in the smell of decaying leaves, he was feeling pretty good about things. His research was progressing well. He was convinced that a mechanism for not merely avoiding the Interlopers but for fighting back was at hand. Despite its forbidding population of psychic parasites, the world was looking good to Cody as he turned down the street on which he lived.

He eyed the neat, prosperous homes with their desert landscaping approvingly. Thanks to his relentless, covert efforts, his immediate neighbors lived nearly free of Interlopers. As a result, his was a street populated by smiling people and happy families. Unwitting and unawares, they had been blessed by none other than Coschocton Westcott. A psychologist conducting a study of the neighborhood would have been astonished at the abnormal level of contentment to be found there without having the slightest idea as to its cause.

Cody was smiling as he turned into the driveway. Waiting to greet him were Mark and Dana from next door. Uncharacteristically, the expressions on their faces were grim. Frowning, he parked in the driveway, grabbed his laptop, and moved to confront them. That was when he saw that the door to his house was standing open wide. Kelli was not silhouetted there waiting to greet him. The scene made no sense. Why would she leave the door open and not invite their friends inside? Or conversely, not be standing outside chatting with them as he pulled in?

As he started around the front of the car, Mark moved to intercept him. "She's not here, Cody." He gestured at the house. "I've already let your cats out." Behind him, Dana stood with one hand clasped tightly in the other. Her expression was agonized.

The archaeologist swallowed hard, panic rising within him. His gaze swept the Interloper-free yard as well as the one next door. Nothing alien and half-visible mocked him from across the street.

Maybe he was leaping to conclusions. Maybe it was something else entirely. People did suffer from sickness and injury due to other causes. Those Who Abide might be at the root of a large, inexplicable chunk of humankind's cultural grief, but they were not responsible for everything. Not everything.

As he let Mark and Dana drive him to the hospital he clung desperately to that single frantic, forlorn hope.

Eight

Sun◦washed and of recent vintage. most of the hospi◦ tals in the greater Phoenix metropolitan area glowed with comforting earth tones banded with rows of darkened glass windows. The one in Scottsdale that Kelli had been rushed to was no exception. In an East Coast city of older vintage the complex might have been mistaken for a new office building or software park. Entering, one was instantly disabused of any such frivolous notion. No matter their location or lineage, design or décor, on the inside hospitals were invariably similar. And there was always the unmistakable dry tang of disinfectant.

It was not a place in which Cody wanted to find the light of his life. If only she had believed him, if only she had listened more closely to his warnings and explications, this would never have happened!

What would never have happened? he asked himself. As yet, he knew nothing of what had actually occurred.

Though he appreciated their genuine and heartfelt concern, Mark and Dana were not much help. As they hurried down one sterile hallway and then another like rats in an ochre-walled maze, a fearful Dana told Cody that it had happened while she and Kelli were out shopping. The two women had been stocking up at Albertson's market, laughing and chatting and having a nice afternoon; there was nothing amiss, nothing untoward, nothing to indicate that either of them was feeling anything unusual. And then suddenly a peculiar expression came over Kelli's face; she stopped speaking in midsentence, her eyes had rolled back into her head, and she collapsed like a sack of rain-soaked rice.

Dana had managed to catch her as she fell, unable to arrest her fall completely but at least preventing her from cracking her skull on the hard floor of the supermarket. Unable to revive her friend, she'd unashamedly begun screaming for help. The store manager called 911 and paramedics arrived with commendable speed. Dana had gone with Kelli in the ambulance. As soon as they arrived at the hospital, she'd called Mark. Unable to do more than pace the waiting room, unable to reach Cody by phone since he'd already left his office on campus, they'd returned home to await his arrival.

"Where did it happen?" Though he was all torn up inside, he did his best to fight down the nausea and despair that threatened to overwhelm him. His people were supposed to be good at that sort of thing, but as they hurried along the passageways all he wanted to do was start bawling and throw up.

"I told you." Dana was having trouble keeping up with the two men, obliged to break into little, short sprints from time to time to avoid falling behind. "In the market."

"No, not that. *Where* in the market? What *section*? What were you doing, what was Kelli doing, when she collapsed?"

Distraught and concerned for her friend, his neighbor struggled to recall. "We were shopping, just shopping."

She shook her head in disbelief at the remembrance. "It happened so fast. We were on our way to check out and Kelli stopped to look at some new ornamentals that had just come in."

"Ornamentals?" Without breaking stride, Cody looked at her sharply. "What kind of 'ornamentals'?"

"You know." Puzzled at this line of interrogation but too worried to argue, Dana chose to reply without questioning. "Houseplants. Ornamental houseplants."

"Live, or dried?" At any other time Dana would have wondered at the seriousness with which Cody put the query to her.

"Alive, of course. There were some pretty tropicals, some calatheas and a couple like them that I didn't recognize. Lots of coleus, of course. Kelli thought they were all beautiful. She loves unusual things, you know, and . . ."

With Mark leading the way, they rounded still another corner, brushing past nurses and candy stripers, meditative interns and the aimlessly ambling, dull-eyed relatives of the ailing.

"She touched one of them, didn't she?" Cody sounded more accusatory than he intended. "One or more. And then she went down."

"That's right." Having already explained what had happened, his neighbor was not surprised at his reaction. Later, when she had time to think about it, she would wonder at his uncharacteristic and seemingly unjustified vehemence.

For now, though, she and her husband and their friend were adrift in the acute emotions of the moment. "Here we are. Three-twenty. No, Three twenty-two."

Why couldn't the manufacturers of hospital apparatus make their equipment silent, an anxious, fearful Cody wondered as he followed Mark into the room. With all their high-tech skills, why did they have to build devices

that warbled horrid beeps and squeals? The information
the machines provided was relayed to monitoring screens
at the nurses' station anyway. It seemed that the sole purpose of such familiar, seemingly innocuous sounds was
to terrify already apprehensive visitors to the sickrooms
of friends and loved ones.

He caught his breath and his heart missed a beat as
Mark stepped aside to reveal the full length of the hospital bed. Suspended in a sea of milky white, the light of
his life lay unmoving beneath a thin layer of eggshell
sheets and pastel blankets, her hair haloed behind her head
which was gently cradled by an oversized, hypoallergenic
pillow. Her complexion was wan and her eyes were closed,
and he thanked Manitou that she was breathing, albeit
barely perceptibly, on her own. Had her face been ob-
scured by a nest of tubes and hoses he was not sure he
could have handled it.

Moving to the edge of the bed, he stood staring down
at his unmoving wife. Tears came easily, automatically,
as he reached down to pick up her right hand. The un-
accustomed unresponsiveness of those small, strong fingers that under normal conditions pressed so effortlessly
and reassuringly into his own shocked him more than anything else. They lay immobile in his cradling palm, warm
but limp.

"Coma." Mark's voice reached him from somewhere
nearby, from a distant place that barely impacted on
Cody's consciousness. "Some kind of anaphylactic shock.
I didn't get to talk to the attending physician much. We
were in a hurry to get home so we could meet you."

Cody silently cried out for his brain to work, his mouth
to function. "Did the doctor have any idea what might
have brought this on?"

His friend shrugged, eloquently illustrating the help-
lessness he felt. "We thought maybe she cut or pricked

herself on one of the plants, and that she had a violent allergic reaction. When Dana told the paramedics what had happened, that was their first thought, too. Or maybe there was an exotic spider riding on one of the imports, and it bit her when she was checking them out. They're supposed to have been running tests here   " His voice trailed away inconclusively.

"If you want us, we'll be outside, down in the waiting room." Taking her husband's hand, Dana led him out of the room and closed the door quietly behind them. When Cody did not turn or speak or otherwise acknowledge their departure, they were not offended. They understood, which is the best thing good friends can do.

Left alone with his unforeseen, intimate disaster, Cody found he couldn't move. All he could do was stand by his wife's bedside and stare down at her, as if by the sheer force of his gaze he could somehow break the venomous spell that had overwhelmed her. She continued to breathe easily on her own, her chest rising and falling as gently as tissue in a warm summer breeze.

Unexpectedly, a soft moan escaped from her lips. Beneath the sheets, her body twisted, and her head fell toward him. The peaceful, unpained expression on her face contorted as something dug at her, probing and disquieting, unsettling the trance into which she had fallen.

The small, fist-sized head that welled up from her throat was particularly ugly; a warty, leprous mass of pustular knobs and protrusions. A single ichorous eye gazed unblinkingly up at Cody. Frozen in mid-breath by an overwhelming rush of fear and fury, he could only twitch and jerk back slightly as his eyes locked onto that pernicious, unwholesome gaze. And the abomination was not alone.

A clutch of barbed tendrils pushed up and out of her forearm. Reflexively, he pulled his hand back as they lashed in his direction like so many stinging anemones hunting undersea prey. Emerging from her ear like a snake sliding out of its burrow was a banded length of drab-toned alien corruption. Split into four sections, its nether end probed and felt of its immediate surroundings. Each of the four slender sections was lined with tiny, dark-stained teeth. These were designed for feeding; not on material as prosaic as ordinary flesh, but on something else. Something at once less obvious and more vital.

Interlopers. Several of them, feeding on his beloved. In shape and state they were as horrible as any he had yet encountered.

He didn't even know what they consumed, much less have any insight into the process. For all that he had learned, for all the arcane knowledge he had studied and gleaned from the glyphs and carvings of the long-vanished Chachapoyans, he felt as if he were drowning in a deep, dark well of oily ignorance. Certainly, obviously, they were the cause of his wife's present condition. Despite his warnings and forgetting his admonitions, preoccupied with casual sociable chatter, she had made contact with a living plant, or with several. At least one had been the abode of an insatiate, waiting Interloper. Apparently more than one. Or maybe she had caressed and inspected several tenanted plants before their incursions had taken full effect.

Without knowing what they were doing to her or how they were doing it, there was nothing he could do for Kelli. He could not help, could not relieve, could not make her better. Nor could any traditional physician, no matter how many elegantly gilded testimonials from prideful institutions of advanced study hung on the walls of expensive offices filled with deep-pile carpet and soft music. Kelli was afflicted beyond the call of modern medicine. No known drug would alleviate her symptoms, no conventional course of treatment would restore the color to her cheeks or the brightness he knew so well to her eyes.

Was she going to die? Lie in a state of living death until all the wondrous, vibrant life that sustained their love leaked out of her, with neither him nor anyone else able to stanch the seepage? He would not allow it!

Reaching down, he swung with a vengeance at the ghastly shapes that protruded, writhing and contorting, from her helpless form. They twisted as his clenching fingers passed through them, fluttered briefly as his fists battered the space but not the place they occupied. With mouths that bloated and shriveled, ballooned to turgid proportions only to be swiftly metabolized, they mocked his futile efforts: moaning, whistling, enouncing in measured, whispered tones that echoed with the icy indifference in which they dwelled. Spicing the grisly, pianissimo chorus of corruption that arose from his wife's inert body was the faintest possible, barely perceptible insinuation of distant, giggling laughter.

He could stand by her side and fume powerlessly. He could weep and whimper and bemoan her fate. Or he could do something. Return to the university, bury himself in his work as never before, and try to find a solution, if not an outright cure. Having had ample opportunity to observe firsthand the effects of infecting Interlopers on a wide variety of human beings, he knew that their influence varied as much as their sizes and shapes. Whatever had struck down Kelli was more harmful than a recurring headache but less so than the sudden urge to leap off a bridge or drive into oncoming traffic. As long as she lay in a limbo of their creation and grew no worse, there was hope.

She was stable, the attending physician informed him later. Her vitals were strong, from her heartbeat to her blood pressure to her subdued but regular respiration. Insofar as he could tell, she was in no immediate danger. But neither did she show any sign of emerging from the comatose state into which she had inexplicably lapsed. Oh—and they were still searching for possible cause, concentrating on the plants she'd been browsing in the market. Samples had been brought in for analysis. Her blood was being minutely screened for indications of sensitivity to the relevant plant matter, and also for susceptibility to a wide range of insect and arachnid venoms.

A distressed and distracted Cody listened with only half a mind. He knew that the hospital lab's search, however thorough and well-intentioned, would find nothing. Kelli had been bitten, all right. As a consequence, she was infected by something that their expensive and state-of-the-art equipment would not, could not, detect. He already knew the source and the nature of her infection.

It was dark when, exhausted, he knew it was time to go. If she was in any way at all aware of his presence, or that of any other visitor, she gave no sign. Every time she had one of her small, subdued episodes of arching and grimacing an ache shot through him no painkiller could snuff. Those Who Abide were hurting her. Doing what to her imprisoned psyche and self he could not imagine.

He rose to leave. Not because he could no longer stand seeing the mute agony in her face, but because it was clear that in staying he was doing her no good at all. Any answers, any succor for her condition, were to be found not at her bedside but back in his office and the archaeology department's basement lab. He had to go to work.

The hospital bustle that had greeted him earlier was at this late hour much subdued; the ebb and flow of those employees and visitors and patients who remained was considerably reduced. Mark and Dana had long since departed, but not before making him promise that if he

needed anything, anything at all, he was to call them either at home or work, regardless of the hour. It was good
to have friends, he told himself as he strode purposefully
down the hall, even if there was nothing they could do.
It was all up to him now. All up to him.

He turned corners and traversed passageways until it
occurred to him that he might be lost. He was more irritated than angry. It was the nature of whoever was responsible for the planning of hospitals to construct them
in such a fashion as to make their interiors as confusing
as possible for unknowing visitors. Theseus himself would
not have been able to follow the "simple instructions"
that were commonly provided to preoccupied visitors. To
indicate direction, large urban hospitals resorted to strips
of colored tape affixed to floors and walls, when what
each visitor really needed was an individual, hand-held
GPS.

Finding himself in a comparatively busy corridor that
looked exactly like the dozen or so corridors he had already traversed, he confronted a tall, preoccupied intern
clad in surgical greens. A cap covered his head and hair
and a white mask hung from his neck.

"Excuse me. I'm lost, and I was wondering if you
could show me the way out." Despite his distress, Cody
somehow managed a smile.

"The way out?" The intern smiled. He had a narrow
but pleasant face accented by a distinctively hawkish nose.
"Most people use the Eighth Street exit." Raising an arm,
he pointed. "Keep straight on that way and go through
the double doors. Turn at the first right and you'll see another set of doors. There's a security station on the other
side, and beyond that, the street."

"Straight, right, straight," Cody repeated mechanically.
"Thanks."

"You're welcome." The intern grinned widely. "Of

course, that's the exit everyone else takes. For you, Coshocton Westcott, there is no exit. Not now. Not anymore."

Shocked out of his suffering, Cody stumbled away from the intern's glacial, slightly twisted smile. As he stared at the other man, he saw that his eyes were completely glazed over, like a window on a particularly frosty morning. Small, many-legged creatures bulged in the middle and translucent of aspect milled about on the surface of his corneas—or in that general psychical vicinity. Somewhere behind those squalid, transient cataracts there lived a decent, caring, concerned medical professional. But at the moment, his entire system, from eyes to ears to mouth, had been taken over and was under the tenacious control of Interlopers unknown in strength and number.

One corner of the man's smile imploded, as if the parasitic aberrations fighting to command his body were imperfect in their understanding of his motor functions, unable despite their skill and power to operate the complex human machinery they had taken control of with the same ease as its evolutionary landlord. The left side of the intern's face hung slack, as if he had suffered a serious stroke. It rendered the ghastly grimace even more grotesque. Expression-wise, before Cody's eyes the unfortunate intern metamorphosed into a cross between Dr. Kildare and the Phantom of the Opera.

The archaeologist didn't give a good goddamn what the man looked like. When he spoke, he knew he was addressing anything but a bewildered apprentice physician.

"What have you done to my wife?"

"She sleeps." The intern was weaving on his feet now, caught in the grip of and manipulated by purposeful nightmares. "Not dead but not alive." The scornful sneer grew more contemptuous. "She is become food."

Howling, Cody launched himself at the other man. Veering away from the archeologist's lunge with preternatural grace, the haunted physician whirled and sprinted down the hallway. Blind with rage, Cody pursued without stopping to consider what he would do if he actually caught his tormentor. Whoever he actually was, the poor intern was not responsible either for his scornful words or his taunting actions. Interlopers operated his muscles, his tongue, his palate, making clumsy use of them to convey their feelings in terms a human could understand. Catch the man, tackle him, bring him down, and carry the confrontation further, and observant hospital personnel in the vicinity might readily assume that the tall outsider was assaulting one of their own. Cody would be swarmed by security officers, dragged off his inculpable quarry, and arrested. Little good could he do Kelli in jail.

None of which penetrated his anger sufficiently to slow him down.

They passed a wide-eyed night nurse and a startled janitor, a grieving family on their way out and a pair of assistant administrators necking in a phone alcove. The chase continued down a glut of corridors that were new to Cody. As he penetrated deeper and deeper into the hospital complex, he encountered fewer residents, fewer people.

It struck the panting archaeologist that the overhead fluorescents were growing dimmer. The change was so gradual he hadn't noticed it at first. Shifting his attention to something other than the running man he was chasing, he saw that the reduced illumination was not a consequence of his sharpening fatigue. The glow from the glass tubes overhead was markedly feebler.

There was no one else around. Come to think of it,

they hadn't passed anyone in quite a while. Where was he? An infrequently visited service corridor might reasonably be expected to be fitted out with subdued lighting, weaker bulbs being utilized to save electricity. Or was he being led by the tip of his anger into less prosaic regions that bordered not just on the hospital complex, but on reality itself?

Coyotes would send out one of their own, tongue lolling, prancing amicably, to make friends with a neighborhood dog, or simply to irritate it into defending its territory. The dog would track its wily relation into the hills or out into the desert, where the rest of the pack would be waiting to pounce on and devour their domesticated cousin. Was he following—or being coerced? What, exactly, was he accomplishing by continuing this aimless chase, when he could not even hope to gain honest satisfaction by eventually flailing away at the body of an innocent man?

The Interlopers lived in *this* world—but they came from, they originated, somewhere else. What, he found himself wondering as he slowed to a stop, might that somewhere else be like? Was it above ground, below ground, under water? And more meaningfully for the moment, was it a place that favored subdued lighting?

Ahead of him, his target had also halted and turned. A hand beckoned. "Think of your wife-food, Coschocton Westcott! Have you propitiated your anger already?"

"Oh, no." Slowly, Cody began backing away. If the man came after him, he would fight. Though no football player, the archaeologist was of good size, and in excellent condition thanks to years of digging and climbing. The possessed intern did not appear to be armed.

Reversing direction, he lurched unsteadily toward Cody. "You—were—warned. Not to interfere. Not to intervene. To drop a certain line of research. You are a clever man, Coschocton Westcott, but you cannot watch everywhere and everything at once. Any human can be reached, even one who can perceive. And if he cannot, others who are near to him can be made to abide. You were warned."

The admonition echoed, burned in his ears as Cody turned and ran. "You were warned! Warned . . . warned . . . warned . . ."

Was that the last turn they had made? Ducking to clear the occasional low-hanging light fixture, avoiding the pipes and conduits that lined the walls and ceiling, he ran on, ignoring the strain in his legs and the pounding of his heart. He found himself hungering for the sight of another human being: a security guard reading a girlie mag, a bored nurse delivering nightly medications, a housekeeper pushing a voluminous laundry cart—anything with a human face and eyes that were not windows into the depths of horror. But there was no one. Only the murky glow of the oddly muted fluorescents, an occasional rattle or gurgle from one of the pythonic pipes, and the steady slap-slap of his shoes hitting the smooth concrete floor as he fled.

The wholly manufactured nature of his surroundings gave him hope. There were no stones for him to step on, no Interloper-inhabitable trees or bushes for him to bump into. If they had been trying to lure him into some nebulous border region where his soul and self would become more amenable to their manipulations, they'd failed.

Or had they? Wasn't that the intersection he wanted just up ahead? Didn't he turn left there? He slowed, hesitating. Or was it right? Was the main corridor that led to the reception area to the right or the left? Did they have him running in circles? Were they watching and laughing, just waiting for him to collapse from exhaustion, to pass out, so they could send dumb and deceived vassals like the unfortunate, unwitting intern to fetch him back to nether regions just this side of the particular Hell they called home?

His throat burned as he impulsively chose the left-hand corridor. Almost immediately, it seemed as if the light ahead began to brighten slightly. Enclosed by walls of concrete and plaster, paint and plastic, he felt comparatively safe from direct assault. If they were going to get him, it would have to be through the use of deluded, victimized proxies. He knew them too well, could see them too clearly. Only his rage at what they had done to Kelli had momentarily blinded him to their propinquity. It had taught him a valuable lesson, one he would not repeat. Nothing, absolutely nothing, would cause him to let his guard down ever again.

If he was going to restore his wife, he would have to stay clear of their grasp. Not to save himself, but to save her. In her current comatose state, how long could she tolerate their loathsome "feeding"? How much time did he have?

How much time did *she* have?

Voices. He heard voices. Following them, he stumbled into a brightly lit hallway, nearly bowling over a sleepy, startled orderly as he lengthened his stride. Eyes both bemused and tired looked up at him sharply. The majority of visitors seated in the reception area ignored him. Breathing hard, perspiration pouring down his cheeks and neck to soak his shirt collar, he slowed to a less conspicuous walk. Without pausing, ignoring the few stares, he strode past them and out into the entryway atrium. From an overbearing but sickly philodendron, grasping pseudopods reached for him. He avoided them absently, almost contemptuously. There was no sign of the abiding intern whose taunts had led him on a fool's chase that, had he not come to his senses, might well have turned into a fatal one. Nor did he expect to see that poor, pitiable creature here, wandering about beneath bright lighting and energetic, healthy, uninfected people.

Nothing intercepted him as he made his way to the parking lot and his waiting car. The warm post-midnight air was alive with the sounds of the city: cars accelerating, the occasional horn protesting, a distant siren wailing to or from some minor disaster, the muted night-subdued chatter of visitors and employees entering or leaving the hospital.

There was that, and then there was the steady susurration of spectral sniggering that had become his constant companion. It was a little louder now, a little closer, uncomfortably familiar, insinuatingly intimate. He shut it down, refusing to hear it. It became pervasive only if he granted it permission. He locked it out just as he shut out everything in his life save one overriding, all-important matter.

He had work to do and nothing, not on Heaven or Earth or any as-yet unknown regions tangent or between, was going to stop him.

Nine

Of one thing he was sure, of one conclusion he was already certain: He needed help. Given enough time, he felt he could find any remedy, any solution to Kelli's condition that might exist—if one existed. And one *had* to exist. But he had no idea how much time he had. Parasites usually tried to keep their hosts alive, but the Interlopers could not be compared to the simple organic parasites familiar to generations of beginning biology students. Who knew what whims might drive Those Who Abide? He had no way of knowing when her already weakened condition might fail, when her critical bodily functions might shut down one by one. He might have years in which to search for a cure—or he might have months. Or he might have no more than . . .

He threw himself into research with a fervor that astonished and troubled his colleagues and friends. They ascribed his sudden fanaticism to a desire to lose himself in work in order to avoid having to ponder his wife's hapless condition twenty-four hours a day. Even the best intentioned of them did not understand. He could never put Kelli out of his mind for more than an hour.

Kelli, Kelli—how did the Interlopers "feed"? What sustenance did they draw from a human being, comatose or active? The abiding servant Uthu had spoken of some form of nutrition. It was not physical, or if it was, the effects were not visible or detectable by the usual means. If he knew *how* the Interlopers fed, he might be able to find a way to prevent them from feeding, or to poison them, or to in some fashion, way, means, interfere with their living processes. In his research, thorough as it was, he was striking out in a dozen different directions into the unknown. He did not even know what he was looking for, or if he would recognize it when he found it. He only knew that his life, his happiness, his future, depended on looking.

He needed help.

But where to begin searching for that? As far as he knew, except for some long-dead Chachapoyan shamans, he was the only human being uninfected by the Interlopers who was aware of their presence. It seemed unlikely that among the billions and billions who populated the Earth there was no one in that singular position except him. Doubtless another, somewhere, whether by accident or design, was suffering from the same cursed knowledge and awareness. How to find them, make contact, establish a rapport so that they might help one another, or at least find companionship and common cause in the fight against the empyreal body-dwelling parasitoids?

Foolish as it made him feel, he began by searching the columns in the daily paper under headings such as *Psychic Readings, Your Future Foretold,* and *Secrets of the Ancients Revealed*! (only $29.95 plus shipping and handling!). Unsurprisingly, there was nothing listed under "Interlopers" or "Intruders" or "Those Who Abide." Follow-ups to the ads quickly disabused him of any notion that they might prove helpful, or that the advertisers were anything but frauds or, at best, well-meaning quacks who had nothing to offer. Most wanted money.

It was the same with the television spielers, those with 900 numbers that promised free consultations and readings. When he tried to talk about invisible creatures that fed on something undefined within the bodies of ordinarily unaware humans, the more adept individuals on the other end of the line consistently tried to steer the conversation around to whether Cody was married, whether he loved his parents or not, if he was having trouble at work, in his love life, or sleeping, what his favorite television shows were, and more than once, what the numbers were on his primary credit card (for reference purposes only). The less skilled, if that was not an oxymoron in the call-in psychic hotline business, quickly dropped off-line when he started talking about Interlopers that inhabited natural objects such as trees and rocks.

He had expected nothing less, but felt bound to try every possibility. Having thoroughly exhausted the exceedingly limited capabilities of the more professional manifestations of the country's fascination with psychic silliness, he moved on to more reputable sources. Researching the studies carried out and reported on by the distinguished CSICOP organization and its venerable journal *The Skeptical Inquirer* saved him a good deal of time by allowing him to quickly ferret out associations and groups that cloaked themselves in a veneer of scientific respectability. Reading about fraudulent individuals who had already been exposed allowed him to concentrate on those who had not yet been thoroughly investigated.

More and more, he found himself drawn to police files and records. These, at least, were full of unexplained, seemingly irrational incidents. The postal clerk who arrives at work one morning with automatic weapons in the pockets of his uniform, the "good kid" who suddenly and for no apparent reason goes berserk and hacks his family to death with an axe, the preteens who gun down their teachers and schoolmates, the active athlete suddenly brought low by a crippling disease alien to his lineage: All these and more drew Cody's attention in his desperate search to find something relevant to his wife's condition.

So many appalling incidents that defied rational explanation; they piled up in his office, filling the previously empty corners and overwhelming his neat desk and file cabinets and bookshelves. Tribal warfare in the Balkans, endless misery in Bangladesh, religious warfare in the Middle East, a successful banker convicted of murdering his co-workers in Zurich, a garbage collector from Des Moines committing suicide while on vacation in Colorado—all were components of the unending, dismal, inexplicable liturgy of dementia and irrationality that afflicted mankind. Nor was it anything new, Cody knew. It had ever been so, throughout human history.

He could not help but wonder how much of the gloomy record of misery and wretchedness he was accumulating was inescapable, and how much due to the presence and interference in human affairs of the still mysterious aggressors whose hapless hosts referred to them as Those Who Abide. Were they evenly spread throughout human civilization, or were there regions where they thrived and others where they were scarce? What percentage of the population of Northern Ireland was infected? What of Russia and the Congo, of India and southern Mexico? Was the bulk of Polynesia relatively infection free and that of downtown Washington D.C. otherwise?

Gradually he began to build a picture of human history that owed as much, if not more, to the possible intervention of the Interlopers than to the exercise of human logic and free will. Contemporary affairs were only the tip of the metaphysical iceberg. The present had no monopoly on the inexplicable. Decisions that had been made since the beginning of recorded time he now viewed through the lens of a new awareness. Perception granted him a unique perspective.

What was really behind the burning of the great library of Alexandria? Did its thousands of scrolls containing the collected knowledge of the ancients include among them the formula for a potion similar to that which had been discovered independently by the Chachapoyans? What actually caused the decline and fall of Rome and the end to the wondrous Pax Romana that had kept comparative peace in Europe for some five hundred years? How did Genghis Khan and his successors really manage to defeat the combined forces of nearly half the known world? Did he have unknown, unseen allies that sowed confusion and dissension among his adversaries in expectation of the mass murder and devastation that would follow?

Every significant human event that confounded reasonable, intelligent thought had to be viewed in this new light. It was terrible for Cody to think that he might be the only one with his finger on the "view" switch. Without incontrovertible proof, no one would listen to him, ponder his theories, or make an effort to substantiate his reasoning.

The revision of human history would have to wait, he decided. What mattered now was Kelli. His immediate efforts must be directed toward saving his wife.

If there was anyone else like him out there, they might very well have already traveled down the same desperate path of seeking he was currently following. What would *they* do next? How could a poor farmer in Pakistan make contact with a kindred spirit in Paris? How might a hunter-gatherer in Papua New Guinea exchange knowledge and observations with a gem miner in Minas Gerais? How could an archaeologist in Arizona hope to find a fellow perceiver in Antigua?

Newspaper ads seemed the most likely place to start. He commenced a comprehensive search of the personals in every paper he could get his hands on. In that regard, it was more than a little helpful to have full access to the university library. His telephone bill skyrocketed as he placed regular, hopeful calls across the country and to the far ends of the earth. The responses he gleaned varied from the absurd to the outright deranged. In less than a month he had personally held conversations with more psychotics and genuinely disturbed people that the psychiatric outpatient center at his wife's hospital dealt with in a year. Not one of them, not even the hundred or so calls he placed to various locales in Southern California, contained an iota of useful information.

Only when he felt he had exhausted the more traditional resource of newspaper ads did he turn wholeheartedly to the Internet. Anyone could place a newspaper ad, but not everyone had access to the Net. While maintaining the steady flow of newspapers to his home and office, he began to spend more and more time accessing search engines and composing his own eclectic messages to be posted on as many bulletin boards as he could manage.

The result was a flood of information that threatened to inundate the computer in his office and the two he and Kelli kept at home. He bought and added more hard drive storage than a small business server would need, spending money he didn't have to install a full-scale designated server in his den. Additional research eventually enabled him to import filtering software that screened out a great deal of the electronic chaff, winnowing out what was irrelevant so he had time to skim to the articles he absolutely felt he could not ignore.

He learned a great deal, absorbed an enormous amount of pertinent material, and built the most powerful anti-spam firewall possible to fend off the resultant flood of E-mail requests for, yes, his credit card number and free opportunities to consult 900 numbers. As Kelli's condition seemed to worsen slightly, his melancholy and discouragement grew. The abundance of cybercrap was no different from what he had previously encountered in its traditional print-and-paper counterparts.

He answered as much of the material that flowed to his computer and mailbox as time and money would allow. He stopped shaving and lost weight despite Mark and Dana's goodhearted attempts to have him over for dinner as often as possible. His work at school suffered noticeably, with lectures skipped, papers left unread, and a dearth of publication in the professional journals that had come to expect regular contributions from him and his wife. Only his semi-celebrity status within the field as the interpreter of the Chachapoyan codex allowed him to retain his position at the university, tenure notwithstanding. He didn't know what to do except to keep digging, both into the Chachapoyan glyphs and the deluge of irrelevant, often unintelligible material that flooded his home and office.

He also had to deal with would-be hopefuls in person, though this was infrequent. No psychic search service was going to send personnel at their own expense to try and induce him to retain their services. No metaphysical detective living in North Platte was going to pay his or her own way to fly down and visit him. Where confident, self-assured astrologers and soul dowsers and inventors of devices for seeing into the other world were concerned, a lack of willingness on Cody's part to commit money to their diverse enterprises was usually a sure means of terminating further dialogue.

So he was somewhat surprised to answer the door one Saturday morning to find standing on the walkway in front of the steps a small, unassuming, elderly gentleman nattily decked out in pin-striped suit complete with bow tie and hat. Brushing his long and currently unwashed black hair back off his forehead, Cody gazed at his latest visitor out of tired, aching eyes beneath which premature bags had begun to form.

The little man won points for neatness, anyway. As near as Cody could tell this early in the morning, his visitor was unpolluted and therefore not another minion of the Interlopers. Nothing untoward abided within him, except perhaps a tendency to stare without blinking. Not that he was any saner than the multitude of mostly well-meaning nuts who had preceded him. The furled black umbrella he was leaning on, not jauntily but as if he actually might need the support, was proof enough of that. Only those who had no choice in the matter wore suits and ties in Phoenix in late September, and nobody actually carried umbrellas. Overhead, the intensifying sky was a flat sheet of blue from which heat radiated like the flame of a gas stove.

But the bow tie was a nice touch, Cody had to admit. And the umbrella was less threatening than some of the objects the more disturbed of his recent visitors had carried with them.

Though his profession had given him some experience at reckoning an individual's ethnic background, he couldn't quite place the man standing before him. He was fair-complexioned but not Nordic, with fine features and slightly oversized ears. Feminine, even. Nor did he look particularly Slavic. He might well have been Romany save that his skin was really too light. His ancestry remained a mystery. From beneath the expensive fedora, which boasted what looked like a small fly-whisk tucked neatly into the hatband on the left side, emerged white, slightly curly hair that in places still showed insinuations of blond. His appearance suggested someone who did not lack for money, but who was not conspicuously wealthy, either.

Cody sighed. Those charlatans who put up a good front usually waited at least half an hour before making the first practiced request for funds. "Can I help you?" He had learned to be polite instead of churlish even when confronted by visitors who invariably wasted his precious time. There was enough woe in the world without his having to add to it. He would not do the Interlopers' work for them.

The dapper visitor smiled, displaying what appeared to be all his own teeth, with the exception of one that was conspicuously and unapologetically gold. It flashed in the morning light.

"Vielleicht," he replied. "Perhaps." His accent was strong, and quite different from what Cody might have expected. German, he decided immediately. Which meant that his visitor might equally be from Germany, or Austria, or Switzerland. Or Chicago. Or anywhere, including the greater Phoenix metropolitan area.

"It is I who may be able to help you, Herr Westcott." Raising the umbrella, he gestured slightly with the tip. "Might I come in? It is very hot out here, much more so than I am used to."

Not from Phoenix, then. Cody hesitated, then sighed and stepped aside. At least this one was well-groomed and didn't smell. "Come on in, then. You've got five minutes to convince me you can do anything for me."

The man nodded and walked with measured stride past the far younger, much taller archaeologist. As Cody led him to the den, he noted that his visitor's eyes were never

at rest. They were in constant motion, darting from left
to right, searching, hunting. A quintessential characteristic of the paranoid, he knew. Four minutes left. He had
work to do and no time to waste today coddling the deranged fantasies of even well-dressed eccentrics.

He directed the man toward the one chair that was not
buried beneath piles of printouts, stationery, books, magazine excerpts, and letters both opened and still sealed.
"Everyone calls me Cody. Or Professor Westcott."

Settling himself in the empty chair, his eyes still flicking from place to point as he rested both hands on the
end of his umbrella, Cody's elderly guest smiled politely.
"Very good to meet you, Herr Professor. I am Karl Heinrich Oelefsenten von Eichstatt. You may call me Oelefse."

Leaning against shelves overflowing with papers, Cody
crossed his arms and frowned. "The Oelefse part doesn't
strike me as fitting with the rest."

The fedora bobbed, head and hat performing an odd
little miniscule nod. "That name was a gift from someone else I was able to help. Many of us have gifted names
in addition to those given to us at birth."

Uh-oh, Cody thought. Making no effort to disguise the
direction of his glance, he peered meaningfully at his
watch. "You don't have much time left. Where are you
from? L.A.? San Francisco?" There was a sizable German-
speaking community in the city by the Bay, he knew.

For an old man, the visitor's tone was steely. "If you
keep asking me questions, Herr Professor Cody, I will not
have time to explain how I may be able to help you. I
have come from Heidelberg."

Cody lowered his arms. "Pennsylvania?"

"Germany."

A little more than one minute left. Already, the archaeologist's thoughts were jumping ahead, to the work
he'd been doing before the doorbell had disturbed him.

No nut was going to come all the way from Germany to Arizona to indulge his fantasies, not even one with money. He hoped the old boy wouldn't put up a fuss when it was time for Cody to show him the door.

"You expect me to believe that you've come all the way from Germany, at your own expense, just to help me, a stranger you've never met?"

"Of course. We saw your plea on the Net. And I did not come at my own expense. The Society paid my way."

Definitely time to go, Cody decided. "Well, that's very thoughtful of you, Oelefse. And I truly appreciate it. But I'm very busy and there's a lot I want to do still today." Standing away from the shelves, he gestured toward the hall that led to the front door. "I hope you enjoy your visit to Arizona."

The old man made no move to rise. "You do not believe me, young mister Cody."

"Now, now, did I say that?" The archaeologist plastered a big, fat, fake grin on his face. He'd been down this road with others of Oelefse's ilk, many times before, and had formulated a routine for dealing with them. The important thing was to remain calm, and friendly, and sympathetic to their beliefs. "You're not going to give me any trouble, are you? Because I really am busy."

"*Verdammt*, do you think you are the only one? The only person who is troubled by Those Who Abide?"

"No, of course not." Cody was already halfway down the hall. He glanced back at his visitor. "I'm just one of the busiest ones."

His visitor sighed. "Two blocks from here there is an artificial cataract that decorates the entrance to this neighborhood. It has a big sign on the bottom and is constructed of native stone." Small, intense blue eyes locked on Cody's. "Presently, it is home to not less than two and not more than four Interlopers, of at least two different types."

Cody stopped walking toward the front door. Pivoting sharply, he returned to the den. "How do you know that?" His visitor was right, of course. Cody saw those particular Interlopers every time he drove past the waterfall.

"I see them, of course. Your house, by the way, is clean."

"Yes, I know." Hastily shoveling papers out of another chair, he sat down opposite his visitor, whom he was now seeing in an entirely new light. Could it be that the man's inner strength, his tone of voice, his self-possession, were not manifestations of madness, but of something else? "The question is, how do *you* know?"

"I told you. I can see them. Anyone who belongs to the Society must be able to perceive."

Cody swallowed. He was too unsettled to be polite. "You're from Germany and you belong to an organization that's aware of Those Who Abide?"

His visitor took the archaeologist's astonishment in stride, exactly as if it was something he had encountered before. "The translation in German is different. Why should you be so surprised? We have had more than our share of troubles with Those Who Abide."

Cody found himself nodding slowly, aware that he had gone from cool skepticism to grudging acceptance of his visitor's legitimacy. "That would explain a lot."

"There are many explanations awaiting you, my young friend. Not everyone is of a mind sufficiently open to accept them."

"Oh, I'll accept them, all right." Cody spoke with feeling. "I'll accept anything that might help my Kelli."

"*Ah ja*, your wife." Oelefse was nodding slowly to himself. "From the description accompanying your entreaty, a most unfortunate, but hardly unique case. You made it quite clear to anyone capable of reading between the lines that she has been infected. I am truly sorry."

Ashamed at the way he had treated his visitor, Cody now strove to make amends. "Look, I'm sorry if I was a little abrupt with you at first. You have to understand that in the course of trying to get help for Kelli, I've had to deal with a lot of people who were pretty shaky upstairs."

"I am not offended, Cody." Raising the umbrella, the elderly German pointed toward the other end of the house. "You will now offer me something to eat and drink. Nothing too heavy, please, and tea would be nice."

Cody immediately started toward the kitchen. "Coming from Europe, I would've thought you'd prefer coffee."

"I would," Oelefse conceded, "if I could find an American who knew how to make it. Tea will be fine."

Rummaging through the filthy, half-abandoned kitchen, the archaeologist managed to find both tea bags and a box of cookies that was not too far past the expiration date stamped on the wrapping. When the tea was ready, he brought it and the accompaniments into the den, to find his visitor blithely reading through a stack of magazines.

"Nothing in any of those." Cody put the tray down atop the pile of books that concealed the coffee table. "Sugar?"

"I will help myself." Putting the magazines aside, Oelefse resumed his seat. His manner in preparing his tea was as precise as everything else about him, his movements almost dainty. He ate and drank with the air of an impoverished aristocrat. "Nothing for you, my friend?"

"Me? Oh, yeah." Revisiting the kitchen, the archaeologist returned with an open beer. This he used to salute his guest. "To your health."

"Prosit." The elderly gentleman gestured slightly with his cup of tea. "You Americans do not know how to make beer, either."

"I hereby apologize in advance for all my country's deficiencies." Cody struggled to rein in his impatience. "How can you help Kelli?"

"First I must see her. In your communication you stated that she lies in a comatose state."

Cody nodded. "She breathes on her own, and she's getting fluids and sustenance intravenously. Her body seems to be processing everything properly, but her blood pressure lately has been trending downward." He bit back the lump in his throat. "The doctors try to be reassuring, but I can see that they aren't hopeful."

"Why should they be?" Oelefse spoke with unconscious coldness. "They cannot know what is wrong with her. I must see her."

"Of course, of course." The surge of hope that Cody felt nearly caused him to drop the perspiring bottle he was holding. "*Can* you do anything for her? Is there a pill, or some kind of injection?"

"Diagnosis first, then prognosis, then treatment. If such is viable."

Hope evaporated as quickly as it had materialized. "What do you mean, 'if'?"

"I will not lie to you, Cody Westcott. The Society has no time for comforting prevarications." Blue eyes narrowed at him over the rim of the teacup. "Those Who Abide vary enormously in their ability to affect human health. Not so much the physical aspects of it as the mental. Your wife might emerge from her coma—changed."

Cody's lips tightened. "Changed how?"

Oelefse sipped delicately. Steam rising from the cup curled over the bridge of his nose. "Her memory may be damaged. She may feel differently about certain things. She may feel differently about you."

"I'll take that chance." The archaeologist knocked back a long swallow.

"There may be other kinds of impairment. Her sanity may be damaged."

"Just bring her out of the coma. I'll deal with whatever consequences arise."

"Will you? You are nothing if not confident. That is good. You are going to need all the confidence you can muster, my friend, if we are to have any chance of saving your wife. Now then: I do not suppose you can identify the Interloper, or Interlopers, who have come to abide in your mate's body?"

"I don't know names for any of them, if that's what you mean. I suppose this Society of yours does?"

Oelefse smoothly poured himself a second cup of tea, emptying the small pot Cody had prepared. "Over time, one learns to put names to things. It is the human way. The Society is very old, and the litany of Interlopers quite long."

"How long?" Cody prompted his visitor. "How many different kinds are there? I know that I've seen dozens."

"There are thousands of different types," the German told him quietly. "And they number in the millions. They have afflicted mankind since the beginning of time. Some say they came down from the trees with us. As for the Society, as an archaeologist you would know the ten- to fourteen-thousand-year-old cave paintings from Lascaux in France and Altamira in Spain."

Cody nodded. "They show bisons and cave bears and lions living beside humans in Neolithic Europe."

"And Interlopers." Oelefse smiled at the younger man's startled reaction. "*Ja*, they too are depicted on those same ochre-stained walls. What appears abstract or incomplete

to the average anthropologist is perfectly obvious to those
of us who know what we are looking at. In Australia
there are similar ancient paintings, and also in Damara-
land in southwest Africa. Primitive peoples knew the Interlopers, but that does not mean they knew how to fight
them. Some did, and survived. Others did not, and perished beneath the weight of their own ignorance. We have
records of such vanished peoples." Blue eyes twinkled.

"Heidelberg has been a repository of such knowledge
for thousands of years. Not for nothing has it been the
intellectual center of Germany."

"And yet in spite of all that knowledge, you suffered
Kaisers, and Hitler."

His visitor took no offense. "The stronger resistance
is to Those Who Abide, the more energetically they strive
to locate and obliterate its source. Germany has suffered
more than most from their depredations. Why do you
imagine that Heidelberg was spared the devastation that
consumed my country during the Second World War? Why
do you suppose that Rothenburg-ab-den-Tauber, the best
preserved medieval town in Germany, was spared destruction towards the end of the war? It was because the
general commanding the American forces in that area
knew it as a centuries-old center of resistance to the Interlopers, was a member of the Society, and interceded
to see that it was not bombarded. In the great punishment
museum of Rothenburg there are devices for restricting
the movement of Interlopers, and of those people who
were afflicted by them." He smiled knowingly. "Their true
function has never been divined."

Draining the last of the beer, which if not up to his
visitor's Continental standards was still satisfying to him,
Cody considered opening a second. "I know from my own
work that the Interlopers are not a new phenomenon."

"Indeed. You worry about the abiding that has paralyzed your wife. Your immediate concern is, understandably, personal. In contrast, we of the Society have charged ourselves to worry about entire countries, whole governments. Consider, my young friend," Oelefse enjoined his host, "human history. You are better placed than most to do so. Contemplate the lapses of reason, the irrationality of important decisions, the insanity of many of mankind's actions. As a species, we think, we analyze, we are capable of the most abstruse logic, and yet we so often choose to act in a collective manner that is embarrassing to our simian predecessors. Why is that? Is it simply our nature, our fate, to stumble and bumble about like blobs of mindless protoplasm with no more sense than a colony of clams? Or are there other forces at work, other influences that lie beyond the collective cognizance of the great mass of humanity?"

Cody badly wanted another beer, but found himself transfixed by the oldster's words. "The Interlopers. Yeah, I've thought about it."

His visitor leaned back slightly in the chair. Outside, the late summer sun baked backyard and city and the desert that surrounded it. "Their influence is not absolute, but it is the single most important factor in mankind's lack of advancement. Where we should be forging ahead to a bright and brilliant future, we instead trip and flounder and sometimes even fall. Because of Those Who Abide. The world wars you alluded to, the Dark Ages, Africa today: All are the consequence of severe Interloper activity. These things the Society is pledged to fight." Oelefse's smile was warm. "When we can, when it seems feasible, and when one of us can be spared from greater concerns, we even help individuals."

"I'm more grateful than I can say." Cody felt an overwhelming sense of gratitude even though Oelefse had yet to do anything for Kelli. Just the older man's presence, the revelation that the archaeologist was not alone in the world in his ability to perceive the infectious horrors that had struck down his wife, had a consoling effect. "So these creatures do affect not just individuals, but the course of human events."

"*Ja.* As one of the Sighted, you must be made aware of the bigger picture, as you Americans say. It is assumed by me and my colleagues that you acquired this competence in the course of your professional work."

"There was a formula for a potion. Working together, a friend of mine and I prepared it. I drank some, he didn't. He died before he could sample the results of his own handiwork. The Interlopers killed him. Or arranged events so that he would die."

"I am sorry. He passed away in a good cause and in good company. Famous company, which you will learn about in due course. As a member of the Society, you will have access to a store of knowledge vaster than your dreams."

Cody hesitated. "Member? Do I have to undergo some kind of initiation or something?"

Oelefse laughed softly. "You are already a member, my friend. Anyone who can perceive, anyone who is Sighted, is automatically so. *Willkommen*—welcome."

"Thanks—I guess." He glanced at his watch. Far more than the five minutes he had intended to grant his guest had expired. "So Those Who Abide affect the course of human events. How? And why? Why should they care what we do or how human society evolves?"

"I should think you would have grasped that by now, Cody." The old man carefully set his cup aside. His gaze was as hard as his voice. "It, everything, has to do with how they feed—and what they feed upon."

Ten

The archaeologist was silent for a long moment, contemplating questions he wasn't sure he wanted answered, knowing that if he wanted to help his wife he had no choice but to hear them.

"That—that was one of my main questions. I know it has something to do with human unhappiness."

"Truly it does." Oelefse shifted in the chair. "Tell me, my friend: Have you ever felt ill without knowing the source? Irritable, angry for no discernible reason, upset with a moment in life that was really of minor consequence? Have you ever yelled at others only to wonder why afterwards? Hurt another person for no good cause? Suffered from headaches that no pill would alleviate, such as migraines that seemed to materialize without cause? Acted in an irrational fashion that left you feeling later as if you had been acting in a dream?"

"Who hasn't?" was all Cody could think of to say.

"Who indeed? Most of the time, such behavior can be traced to natural causes. But sometimes it cannot. The most severe examples arise from roots beyond the ability of medical science to detect. Though not beyond that of modern physics. How is your knowledge of subatomic particles?"

The change of subject took Cody aback. "Pretty limited. There's not much call for it in archaeology, except for those of us who specialize in dating."

"I will not go into details. Those Who Abide *are* detectable by devices that measure such things, but we who search them out and confront them cannot carry particle accelerators around with us." Unexpectedly, he grinned. "They will not fit even in a German car.

"Different kinds of Interlopers induce different reactions. What they feed upon, what they derive from their incognizant human hosts, is misery. Unhappiness, despair, grief; these are all powerful emotions that generate particular sets of electrical impulses in the brain. As near as we have been able to determine, this is what the Interlopers feed upon. The greater the distress, the more extreme the anguish, the more food there is for Those Who Abide." His voice fell slightly.

"Is it any wonder that they would revel, and multiply, and thrive, during a war, or a period of widespread misery in human history such as the Dark Ages, or the time of the Black Plague?"

"But that's when their human hosts would perish in the greatest numbers." Cody considered the ramifications. "That doesn't make any sense."

"The only time an Interloper can move from one human to another is when the original host dies. At times of great crisis, people are always being buried. For the Interlopers, transfer then becomes a matter of picking and choosing among many potential new hosts, not of finding one.

"At the same time, while they are feeding, they can sometimes control more than their host's emotions. Surely you have by now encountered evidence of this adaptation?"

Cody remembered: the auto accidents he had observed, people happy one moment and fighting the next, parents berating bewildered children: all evidence of the malicious intervention of hungry Interlopers.

"So they don't just *feed* on negative emotions; they actually stimulate them."

Oelefse nodded somberly. "Just as certain ant species stimulate aphids to secrete a sugary nectar for the ants to feed upon. To Those Who Abide we are cattle. Desolation and misery are their crops, which they cultivate wherever and whenever they can. A headache is a snack, a marital row a meal, emotional disintegration a dessert. The great causes of mass human suffering such as epidemics, natural catastrophes, and especially war, are banquets: troughs of despair in which they wallow ecstatically."

"And there's nothing we can do about it." Overwhelmed by the dismal revelations of his guest, Cody would have slumped dejectedly, if not for the realization that it might serve to excite and attract any Interlopers in the immediate vicinity. No wonder the restorative properties of humor were always being lauded by physicians. A joyful individual would present a dearth of nourishment to an Interloper.

"On the contrary, my young friend. We can fight," Oelefse told him. "We of the Society have being doing so for millennia. If there was no resistance, civilization as we know it would be even worse off today than it is. What progress we as a species *have* made is a consequence not of fatalistic acquiescence, but of a will to resist." He wagged an admonishing finger at the despondent younger man.

"Laughter, my friend, is a powerful weapon. It is to the Interlopers what insecticide is to bugs. While it cannot cure an infestation, it *can* help to ward one off or to mitigate its consequences. Remember that always."

"That's it? All we can fight these things with are jokes?"

"There are other means. If there were not, there would be little hope. The members of the Society have calculated that were it not for the Interlopers, civilization would be at least a thousand years more advanced than it is now. We would long ago have seen an end to the kind of tribal warfare that roils the Balkans and the Caucasus, Africa and the Middle East. We would be done with fossil fuels and their attendant pollution, and would long ago have settled the other worlds of our solar system, if not those of other stars. Always, the Interlopers are there, holding us back, eagerly abetting our worst instincts. Every time it seems that we are ready to spring forward, there is an inexplicable, seemingly unavoidable war, or a new crisis over something as stupid as money, or territory, or religion, that holds us back. Or a new plague rears its microbial head, its spread facilitated by zealous Interlopers." His gaze narrowed, and there was nothing of the senile about it.

"The new drug-resistant tuberculosis, chloroquine- and fansidar-resistant forms of malaria, mutated kinds of venereal disease: All have Those Who Abide to thank for their rapid spread, if not their origins. And then there is AIDS. All this in addition to the ubiquitous scourge of cancer. To Those Who Abide, a suffering human is a fertile field. The person who coined the English phrase 'misery loves company' had no idea what kind of company he was describing.

"At the moment we live in one of the more comparatively peaceful, sane periods of recent centuries. It has been a protracted, enduring struggle, but human science is slowly coming to grips with the effects Interlopers can induce, even while remaining ignorant of the true cause. As a result, Those Who Abide are restless. They are building toward another great catastrophe in hopes of throwing us back, of casting us once again down into the Pit. The development of worldwide communications is potentially a boon to their destructive efforts, allowing them to reach much greater numbers of people simultaneously. The Society is fighting this where and when it can.

"Because a new international crisis approaches, there was some debate over whether my services should be spared to help you with your purely personal concerns."

"I see," Cody replied quietly. "Why *did* you—the Society—decide to help?"

"Because you are valuable, Coschocton Westcott. To the cause. Not only are you Sighted, but your field is one in which expertise is always needed and not often found."

The archaeologist eyed his visitor evenly. "And if I was a plumber, or an insurance salesman, or a broker, you would not be here today, because I would have nothing to offer the Society?"

The older man's lengthy pause was eloquent. "Our resources are limited, my earnest young friend. They must be deployed daily in the service of all mankind. We cannot win every individual battle, but we *must* win the war. Otherwise, we are doomed to dwell forever in the depths of our own despair. Sadly, in great conflicts it is the civilians who invariably suffer the most. I am a soldier. You, like it or not, because of your abilities and skills, now also become a soldier."

Cody did not feel especially martial. "Sounds to me like what you need in this clash is not archaeologists, but an army of comedy writers."

His guest smiled, the one gold tooth gleaming brightly. "What makes you think they are not counted among the ranks of the Society? Their aggregate is small but significant, and their influence out of proportion to their number. Every day they wage war on behalf of those who

would be dominated by the Interlopers. Often they win,
sometimes they lose. If you wish to gauge their ability,
you should watch more television comedy. As you do so,
consider how many terrible programs are broadcast, and
how many good ones inexplicably fall by the wayside.
Consider how programming decisions are made by executives with no experience in professional comedy, little
sense of humor, and the inability to understand any wit-
ticism more complex than the writing on the walls of a
public restroom. Unable to stand the therapeutic effects
of human laughter, Those Who Abide are particularly keen
to infect and dominate network programming executives
and their ilk. This holds true in the rest of the world as
much as it does in America, though because of the influence and pervasiveness of your television programs,
Those Who Abide are particularly active in your industry."

Remembering some of the hideous excuses for sitcoms
he and Kelli had suffered through during the past year,
Cody could well believe what his guest was telling him.

"You said there were other things besides laughter that
could be used to fight these predators. Can any of them
be used to help my wife?" Cody inhaled deeply, his mind
already made up. "If you can do anything for her, anything at all, then I'm yours. I'll resign my position at the
university, do research for you, let you guide my entire
future. I'll do anything, anything you want. I'll even move
to Heidelberg."

Oelefse raised a hand to calm him. "That will not be
necessary, my friend—though you would like Heidelberg.
The Society is already strong there. Where we need assistance is elsewhere. As to helping your unfortunate mate,
no course of action can be prescribed until the severity
of her condition has been ascertained and her prospects
for treatment have been appraised." Setting the empty

teacup aside, he rose from his chair. For a moment, he towered over the seated archaeologist, and not only physically.

"Believe me, my friend, I understand what you are feeling. It is a terrible thing to watch a loved one's life slip away, to see them drown in anguish not of their own making. Depression can kill as surely as any heart attack. It is the cancer of the mind. I know, because I have seen it happen all too many times." His voice shook ever so slightly as he seemed suddenly to be looking not at Cody, but past him, to a distant place and time.

"The first time, it was my wife. Then it was my children. A little girl, beautiful she was, with golden hair and dancing eyes. My boy lived longer, but he died just the same. Driven to throw himself over a precipice in the Alps. I never understood, never knew why I had been singled out for so much unhappiness. The Society found me. They saved me from the Interlopers who had bled my family emotionally dry and then discarded them the way a spider discards the empty husk of an insect it has finished feeding upon. They cured me, and tutored me, and allowed me to learn." He straightened.

"Now, and for many years, I have been a soldier in the Society. When and where it is both possible and feasible, I perform the same service for others that the Society performed for me. They gave me back my life, a reason to go on living. My goal is the same as theirs: disrupting the machinations of Those Who Abide, helping the unwitting who suffer from their afflictions, and striving for their eventual and complete extermination." A thin smile creased his mouth. "The Interlopers can sense these things, my friend. They do not like it, and they do not like me. They hate anyone who can perceive them." Once more, his eyes met Cody's. "They hate *you*."

The archaeologist did not flinch. "The feeling's mutual."

"Good!" Reaching forward, the older man put a firm hand on Cody's shoulder. "But manifest your antipathy as laughter, and laugh at them. Hatred they can deal with. Laughter—laughter drives them into a frenzy. They have no way to fight it. Laugh long and hard enough, even to yourself, and you can drive off any Interloper. That is one way we fight them." He stepped back.

"Now come, my young friend, and we will see what can be done for your wife."

Snatching up his car keys and wallet, Cody followed the elderly German out into the hall. "Tell me, Oelefse: You say that you're a soldier now. A soldier in the Society. What were you before—before . . ."

The older man didn't hesitate. "Before my family was taken from me? Before my former life was destroyed? I was a physicist, young Cody. I worked much of the year in Switzerland, at the CERN supercollider facility in Bern. There are a number of physicists in the Society. We are always arguing with the biologists among us. One of the great questions that consumes us is whether the Interlopers are composed of waves or particles, or a combination thereof."

"What's the prevailing opinion?" They were approaching the front door.

"That it does not matter," Oelefse told him, "so long as they can be made to die."

For the first time in many weeks, Cody allowed himself a small surge of hope. "Then they can be killed. By laughing at them?"

"Laughter is a means of defense, not attack. It can drive them away, but sustaining honest, effective laughter long enough to kill even a small Interloper is nearly impossible."

"I guess the safest people in the world would be professional comedians." Before opening the door, Cody armed the in-house alarm system. His visitor watched with interest.

"On the contrary, there are many such who suffer from the attentions of Those Who Abide. Professional comedians are among the most unhappy, morose, melancholy inhabitants of the planet. Where do you think professional humor comes from, anyway? From a lifetime of fighting off the effects of Interlopers. Funny is painful, my young friend."

"Then there are other ways to kill them. You indicated as much."

Oelefse patted his jacket. Was that a bulge where an inside pocket might be? "No, it is not a gun." He grinned at the archaeologist. "The Interlopers are patterns of otherworldliness. Generating and projecting the right electromagnetic field can play havoc with such patterns. It depends on the Interloper. The *atrix* is not a panacea, but long years of development have gone into its manufacture." He wagged a finger at Cody. "Solid-state physics, advanced chip masking technology, even the development of smaller and smaller batteries have made such devices possible. Those Who Abide fear them, and their improvement. Is it any wonder they strive to thrust the world into another crisis, whether through disease or politics? For example, you cannot imagine how many important people are presently afflicted in India and Pakistan."

"How can you prevent adverse events from taking place halfway around the world?"

"The Society has operatives everywhere. Sometimes we are successful, such as in Peru and Ecuador. Sometimes we are too late, as in the Congo. We fight on because we must. Mankind has come too far, reached too lofty a height, to collapse under the weight of another great plague or war. Science abets our work, but knowledge is our armor."

Cody hesitated with one hand on the door handle. "If you have a device that can kill Those Who Abide, why not mass-manufacture it, hand thousands of them out to a Society-inspired army, and kill every last Interloper?"

"It is not so easy, my friend. The *atrix* and its companion devices are not easy to use. Teaching others how to calibrate one takes time. And they are not always effective." His expression darkened. "There is some concern that the Interlopers may have the power of rapid mutation that is found in insects and smaller creatures: the ability to evolve defenses against new forms of attack, as has happened over the years with malaria and other diseases. Employ the *atrix* too much and too often, for example, and the risk is run of rendering Those Who Abide immune to its effects. We must move carefully.

"For now, our principal concerns are further research, preserving civilization—and helping your wife." A broad smile creased his face. "They say that the last shall be first. Excuse me."

Stepping in front of Cody, the old man took the handle and opened the door very slightly. As he stood peering out, Cody wondered at his caution.

"If you're looking for Interlopers, I check the neighborhood every morning. Except for the ones that are resident in the stones of that artificial waterfall you saw on your way in, this area is clean."

"Is it?" Oelefse did not look up from his examination.

"You bet," Cody assured him. "They can't move around on their own. They need— A sudden thought made him hesitate. "Is that what you're looking for?"

"My young friend, I have already told you how they have influenced the course of human history to its detriment by afflicting important players throughout time. What makes you think anything has changed? Ah!"

Cody was instantly on guard. "What—what is it?"

Oelefse stepped aside. "See for yourself. The far street, around the corner. A white sedan of domestic manufacture. There are two men sitting in the front, both wearing dark suits."

The archaeologist located the car and noted its occupants. "Infected?" His guest nodded. "How can you be certain?"

"What fools wear dark suits in the desert in late summer?"

Cody eyed the older man significantly. "How do I know that *they're* not the representatives of this Society you speak of, and you're not an infected, manipulated decoy sent to lure me out of the house?"

Oelefse spread his arms wide. "You are Sighted, my young friend. Do you detect in my person any evidence of infestation?" Though it was not necessary and really made no difference, he executed a slow, theatrical pirouette. He was still smiling.

"Okay, so they're the bad guys and you're not. That still doesn't explain why you're dressed as impractically as they are."

Oelefse made a show of adjusting his bow tie. "I take great pride in my appearance, Cody Westcott. It is a good sign that someone is not afflicted. Those who suffer from the debilitating, gnawing presence of Interlopers rarely take any care with their bearing or attire."

"So the well-dressed are unpolluted?"

"Usually. Remember that, where Interloper presence is concerned, nothing is for certain. But the two in that car, they have about them a certain aspect that is detectable even at a distance. Experience enables one to recognize such signs. They are minions of the Interlopers, their actions and activities directed by Those Who Abide within them. Such constant control is difficult for the Interlopers to sustain without damaging the host."

"Uthu," Cody muttered. More loudly he added, "I've already encountered one who's been damaged. He came to warn me to stop my research. That was before"—he swallowed hard—"before Kelli was infected."

Oelefse's expression was somber. "They have no sense of mercy, you know. They will feed upon young children as readily as on an adult. They devour misery the way you would a good dinner. Can you remember anything distinctive about the person who came to see you?"

"He isn't either one of the two men in that car, if that's what you mean. What do we do now?"

"Do? We take my car, Cody, and we go to help your wife. But first, we make a little detour." He winked mischievously. "It takes time for the Interlopers to impose their will even on hosts they control so thoroughly. Reaction time is slowed. On the other hand, there is nothing wrong with my reflexes." Stepping through the open door, he headed down the winding path that led to the driveway and the silver Mercedes parked there. "Have you ever been to Germany, my young friend?"

"No." Cody tried hard not to look in the direction of the white sedan parked around the far corner.

"Ah! Then you have never been on the Autobahn." Walking around the front of the car, Oelefse used a small remote to unlock the doors. "I honestly do not know how you Americans manage to get anywhere in your cars, with these frivolous speed limits of yours."

"Frivolous speed limits?" Cody slid into the seat on the passenger side, unaware that in the thirty minutes to follow he would learn more about reaction times than he really wanted to know.

"Which way is the hospital where your wife is being

looked after?" Looking determined, Oelefse slowed to a halt at the stop sign where the last neighborhood street met the first main thoroughfare.

"Turn left here and head due north."

"Ah. Then we will go *this* way." Turning sharply in the opposite direction, the elderly German pulled out directly into traffic flowing past at no less than fifty miles per hour.

"Jesus!" Cody flinched as a big van swerved to miss them and an irate woman in a small Cadillac mouthed angry words from within its tinted window, air-conditioned interior.

"Remember, my friend," Cody's seasoned driver reminded him, "that while the Interlopers cannot be killed by normal means, their human hosts can."

As they sped without slowing through a double lane change, Cody forced himself to consider his wife's condition as unemotionally as possible. "Then the ones inhabiting Kelli won't let her die, because that would mean they would be trapping themselves in a lifeless, useless body—unless they can make sufficient contact with another motile form."

"That is probably true for a little while, at least. They will conspire to sustain her on the edge of life so that they can continue to feed off her enduring suffering. Only when they have had enough will they allow her to expire in a final orgy of feeding." Seeing the stricken look on his companion's face, he added, "I am sorry to speak so bluntly, my friend, but while there is ample room for compassion in the Society, there is neither time nor space for convenient euphemism. But do not worry: We will do our best to save your Frau."

" 'Our *best*'?" Cody turned sideways in the seat, fighting to ignore the seeming indifference with which Oelefse was weaving crazily through traffic.

"Where the Interlopers are concerned, nothing is absolute, nothing is for certain." The older man's tone was unyielding and unrepentant. "As I told you, I myself have lost loved ones to Those Who Abide. I will attend to your wife as if she was my own. More than that I cannot do."

"I— I'm sorry." Overwhelming emotion welled up in the distressed archaeologist as he sat back in his seat. "I know—you'll do everything you can. It's just that these past weeks have been harder on me than anything I ever imagined. You know, you joke with someone every day, argue with them, share food and fun and work and sleep with them, and you don't think about it. You just accept it. Until suddenly they're not there anymore."

"That has been my life for many years now, my friend." With the skill of a Grand Prix driver Oelefse eased the big car around a pair of convoying big rigs. "All you can do is channel those emotions into useful avenues of endeavor. Frustrating Interlopers, for example." His gaze flicked up to the rearview mirror. "Are they still following us?"

"Following . . . ?" Whirling in his seat, Cody stared out the back window. For an instant, the traffic was devoid of menace. Then a white sedan hove into view, swinging out from behind the same pair of trucks the Mercedes had just passed.

"I wasn't thinking, I was—yeah, they're still behind us." He squinted. "I'm almost positive it's them, but if so, they're hanging back a ways."

Oelefse's expression was set knowingly. "They are doing their best to remain inconspicuous."

"Why are they bothering? If they've been keeping track of my movements since before your arrival, they already know where Kelli is."

"*Ja, richtig*, but they *don't* know that you are taking me to the hospital. We are in my car, so maybe they are

thinking that I am taking you somewhere else. To the airport, for example."

Cody frowned uncertainly. "Why would you be taking
me to the airport?"

Instead of responding to the query, Oelefse. suddenly
wrenched hard on the wheel and yelled, "Hang on, young
Cody!"

Cody knew he must have paled as the oldster cut across
two lanes of horn-blaring, finger-thrusting traffic to launch
the Mercedes at the last possible instant onto the ramp
for the Pima freeway. When he'd recovered his equilibrium sufficiently, he turned in the seat to peer out the
back window.

"I don't see them anymore."

"*Gut!* We will make certain."

Oelefse was as good as his word. Not only did he lose
their pursuers, he almost lost the archaeologist as well as
he put the big sedan through a series of evasive maneu-
vers that were more aeronautical than automotive. When
they finally abandoned the freeway for a return to surface streets, Cody was perspiring as if he'd just finished
a three-mile run.

Glancing to his left, he saw that the elderly driver was
not even breathing hard. Also, the younger man noted,
not once had Oelefse taken either hand off the steering
wheel.

"I haven't been this frightened in a car since the time
Kelli and I had to drive from Chachapoyas back to base
camp in the dark."

Oelefse's expression did not change, nor did he take
his eyes off the road ahead. "You should try coming up
on a long line of intercontinental trucks traveling at fifty
kilometers an hour when you are doing two twenty, only
to have one pull out in front of you at the last minute as
you are trying to pass. On a bridge. With no shoulder.

The Autobahn is wonderful for driving, but wide shoulders for parking and passing and emergencies is an American invention." He glanced briefly to his left. "At such moments a man's heart may stop before his vehicle does. Are they gone?"

Cody scanned the roadway behind them until he was sure, or as sure as he could be. "I don't see that car anymore."

"I thought not. It takes time for Interlopers to communicate with and to influence their hosts. Reaction time, remember? Now then—which way to this hospital? Just to be safe, let us use a roundabout route."

"If you'll promise to keep it close to the speed limit," Cody insisted.

"Provided we do not encounter a certain white sedan, I am happy to take my time and enjoy the scenery. Your American West, you know, is so very popular in Germany."

Cody was not sure Karl Heinrich Oelefsenten von Eichstatt ever "took his time," but he was far too drained to challenge the older man.

Eleven

Despite Cody's assurance that he had not seen a trace of the white sedan for over an hour, Oelefse insisted on circling the several blocks surrounding the hospital, spiraling into a covered parking lot instead of heading there directly. No one tailed them from the lot to the lobby, or followed them into the elevator. All the while, both men kept careful watch on everyone from nurses to janitors to visitors. All appeared clean and uninfected, as did the colorful boulders that adorned the fountain on the third level.

Since it served the most seriously ill patients, the floor where Kelli lay was quieter than most. There, everything and everyone seemed to move more slowly than elsewhere in the complex. Nurses spoke more often in whispers, and doctors smiled less. There was no need for such courtesies anyway; not when the patients for whom they might have been intended could neither see nor hear those who were attending them.

Kelli's room was at the far end of the hall. As he did every time he paid a visit, Cody pictured her walking, perhaps tottering a little, in her white hospital gown as she came through the door. Saw her glancing up to see him approaching, her face breaking out in the irresistible, sunny, slightly sardonic smile of affection he knew so well. And as also happened every time, no recuperating Kelli emerged to greet him. Nor did he find her standing alone inside, gazing longingly out the window at the sun-kissed cityscape beyond, waiting to whirl around happily at his arrival.

The body in the bed was pallid and immobile, unchanged from the last time he had seen her. In his absence he knew that nurses turned and cleaned her, that doctors prodded here and poked there. But she always looked the same to him; flat on her back, eyes closed. She did not look up as he entered, nor react in any way to his touch.

Something else did, however. It always did.

This time it took the form of a small white worm limned in pale bluish stripes. It emerged from her upper arm to stab several times in his direction before retreating back into the living form that provided it with sustenance and shelter. He did not make a grab for it. Had he done so, he knew that his fingers would have passed completely through it. Likewise, the inhabitants of his wife's body, her abiding tormentors, could not move from her to him in the absence of a natural vector such as a rock or tree. And not just any rock or tree. Many, he had learned from Oelefse, were unsuitable homes for the creatures. Otherwise, every inch of the Earth and every growing thing would have boasted its own coiling, twisting, loathsome inhabitant. Drawing back, he mentioned as much to his mature companion.

"Your American Indians and other animist peoples were right all along, my young friend." Never stopping, never pausing for rest, Oelefse was investigating the room foot by foot, section by section. "They worshiped many things: the forest, the animals within, the rivers and lakes, the mountains and valleys. For them, each had its own spirit, to be avoided or propitiated. They were more right than ever they knew." Using the tip of his umbrella, he flipped open a cabinet and leaned forward to peer carefully inside.

"The animals have their spirits, but they are natural to them. They are not Interlopers. And Those Who Abide cannot be assuaged with prayers. The practice of human sacrifice throughout the ancient world had a very real basis in sound medical practice. It was the ultimate means of ridding individuals of the Interlopers who had taken residence within them and emotionally and spiritually sucked them dry. Of course, as a consequence of this method of cleansing the host also perished, but it was the only way the majority of our ancestors had of coping with the spread of Those Who Abide. When your Iroquois or Ute or Sioux prayed to the spirit of a particular rock or river, more than likely a tribal shaman had already identified it as the home of a waiting Interloper."

Fascinating as the older man's discourse was, Cody listened with only half an ear. His attention was on his motionless wife. "So the Chachapoyans weren't the only ancient peoples with access to such knowledge."

"*Nein*, my friend. The proper combination of drugs to take to enable one to perceive was once widely known. It is less so today, due not to the myopia of physicians and scientists but to a concerted effort on the part of Those Who Abide to constrict the spread of such knowledge." Concluding his inspection of the room, he carefully set his umbrella aside. "Now, let me have a look at her."

Reluctantly, Cody made room so that the older man could stand next to the bed, close by Kelli's upper body. Oelefse contemplated the recumbent form: the gentle, barely perceptible rise and fall of her chest, the occasional fluttering of closed eyelids, the soapy drip of nutrients through plasticine tubes. Reaching out, he gently stroked one exposed arm, his fingers journeying as delicately as a surgeon's from cheek to neck to shoulder, down the promenade of bare flesh until they reached the hand that was lying palm downward on the blanket. Collecting the limp fingers in his own, he squeezed gently while murmuring under his breath.

"What's that?" Leaning forward, Cody tried to make out the words. "What are you saying? I don't underst—"

Crunching and gnashing unearthly fangs, a mouth mounted on a weaving stalk burst from the tip of his wife's waxen index finger. It snapped at the oldster's cradling fist, the razor-thin teeth slashing harmlessly through his flesh. Oelefse's hand shuddered slightly, but he maintained both his grip and his incantation. Frustrated, the emergent jaws withdrew swiftly back into the finger from which they had erupted. Giving a little shake of his head, Oelefse released Kelli's hand and laid the slack fingers gently down on the bed. Turning back to an anxious, expectant Cody, the older man sighed heavily.

"I have not the inclination to play the diplomat. Her condition is grave."

"I can see that," the archaeologist snapped testily. "Tell me something I don't know. Can you do anything for her?"

"I will try. First I must get some things from my car." Leaving Kelli's bedside, he strode past the anxious archaeologist. "I will be right back."

Cody resumed his stance beside the beautiful, motionless woman in the bed. "Don't touch the rocks around the fountain on the way out. They're contaminated."

Oelefse smiled knowingly on his way out the door. "I know. I saw that on the way in."

What was he thinking, pointing out the obvious? Cody

chided himself as the door closed quietly behind the oldster. Oelefse was the nearest thing he had encountered to
a professional Interloper hunter. It was just that Cody was
still not used to the idea that there were others at least
as adept as himself at ferreting out the hiding places of
the intruders. It helped considerably to know that he was
not alone in the world, was not the only one with the
ability to espy secret horrors lurking in innocent-looking
pools of water and unworked stone. There existed a mysterious brotherhood in which he had automatically been
granted membership by virtue of his ability to perceive.
Where Kelli's still abject condition was concerned, he
could dare to hope. He no longer felt completely alone.

As he always did during such visits he talked softly
to her, not expecting a response. Nor did he receive one.
There was no way of knowing if she heard what he murmured lovingly. The doctors said that it was possible, but
they were the same doctors who were baffled by her condition. Without clearance to stick his head into other
rooms, Cody could only wonder how many of the hospital's other patients might be suffering from similar Interloper infestations.

They fed off human misery and suffering, Oelefse had
assured him. A hospital, therefore, would seem a logical
place to find them in great numbers. How much of it did
they cause? How many afflictions did they directly induce? These were sobering thoughts to which he could
only direct a small portion of himself. His focus, his primary concern, remained Kelli.

True to his word, Oelefse was not gone long before
returning with a large briefcase in hand. Except for its
size, it looked like an ordinary businessman's attaché; just
the sort a European of Oelefse's class and station in life
might carry. Setting it down on an empty chair, Cody's
new friend popped it open with a remote radio control.

Seeing the archaeologist's expression, the older man explained.

"Those Who Abide cannot of course open metal latches or tumblers, but their human minions can. Of necessity, we of the Society are very security-minded." Flipping up the top, he began removing an assortment of materials, laying them out neatly on the empty, four-wheeled food-service tray nearby.

"Lock the door," Oelefse instructed him. "And the windows. Draw the blinds." He gestured. "Jam the back of that chair against the door latch."

As Cody complied, the diminutive, smartly dressed Oelefse proceeded to remove his clothes, stripping down until he stood naked in the hospital room save for his briefs. Though reflective of his age, his pallid physique was more developed than his well-cut suit might have suggested. As the archaeologist looked on, he began to paint himself.

Cody was a more than competent professional. He prided himself on being well-read in his field, and not just within his specialty of western South American studies. But he had never seen anything resembling the patterns that the dignified German was now daubing upon his nude form. Slashes and spirals, curls and chevrons, groups of dots and mysterious anthropoidal shapes began to color his blanched, exposed skin. He went about this artistic self-embellishment in silence and as efficiently as if he were preparing to go to the opera.

Finished with the paints, he began to slick back his white hair with a handful of glistening, oily material scooped from a stubby, wide-mouthed jar. A powerful stench filled the room, magnified by the lack of outside ventilation.

"What the hell is that?"

"Bear grease." Concluding the procedure, Oelefse

moved to the sink to wash his hands—and only his hands. "Infused with distinctive chemicals. The byproducts of certain animals have powers undreamed of by most men. The Orientals know this, and suffer a good deal of criticism for it."

Cognizant of the worldwide trade in animal parts, Cody frowned unhappily. "Rhino horn? Tiger genitals?"

"Nothing like that. Some among the Oriental herbalists are knowledgeable, but most can do no better than random guessing. The Society has made a study of such things."

The archaeologist's nose twitched. "I can see where that stuff might repel Interlopers—and everyone else."

"Not at all." Reaching once more into his open briefcase, Oelefse removed a sequence of necklaces and placed them one at a time around his neck. "It is not the odor, but a combination of other chemicals that are released into the air. Smells have power just as do tastes and sounds and visuals." Holding up a small, exquisitely incised gourd that sat on one end of a stick decorated with feathers, beads, and seashells, he shook it in Cody's direction. Small hard objects unseen within the gourd produced a satisfying rattle.

Setting it momentarily aside, Oelefse removed several lengths of gleaming, beautifully machined stainless steel and began screwing them together to form a long pole, at the end of which he attached a colorful explosion of feathers, bone, and shell. Thus equipped with rattle and staff, paint and grease, he looked preposterous indeed as he stood nearly naked in the middle of the hospital room: a modern parody of some Neolithic witch doctor.

His expression, however, was deadly earnest. "Now, we begin. Watch the door, my young friend. Do what you must to see that I am not interrupted."

"What are you going to do?" The archaeologist within

Cody was more enthralled than amused by the older man's appearance. Though he recognized none of the patterns painted on the slim, elderly body, nor any of the contrivances Oelefse carried, they hinted at a collective lineage that was hoary and respected.

"Medicine," Oelefse declared, "is an evolving science that all too often looks down upon its roots. Many of those roots are false, but others are fixed in real knowledge. Some day I will show you the medical library that the Society has maintained for thousands of years." He smiled through paint and grease. "Its contents are not online."

Approaching the foot of the bed, he began to chant, shaking the rattle while passing it back and forth over Kelli's feet and legs. From time to time he would raise the instrument toward the ceiling or point it toward different corners of the room. He alternated this with slow horizontal passes of the steel staff over her entire blanketed body.

Thinking himself prepared for anything, Cody was startled when Kelli moaned and writhed beneath the bedsheets. He wanted to ask Oelefse if she was in pain, but seeing the look of concentration on the German's face, observing the tension in his muscles as he sang and moved with studied precision, he dared not interrupt.

The room grew dark, darker than the shuttered windows ought to have allowed. A warm breeze, almost hot, caressed Cody's cheeks. Something on the rising wind sang in his ears that was more than the passage of air. An occasional rumble, as of distant thunder trapped in the mattress, punctuated the breeze. Where wind and rumble arose from in the sealed room he could only imagine.

There came a rapping at the door. "Hello? Mr. Westcott, is that you? Are you in there? What's going on?"

"Everything's fine, nurse!" He had to raise his voice slightly to ensure that his words would be understood above the wind that was now whipping his long hair about his face. "I thought I'd try some music. My wife loves heavy metal."

"You have to turn it down, Mr. Westcott. Excessive noise will not be tolerated."

"I'll watch it!" he replied in response to the admonition. The rapping ceased. Pleased with himself, he turned back to the bed—whereupon his eyes all but jumped out of his head.

A small but intense vortex had formed directly above his wife's body; a wide-lipped, slowly rotating squat tornado of a spiral within which flashes of red light raced like electrified rats skittering for distant burrows. His position unchanged at the foot of the bed, a chanting Karl Heinrich Oelefsenten von Eichstatt conducted this energetic specter with rattle and staff and carefully composed incantation. Cody was certain there was a perfectly good scientific explanation for what he was seeing: it just escaped him at the moment.

The rapping at the door was now replaced by a more insistent pounding. "Open up in there! Mr. Westcott, you must open this door." The voice was demanding, insistent. Glancing in Oelefse's direction for a sign, Cody found himself ignored. When the pounding intensified, the archaeologist responded by pressing his shoulder against the door and leaning his weight into it, more than a little astonished at the position he suddenly found himself occupying.

The wind in the room had risen to a howl, all of it sucked inward toward the flashing, shrieking vortex. As Oelefse's surprisingly strong voice rose to a feverish pitch, a small greenish length of spectral plasm emerged from his wife's abdomen. Fighting to cling to its host, the shape was drawn involuntarily upward, to vanish into the spout-like underside of the vortex. It was followed by a cluster of tentacles attached to a knobbed egg. Eyes dipped and bobbed wildly as a flattened, crablike blob went next. A staring, gaping Cody did not know if he was witnessing multiple Interlopers being drawn from his wife's twisting, moaning form, or pieces of a single, much larger one. Wherever the truth lay, it was clear that her infection was as serious as he had believed all along.

The door shuddered as something heavy slammed against the other side. Tightening his jaws, Cody struggled to find a better purchase on the slick hospital floor as he pushed back against whatever was trying to get in. Whoever was out in the hall had stopped yelling at him and shouting orders in favor of turning to brute strength. With a desperation born of revived hope, the archaeologist held his ground, his efforts abetted by the metal chair he had jammed against the handle. Again the door boomed as something heavy thudded against it.

How much longer, he wondered? The tireless Oelefse showed no sign of ceasing his chorusing or his choreography. When would whoever was on the other side call in Security, or outside police? And when they finally arrived, as it now seemed inevitable that they must, what would Cody tell them? If they got a good look at the painted-up, greased-down elderly German, they might not bother with questions.

Not that Cody cared if he was arrested and incarcerated along with Oelefse. He would suffer any indignity, endure any punishment, if only Kelli's health could be restored to her. And maybe this time she would take his "crazy theories" a little more seriously. Especially after she had the opportunity to converse with her hapless doctors.

She was far from cured yet, however. As Cody held

the door against all intruders, Oelefse stood straight and strong in the darkened room, which was now alive with brief bursts of supernal brilliance and streaks of emancipated crimson lightning. Kelli continued to twist and whine softly within the bed as one grotesque guise after another was pulled from her body to vanish into the slender but irresistible maw of the wailing vortex.

A cluster of saw-edged tentacles suddenly thrust through the door, weaving and flailing. One pierced the archaeologist's forearm, emerging on the other side. There was no blood and no pain; only a slight coolness in the vicinity of his wrist. After writhing futilely for a few moments, the tentacles withdrew. The hospital door was metal and composite. While the Interlopers on the other side could penetrate it as if it were water, in the absence of a vector composed of natural material they could neither infect nor affect the human leaning against the other side.

Cody was wondering how they were going to celebrate, when something monstrous and irredeemably evil suddenly burst through his wife's chest to strike at the vortex. It had a wide, warty, leprous face with burning white eyes and tiny bright yellow pupils that bulged so far forward they seemed on the verge of tumbling out of their inadequate sockets and onto the floor. A great, clawed, four-fingered hand reached up from a muscular shoulder still buried within Kelli to slash violently at the vortex, cleaving it as though it were made of paper. Bits of the compact maelstrom went flying in all directions. One just missed Cody's face and he felt the heat of its passing as it flew past him and through the solid hospital door. The apparent catastrophe had one beneficial side effect, one unforeseen consolation: Something on the other side of the door screamed, and the heavy pounding that threatened to numb the desperate archaeologist's shoulder momentarily ceased.

Abruptly confused, the wind tore at his exposed skin and clothes. The massive yet ethereal hand reached for the chanting Oelefse. Bringing his metal staff down in a swooping arc, the German struck it between its grasping fingers. Red sparks that were not the fire of Earth flew, momentarily blinding Cody. A distant, discordant howl rose from that horrific, swollen face and it promptly withdrew, pulling the single hand down with it, back into Kelli's writhing form. Tears started from Cody's eyes at the thought that something like that might be living within, and feeding upon, the woman he adored.

With the destruction of the vortex the wind began to fade, individual zephyrs slipping away to hide beneath doors and windowsills and in ventilator shafts. Normal, subdued sunlight that had been forced from the room returned, brightening it considerably. An exhausted Oelefse stood supporting himself with one hand on the bed's footboard. His expression was drained and sweat poured in rivulets down his face and naked body, streaking the patterns he had so carefully painted there. For the first time, Cody noted that the elderly man was as muscled as a retired circus performer, the lumps and bulges within his flesh clad in skin the texture and hue of dirty white suede.

Interestingly, the pounding on the door was not resumed. The calm before the accusatory storm, the archaeologist decided. Moving quickly to the side of the bed, he stared down at Kelli. She appeared to be resting comfortably once more, though droplets of sweat now beaded her face. Finding a washcloth, he tenderly brushed away the perspiration. Her eyes remained closed, her expression as nonresponsive as before. Troubled, he turned to Oeletse.

"Is she better? She looks the same. And she's still not reacting."

"Give me a moment, my friend. I understand your distress, but nothing will change if I take a few minutes for myself, and we will present a much more reassuring appearance to the administrative functionaries if I alter mine." Snapping the briefcase shut, he took it with him into the bathroom. Moments later Cody heard the shower running.

Apprehensive as he was, there was nothing he could do to draw an explanation from the older man. He would have to wait. And he had to admit that Oelefse was right. Hospital security would be far less inclined to have them arrested if the German did not appear before them clad in bear grease, war paint, and little else.

Glancing idly toward the foot of the bed, he saw that Oelefse had laid rattle and staff down on the bed sheets. Three-quarters of the way up the staff, the tough stainless steel was partially melted beneath a black streak slightly less than a foot long. Cody went cold inside. The thing that had caused that was living within, and feeding off, the woman he loved. Based on what he knew, Interlopers could not normally affect non-natural objects such as steel. But the events of the preceding half hour had been anything but normal. Certain minor laws of nature had been suspended, existence altered, and perception adjusted. Reality had been tampered with.

Leaving Kelli's bedside, he removed the chair propped against the door and opened the window blinds, flooding the room once more with unfiltered sunshine. By the time Oelefse emerged from the bathroom, once again impeccably attired, there was little to indicate that anything out of the ordinary had taken place. The German was just setting his handsome hat back on his head when two husky security guards burst into the room, closely trailed by a doctor and nurse. As they cast suspicious glances in all directions, Cody looked up curiously.

"Everything all right?"

When the security men gazed hard at the archaeologist, he met their accusatory stares with an expression of bemused innocence. The doctor turned on the bewildered nurse.

"Well? What's this all about, then?"

"I—it sounded like there was a war going on in here. I swear, Doctor! The outside walls were shaking. If you put your palm against them you could feel the vibrations!"

The duty physician turned sternly to face Cody, who was seated on the edge of the bed alongside his gently breathing wife. "My nurses are not subject to hallucinations, Mr. Westcott."

"I told her." Cody shrugged, affecting the air of one who when confronted by a meaningless challenge could not and would not argue with those too daft to accept the obvious. "My wife likes heavy metal. I'm sorry if I had it going a little too loud."

"A little loud!" The flustered nurse's outrage was palpable. "It was more than music that was going on in here!"

Oelefse spoke up, gesturing at the room. "Really, Herr Doktor, do you see anything amiss?"

The duty physician scanned the room. "No. No, everything looks all right." His eyebrows drew together and he gestured with a nod. "What are those?"

As one, Cody and Oelefse's eyes went to the two long objects resting crosswise on the foot of the bed. Rising from his seat, the old man picked them up, prepared to allow the doctor closer scrutiny should he be so inclined.

"Gifts for my young friend here. He is an archaeologist, and as such interested in all manner of primitive objects."

The doctor stared a moment longer. Then he finally relaxed. "They're very handsome. Indian? The metal one is, of course, a reproduction." Behind him, the nurse glowered silently.

"Of course. *Ja*, they are Indian. You are perceptive beyond your field, Herr Doktor."

Feeling good about himself and better about the situation, the physician smiled broadly. "Sorry to have bothered you, then. Please do try to keep the volume down in here, though. Our walls are reasonably well soundproofed, but they're not impenetrable, and not all our patients are heavy metal fans. Especially some of the elderly ones. American or British band?"

Oelefse gestured deferentially. "German, of course. Rammstein. I thought they might be especially efficacious in this case."

The doctor shook his head in amusement. "Heavy metal music. Now that's a therapy I haven't tried." Favoring the bewildered nurse with a withering look of reproach, he turned and led the way out of the room. Relieved of any need to wrestle with recalcitrant visitors, the security men followed without comment.

Cody let out a deep, inward sigh of relief. So preoccupied with the nurse's report and then distracted by Oelefse's colorful gear had the doctor been, he'd failed to notice the absence of a CD player, tape deck, or any other visible source of the sounds that the archaeologist had claimed as the "music" that had shaken the room. The older man began to break down the staff into its component parts to repack in the briefcase. He paused to inspect the scorched, marginally melted section of shaft, running a finger over it speculatively.

"*Donnerwetter.* Very powerful infestation, this. Very, very strong," he muttered under his breath.

"What now? What happened?" Cody glanced helplessly down at his beloved. "Did any of that do any good? She doesn't seem any better."

"Oh, but she is." Carefully, Oelefse placed the rattle in his attaché. The archaeologist noted absently that the interior was equipped with customized holding straps, pockets, and slots designed to accommodate a wide variety of paraphernalia not usually found in such cases. The decorated and incised gourd-rattle fit neatly between an ultrathin laptop computer and a satellite telephone.

"Is that a fact?" Cody cradled his wife's limp hand. "Better how?"

"She was suffering from a multiple infestation. Perhaps you saw, when I drew them out."

"I didn't know what was going on." Was Kelli's pulse stronger? As he spoke, he let his fingers slide affectionately along her wrist. "Are you telling me you performed some sort of exorcism?"

"That word conjures up all manner of irrelevant theological connotations. Rather say that I interfered on a metaphysical level with a number of the Interlopers abiding in your wife's body. Through a combination of sounds produced by a variety of means I rendered them exceedingly uncomfortable."

Cody listened intently. "Okay, so you got them out. I don't pretend to understand how, but you can fill me in on the details some other time. Where did they go?" He indicated the smooth, painted hospital walls. "There are no natural materials in here for them to make contact with, unless the wood in the walls would suffice. In which case," he finished with a start, "they're still here."

"They are not still here. There is very little wood in these walls. Like those of most large commercial structures, they are framed with steel. Having no accessible locus of human contact outside your wife's body, and being unable in the absence of a suitable natural vector to find a way to enter ours, they were inescapably drawn back to their own world."

The archaeologist's gaze narrowed. "Their world?"

"One that exists in tandem with our own. Not parallel, as some theoreticians would have it, but thoroughly integrated. Even as we speak, parts of it are passing through this city, this room, our bodies. Think of a sheet of aluminum foil, crumpled into an irregular ball and then pierced with many long needles. The needles represent the world of the Interlopers. Portions of the needles penetrate and make contact with the aluminum sphere while others either stick out the sides or pass through air pockets within. Where folds of aluminum make contact with shafts of steel, congruency exists. All Interlopers can perceive our world, but only a few among us, those whose sight has been altered, can perceive them. As for their world, well, it is a place best not seen, not even by those who are prepared to do so."

Cody hesitated uncertainly. "By drawing these Interlopers out of Kelli's body and sending them back to their world, you've cured her?"

"Unfortunately, no. I have cured some, and seen it done by other members of the Society, but I am afraid that in this instance my best was not good enough. In your wife were abiding no less than seven different kinds—we do not say 'species'—of Interlopers. As they were drawn from her I recognized *Thalep*, *Ozixt*, *Horok*, *Jaquinq*, *Balemete*, and *Sagravht*."

"That's six," Cody pointed out unnecessarily. "You said you recognized seven."

Rising from his chair, Oelefse walked forward until he was standing at the foot of the bed. Reaching out and down, he put a hand on Kelli Westcott's blanketed ankle and squeezed gently. The softest of moans escaped her barely parted lips.

"*Uninivulk*. Very bad one, very potent. Hard as I tried, I could not break its grip on your wife's vitals. It is too strong, too tightly interwoven with her system. It is always hungry, always feeding. Frankly, I was surprised to see it co-existing with so many lesser of its virulent brethren. Usually a *Uninivulk* will not tolerate company." Eyes brimming with sad wisdom rose to meet those of the anxious archaeologist. "They must hate you very much."

"It's reciprocated." Staring down at his wife, Cody tried to recall in detail the awful phantasm that had risen from her resting form to take a vicious, if ineffective swipe at the older man. It was living inside her, feasting on her discomfort, wallowing in her physical and mental suffering. He could do nothing about it. Without Oelefse's intervention he could not even see it. And neither could the well-meaning physicians who came to check on her condition twice a day.

"That is how I helped her." Oelefse released the covered ankle and took a step back. "Though the worst of the Interlopers remains within, six have been expunged." His expression twisted in wry amusement. "The next nurse or physician who checks the equipment that is monitoring her condition will be very surprised, and encouraged. The improvement is real, but any encouragement is false. For the moment, she is better: physically stronger, her body freed to do battle with the only one that still abides. Sometimes humans can fight off such infestations on their own, through sheer effort of will. That is how seemingly incurable victims of inexplicable illnesses suddenly manage to make full recoveries." The slight smile evaporated.

"That will not happen in your wife's case. Not when her system is forced to deal with an abiding *Uninivulk*. I have never known of anyone infected by so virulent an Interloper to survive. She will be better for a little while. Then its presence, and feeding, will begin to take a toll on her temporarily reinvigorated system. She will again begin to fail, to start on the inevitable, slow descent into paralysis, and death."

Cody could barely control his response. "Then you didn't help her very much after all, did you? All that happened here was that you postponed the inevitable."

"It is only inevitable if we do nothing, and if the *Univivulk* is allowed to continue feeding unchallenged. I said that I had never known anyone infected by that variety of Interloper to have survived. I did not say that survival was impossible. There are things that can be tried." His eyes bored into the younger man's. "It will be dangerous. You must trust me implicitly and do everything exactly as I say."

"Tell me what I have to do." Cody responded without hesitation. "Just don't expect me to trust your driving."

"Good! You can still joke. Remember always how much the Interlopers hate that." Turning, he walked back to his chair and closed the briefcase. Multiple locks snapped shut. "First, you must hire someone to watch over your wife around the clock."

The archaeologist frowned. "Isn't that the responsibility of the hospital staff?"

"I can see that you have never had to spend much time in hospitals. Staff carry out their assignments, and little more. Nurses will bring your wife new bags of nutrients, will check her vital signs manually to back up the work of the machines, and will keep her clean. Doctors will make brief checks on her condition as part of their scheduled rounds. The rest of the time, she will lie here like this. Alone." He indicated the door.

"Reflect a moment on the adverse possibilities. Late at night, a lackey of Those Who Abide enters. He is not noticed, not challenged. He carries a canvas sack containing several large stones, or pieces of wood brought from the forest. He lays these on your wife's helpless body. Each stone and piece of wood contains—"

"All right, all right: I get the picture. I'll see that she gets twenty-four-hour care."

"*We* will see that she does. We must make certain that whatever agency you use, whoever you hire, is Interloper free. It is not a difficult thing to do, but it must be done. Then, and only then, you and I must make a little trip."

"Where to? Drugstores? Someplace that can only be found in a bigger city? It's not far to L.A."

"If we are to help your wife survive to see another birthday, I am afraid we must roam farther than that. You have done much work in Peru. May I therefore assume that your passport is in order?"

Twelve

To Cody's surprise, saying goodbye to his wife while she lay unconscious and entirely unresponsive turned out to be far more difficult than it had ever been when she was alert and mindful. At such times she would always make some little joke to lighten the atmosphere of farewell. This time there was no quip to send him off. It was usually Kelli who would choose the moment for a passionate, parting kiss. This time there was no passion. It was his wife who always had to have the last wave goodbye. This time he was the one in control of the moment. When it came, he did not want to whisper the joke, bestow the kiss, or flash the wave. He did not want to do any of those things, because he didn't want to leave. Especially after the confrontation that had all but consumed the hospital room several days earlier.

He had no choice in the matter, he knew. If he was going to restore her, he had to follow Oelefse's orders, and following those orders meant accompanying the older man back to Europe. It meant leaving Kelli behind, not laughing and absorbed in her own research as had been the case on similar previous occasions, but lying in bed motionless and unaware, more helpless than any kitten.

At least she would not be completely alone. After Oelefse had thoroughly vetted the security company's background and run his own unique brand of surreptitious checks on its staff, Cody hired security personnel to be with Kelli around the clock. Though puzzled, they offered no objections to the strictures the archaeologist and his elderly friend placed on their movements, and on who should be allowed to have contact with the patient. In the absence of a perceiver like Cody himself, this setup was not perfect. But it was better than leaving Kelli exposed and vulnerable to whoever might wander in off the street.

Even when all that could be done had been done and there was nothing left to do, he was reluctant to leave her side. From the doorway, Oelefse's voice chided him gently.

"We have to go, Cody. You can do nothing for her here." The older man checked the Patek Phillipe on his wrist. "We will miss our flight."

"I'm coming." Rising from the edge of the bed, the distraught archaeologist leaned over to gently press his lips against his wife's. Each time he did so, he hoped, and each time those hopes were dashed. A sleeping beauty Kelli might be, but it was going to take more than a lover's kiss to awaken her from the contaminated slumber into which she had fallen.

"Don't worry, Mr. Westcott." Seated at the other side of the bed, a middle-aged, balding concrete block of a man put down the novel he had been reading long enough to offer a reassuring smile. The ex-cop's belly might have gone to flab, but there was nothing wrong with his mind or his reflexes. "My outfit's used to this kind of work, though we're usually hired to watch over injured criminals awaiting transport to jail." He glanced down at Kelli. "Ain't nobody gonna mess with her while me or one of my buddies is here."

Cody could only nod. Lately he had been reduced to nodding a great deal. It left him feeling dead in the water, as if he was neither going forward nor retreating but instead had become trapped in time, a fly in molasses reduced to wriggling helplessly in place.

The mere act of turning away from the bed, not knowing when he might see her again, not knowing if she would even be alive by the time he returned, made him feel as if he were trying to move a parked truck with his bare hands.

All the way through the hospital he kept wanting to turn around and go back, convinced he had forgotten something, wanting to hold her in his arms one more time, desperate to brush his mouth across her lips and cheeks and forehead in the event she could sense such contact. Not wanting to leave. Then they were striding through the entrance atrium on their way out of the hospital.

He was compelled to endure more of Oelefse's driving, but it was a mercifully short ride from the hospital in Scottsdale to the airport. They were not challenged on the way, or subsequent to their arrival. The older man was quick to explain that airports were comparatively secure places, islands of safety in a world alive with Interlopers. Except for the occasional sculpture of wood or stone, everything about them was man-made and therefore unsuitable as a vector for the intruders. Having spent his fair share of time in airports, Cody had always decried their artificiality. Now he embraced it.

It struck him that in agreeing to follow Oelefse's directives blindly, he had neglected to ask even the most basic questions. Such as . . .

"Where in Europe are we going? Germany, to seek the help of your Society?"

"Close, my young friend, but not quite. What we seek lies near to there. I would make the slight detour to show you our library, to introduce you to my colleagues, but time is precious. That friendship and those books will always be there. It is your wife we must be concerned with now."

Cody could not have responded better himself. "Where, then?" His elderly companion held their tickets, which he had not seen.

"Have you ever been to Austria?"

Austria! Land of Mozart and pastry, fine crystal and alpine skiing. "No. My work has only taken me to South America, remember."

"Then this deficiency in your traveling experience is about to be rectified. Though," Oelefse added somberly, "I am afraid there will be little time to sample the delights of that enchanting country. No whipped cream for us, my young friend. No raisin *brot*, no *sachertorte*, no *kaiserschmarrm*. We go in search of blue leaves."

"Blue leaves?" A methodical, barely intelligible feminine voice was calling their flight. Hefting his carry-on, Cody trailed his guide closely, not wanting to lose him in the milling crowd.

"*Ilecc* leaves. Does your wife like tea?"

The flight was full: noisy and busy all the way to New York. From there it was nonstop all the way to Vienna. After overnighting at a hotel connected directly to the airport terminals, Cody once more had to suffer Oelefse's driving as they made their way northwest to Salzburg.

"Why Salzburg?" As the archaeologist spoke he was staring out the window at the increasingly mountainous Austrian countryside.

"It is an ancient and traditional point of congruency."

As always, both of the German's hands were firmly affixed to the steering wheel. His eyes never strayed from the road ahead. "There is a rock there. For some reason, large and distinctive rocks are often the loci of such places. It is as if they were buttons, tying together both halves of a sweater. Only in this instance, our rock fastens together two different dimensions of the same world."

"What happens if the rock gets moved?" Cody inquired only half-jokingly. "Do the two pieces of the world come apart?"

A small smile of amusement creased Oelefse's face. At such moments he looked, Cody decided, like a mischievous watchmaker who repaired cuckoo clocks during the day while quietly assembling an atom bomb in his basement at night.

"In the case of this particular rock that is not a concern, my friend. You will understand when you see it."

It was midafternoon when they entered the old city, a gabled knot of steeples and towers and many-windowed stone buildings. The presence of so much stone unnerved Cody, but Oelefse knew ways through the often narrow, shop-lined streets that allowed them to avoid the attention of local Interlopers.

The German was right in his assertion that the rock in question was in no danger of being picked up and moved. The old city ringed it like a necklace, individual buildings set like faceted gemstones at its base. A flat-topped Gibraltar, it dominated the town and the surrounding terrain; a massive, sheer-sided mass of solid gray-white granite hundreds of feet high. Resting atop this majestic monolith and occupying the entire plateau was the enormous and imposing fortress of Hohensalzburg, ancient home of dozens of kings and rulers of this part of the world.

Unknowingly, they had constructed their fortress atop

one of the buttons that held together the different dimensions that comprised this corner of reality.

Having parked the car, Oelefse led his awestruck companion up a gentle path that wound like a snake between walls of cut stone and gray stucco, until they reached the base of the natural ziggurat. Twenty to forty feet above the ground, Cody could see where small openings had been hacked out of the naked rock. Some were exposed to the afternoon air while others were covered with heavily weathered grates of iron so dark it was almost black. Still others had steps leading up to them, and were barred with wooden doors.

Noting the direction of his stare, Oelefse anticipated his companion's questions. "Those are ancient caves, my young friend. For thousands of years they were home to Neolithic hunter-gatherers. Later, they provided shelter for an order of druids dedicated to fighting Those Who Abide." Tilting his head back slightly, he gestured upward. "This great rock, upon which the fortress is raised, is for some reason yet to be fathomed inhospitable to Interlopers. They do not, and to the best of our knowledge never have, dwelled within. Perhaps instinctively, that is why the castle was begun here. Possibly some court sorcerer recommended the site. We are not sure. For hundreds of years the inaccessible heights offered safety from the depredations of attacking hordes seeking to displace those who lived here in comparative peace.

"Following the druids, the caves were occupied by monks of the Order of Saint Callis. Building upon the knowledge left behind by their druidic predecessors, they too gave battle to the Interlopers for nearly a thousand years. When the Order was dissolved and dispersed by invaders, the survivors regrouped in a river valley to the north."

"And became the Society," a marveling Cody finished for him. "Your Society."

"Yes." Oelefse nodded solemnly. They were nearing the end of the path and approaching a structure that was built into the rock. "Now we must rest in this sacred place, and have something to eat."

"Eat?" Cody blinked. "Here?"

"Do you not see the sign?" His guide pointed upward, to the lintel above the doorway they were approaching. "My friend, here in the catacombs district of St. Peter's Abbey is the oldest continuously operating restaurant in Europe. It was founded by the Society and has been providing rest and sustenance for us, and for other travelers, ever since."

Cody noted the sign but was unable to read it. As they passed beneath, Oelefse translated for him. "Open since 803." He smiled slightly. "That is the year, my young friend, not the time of day."

Inside, once a few whispered words had passed between Oelefse and a waiter, they were directed deep into the establishment, where they took seats in a room lined with vaulted brick. One wall was bare, unworked stone: the naked rock of the granite monolith itself. Somewhere high above their heads the yellow-and-brown patinaed wall of the fortress guarded Hohensalzburg's impregnable approaches. It was cool and dark and very, very quiet in the chamber. The other half dozen tables, immaculately set, stayed empty. When food finally arrived, Cody knew what it was like to eat a fancy meal in a simple cave.

"This is a special place." With the grace of a visiting nobleman dining at Versailles, Oelefse cut away small, bite-sized pieces of his schnitzel and placed them fastidiously in his mouth. Watching him, Cody was sure that had one been available, his guide would have preferred the use of a scalpel to an ordinary knife. "Society members have met here and planned strategy against Those Who Abide for thousands of years. For the past millennium we have also dined here, first in caves like this, later in the rooms that have been added onto the exterior of the establishment." He gestured with his knife.

"Above our heads are millions of tons of solid rock, none of it, insofar as we have been able to determine, ever inhabited by Interlopers. Why this should be so, why they should shun this stone while infesting others like it, we do not know, but from prehistoric times the rock was recognized as one of those rare places that are a part of the natural world that is safe from infestation. It provides advantages for defense, and for study."

"So there have always been members of the Society active here?" As he spoke, Cody was slathering fresh butter on dark bread.

"Even before there was a Society. Recognizing the uniqueness of the site, one of our more prominent European members, the Archbishop Gebhard, laid the first foundations for the fortress in 1077. It took six hundred years of continuous work to bring it to the condition you now see. Much of the most important work was done by another of our venerable members, Leonhard von Keutschach.

"Recognizing this place as a center of knowledge and resistance, Those Who Abide have made various attempts down through the centuries to destroy it, most notably by influencing those they dominated to gather in sufficient strength to attack. The last such attempt was made by a group of angry farmers."

"When was that?" Cody inquired over his excellent meal.

"Let me think." The older man's brow furrowed. "I believe it was in 1525."

"So the fortress has been secure since then?" Here was

a place where even Kelli could be safe, the archaeologist mused.

"In a sense. The Society abandoned it as no longer necessary to its efforts back in 1861, when all archives and study facilities for this part of the world were consolidated at Heidelberg." Sitting back, he swept an arm upward to encompass the dark, somber room in which they were dining. "But there are times that demand one or more of us visit here, to make use of the rock's unique properties."

"Like providing a home for a plant with blue leaves?"

"Among other things, yes." Oelefse's expression fell slightly. "One hopes the *ilecc* bush may still be accessed here. If all goes well, we will find out tonight."

Cody frowned. "Why tonight? Why not now?"

"You will see, my young friend. You will see." Smiling, the older man indicated Cody's plate. "Finish your meal. You will need your strength."

The archaeologist assumed he would need at least some of that strength to scale the mountain, but as it developed, very little effort was required. Though it was possible to follow in the footsteps of the thousands who had gone before and climb the steep, winding road that led from the old city to the fortress, Oelefse opted to take the funicular, or inclined railway, that had been bolted to the sheer side of the rock. Designed to convey lazy tourists to the top, it provided a means of ascent that enabled both men to conserve their strength. For what, Cody could only imagine.

Once inside, the magnitude of the fortress astonished him. Exploring it from within was the only way to appreciate its vast extent and the effort that had gone into its construction and expansion. Surrounded by the massive stone walls of the granary, the arsenal, and the extensive living quarters, he could well believe it had taken six hundred years to complete. Now it swarmed with laughing children and their curious parents, doe-eyed honeymooners and picture-snapping foreigners.

"You rarely see anyone acting unhappy or sad up here," Oelefse remarked. Walking to the edge of a wall, he inhaled deeply of the fresh air as he gazed southward toward distant Heilbronn Palace and the snow-clad Alps beyond. "This is a safe place." Kneeling, he picked up a handful of grit and let it sift away between his fingers. "Clean stone. Such gateways are vital to our understanding of Those Who Abide, and to our unceasing efforts to wipe them out."

"Gateways?" Looking around, Cody could see a number of entrances; to the inner keep, to the royal residences, to kitchens and living quarters. They ranged in size from small arched openings blocked by wooden doors to massive double gates bound with iron strapping and nails. "Which one is ours?"

"You cannot see it from here." Turning away from the spectacular view of the Austrian countryside, Oelefse led his young companion down broad stone steps. "If it was easily accessible, some maintenance worker or tourist might stumble into it. That would like as not prove fatal to the curious." Seeing the look on the archaeologist's face he added, "I told you this could be dangerous. If you wish to wait behind, I can go on alone and—"

"We'd argue about the philosophical underpinnings, just like we argue about everything else, but I must remind you that I'd die for Kelli." Cody regarded his elderly guide without blinking.

"*Ja*, it is true: There is no logic in love. I would have done the same for my Ingrid, but—she died first. Come." Holding tight to his briefcase, he led the way northward, against the flow of tourists and other visitors. "We will make ready."

Preparations consisted of taking the last guided tour of the day. As they were shown the state apartments and fabulous ceramic medieval room heaters and other highlights of the fortress, Cody tried not to become too absorbed in the guide's talk. The history of the castle was fascinating, but he hadn't come all this way to play tourist. Halfway through, as they were about to leave the Reckturm, or prison tower, Oelefse gestured for him to hang back. Gradually, the voices of the tour guide and his flock receded into the distance, the murmur of their voices swallowed by their stony surroundings. The two men stood alone in a low, narrow passageway.

Opening his briefcase, Oelefse removed a massive wrought-iron key half the length of his forearm. Inserting this into the coal-black iron lock of an ancient door opposite, he turned it as gently as possible. Metal ratcheted against metal and the door opened at a push.

Entering, the dapper German shut the door behind him and relocked it from the inside. Removing a pair of compact flashlights from his case, he handed one to Cody and switched on its mate. The lights revealed a passageway and stone stairs leading downward. After descending through a couple of corkscrew turns they encountered a second door of far more recent manufacture. The alloyed metal was secured by a pair of electronic locks. When Oelefse keyed in the combination, the barrier slid upward into the ceiling to allow them entry.

Eventually the corridor leveled out. No windows dimpled the ancient stone walls and no light entered from outside. Oelefse halted outside a third door.

"Where are we?" the archaeologist finally felt compelled to ask.

"Inside the mountain, near the center of the fortress and the loci." The older man pointed upward. "There is a huge old lime tree not far above our heads. No one knows when it was planted, but it still produces excellent limes."

Cody blinked. "We're practically in the Alps here and there's a lime tree growing out of this bare rock?"

"Astonishing, isn't it? But then, we are standing in an astonishing place." Glancing around, Oelefse found a stone bench, sat down, and checked his watch.

"It's just past five o'clock, almost closing time for visitors. Soon Security will begin rousting teenagers from their hidden corners and hustling the romantically inclined in the direction of the road or the funicular. There are certain nights during the year when the fortress is kept open after dark for special celebrations. Tonight is not one of them. We will be able to do what we must without being disturbed."

"What about after-hours security? Aren't there watchmen?"

"Only at the main walk-up entrance. There is no other way to reach the castle after dark, unless one is an experienced mountaineer. Scaling the rock in such a fashion is against the law. Of course, that has not prevented people from doing so, but to my knowledge, it has never been attempted at night. Not only would that be exceedingly dangerous, there would be none of the publicity such people seek." Folding his hands in his lap, he settled himself back against the cold, unyielding wall.

"You mentioned something about loci?" Cody queried him.

"You remember my description of the habitat of the Interlopers as being akin to needles thrust through the aluminum ball that is our world? One such 'needle' passes through this rock. Because the great massif is hostile to Those Who Abide, yet so close to our reality, they tend to congregate in its vicinity. Beyond this stone lies a meeting place of our world and theirs." He checked his watch again. "In the realm of midnight we will have to pass through one more door, and then we will go looking to pick the leaves of the delicate blue *ilecc*."

"What do we do until then?" Cody felt the weight of stone, not to mention ages, pressing down upon him.

Oelefse smiled reassuringly. "I have a deck of cards. And a portable chess set. Do you play chess, Cody West-cott?"

"A little. Kelli and I . . ." Choked, he found he could not finish the remembrance.

"Good." Digging once more through the contents of the briefcase, the German took out a chessboard and began to set up individual pieces. Cody started to help, but was forced to stop.

"What's that? And that?" He pointed to several pieces whose appearance was confusing.

"The first is a rook, the second a knight." Having set up his own side, Oelefse began to do the same for his young friend. "Their shapes are not of this reality, but of that which is home to Those Who Abide. You should learn to recognize them."

"Why? For a couple of games?"

"No." Playing black, the older man waited for his opponent to make a move. "Because in a few hours you may be seeing the beings upon which these carved pieces are based, and you will want to avoid them." In the dim glow of their flashlights, his eyes glittered hard and efficient. "They will do worse than try to checkmate you, in a game that is considerably more serious."

The preoccupied archaeologist was inordinately pleased to win two of the five games they played, though there were a couple of times when he suspected that his opponent was making foolish errors just to keep him in the game. He fully intended to query Oelefse about it, but when the older man abruptly swept the pieces into a

waiting box and folded up the board, he forgot all about
the trivialities of time-wasting amusements.

"Are you sure you are ready for this, my friend?" No
avuncular figure now, Oelefse seemed to have sloughed
off thirty years as he faced the door on the far side of
the chamber. "You can still wait for me here."

"Not a chance." Cody was emphatic. "Whatever lies
ahead, whatever getting these leaves entails, I'm with
you."

The older man nodded solemnly. "Keep close, then,
and do as I tell you."

Unlocking the door, he stepped through, waited for
Cody to follow, and shut the barrier behind them. They
were committed. Keeping his breathing steady, the archaeologist followed the German, their feet tapping on
stairs that now wound upward in a wide spiral. Diffuse
light began to illuminate the steps and he found he no
longer needed the flashlight, which he promptly slipped
into a front pocket of his jeans. Spilling straight down
into the winding stairwell was the light of a full moon.

Two full moons.

They hung side by side in the night sky, impossibly
close together. Gravity ought to have torn them apart, but
perhaps gravity did not act here as it did in his reality.
Certainly nothing else did. Cody saw as soon as he stepped
out of the stairwell and found himself standing on the
surface alongside Oelefse.

The fortress, all tens of thousands of tons of it, was
gone. For that matter, so was the city of Salzburg that
had been dreaming below, and the distant silhouettes of
the Alps. In their place was a forest rooted in imagination that sprouted from soil sparkling with tiny crystals.

"This is beautiful." Reaching out, he touched a single
leaf that was longer than he was tall. Dark ripples spread
from the tips of his fingers along the length of the leaf,

as if he had dipped them in a still pond. He had made contact without truly touching.

"It is also lethal, my young friend." Eyes as wary as those of an old survivor alley cat, posture alert, Oelefse was turning a slow circle as he examined their immediate surroundings. Behind them, a gaping cavity in the crystal-dusted earth marked the way back to the fortress, back to Salzburg. Back to reality.

In spite of his resolve to be mindful of the older man's warnings, Cody was overcome by the splendor into which they had emerged. Having expected something entirely different, insofar as he had anticipated anything at all, he was taken aback by the spectral wonderland in which they found themselves. He had been prepared to encounter a landscape by Doré or Breughel or Giger. Instead, he found himself in surroundings that sprang from Rackham and Nielsen. All that was lacking were tiny slips of fairies darting to and fro.

As if on cue, a pair of misshapen pixies materialized and swerved in his direction. Instead of elfin, pre-pubescent bodies draped in glowing gauze, they had flat, dun-colored faces with wide mouths. Their arms were long, hung down well below their bodies, and were tipped with single quills instead of hands. In place of buttocks, bloated abdomens bobbed in the sultry air. They had no eyes and twinkled like bumblebees that had been dipped in glitter. In the dual moonlight, they were figures of myth and magic.

"Get down!"

Something hit Cody from behind, between the shoulders, knocking him to his knees. Reaching forward as he fell, he threw out his open palms to absorb the impact. Where his palms struck the earth, puffs of rainbow-hued dust rose from between reflective blades of crystalline grass. Everything seemed to be happening in slow motion.

Glancing backward, he saw Oelefse assume a kneeling posture. His briefcase lay near his feet, unlatched and open. A device he'd removed from one of its copious pockets was gripped firmly in both hands as he aimed it at the shimmering, oncoming phantasms. It looked like a toy molded from plastic, with brightly colored protrusions emerging from its sides and top and a muzzle that flared wide as a saucer in the style of an old-fashioned blunderbuss. A child's gun.

"Hey," Cody started to ask his friend and guide, "is that really neces—?"

Reaching over, Oelefse gave him a hard shove with his left hand, knocking the unsteady Cody onto his side. An instant later, the glittering specter nearest the two men spat something from its flat face. At the end of the long tongue, which gleamed like a neon tube in the moonlight, was a small, barbed ball. It struck a very small, glittering bush behind where Cody had been kneeling. Immediately, the bush collapsed inward upon itself and shrank to the size of a walnut. When the tongue retracted, the shrunken bush was ripped from the ground and sucked down into that featureless, alien face.

Oelefse fired. The exquisite floating deformity blew apart in a shower of colorful sparkles that sifted to the ground like electric snow. A second shot caught the other flyer with its tongue halfway extended in the older man's direction. When it exploded, it emitted a muffled popping sound, like a water-filled balloon coming apart. Relaxing his arms but with every sense alert, Oelefse turned to check on his companion.

"Are you all right, my friend?"

Shaken, the archaeologist was watching the last twinkling fragments of a misshapen existence filter down to the ground. "What the hell were those?"

"There are almost as many different varieties of In-

terloper as there are creatures on the face of our Earth.
They are a multitude, Cody Westcott, and each one is as
dangerous as the next. Anything that moves here, wherever here is, can infest, infect, or contaminate. Look, yes,
but touch nothing. In our reality there are also many beautiful things that can kill." Reaching down, he extended a
helping hand.

Waving him off, Cody rose on his own, wiping from
his palms dust that sparkled in the moonlight like pow-
dered gemstones. All around him was unimaginable,
empyreal beauty. And if Oelefse was to be believed, every
inch of it potentially deadly. Even after surviving the attack
by the two floating oddities, it was difficult to reconcile
so much glistening splendor with implied danger.

Touch nothing? How could he resist caressing the blossoms of translucent pink that burst forth in lacy profusion from the bushes that lined the path they were taking?
How could anyone expect him not to push gently against
the cascade of shimmering liquid purple that spilled from
a crack in crystal-dusted rocks? Oelefse kept a watchful
eye on him. As long as the older man did not protest,
Cody felt free to sample the tactile delights of the oth-
erness into which they had stepped.

Only once more did his guide interfere physically. The
archaeologist had reached out to pluck a nearly transparent, diamond-covered bloom the size of a cabbage from
its stalk when Oelefse's hand clamped with surprising
strength on the younger man's wrist.

Shaking an admonishing finger at the archaeologist,
the elderly German used the flared tip of his pistol to
gently nudge the blossom's petals aside. Beneath, crawled
half a dozen fat caterpillar shapes. Miniature lightning
scrolled down their backs in colorful streaks. When
touched by the hard edge of the gun, their heads expanded
to ten times their normal size, displaying a ring of inward-

facing teeth that looked sharp and brutal. At this unexpected, implicitly deadly flowering, Cody drew back, remembering what Oelefse had said about deadly beauty.
It was warning enough. Thereafter, despite a flourish of
temptation, he kept his hands to himself and contemplated
the surrounding dazzle with eyes alone.

They had long since left the stairwell to reality behind.
Cody wondered how Oelefse knew where they were going.
There were no paths, nothing to indicate direction, and
little that could be used as a landmark. Towering growths
would shrink with notable speed into the ground at their
approach, only to reappear like launching rockets in their
wake. The entire glittering, glistening, shimmering realm
was in a state of permanent agitation, as if by remaining
too long in one place or form its inhabitants were inviting affliction. The light and color were staggering in their
diversity. Oelefse was leading him deeper and deeper into
a world composed of reconstituted rainbows, much of it
potentially murderous.

A supple figure of winged, flaming green sparks danced
past his head. It was one of the most beautiful things he
had ever seen, and he didn't dare touch it, or try to cap-
ture it in his cupped hands. Oelefse's admonitions had
firmly taken root. In the dimension of Those Who Abide,
the archaeologist had learned, beauty packed a nasty bite.

Thirteen

"There!"

Oelefse paused in a patch of knee-high ropes that fountained silver sparkles from their extremities, like so many eels vomiting enchantment. Coming up behind him, Cody strained for a better view. In the clash and confusion of mutable radiance, it was difficult to isolate any one shape or configuration. Only when his guide pointed it out did the younger man espy the cluster of *ilecc*. Just as Oelefse had told him, its leaves were an intense cobalt hue that twinkled as if illuminated from within by a million miniscule blue bulbs. Even in the convulsion of color that surrounded them, the several *ilecc* bushes stood out. Though without Oelefse's trained eye, Cody doubted he could have found them on his own. Singled out and isolated by his line of sight, they were as spectacular as any of the transcendental growths he and his companion had encountered thus far.

Oelefse retained the lead as they tentatively approached the cluster. Nothing sprang from the surrounding inimical fairyland to lay claim to their souls. Nothing reached forth to tear them asunder. Bending slightly, the older man handed Cody his outré pistol.

"Keep watch." Reaching into his briefcase, he pulled out a knife that was breathtaking in its ordinariness. Simple handle, single unadorned steel blade. Or was that a line of electricity running along its cutting edge? Before Cody could manage a better look, Oelefse had him peering back the way they had come, watching for—anything that moved toward them, the German cautioned his apprehensive companion. Once he felt confident that the archaeologist was on alert, Oelefse began to prune selected leaves from the largest of the several blue bushes, wielding the knife with a surgeon's skill. One by one, the excised leaves were placed in a waiting plastic bag. Soon the bag itself began to glow with an incredibly opulent, vivid blue light.

Anxious to return the unfamiliar weapon to its owner, Cody nonetheless did his best to keep a sharp eye on the outlandish, exotic landscape. Despite his resolution, his attention was continually being distracted by shimmering, lazily perambulating perceptions of incomprehensible beauty.

A line of flickering green veils danced across his field of vision, drifting from right to left like dancers in some ethereal slow-motion ballet. Emerald stars twinkled within their slender, diaphanous bodies and they stared at him out of eyes that were wandering bits of comet. Lumps of phosphorescent orange trundled along the ground, living diadems of gold and glistening padparaschah. Everywhere he looked there was light and color and coruscating brilliance, as if he had stepped into a world permanently bathed in cold fire.

Overhead, growths that were not plants shivered with ecstasy beneath the rain of lambent moonbeams. Some moaned softly while others were silent. He felt himself adrift in visual Debussy. Only something like gravity kept him bound to the earth; otherwise he felt certain he would have taken flight, soaring skyward while born aloft on streamers of scintillating aurora.

Alerted by some subtle shift in his companion's manner, Oelefse glanced up from his work. "Beauty kills," he reminded Cody curtly. "In this place even daydreaming can be deadly."

His thoughts wrenched back to reality by his companion's cool tone, the archaeologist blinked away incipient fantasies. "I'm on it, Oelefse. Tend to your snipping. How much longer?"

"Almost done. Almost have enough." He resumed his horticultural cropping.

It was a song that finally snared Cody. Not some beauteous wayward shape, not something glistening on the ground that dropped diamonds in its wake, but a melody. A hymn so pure it could only arise from a source immaculate and unsullied. Entranced, he stepped forward, certain that as long as he kept Oelefse in sight neither of them was in any real danger. He had to find the source of that unearthly music.

It hung in the air behind a baobab-shaped organic tower through which lights ran from bottom to top before sparking off into the enchanted sky. In outline the singer was amorphous, a hovering mass of shifting transparent silk some ten feet tall. Within its core, chanting crystals swam like bioluminescent squid on a dark Pacific night. Each emitted a slightly different tune and color. Combined, they melded to create a transcendent harmony that tantalized both ear and mind. A chorus of trained angels could not have generated so euphonious a sound.

Later, he was not sure if he fell into it, or it ate him.

He was suddenly and unexpectedly engulfed. A thickness, rancid and cloying, clogged his nostrils and threatened to fill his throat with mephitic glue. The singing crystals had become small round suckers lined with barbed teeth. They were drifting toward him, opening and closing with a horrid pulsing that suggested the muscular action of unmentionable orifices. Abruptly frantic, he tried to get away, only to find that he could hardly move. He was trapped in something like glistening, transparent gelatin. It severely inhibited his movements and restricted his ability to defend himself. He could not even bring the weapon he still held tightly in one hand to bear on the vicious, degenerate mouth-shapes that were advancing inexorably toward him.

A ringing filled his ears. It was loud and insistent, but not unbearable. He felt himself beginning to torque as the protoplasmic material in which he was embedded responded to the rising whine. There was nothing he could do to stop it. His body curved, then bent in the middle, forcing him to arch backward until he thought his spine would snap. The fanged suckers had ceased their movement toward him and were swirling about in aimless confusion. Still the whine intensified, until it reached a profound level of auditory disturbance. Then the world exploded.

Or rather, the Interloper that had engulfed him did. Coated with clamminess, he found himself sprawled upon the ground. Their internal glow muted, the brilliant singing crystals were crawling away in all directions, seeking shelter in the surrounding scintillating growths. Whenever he blinked, they would change from exquisite crystals to obscenely pulsating fanged suckers, and back again.

Oeletse was standing over him, briefcase in one hand and a most peculiar-looking tuning fork in the other. It was the source of the ascending whine that had disturbed Cody but had proven fatal to the organism that had enveloped him. Abashed, he rose slowly and tried to wipe the clamminess from his exposed skin.

"I'm sorry. It was—it distracted me."

"The chant of the *Acryalaq* is lulling, but it is an Interloper like any other." The older man indicated their fairy-tale surroundings. "In their own dimension, or whatever place this is and however one chooses to label it, they take on a beauty that is as striking as it is false. Here, only our being alien protects us. If we react, or draw too much attention to ourselves, then our intrusion becomes magnified, like the beating of a drum. We become to the Interlopers in their world something like what they become to us in ours." He held up the tuning fork. It had a visually disorienting shape, as if there were three bars to the fork instead of the usual two. The optic confusion tormented Cody's eyes.

Oelefse smiled. "People have sketched this little device for years, thinking it no more than an optical illusion. Only the master craftsmen of the Society know how to actually make one. The vibrations can be deadly to Those Who Abide. They are more profoundly affected by sound than by the usual variety of prosaic physical assaults."

"In Kelli's hospital room, the rattle and your singing were what drew them out," Cody remembered.

The older man nodded. "Laughter too has its own distinctive pitch. Why do you think music has traditionally been thought to have medicinal effects? It does! The right sort is intolerable to Interlopers. Among composers, Brian, Bantock, Janacek, Mahler, Tournemeire, Pingold, Beethoven, and a few others have been shown to have particularly therapeutic effects. In Germany, a group called Scorpions often used to hit just the right notes. There are many more." He continued tolerantly. "So you understand, we are not helpless, not even against that which is to most people invisible." He looked past the embarrassed archaeologist. "Now we must hurry to leave. The act of your being momentarily fed upon has alerted this place to the actuality of our intrusion."

"I'm sorry." Still wiping at himself, Cody hustled along in the other man's wake. "I don't *feel* partly consumed."

"How about unhappy, downcast, dispirited?"

"Well, yes, but that's because I acted in such a thoughtless, stupid manner."

"It is not. It is because you were temporarily affected by the *Acryalaq*. To feed upon the depression and sorrow of mankind in *our* world, an Interloper must be swallowed by a human body. To feed upon you here, the *Acryalaq* must swallow *you*."

"What—" Cody gulped hard, "What would have happened to me if your tuning fork hadn't worked, if you hadn't been able to rescue me?"

"You would have fallen into a trancelike state of deep despair. Depression, you know, kills more people than most any disease worthy of the name, yet it is still not recognized as such by many doctors. Through dint of perseverance and science, humankind makes progress; a little here, a little there, against Those Who Abide. For the first time, we have medicines that can help us fight off an Interloper infestation. Prozac, for example. Before that, Saint John's Wort. While these do not affect the physical fabric of the Interloper, they break down its food. Judicious application of such curatives can sometimes starve an Interloper to death. But it is not common, and Those Who Abide slowly develop a resistance to such drugs and herbal extracts. That is why something like Prozac may help a severely depressed person for a while, but not permanently. It is not that the drug fails; it is that the inhabiting Interloper or Interlopers gradually develop a resistance to repeated applications. Music is better. So is laughter. There are beneficial side effects, and both are less invasive. There are better ways to alter the chemical composition of a person's mind than with heavy doses of immoderate pharmaceuticals."

Ripples of refulgent elegance bowed in an unfelt breeze as first Oelefse and then the archaeologist leaped over them. Silver radiance trailed from Cody's feet where they had struck the wheat-high growths. From their midst erupted a flurry of iridescent, silver-winged sylphs that took the shape of orchids with legs.

"But everything here is so beautiful."

"I know that." The older man sprang like a wizened hare between two opalescent, sky-scraping spirals; twinned pairs of outgrowths forever entwined in intangible love. "In our world beauty is deceptive. Here it is both deceptive and lethal."

"But down below (Cody's brain screamed for direction in this dimension of shimmering sighs and electric silhouettes), the Interlopers I perceive are grotesque distortions of traditional life forms, all teeth and claws and suckers and clutching tentacles."

"Ah, perception!" Oelefse hurdled a log composed of glistening strands of dew that throbbed like a longitudinal heart. "What you see here is truth, and what you see there is truth. Your eyes tell you true. It is your mind that is confused. Your experiences with perception should have taught you by now: Trust everything that you see, but not how your brain interprets it."

Cody's thoughts tightened into a Gordian knot. "I don't understand."

"You will, I hope—if you live long enough. And be careful where you wave that pistol."

With a start, Cody realized he was still clutching the wide-mouthed weapon that Oelefse had used earlier. Gripping it even tighter, he raised it into firing position. He didn't know if it was armed or loaded; still, it made him feel that he was not entirely helpless, nor completely dependent for his survival on one elderly, somewhat punctilious German. Oelefse continued to hold the now silent tuning fork out in front of him like a sword. It was better than that, Cody knew. Here, a blade was useless, and probably bullets too. Sound was the ammunition they could not afford to extinguish.

His usually reliable sense of direction having long since deserted him (being engulfed whole has that effect on people), he was amenable to following Oelefse's lead. Certainly, the older man seemed to know where he was going, though the archaeologist felt they were taking an awfully roundabout route back to the stairwell that led to the corridors of Hohensalzburg Castle. Or maybe it was just his aching legs that made him feel that way.

The blue leaves! The cobalt-hued bracts of the *ilecc*! He had seen Oelefse place them one by one in a plastic bag, but where was . . .?

In the briefcase, you idiot, he told himself. His knowledgable companion would not carry so precious a cargo loose in one hand. Surely the leaves were inside the briefcase. In any event, having run so far from the place where the bushes grew, he was not about to reveal his ignorance by wondering aloud if Oelefse had left them behind. The older man's mind was full to overflowing, but in the time they had spent together Cody could not remember his guide exhibiting any especial tendency to forgetfulness. Relying as he was on the other man to preserve their lives, Cody had no choice but to trust him in the vital matter of a handful of blue leaves.

They were better off in the German's possession anyway, the archaeologist mused. At least Oelefse had managed not to get himself eaten.

"We are almost there." Now the older man's tone was

showing signs of fatigue. They were the words Cody had been waiting to hear. His fears, the ache in his legs, faded noticeably. A quick plunge down the aurora-rimmed aperture and they would be safely back in their own world. True, they still had to confront the alerted Interlopers who dwelled there, but at least his environs would not sway, and moan, and sing songs of vaporous, virulent loveliness. The world might reflect, but it would not glow, and there would be only one moon hanging in the bilious sky.

Oelefse slowed and the archaeologist, who had experienced no difficulty keeping up with the shorter, older man, had to put on the brakes to avoid running right over the top of his guide. Perspiring profusely in the dual moonlight, expensive briefcase grasped tightly in one fist and gleaming metal fork in the other, he looked like a mad piano tuner stalking some fabled feral Steinway.

They stood gasping in the middle of a small meadow composed of transparent shards tinged sapphire and ruby, glistening ankle-high fronds that rustled with a soft, shy radiance. Deeper in the jungle of shimmering impossibilities, the rising tinkle of bells heralded the approach of unseen dynamics as lethal as they were beautiful. The ground began to shake beneath the gathering of forces that were without weight but not devoid of substance.

The stairwell was gone.

In order to cover more ground they separated, but were careful to stay within clear sight of one another. Overhead, the splay of unfamiliar stars assumed an ominous cast, and in the distance something mewled obscenely. From within the density of flickering, glittering growths, small hungry lives looked on expectantly.

Tired and anxious, the two men met on the far side of the coruscant field. "We have to find it." Oelefse was breathing with some difficulty. For the first time since they had entered the dimensionality of the Interlopers, he looked his age. "It is the only way back." His gaze was focused on the high, waving fronds of twinkling transparency that surrounded the meadow, and on the sound of tinkling bells that was drawing steadily nearer. "And we have to find it fast. We have become too conspicuous."

Panting, Cody turned and gestured helplessly. "I've been over every foot of ground on my half. There isn't even a rabbit hole."

"An apt choice of words, my young friend." Oelefse started back toward the center of the meadow. "Come—we must look again."

"Couldn't we hide in the forest—or whatever this is—until it's safe to come out?"

His guide shook his head sharply. "There is no place here for us to hide, Cody Westcott. We stink of alternate reality."

As he followed the other man, the archaeologist kept his gaze on the ground, searching desperately for any suggestion of a hollow or opening. "We're not exactly defenseless. We have your pistol, and the tuning fork. And we can always fight back with laughter."

"Have you ever seen a person overwhelmed by deep depression?" Oelefse challenged him. "Terminal melancholy rendered as a solid, motile form instead of a feeling is not a pretty sight. It can prostrate even a professional comedian." He nodded in the direction of the approaching tintinnabulation. "I do not want to be standing here waiting to greet it when it arrives."

Watched all the while, they continued their desperate search. If there had ever been a hole in the meadow, it was now gone, swallowed up by circumstance, camouflaged by coincidence.

Camouflaged . . . Edging away from his tall companion, Oelefse pivoted and rushed back to the center of the meadow. As Cody looked on, the elderly German began jumping up and down like a maniac—but a maniac whose mania of the moment was under control, and brought to bear with purpose.

"Here!" Oelefse was shouting excitedly. "Over here, Cody!"

The tinkling, which had grown to clanging, was very near now, as if the meadow was about to be assaulted by an army of runaway church bells. The archaeologist hurried to rejoin his guide. When he arrived, disappointment settled on him like the reek of cheap whiskey. Glittering glassy-grassy, the ground looked the same as every square foot they had previously covered.

"There's nothing here," he commented disappointedly.

"There is always something there." Taking two steps forward, a grimly grinning Oelefse began to jump gingerly up and down. As he did so, the earth beneath him responded like the surface of a too-taut trampoline. Seeing the look on the younger man's face, he explained, "Some kind of membrane. It formed over the opening while we were searching for the *ilecc* bush, like a scab over a wound."

As near as Cody could tell, the surface on which Oelefse was standing was identical to that which surrounded them, right down to the glittering mat of eight-inch-high multihued growths.

"How do you know it's the entrance?" he asked. "Maybe it's a lure, like the appendage that grows from the forehead of the anglerfish?" He indicated the spongy covering. "Maybe that's the opening to a mouth."

But Oelefse was not listening to him. Instead, he was staring, focused on something beyond the archaeologist's right shoulder. Cody turned, and beheld the Snark.

How to describe a sense of horror that derives from the sight of overpowering beauty? He was unable to do it. His voice caught in his throat and he could only stare. It loomed above them, pealing like doom, singing a song of shattered desire and overpowering despair. Cody felt himself drawn to it, inclining toward the pulsating mass of jangling lips and bottomless maws, leaning in the direction of a falling forward that would have seen him ingurgitated like paste, reduced to little more than emotion-bereft human slime.

Something grabbed his left wrist and pulled. Hard.

"Cody—jump! Now!"

He no longer had any control over his body. His neuromuscular system stood paralyzed by the sight and sound of the bells, by their beauty and temptation. It was, he remembered later, akin to optical heroin. The sight would haunt him for the rest of his days.

But it would not consume him. Not today.

Losing his balance, he felt himself yanked backward. Who would have thought to look at Oelefse that there were such reserves of physical strength in that well-preserved but unassuming patrician body? Tuning fork shoved in his pocket, briefcase gripped securely in his left hand, the elderly German had wrenched the much bigger and younger man backward. They tumbled in tandem, falling hard against the very spot where Oelefse had chosen to do his demonstrative bouncing. As they fell, a murderous pealing reached for them. There was a tender, ripping sound, as of a bedsheet splitting down the middle in the distance. Blackness descended.

Cody's head slammed against something unyielding and did a little bouncing of its own. A different class of stars from those that had pockmarked the heavens of elsewhere filled his vision. Oelefse had landed on his side and was now rolling to a sitting position. It took him a minute to find his flashlight.

It was dead silent, the archaeologist noted, which was

a prohibitive improvement on the silence of the dead. As soon as the older man's light winked to life, Cody's slowly clearing vision revealed walls of cut stone, the same material that was presently cushioning his backside. It looked familiar, was familiar.

They were back in the chamber, back in Festung Hohensalzburg. Back in their own reality.

Overhead—if one stood precisely in the center of the chamber and listened intently—there was a barely audible, distant clinking of tiny bells. Or it might have been a baffled, frustrated roaring. Cody sensed that his ears were not working too well. A consequence of the blow to the back of his head occasioned by his fall, no doubt.

"How come we can break through the barrier but they can't?" He was startled at the sound of his own voice in the echoing chamber.

"It is all a matter of relativity, my friend." Standing straight if not tall, Oelefse was brushing himself off. "Remember, to be active in this world every Interloper needs a host, and to enter a host they must first exist in a vector." He indicated their cold, comfortingly solid surroundings. "This stonework is uncontaminated, and has stood thus for hundreds of years. Otherwise it would not be possible to make use of such a portal." Reaching up, he clapped his companion on the back. "Enough sightseeing, *ja*? We are alive, uninfected, and we have secured the blue leaves of the *ilecc*. It is time to depart."

"I'm with you, Oelefse." Fumbling in a pocket, Cody found and extracted his own flashlight. Together they started off down the corridor. Behind them, distant outrage took the form of a momentary incursion of fetid fairy-dust that rapidly and unobserved evanesced from the chamber.

They emerged at last into the subdued light of a quarter moon, the walls of the fortress buildings towering sentinel-like above them.

"What now?" Around them, all was silent and still. It was too late and they were too high to hear much of the sound of the city below. Somewhere distant, the horn of a Peugeot blared mournfully. It was so hauntingly ordinary, so immediate, that Cody wanted to cry. Had the unknowing driver been within reach, the grateful archaeologist would have hugged him.

"We go down, of course. Back to our nice, comfortable, Interloper-free hotel. Back to reality, although we are back in it now, even if it does support within its walls the weight of ages." Strength and confidence regained, the elderly German chose a path that would take them toward the main entrance. "We cannot leave by the tourist gate, of course. It will be locked. But there is a small gate that is used by people who work here." He smiled. "The Society has a key. It leads to a separate path that is negotiable even in the dark. Going down, it will be easy."

Feeling quietly triumphant, Cody walked effortlessly alongside his guide. They had been to a place where man was not meant to be, and had survived to return. And now they had the makings of a medicine to drive out the horror that continued to abide within his beloved. He was feeling very good.

"What about the night watchman? Won't he wonder what we're doing here?"

"What night watchman? When not in use, the fortress is sealed and inaccessible. There is no need for night watchmen within as long as the entrance is patrolled outside."

"Then who," the suddenly uneasy archaeologist murmured as he raised a hand and pointed, "is that?"

fourteen

Oelefse halted sharply. Shambling toward them in the pale moonlight were more than a dozen human figures as diverse in shape and substance as could be imagined. A baker's wife advanced alongside an off-duty airline pilot, who in turn was flanked by a taxi driver. An old woman in traditional Tyrolean garb was escorted by a pair of extensively pierced teens a quarter her age. There were construction workers and a second-form teacher, an assistant brewmaster and a tour guide. Other than their presence there together in the venerable fortress in the middle of the night, they had only silence in common. That, and the fact that they carried rocks. Some bore only one rock, others two or more. The rocks had something in common, too.

They were tenanted.

"Away!" Clutching at the immobilized archaeologist's arm, Oelefse was pulling him backward, back the way they had come. "They are armed!"

The gaping archaeologist could see that. If truth be told, the eccentric grouping they were confronting was heavily, if unnaturally armed. Because every stone they carried was home and vector to a sojourning Interloper. Tendrils writhed, tentacles clutched, multiple mouths snapped, and eyes variously rolled, bulged, blinked, and gaped. In the self of each of the dull-visaged, shambling, stumbling Austrians dwelled one or more controlling Interlopers. Exerting themselves to the maximum of which they were capable, they had assumed control of their respective hosts.

Equipping themselves with weapons in the form of vectored others of their hostless, hungry kind, they had come looking for the healthy humans who had dared to make the passage between planes of existence. It had been decided that immediate infection would be the reward of the trespassers, ceaseless melancholy their destiny. In this judgment, Cody and Oelefse were determined not to concur.

Their assailants advanced slowly, almost ponderously, like marionettes being operated by inexperienced, clumsy puppeteers. But not so slowly that evading them would be easy. Once more, Cody and his elderly companion would have to stand and fight. He readied himself. They were not defenseless. They still had the pistol and the tuning fork.

Oelefse had something more substantial in mind. Opening his briefcase, he withdrew not one but two tuning forks, placing the one he had been carrying carefully back into its waiting strap. Like their smaller predecessor, the new pair he removed had been drop-forged of gleaming, highly polished steel. Each was as long as the briefcase was wide, nearly the length of the older man's forearm.

"Have you ever used a sword, my friend?"

Cody responded with a short laugh that was not forced. "Sure. Every day, during my lectures. And also when I'm in the field, to remind the local help who's in charge and to keep them from getting too cocky."

Oelefse muttered to himself. "The old arts die by the
wayside and are replaced by the new. I suppose if I offered you a video-game joystick you would be able to
handle it blindfolded. Here." He handed Cody one of the
two gleaming devices. The archaeologist hefted his ex-
perimentally. It was solid, and gratifyingly heavy.

"Surely you have at least seen some movies?" As-
suming the stance of a trained fencer wielding saber instead of foil or epee, Oelefse speedily demonstrated a few
basic moves. "Like this, see? Do not try to get fancy. Cut
and slash, cut and slash, keep your distance." Their assailants became visible again, advancing around a precipitous wall of solid stone. Mute and focused, they hefted
their adulterated stones in expectation.

"At all costs you must avoid contact with one of the
contaminated rocks."

"I know that much," Cody snapped irritably. He was
not a child. "How long can we just keep retreating?"

Oelefse glanced skyward. "Not long enough. They
know that. I do not think even the presence of curious
tourists would be sufficient to forestall an assault by this
group. Their abiding Interlopers seem very determined.
Our presence here has upset them even more than I presumed." When he grinned, he looked twenty years
younger. "That alone is justification enough for our visit."
Halting, he reached for something and passed it to his
younger companion. "Here, this will be very useful."

Cody looked down at the lid from a plastic garbage
can that his companion had handed him. "We throw this?"

"No." Oelefse held up a lid of his own. "They will
serve as shields against flying stones and their inimical
inhabitants." He lowered the triple tip of his tuning fork.
"Those Who Abide can do nothing with plastic. Now
come: before they think to try and encircle us. They will
not be expecting an attack."

Neither was Cody, but he rushed forward alongside his elderly guide, trying his best to imitate the other man's movements. When Oelefse swung his long tuning fork downward to strike the ground and set it ringing, the archaeologist did the same. He felt utterly absurd, swinging the metal rod in front of him, holding the slightly aromatic plastic disk in his other hand like an extra at the rear of a battle scene in some cheap Italian sword-and-sandal flick. Somehow Oelefse managed to hang onto his briefcase as well as the garbage can lid he had appropriated for his own defense.

"Watch out!" Even as Oelefse shouted a warning, he was raising his improvised shield.

The first rocks came flying. Each sprouted various combinations of unearthly but deadly arms and limbs and teeth, anxious to sink themselves into the vulnerable essence of the two onrushing humans. One fist-sized chunk slammed into the plastic disk Cody was carrying, only to bounce harmlessly off to the side, the nebulous limbs of its resident Interloper flailing furiously. Without actual physical contact between stone and human flesh, it could not escape its granitic prison.

Confronted by a raver-rocker-student, the archaeologist swung the singing tuning fork in her direction. Not at the young woman, but at the stone she was carrying. The danger lay within that uneven rock, not in her vacant, disconcerted gaze.

Something with a mouth three sizes too large for its body and a quartet of bony arms reached toward Cody from the depths of the rock. Clutching fingers clawed briefly at his shoulders and chest with false damp, chilling him slightly. As the teen thrust the stone forward in an attempt to touch it to Cody's ribs, the oversized tuning fork made contact with the softly moaning, clutching Interloper.

Light reminiscent of the pseudo-bioluminescence he had seen on the other side of the stairwell exploded in his face, a momentarily blinding burst of violent yellow and green. No sound accompanied the detonation, no concussion rocked his eardrums or rattled his nervous system. More disoriented than he, the student stumbled backward. Dazed but determined, he pursued and thrust the tuning fork at her exposed midriff, making light contact with the smooth skin just above her ring-bearing navel.

A second burst of light engulfed her, as if she had swallowed a flare. Insensate and silent, it spewed vertically into the night sky as her inhabiting Interloper vanished in a blast of cold crimson embers. After months of avoiding and dodging, he had finally slain one of Those Who Abide.

It felt good. Real good.

As the young woman fainted harmlessly to the ground, unconscious but cleansed, the others tried to surround the two men. Transparent tentacles only the imperiled could see thrashed and flailed in impotent rage. Mouths snapped and bit at flesh they were determined to feed upon from the inside out. Bodies dipped and thrust. But their movements were sluggish. It took time for them to respond to the commands and directives of those abiding within them. Though outnumbered, Cody and Oelefse reacted with a speed and sense of purpose their internally dominated antagonists could not match. Interlopers traditionally infected other humans through stealth and accident. The kind of frontal assault they were attempting to mount within the castle walls was proving clumsy in its execution.

That did not make it any less deadly, Cody knew. A single extended contact with an Interloper-bearing rock was all that would be necessary to render him as helpless as their hapless attackers, or as afflicted as his poor Kelli. Keeping a firm grip on his garbage can lid, which had long since ceased to be a source of dry amusement, he swung and stabbed with the tuning fork.

An Interloper-laden chunk of smooth-sided river rock was rammed in his direction. With growing confidence, he swung the tuning fork at the squat, particularly ugly Interloper that was frothing forth from its surface. The three-pronged device sliced through its midsection.

Nothing happened. There was no outburst of brilliant light, no despairing moan as the Interloper shriveled and died. It continued to claw at him, its grasping fingers passing repeatedly through the flesh and bone of his arm. Backing up, he brought his arm down, catching the hideous manifestation with a strong backswing. The second blow had no more effect that the first. Pushing forward, the middle-aged man holding the stone came within inches of touching it to Cody's right thigh.

Steel flashed in the moonlight, slicing the mewling Interloper in half. It blew up and died in a satisfying shower of sparks and silent energetic discharges. Oelefse was at Cody's side, shouting at him.

"Do not forget to strike your fork against the pavement from time to time, Cody Westcott! Not every useful device in this world is powered by batteries, you know." Swinging his shield around, he caught a flung, Interloper-inhabited stone and bashed it aside as he returned to the fray.

Cody did not forget again. From then on he took every opportunity to bounce the tips of the tuning fork off the paving stones beneath his feet. As he and Oelefse battled on, a strange sort of exhilaration overtook him. It was more than a surge of endorphins. Hundreds of years ago, thousands of other men had done battle on these castle walls, with sword and spear and shield. They had been fighting one another, but how many had done so under the influence of unseen, unsuspected Interlopers? How many of Those Who Abide had been present at such times of carnage, fattening themselves on the ultimate human misery that was war?

Now he was doing the same, fighting to save himself and his wife alongside an old man whose store of knowledge was exceeded only by his uncommon energy and determination. Only, they were not fighting with their own kind, but with the unseen instigators of a vast proportion of human woe. Instead of watching while Oelefse chanted and played, he was finally striking back himself, and in a fashion that was visually as well as physically inspiring.

Somewhere in a far distant grave, he felt, a long-dead Chachapoyan shaman or two might be looking on with pride as he carried on the fight that the Chachapoyans had waged and eventually lost.

"Oh look, honey!" The well-dressed woman clutched at her husband's arm and pointed. Raising his glance, her husband followed the direction of her stare.

"It's beautiful, isn't it?" Clinging to his arm, she hugged him tight.

Equally well-attired, and sated from a fine late-night supper, her spouse frowned as he contemplated the flurry of colored lights that were flaring forth from the ramparts of Hohensalzburg Castle. With a gesture and some weak German, he intercepted a pedestrian heading the other way.

"Excuse me, sir." When the man stopped, the husband gestured castleward. "What does this show signify?"

"Show, show?" His stroll interrupted, the Salzburger turned to look in the same direction as the two visiting Britons. When he saw the intermittent glare, his face creased into a frown beneath his hat. "That is strange. I had not heard of a show being scheduled for the fortress tonight."

"They do put on such light and sound shows, though," the woman ventured hesitantly.

"Oh *ja, ja,* many times during the year. Light and sound, sometimes telling the history of the fortress, sometimes recalling the many wars of the past." His frown did not go away. "My wife and I and our friends come sometimes to see them ourselves. Though, living here, one grows used to such events." He squinted upward, at the towering bulwark of ancient stone. "Odd for the city to have one on a Thursday night." With a shrug, he turned away. "Perhaps it is a special, unscheduled presentation for some visiting dignitary. Who can say? I wish you a good night."

Long after the citizen had vanished down the narrow street, the two tourists stood watching until at last the spray of light and color on high came to an end. Pleased by their unexpected good fortune, they turned and resumed the stroll that would take them back to their hotel. They had another story, another detail to add to the history of their vacation with which to regale their friends when they returned to Birmingham. Concerning the true nature of what they had just witnessed, a battle for the minds and bodies of two of their fellow humans that was unprecedented in recent European history, they had not an inkling. It was no historical pageant, nor a compilation of preprogrammed recordings and strobe-light effects. They had been spectators instead at one battle in an invisible but incessant war. Of this they knew nothing: only that they regretted the absence of their camera, left in a drawer back at their hotel.

•   •   •

Unaware that their fight to preserve their independence and humanity had been viewed from below as a charming entertainment, a visual bagatelle, a casual diversion for the meandering curious, Cody and Oelefse put aside their shields as they went from body to body, consoling a cluster of fellow humans as diverse as they were presently bewildered. All had survived the excision of their resident Interlopers, struck from their selves as cleanly as one infestation after another had been blasted from their vectoring rocks. As near as the two perceiving men could tell, not a single one of Those Who Abide had survived the brawl, not those inhabiting dominated human bodies nor those residing hopefully in stone. Their respective humans now stood free and uncontaminated, unaware as ever that they had only moments ago been grievously infected by something they could not see, hear, or feel. To the last man and woman, however, they now suffered from a severe but not serious collective headache.

Only when he was certain not one Interloper had survived the desperate conflict did Oelefse retrieve the long tuning fork from his young companion and slip it back into its holding straps inside the briefcase. Following Cody's with his own, he snapped the case shut and prepared to resume the planned nocturnal departure from the fortress that had been so contentiously interrupted.

Ambling downhill alongside the older man, the winded archaeologist wiped perspiration from his face and neck. Glancing backward in the direction of their dazed former assailants, he wondered aloud at their immediate fate.

"For them, it will be like waking from a dream." Oelefse gestured and they turned to the right, off the main avenue and down a narrower side path. "They will look at one another and begin to question what happened to them, why they are here. None will have a proper explanation. When morning comes and the castle reopens to tourists, they will stumble back down to their jobs and homes. The ache now pummeling their heads will last no more than a day. By nightfall there will not be one among them who does not feel better, healthier, and happier." He visited a hearty slap on the archaeologist's back. "It is a good thing we have done here tonight, my young friend! In the course of saving ourselves, we have also helped others."

Cody nodded pensively. Already a faint suggestion of light had appeared in the eastern sky, foreshadowing the dawn. "Now if we can only help Kelli."

"We shall, we shall, my friend." The older man tapped his briefcase. "We have gone on such an excursion as few men ever dream of, and returned alive, and with the blue leaves of the *ilecc* safely in our possession." In the strengthening light, his wink was easy to make out. "We will go back to America, to your dry and well-paved desert, and by Heaven, we will make some tea."

"Tea," Cody murmured. "I wondered how you were going to use the leaves. And by the way: Do you know where I can get a briefcase like that one?" He indicated the still immaculate, unscratched case Oelefse cradled beneath his left arm.

"Like this?" His guide shrugged. "It is only a briefcase. Surely in your home city there are establishments that sell similar attachés?"

"Similar, maybe, but not the same." Cody was eyeing the old man closely. "It seems to hold a lot more than it should."

"On the contrary, my young friend, it holds no more than it should. But if you really want one, well, I will see what I can do. Our supplier is somewhat exclusive." He smiled encouragingly.

"Exclusive, or elusive?" Cody smiled back. Not all the wonders he had encountered in Oelefse's company were overwhelming. The smaller ones had their own unique attractions.

Oelefse was stating the obvious when he remarked that their activities seemed to have drawn a good deal of unwanted attention. Consequently, he put in a much greater effort and spent a good deal more time in planning their return to America than he had their departure. Instead of flying directly home, and despite Cody's desire to not spend a moment more than was necessary in travel, the old man insisted on taking a roundabout route with multiple stops. So it was that they drove, not back to Vienna, but to Zurich, keeping a wary eye on the stone ramparts of the Alps through which they cruised. From Zurich they boarded a plane going to Madrid, from there flew to Miami, and only then did Cody find himself on a flight heading homeward.

Exhausted by his European ordeal, but elated at the prospect of having his wife restored to him, the archaeologist made a conscious effort to relax on the plane. He expected Oelefse to do the same, but his elderly companion was a composed, controlled, ceaselessly active ball of white-haired energy. Most notably, the first thing Oelefse did subsequent to boarding was put in a request to look at the cockpit. This was a treat usually reserved for youngsters, but so charming and persuasive was the genteel German that the flight crew acceded to his request. Cody was not surprised. Oelefse had made the same petition at the beginning of every flight they'd made. Not to view the cockpit and learn about its controls, but to ensure to his own satisfaction that no member of the flight crew was contaminated by something that might compromise their safe journey.

When the archaeologist had questioned him about this particular interest, Oelefse had been quick to explain. "Occasionally, commercial aircraft are lost for no apparent reason, my young friend. They report some minor problem, say they are dealing with it, and the next thing you know, you are watching the appalling details on the evening news. It has happened to planes from every major international airline. Except one, and there is a specific reason for that."

"Interlopers." Cody had responded without prompting. And Oelefse had nodded. It made all too much sense. In the course of an airplane crash, the food of despair would be present in plenty. Only the fact that it was of short, if intense, duration kept a greater number of such catastrophes from taking place.

It did not make for reassurances as they boarded one plane after another.

As Oelefse assessed the flight crew on the pretense of examining the cockpit, Cody's thoughts were only of his wife. There had been no contact with the hospital in Scottsdale since he had left for Europe. What was her current status? Had her condition changed for the better? For the worse? But for his guide's admonition, he would have called to find out.

"You never know who is on the other end of the line, my friend," the old man had warned him. "You never know what abides within them, waiting and ready to partake of whatever information as well as whatever unhappiness may come its way. Better that you should wait, difficult as I know it must be for you to do, until you are once more at your wife's bedside. Then you can make your inquiries with a better assurance of receiving truthful answers."

So the agitated archaeologist let only his eyes make contact with one public phone after another, both in Europe and on their return to the States. His car was waiting, dusty but undisturbed, where it had been left in the covered parking facility. He ought to go home first, he knew. There would be bills to pay to ensure that vital utilities were not shut off, and phone messages to answer. None of them meant anything anymore. Only Kelli was important. Only Kelli mattered.

It was not necessary for Oelefse to be able to read thoughts. He could read the intentions of the younger men in his eyes, his attitude, and his gestures. Leaving the airport, they rushed along the freeways until the time came to exit, not for the Westcotts' neighborhood, but for the broad commercial plain that boasted among its many large, wholly air-conditioned buildings the hospital to which Kelli Westcott had been committed.

They were pulling into the parking lot when Cody shouted an oath and slammed on the brakes. The hospital loomed directly ahead, a shining fortress of pink and white concrete, glass, and steel girded by half-filled parking lots. Overhead, the late summer sun burned mercilessly, heedless of man's efforts to tame the desert by unrolling across it his pathetic little strips of asphalt and schools, strip malls and cookie-cutter housing developments.

Blocking the entrance to the hospital was a veritable company of Interlopers.

Three thousand tendrils flailed in the direction of the car carrying the two men. A thousand unearthly mouths of every imaginable size, shape, and dentition probed and pulsed in their direction. Unclean protuberances puckered and drooled from the midst of the virulent mass while coarse antennae traced twitching, jerking patterns in the air. The writhing mass of otherworldly foulness exuded the stink of sorrow.

"Why me?" Clinging grimly to the wheel, Cody gritted his teeth as he stared through the windshield and tried to decide what to do next. "Why pick on Kelli and me?"

"You delved into mysteries that Those Who Abide

would prefer to keep hidden." Oelefse's tone was gently avuncular. "The more success you have, the more attention you draw to yourself. You are a prize to be taken, you and your wife. If knowledge is happiness, then the Interlopers have a great many reasons to hate you."

"How can we get past that?" Keeping both hands on the wheel in unconscious parody of the older man's driving style, Cody considered the mass of psychical spoliation that loomed before them.

"All hospitals have multiple entrances," Oelefse murmured.

"Around back!" Throwing the car into reverse, Cody burned rubber as he sent them screeching around to the north side of the medical complex. His was not the only brain to recognize the possibility of an alternate ingress, however. No matter how fast the car moved, or how skillfully it was maneuvered by the furious archaeologist, the company of Interlopers kept pace. Whenever Cody slowed, that seething mass of tentacles and suckers and bulbous eyes was there to block any approach to the building.

"How come there's no panic?" Breathing hard, the car idling in the suffocating heat of afternoon, Cody regarded their rapacious multilimbed adversary. Were they facing dozens of Interlopers all crammed tightly together to form a barrier, he wondered, or a single organism monstrous beyond anything they had yet encountered? Without the kind of close inspection that was required to tell, it was a question whose resolution remained out of reach.

"Those who cannot perceive must see something else. When they choose to really exert themselves, the Interlopers can twist reality in distressing ways. Usually, it is a device employed to cause accidents and thereby generate fresh misery. But this time—here, try these."

From a coat pocket Oelefse removed a tiny plastic bottle with a small nipple on one end. Squeezing a drop of the contents into each eye, he blinked reflexively as he passed the container to his companion.

Cody eyed the vial uncertainly. "What's in this?"

"Eyedrops. For clarifying one's vision."

Without further hesitation or additional time-consuming questions, the archaeologist tilted his head back and applied the drops. As his vision cleared he heard Oelefse's muted grunt of satisfaction.

"Perception," the older man was muttering, "is everything."

Squatting directly in front of them was not some gargantuan multilimbed monster, but rather a monster of a truck. The driver of the idling eighteen-wheeler wore an expression of thoroughgoing befuddlement, as though more than his sight had been clouded. The load on his open-bed vehicle consisted of dozens of bound-together slabs of heavy, earth-red flagstone hauled down from a quarry in the northern part of the state and destined for points eastward. These were secured vertically on the back of the flatbed like so many dull, ochre, irregularly shaped dinner plates, each the size of a dining room table.

And every one of them was home to a resident, hungry, agitated Interloper.

The tentacles had not gone away; the suckers and fanged mouths continued to snap at the air, but now Cody could see that they originated in natural stone and not in some ponderous otherworldly bulk. They could not move about of their own free will. No Interloper could do that without a host to convey it. But by masking the perception of the two men, the Interlopers whose movements were restricted to the flat rocks in which they dwelled had managed to give the impression of a highly mobile mob of deadly abiders. And by controlling the truck's operator via the Interloper that occupied his thoughts, they were able to repeatedly block the approach to the hospital of Cody and his distinguished friend.

Now that the two men knew what they were dealing with, Oelefse proposed that they enter the multilevel parking facility and take the covered, third-level walkway across to the hospital, rising by many feet above the threatening load of truck-borne Interlopers.

"They can't do anything to us in this world unless we make direct physical contact with the vectors, the rocks, in which they're living." Cody recited the mantra aloud even as he was backing the car slowly away from the haunted big rig. "Why don't we just walk around the truck?"

"Because while Those Who Abide cannot hurt you emotionally, they still possess the means to injure you physically." Oelefse gestured forward. "If that truck backs over you, it will not make much difference if you touch an Interloper-infected stone or not."

So hard had Cody been concentrating on the potential psychic dangers posed by the Interlopers that he had forgotten about their ability to influence their physical surroundings by adversely motivating those humans who were thoroughly under their control. Leaving the car in the parking facility, the two men hurried to and across the covered catwalk that led to the hospital proper. Beneath them, dozens of enraged Interlopers fumed and flailed upward from their stone prisons on the truck bed. Tendrils and creepers pierced the concrete walkway to flutter madly in the faces of the two determined men. Several clutched at Oelefse's briefcase, but none had the power to dislodge so much as a finger of his real-world grasp, or to impede either man's stride.

Cody walked right through an ichorous maw the size of a cement mixer without hesitating. Fat, leprous lips contracted around him, passed through him, appeared behind him as he increased his pace. A brief chill flustered him for less than a few seconds. No matter how many times he passed through the substance of an Interloper without suffering any ill effects, it remained an unnerving, unnatural experience. Moments later, they were safely inside the hospital.

Used to entering through the main entrance, they were forced to pause for a minute to reorient themselves. Courteous hospital employees corrected their mistakes and offered helpful suggestions. Soon the expectant travelers were in a section of the facility Cody thought he recognized, hurrying through the pediatrics wing past anxious mothers and wide-eyed children. Had he paused a moment to consider where he was, warning signs would have been raised. But so close to the woman he had not seen in weeks, his thoughts were preoccupied.

He did not take time to reflect that any place packed with sobbing, ailing, unhappy children would constitute a natural feeding ground for gluttonous Interlopers.

A holdover from simpler times, Lincoln Logs were pre-cut sections of tree trunk and tree limb designed to fit together to form cabins, Western-style forts, and various other child-friendly structures. In addition to the standard line there were also mini-sets and oversized editions. It was one of the latter that two prepubescent boys and a girl were presently attempting to assemble into a small house. Scattered about the play area were a host of as yet unused logs, none longer than three feet, with shorter connecting pieces.

Reaching for a long log with which to complete a wall, one of the boys kicked it before he could reach it. Or perhaps his leg was impelled by a force he did not understand. The log rolled toward a covey of mothers seated behind a low table piled high with a tattered assortment of housekeeping, health, and beauty magazines. Striding single-mindedly between knees and kids, Cody barely noticed the toy log rolling toward him.

Oelefse slammed into him from behind, throwing him off-balance and knocking him forward. The startled archaeologist had to scramble to maintain his footing.

"What the hell was— ?" As he caught sight of the log, he broke off, staring. Disapproving of his mild profanity, a couple of the mothers had glanced up from their magazines. When they saw him looking in their direction they promptly returned to their reading.

The oversized, umber-stained, notched wooden dowel had rolled to a stop against the foot of a young woman in her twenties. From within the log a sinuous, two-foot-long shape was oozing out of the wood and into her leg. It had stubby membranous wings and multiple eyes and a ration of gnarled transparent teeth that looked like a plateful of overcooked hash browns. Oblivious to the infection in progress, the woman shuddered slightly, as if from a sudden chill, and went back to her reading.

Approaching the log, the little girl who had been helping to build the house smiled and murmured something to her mother. This brought forth a retort so excessively sharp that the child immediately started crying. The other mothers looked up but said nothing. It was not their child who was being rebuked. Truth be told, it was not the mother who was doing the berating. No longer wholly her own self, she had absorbed the infestation that had been meant for Cody.

A small, strong hand was tugging at him, and a voice was whispering urgently. "Come, my friend. There is nothing we can do for her, and we have business elsewhere."

Still staring at the woman, who now slammed her magazine down hard on an end table, Cody allowed himself to be drawn toward the next corridor. Behind him, the children continued to fumble innocently with the toy logs, including the quietly sobbing, unfortunate little girl whose mother had now become unwitting host to one of Those Who Abide.

"You must never let down your guard like that. Didn't I warn you?" Oelefse's words were reproving as they strode past a tall service cart laden with trays of styrene-covered, rapidly cooling food.

"I—I wasn't thinking." Cody was simultaneously relieved and embarrassed by his narrow escape. After all he had been through, both here and overseas, he had nearly been trapped by a child's toy. "I thought it was probably plastic and so I didn't take a good look at it." His tone was defensive. "Isn't every other kid's toy these days made of plastic?"

"I suppose you cannot be blamed for that. Most everything in your country is. In Europe we still believe that children should grow up with some toys fashioned from natural materials. As you nearly found out, while aesthetically pleasing, that can be dangerous. A number of the Society's members work in the toy industry solely to vet such materials before they can pass into the hands of our children."

"It won't happen again." Cody wondered which of them he was trying to convince.

"Not until after we have treated your wife, anyway." They were in the last hall, approaching the room where Kelli Westcott lay in stasis. Nothing could stop them now. The intern and nurse they warily passed were clean, and carried nothing that could be considered a threat.

A young woman, little more than a teenager, was standing outside the door of the private room next to Kelli's. In her arms she held a softly squalling infant less than a year old. A glance in her direction assured the perceptive Cody that she was uncontaminated. So close to his wife now, he had to resist the urge to break into a run. But running would only have drawn attention, and they were nearly there anyway.

As he passed the teenage mother, he absently noted her drawn expression, the lost look in her eyes. That was not unexpected in a mother of sixteen or seventeen. What he did not, could not, anticipate were the actions of the baby. Reaching down in a most non-infantile manner, it brought something up from within its powder blue blanket and threw it in the archaeologist's direction with more force than such tiny, undeveloped arms ought to possess. Instinctively, he flinched.

It was a rock the size of a silver dollar, smooth and shiny as if it had just been plucked from the bed of a sparkling mountain stream. From its reddish depths a pair of insectlike ovipositors extended outward. At the tip of each was an eye, and a small, piercing mouth.

He did not even have time to shout before it struck him on the neck.

fifteen

Anyone else would have felt nothing but the momentary chill. Cody was cursed with the ability to see as well as feel what was happening to him. Boring into his neck, the Interloper's mouths and eyes entered his self, the rest of the attenuated, loathsome form following rapidly. It flowed out of the stone even before that tumbling vector began to succumb to the pull of gravity. By the time the rounded rock struck the floor, nearly all of the Interloper had passed into the alarmed archaeologist. The distraught young mother barely glanced in the direction of the staggering professor. A stunned Cody now understood the reason for her distress: She was not and probably had never been infected—but her infant was.

Before he could react, something cold and hard smacked him in the mouth. Eyes flicking downward, he saw Oelefse straining to jab something into his face. He barely had time to recognize it before an incredible pain shot through his entire system. It was as if he'd suddenly bitten down on a live wire and could not open his jaws.

He nearly fainted from the pain. The older man was there to catch him as his legs went numb. Once again he felt the surprising strength in that elderly body. Then his own system responded, recovering from the initial shock, a burst of adrenaline helping him to regain control of his legs. Trembling slightly, he found himself leaning up against the wall. The far wall, away from the hollow-eyed mother and her malevolently precocious, subtly manipulated child. It glared at him out of beguiled baby eyes, unable to assault him further.

Looking down, Cody saw the river rock lying innocently on the floor. Bending, the young mother picked it up and handed it back to her child. The infant took the rock in its tiny hands, turning the cool smoothness over and over, cooing and gurgling.

What, Cody wondered fearfully, of the Interloper that had sprung from the rock into his neck at the instant of contact? Reaching up, he felt the skin there. Naturally, there was no sign of entry, nor would he find one in a mirror. No puncture mark, no miniscule wound, no millimeter-long telltale gash. Was he contaminated? Was it even now sequestering itself deep within him, making itself comfortable, adjusting to its new surroundings preparatory to taking control of his thoughts and actions?

"You are clean." Gazing up at his young friend, Oelefse took a deep breath. "Though it was a near thing."

Dwindling waves of pain dribbled from the archaeologist's lips like a rapidly receding tide on a beach. His jaw throbbed where the old man had struck him. "What did you do to me?"

"I had to strike before it could establish itself." Reaching into his pocket, Oelefse removed a small, familiar object. "I barely had time enough to rap this against the wall and smack you in the teeth with it. My apologies for hurting you, but the only way to counter the influx of an Interloper is with a greater shock to the system."

Cody considered the small tuning fork and tried not

to remember exactly how it had felt when the rapidly vibrating steel had made contact with the nerves in his teeth. "Then it's dead? Just like the ones we killed in Salzburg?" Oelefse nodded. "Christ, I thought my head was going to come off!"

"At least it is still your head." Turning, Oelefse headed for the last door on the left-hand side of the corridor. "Come. We have tea to brew."

The last obstacle to his reunion removed, Cody hurried forward, passing Oelefse and shoving the door to the room inward. Instantly, something large and aggressive was in his face, shoving him backward and through the doorway.

"Who do you think you are . . . sir?" The man gripping the front of the archaeologist's shirt was not particularly tall, but very wide.

"Take it easy!" Cody struggled to free himself. His adversary released him, but continued to block the doorway with his bulk.

"No one gets in here who ain't first been cleared by my office."

"Glad to hear it." More relieved than ruffled, Cody strained to see past the guard. "Call them, then. I'm Coschocton Westcott, the husband of the woman your company was hired to keep watch over." Less challengingly, he added, "She is still in this room, isn't she?"

The other man's expression remained guarded. "Yeah, she's here. Just stay there a moment." Pulling a cell phone from a pocket, he called in, making Cody and Oelefse stand outside in the hall while he waited for a reply. Anguished and apprehensive, the archaeologist had no choice but to wait. There was nothing to be gained by causing a scene that might bring security personnel running.

The guard looked up from the phone. "Let's see some ID."

Fumbling for his wallet, Cody produced driver's license, university identification, and credit cards. After a short exchange over the phone, the guard finally stood aside.

"Sorry, Mr. Westcott. Just doing my job."

"Real well, too," Cody blurted as he pushed past him and into the room. Following, Oelefse smiled sympathetically at the man.

"Mr. Westcott thanks you for your professionalism on behalf of his wife. You must be tired. While we are visiting, why not take a small break?" He checked his watch. "If I am not mistaken, the hospital cafeteria should be serving lunch now."

"I brought my lunch. We always bring our own. Something hot for a change would be nice, though." He hesitated. "I really oughta wait for my relief."

Oelefse patted him on the arm, urging him through the doorway even as he was pulling it shut. "We will be here for a while. Everything will be all right. Mr. Westcott has been away and is not about to leave his wife's side for some time."

"Well—okay. If you're sure. Who are *you*, anyway?"

"I am his uncle. I am your uncle, too."

"Yeah, right. Funny." The guard gazed longingly down the hall. "I'll be back in an hour. No more."

"Life is short, my friend. Take two." From the gap that remained between closing door and waiting wall, Oelefse smiled encouragingly. "We will be here when you return."

Having seen the guard off, the old man shut the door and stepped into the room. Cody was seated on the edge of the bed, holding his wife's left hand. It was a tender tableau whose parameters were unchanged from the last time they had visited. The archaeologist was silent, but tears were running down his face.

Seeing his mentor approach, Cody struggled to control his emotions. "Look at her, Oelefse. She's worse. Don't you think she looks worse?"

Bending over the bed, the older man considered the inert, softly breathing form. The plastic spaghetti of feeding tubes and monitoring cables still ran from her face and body into an array of medical machinery on either side of the bed. The beautiful face was paler than he remembered it, the pulse in her wrist lagging.

As he stared, something that was all glaring eyes and gnashing teeth rose up from her chest to snap at him. At the same time, half-a-dozen eel-like shapes bit at Cody, coiling around his arms and gnawing futilely at his face. Both men ignored the ferocious manifestations of Those Who Abide. They could not be harmed by them, just as puzzled doctors could not detect the monstrosities or their insidious influence on the inexplicably nonresponsive patient in room 322. Cody almost wished some kind of minimal contact with the infesting Interlopers *could* be gained, if only so he could wrap his fingers around the throat of at least one of Those Who Abide, could feel it writhe and die beneath him instead of under the striking but physically removed vibration of one of Oelefse's lethal tuning forks.

Impotent to influence the two unpolluted visitors, the grotesque, hideous shapes withdrew back into the human they were slowly destroying. Wanting to plunge his hands deep into his beloved, to drag them out with his bare hands, Cody could only sit by her side and hold her hand while Oelefse attended to necessary preparations.

These were simple and few in number. From his briefcase this time he withdrew a different kind of rattle, narrow and more tubular, decorated with different symbols and feathers the like of which Cody had never seen. He wondered at the kind of bird from which they had been plucked—or if they even belonged to any creature he would recognize as a bird. In contrast to their previous visit, Oelefse kept his suit on and put no paint on his face. Setting the rattle aside, he removed from the case a tiny, compact coffee brewer of German manufacture. Noting the direction of his young friend's gaze, the old man smiled.

"This is designed to make a decent cappuccino even in the wilds of Mongolia. It will, should circumstances demand, also brew tea." He nodded in the direction of the door. "I understand your feelings, having not seen her in so many days and after so much drama, but it will benefit her more if you keep watch at the door rather than hold a hand she cannot feel."

Reluctant, but deferring to the older man's wisdom, Cody gently let his wife's limp hand fall back to the bed as he rose and took up a stance next to the entrance. Recalling a previous similar situation, he thoughtfully jammed a chair under the handle as tightly as he could.

The miniature brewer hissed softly as Oelefse added water from the tap in the bathroom. Chanting softly, he began to crumble between his palms the blue leaves of the *ilecc* he and Cody had fought so hard to acquire. As each fragment of leaf fell into the rapidly heating water, it emitted a single, brief, cobalt-blue spark.

Within minutes the water was boiling. Closing the plastic lid, Oelefse raised both arms and began to make studied passes over the coffeemaker, his chanting growing louder. Despite the presence of the splatter-preventing translucent brown lid, blue sparks continued to fly from the fermenting brew, shooting through the protective plastic as if it did not exist.

Picking up the rattle, Oelefse shook it several times over the coffeemaker. There was no ultimate burst of flames; no geyser of embers or flurry of electrical discharges. Ceasing his chant, he put the rattle back in the briefcase and switched off the brewer. Passing the open container beneath his nose, he inhaled but did not taste of the final concoction. Cody thought it had grown a little brighter in the shuttered room, but could not be sure.

"Ice. We need ice. And we don't want to call for it." Without waiting for his young friend to respond, Oelefse reentered the bathroom. Leaning to one side, Cody could see him place the hot container in the sink and run cold water around it. More minutes passed, during which the archaeologist tried to divide his time between his motionless wife, the door, and Oelefse's inscrutable actions.

When at last the old man thought the brew had cooled enough, he returned. Objection sprang unbidden to Cody's lips, but he said nothing as Oelefse carefully removed one of the plastic bags supplying glucose solution to Kelli's unmoving form and poured the tea into the bag. Nearly empty, it promptly turned dark blue with the tea as Oelefse hung it back on its hook. The cobalt-colored liquid swiftly began to flow through the tube and into the ashen arm of the comatose woman in the bed. Adjusting the controller on the tube, the oldster increased the flow to maximum.

If a nurse or doctor should walk in now, Cody knew . . .

None did. Moving to the foot of the bed, Oelefse armed himself with rattles both old and new—and waited.

Unable to restrain himself any longer, Cody finally asked, "Is this how it's usually done?"

"This is not 'usually done,' my young friend. In fact, I have never seen it done myself. The use of the leaves of the *ilecc* is described in the records of the Society. Given the gravity of your wife's condition, I believed from the first time I saw her that this was the only chance she had." His lips tightened slightly. "The accounts say that the tea is to be sipped." He indicated the intravenous tubing that was conveying the precious blue liquid.

"Though no mouth, no throat is involved, I estimate the rate of ingestion to be sufficient."

Cody stared at the steady flow of cerulean fluid that was sliding from the bag into the arm of the woman who meant to him more that life itself. Had they really been friendly antagonists once, in the high green mountains of another continent? It seemed so long ago. Back when the world had been a safer, saner place. Both of them had been happier in the bliss that ignorance brought. They would never, could never, be ignorant again, he knew. That happy, childish state was denied to them even as it was granted to most of the rest of humankind. Such was the inescapable burden of knowledge.

"Then you've never done this before," he commented quietly.

An extravagantly decorated rattle gripped firmly in each hand, Oelefse shrugged. "I can still stop this, if you wish."

"And do what?" Cody's tone was anguished. "I have no choice. *She* has no choice." His expression pleaded. "Do we?"

"Not if you want her restored to you. There is no other way in my realm of knowledge."

The archaeologist replied tightly, "Then let her body drink, and Those Who Abide be damned."

The bag was almost completely drained when Kelli's recumbent form gave a twitch as violent as it was unexpected. Her muscles reacted sharply to some inner stimulus. Arching at the waist, her whole body rose high off the bed, like a gymnast doing a back bend or a wrestler demonstrating a neck bridge. Trembling like an electrified wire, she let out a long, extended gasp, as if she'd been trapped underwater for some time and was expelling every ounce of liquid she had swallowed in a single furious, heaving exhalation.

Emitting a triumphant cry, Oelefse launched into a chant as enthusiastic as it was intense, shaking both rattles at the undulating figure on the bed, the elegant Continental gentleman Cody knew so well transformed once more into a barbarous bishop engaged in blessing the uncognizant afflicted.

Without waiting for instructions, the younger man leaned over and grabbed his wife's shoulders, holding her down as she surged and sputtered. No ambiguous blinking for her, no Sleeping Beautyish delicate fluttering of eyelids. Her eyes were wide open and staring. What they saw he did not know, but so far, her range of vision did not include him, or the old man singing energetically at the foot of her bed, or the room that had been her living tomb for many weeks. They were focused on something beyond reality.

Holding her arm as stationary as he could by leaning his greater weight against it, he carefully removed the intravenous tubing. Slipping the tubes out of her face was more difficult because her head tended to jerk uncontrollably from side to side, but he managed to accomplish that as well. Seeing her freed from that medicinal Gordian knot of plastic piping was almost as encouraging as her movements. The removal of the IV drips that had kept her alive did nothing to slow her movements. If anything, they allowed her to convulse more explosively than ever. Though he outweighed her by a hundred pounds, on several occasions her arching form lifted him right off the bed.

Full of Those Who Abide she was—and now they were coming out. Not voluntarily, not to see what was happening, but because they were being forcibly purged. And they were not happy about it.

Flying eel-shapes that were half-slavering jaws spurted from her widely parted lips. They flickered brilliantly in the subdued light of the hospital room, bursts of anemic blue and green light running the length of their malformed bodies like sickly lightning. Upon contacting either of the two men, instead of passing through them as they normally would, they recoiled as if singed. Drifting, floating aimlessly, they sought refuge. But in the sterile room there was no defenseless host available for the taking, no natural vector in which they could find temporary haven.

They began to die.

One by one, the blinding light of exploding blue and green flares filled the room. Though their aspect was wholly sinister, the volatile passing of the Interlopers reminded Cody of colored strobe lights flashing in a discotheque. Except that strobe lights did not moan when they were turned off, and did not bestow individual looks of hatred upon those dancing beneath them.

A corpulent, one-armed shape devoid of flesh emerged from the vicinity of Kelli's stomach. So hideous was it in appearance, so overwhelmingly gross, that Cody drew back slightly in spite of himself. But he did not let go of his wife. If this worked and she was restored to him, he'd vowed, he would never let go of her again.

The deformed abomination waddled clear of the young woman's body on a quartet of squat, porcine legs. Bleating threateningly, it hopped froglike down the length of her blanketed body, heading straight for the sing-songing Oelefse. The old man was ready for it. When it leaped at him, with a mouth as wide as its entire body agape, Oelefse brought both rattles together on either side of the bloated, lop-sided skull. It ruptured and died in a spectacular bloom of silent fireworks. Greenish fragments of Interloper clung briefly to the German's face and shoulders before fading away to nothingness, like embers thrown off by a dying fire. It was the last of the Interlopers that had been

dwelling within Kelli Westcott, and its incendiary passing coincided with the easing of her violent convulsions.

Held and comforted in her husband's arms, she began
to settle down. Her back no longer arched acutely, and
her eyelids began to flutter. Gradually, her respiration
steadied. Oelefse's chant faded into the aural distance as
ethereally as one orchestrated by Holst. The movements
of his hands slowed, the rhythmic chattering of the two
rattles quieted as he considered the young woman breathing almost normally in the bed. Stopping, he carefully
placed the two rattles back in the briefcase. It was once
more as quiet as an ordinary hospital room.

"Kelli?" Leaning toward his recumbent wife, a solic-
itous Cody Westcott moistened his lips, hardly daring to
breathe. "Kelli, can you hear me?"

Eyes open, head framed by her halo of shoulder-length
hair, she turned toward him. Still trembling, her lips struggled to form words.

"Cody? That is you, isn't it? Oh, Cody!"

Throwing his arms around her shoulders and back,
tears streaming down her face, he lifted her upper body
out of the bed, trying hard not to crush her with the trembling force of his grateful embrace. Though weak from
lack of activity, she reciprocated, her own arms going
under his to hold him as tightly as she was able. She was
crying, too.

A paternal smile on his face, Oelefse looked on wordlessly. Such moments required no commentary. Turning
away from the restored couple, he glanced around the
room. There was nothing hiding in the shadows or glowering malevolently from the corners. It was once again
all that a hospital room should be: clean, hygienic, and
uncontaminated.

Realizing she was still weak and needed room to
breathe, Cody reluctantly broke the embrace. "There were

too many times, hon, when I wondered if this moment would ever come. When I wondered if"—he swallowed with difficulty—"I'd ever hear your voice again."

She was staring straight at him. "I don't even know what happened, Cody."

"Interlopers, Those Who Abide, Remember patronizing my efforts to explain them to you? You were infected. Real bad. Were you—in pain?"

"I don't remember. I don't think so, but I really can't remember. Everything is just one big haziness and a vague feeling of bad dreams." She continued to stare at him. "Then there finally *was* some pain, and I woke up, and now you're here." Her voice fell slightly. "I don't think I'll be challenging you on the existence of these things any time again soon. How long—how long have I been asleep?"

"You've been in this hospital room for weeks. How long exactly I don't know offhand. I'd have to check the calendar. I've been busy with my friend Oelefse trying to find something that would cure you, would drive the Interlopers out of your system. While you were in a coma we've been all the way to Europe and back and now—" Realization caused him to break off abruptly. She was still staring at him, only—she was not staring at him. Something was wrong. Very wrong. It took an effort of will for him to voice the question that could no longer be avoided.

"Kelli? You—you can't see me, can you?"

Her hands reached out to him, once more gripping his arms. A sorrowful smile creased her weary but still beautiful face. "Yes I can, Cody. My memory fills in the blank places."

Cursing under his breath, fighting back the emotions that threatened to overwhelm him, the archaeologist turned a beseeching face to his friend. "Oelefse, what is this? I thought she would be fully restored: both to me and to herself. It—it's a temporary condition, isn't it? It's just going to take a little while for her sight to return, right?"

Having closed and latched his attaché case the elderly German now moved forward to study the figure sitting up in the bed. Taking Kelli's face in his hands, he gently manipulated it to and fro, peering into her open, staring eyes. She bore the examination in silence. Internally, Cody was in agony.

"I do not know." Holding his chin, a concerned Oelefse straightened as he gazed speculatively at the revived woman seated helplessly before him. "This I did not anticipate. There is nothing in the literature about it. Though in cases of such severe infestation, side effects should be expected."

"Side effects?" In the space of a few minutes, the archaeologist's emotions had run the gamut from exhalation to dismay. "Oelefse—she's blind!"

"Possibly. Or perhaps her sight is merely limited. Tell me, my dear, can you see anything? Anything at all? Can you distinguish between light and dark?"

"It's very strange, Mr. Oelefse." Turning slowly, Kelli scanned the room. "I wasn't going to say anything because I thought I was having some kind of hallucinations. But—maybe they're not hallucinations." Turning to face Cody, who had not stirred from her side, she smiled. "I wish now I'd been less critical about your comments and observations, Cody."

"You can see things? Like what?" Taking her hand in his, he squeezed gently. "Don't be afraid, love. Whatever it is that you're seeing, tell us. We won't laugh. God knows we won't laugh. Not after what we saw in Europe."

"Well . . ." She was still reluctant. "Over there, for example." She raised her other hand and pointed. "It looks like the top of a forest, only the trees aren't trees. They're like oversized houseplants, only they have colored lights running up and down their sides, and hardly any branches, and they keep weaving back and forth like they're trying to hypnotize something. The tips of the branches are spitting cold fire." Her hand shifted. "And over there are a bunch of balloons with tentacles and eyes, only they keep flashing like neon signs, and the eyes are on the ends of the tentacles. And next to them is something like a . . ."

"Gott in Himmel," Oelefse murmured when she had concluded her description of the sights she saw around her, "her ability to view the world around her has been transposed. She is seeing into the plane of existence you and I visited at Hohensalzburg! This is most remarkable."

Cody was shaking his head, as if by the very gesture he could make the bad dream he had stepped into go away. "This is crazy! How can that be?"

"It is as I said. Side effects. Because of the danger and difficulty involved in obtaining them, the leaves of the *ilecc* are rarely put to use. No one ever knows for certain exactly what will result from their application."

"Well, do something! She can't live like this. Besides, what if—what if the Interlopers in their elsewhere can now perceive *her*? Won't they come after her?"

"Just because she can see them and they her does not mean physical contact will result." Oelefse continued to watch Kelli, observing every gesture, noting the tiniest reaction. "This is most interesting."

"Interesting, hell!" Cody bawled. "Fix it! Give her back her normal sight, her vision of *this* world. Our world."

Oelefse was slowly tapping a perfectly manicured index finger against his lower lip. "It could be very useful, this. Someone who is fully sighted in the Interlopers' reality." The look that came over the archaeologist's face quickly had the older man making placating gestures. "Take it easy, my young friend. I was only speculating. As a scientist, you must understand that."

"I understand only that I went to Hell and back to get my wife restored to me, and I want *all* of her restored. Every iota. Every cell and sense. That includes her vision of reality. I want to be able to look into her eyes again and see them looking back at me—not some unearthly, translucent irregularity."

"Excuse me, gentlemen?" Calm and controlled, Kelli Westcott sat up in the bed, hands folded neatly in her lap. "Remember me? I don't know what you've been through on my behalf, and I appreciate it, but I have the feeling I've been lying in this bed for much too long. Could we maybe discuss what to do next about me somewhere else? If as you indicate, I'm in a hospital, I'd much rather be at home. Can't we talk about me there?"

So astonished at her sudden recovery were the doctors on duty that they did not even try to hold her another day for observation. With her blindness carefully camouflaged to forestall any objections on the part of the hospital staff, she was discharged into her husband's custody and released. Approaching their neighborhood, Cody was given a reminder of the dangers that had not vanished simply because his wife's coma had been broken. The Interlopers who lived in the artificial waterfall that marked the entrance to the community were still there, still waiting hungrily for the next unwary bystander to lean against them and become an unwilling host. The archaeologist was grim-faced as he pulled into the driveway. Cared for by their good-natured neighbors, the house looked intact, undisturbed, and less troubled than its owners. After the traumatic and extraordinary events of the past weeks, the shock of encountering something so familiar, so domestic and comforting, nearly overcame him.

"Are we home?" Gazing blankly, Kelli fumbled for assistance in exiting the car.

"Yes. Yes, Kelli, we're home. At last. And we're not going anywhere for a long, long time." Holding her against him, Cody escorted her up the winding concrete path that led to the front entrance.

Trailing closely behind, his briefcase an expensive extension of his hand, Oelefse countered the archaeologist's homey assurance. "That is, of course, up to you, my young friend. But if you wish to try and alleviate your wife's present condition, I am afraid it cannot be done from here. At least, I certainly cannot do it from here."

Cody paused outside the front door. Ahead lay his home, his refuge, a castle smaller than Hohensalzburg but to him and the one he loved, no less stirring or vital.

"Then you think there's a chance? You think you can give her back her normal sight?"

"There is nothing wrong with her sight. It is her perception that has become skewed. But I need assistance. I need the help of someone more skilled in such singular matters than myself."

"We've just returned home, Oelefse. I've been away for so long, and Kelli"—he squeezed her tightly to him—"Kelli's been away even longer."

Tilting back her head and speaking to the sound of his voice, she smiled. "What I'm seeing is actually quite pretty, Cody. Deadly, maybe, if everything you've been telling me is true, but still pretty. Otherworldly pretty." She placed her open palm against his chest. "But I'd much rather be able to see you. If your friend thinks he can do something, then we should do what he says."

"I know, I know that." Indecision tore at the archaeologist. "I'll do—Kelli, I'll do whatever you want. You're the one who's been sick. You just climbed out of a hospital bed. Are you sure you're up to going somewhere so soon, or do you want to take a couple of days and rest first?"

She didn't hesitate, turning in the direction of Oelefse's costly and distinctive cologne. "I want to see my husband again, Mr. Oelefse. I want to see him, and my house, and my cats, and blue sky and growing things that don't glow. If you think there's a chance, any chance at all, that you can make that happen, I don't want to hesitate. Let's get on with it, right now." Her smile shone brighter than the polished metal of the medical instruments that had kept her alive. "I'd even like to see you, so I can thank you properly."

Cody checked the emotions that threatened to overwhelm him. "All right, Oelefse. What do we have to do?"

Wizened brows crinkled in thought, and there was a glint in the old man's eye. Or maybe it was just the passing reflection of the midday sun. When he spoke, it was not to Cody but to his wife.

"My dear Mrs. Westcott—is your passport in order?"

Sixteen

Cody thought they would head east, back to Europe. Back to Germany. So he was more than a little surprised when they boarded a Qantas flight.

"Sydney, Australia?" He posed the metropolitan query absently as he and his elderly companion waited for Kelli to emerge from the women's lounge at the airport. "What's in Sydney?"

"Excellent restaurants. Fascinating history. Interesting shopping." Oelefse was scanning the concourse, his eyes ever busy, his mind always alert to the possibility that even in a security-screened public place the wretched minions of the Interlopers might try to intercept them or otherwise interfere with their movements. "None of that, however, need concern us. *Nichts, nada*—nothing."

Cody was watching a tall, cadaverous Scandinavian approach the metal detector. The device would warn of incoming guns and bombs, but not of Those Who Abide. "Then why are we going there?"

"Because it provides the most connections from the western U.S. to Perth which, in case you were unaware of the fact, is the most isolated large city on Earth."

"So we're going to Perth?" The archaeologist shifted his stance, wishing that Kelli would hurry. Although he knew that women in restrooms typically did not hurry, because of her impaired vision he became nervous whenever she was out of his sight for more than a few minutes.

"Only to get to Kununurra."

Oelefse had finally lost him, had geographically dumped him somewhere in the empty northwest of Down Under. He said as much. His knowledgable friend elucidated.

"Kununurra is a small agricultural town in the East Kimberley, almost on the border with the Northern Territories. South of the town lies the Argyle mine, which is famed for its pink diamonds. There is also an impressively big reservoir, Lake Argyle. About two hundred and fifty kilometers drive south from the town is the Bungle Bungle range."

Though he knew Oelefse was being dead serious, Cody could not keep from smiling. "There are mountains in the world that are actually called the Bungle Bungles?"

His friend nodded. "The aboriginal name is more mellifluous. To help your wife we must enter Purnululu. For the local people it is a place of great magic and spiritual significance. Despite its beauty, few tourists go there. The place is simply too isolated. Parts of the range have never been observed close-up and have yet to be visited—by outsiders." Turning his gaze away from the colliding streams of humanity that filled the concourse, he met the archaeologist's eyes unflinchingly. "It is one of those places where the unreality of Interloper existence spikes the truth of ours."

Cody's smile vanished. "I see. If this place is so remote and difficult to visit, how will we know where to go once we get there?"

It was Oelefse's turn to smile as Kelli, feeling her way along the walls, emerged from the restroom. "A member of the Society will be our guide. It is necessary. Otherwise we could well become lost and perish of thirst. The East Kimberley on the border of the Great Sandy Desert is unforgiving country, my friend. It can kill as surely as a hungry Interloper."

The flight from Los Angeles to Sydney was not long— it was interminable. Arriving in Sydney, they slipped past a violent verbal confrontation between a tight-lipped customs inspector and a first-class passenger whose luggage was being dismantled right down to the aspirin bottle in a small medical kit. It was Kelli who spotted the irate traveler's inhabiting Interloper first. It was fluttering in ecstasy, delighting in the mental and emotional discomfort of its distraught host. Feeding in broad daylight.

Throughout the world, international customs are one of the favorite feasting grounds of Those Who Abide," Oelefse informed Kelli and Cody. With his guidance, they had passed without comment through the line of inspectors. As they left the terminal, the enraged protestations of the infected wayfarer could still be heard behind them.

Following a necessary night's layover at an airport hotel, they were up early the next morning to catch the first flight to Perth—another five and half hours in the air. Perth to Kununurra with the requisite stops in between found them in that remote but pleasant town by nightfall. Cody had thought himself used to the travails of long-distance travel, but neither he nor Kelli, leaning on his arm for guidance, had ever experienced anything like this. While they collapsed in an air-conditioned motel room, the indefatigable Oelefse went in search of the local car rental.

"No time to waste," the practical German had responded when Cody had urged him to rest and wait until morning. "We must have a four-wheel drive to reach, much less negotiate, the terrain around Purnululu." Glancing at the night sky he added, "It is late in the dry season. If the Wet hits while we are here, we will not be able to get into the range. I will feel better when we have arranged the necessary vehicle."

"And contacted your colleague." Kelli was seated on the big bed, tracing its outline with her hands. Pain coursed through Cody that she was forced to see with her hands instead of the almost functional eyes she still possessed. She was handling her affliction better than he.

"I doubt we will see him here." Oelefse opened the door, letting in a puff of almost cool night air that slipped down around Cody's head and shoulders like a cloak of gossamer dampness. "We are not likely to be that lucky." He closed the door behind him. "But I know where to find him—I hope."

The journey south from Kununurra along the paved two-lane, shoulderless road euphemistically called the Great Northern Highway wasn't bad. Except for having to hold his breath while the occasional road train came barreling toward them, Cody found it almost enjoyable. He did his best to describe the rust-red, sparsely vegetated ground with its warped hillocks and torturously folded ridges to an attentive Kelli. From time to time a kangaroo or wallaby would bound across the road, while unknown birds mocked them from the shelter of scraggly bushes.

Warmun Community was little more than a collection of dilapidated trailers and a couple of food stores, though a few newer, more permanent houses could be seen hugging the shade of a small canyon.

"This place used to be called Turkey Creek." Oelefse remarked as they pushed through the desert heat toward the largest of the stores. "Like a good deal of this country, the names as well as the land are reverting back to the original owners."

As they walked, Cody marveled at their guide's ability to handle the difficult climate. Living in Phoenix, he and Kelli were used to the heat and absence of humidity. At least, he reflected, Oelefse had finally put aside his elegantly tailored suit in favor of bush shorts, poplin shirt, and wide-brimmed hat. Enveloped by this wilderness apparel, the omnipresent briefcase that went everywhere with him looked distinctly out of place.

Although everyone was soon perspiring profusely, the temperature was not the real problem. Far more aggravating were the flies that assailed them at every opportunity. Refusing to be waved away, they persisted wherever they happened to land—on exposed skin, on lips, or in the inviting cavities of ears or nostrils. Cody and Kelli quickly learned how to perform the Australian salute—the waving of a hand ceaselessly back and forth in front of their faces.

The store was air-conditioned and blissfully free of annoying insects. Behind the counter, a heavyset woman with skin blacker than that of any person Cody had ever seen was unpacking bottled sodas from a cardboard crate and placing them one by one in an open upright cooler. Her features were bold and flattened. When she smiled, the contrast between ebony skin and teeth white as milk was startling.

"What you blokes want? Something cold to drink?"

Kelli wiped sweat from her brow, clinging deftly to her husband's left arm for guidance. The clerk noticed but did not comment. "I'd love a cold cola. The brand doesn't matter."

Oelefse paid. Halfway through their chosen refreshment, he put one hand on the counter and smiled engagingly. "I am seeking Tjapu Kuwarra."

The woman looked uncertain. "You not a government bloke—you got a funny accent, mate. You a friend of old Tjapu?" When Oelefse nodded, she waddled out from behind the counter and retraced their steps to the store's double-doored entrance, parting a sudden influx of laughing coal-black children like an icebreaker cleaving an Arctic sea.

"You see back in the canyon there? Last house—you'll have to walk."

"Is he home?" Cody inquired politely.

The woman chuckled. "Maybe. Maybe not. Doesn't matter. If he wants to see you, he'll be there, and if he don't, he won't." Without a goodbye, she turned to deal with the sudden flash-flood of thirsty children who had inundated the counter with their shouts and laughter.

After downing the last of their drinks, the three travelers left the store and started up the rough dirt track. Overhead, a single scavenging hawk soared silently on rising currents of desiccated air.

"How do you know this Kuwarra person?" Despite her handicap, Kelli negotiated the uneven path gracefully, relying on her husband to notify her of any obstacles in their path larger than a baseball.

Oelefse glanced back. "Why, he is a member of the Society, of course." He smiled. "The Society has chapters in odd places. Wherever Interlopers are to be found, the Society is there: watching, combating, striving to protect those who can not perceive."

Cody had been uneasy ever since they had left their Jackaroo four-wheel drive parked in front of the store. His eyes swept the surrounding terrain: all stone and bush and tree. All natural, and therefore potential home to Those Who Abide. Detecting not a single Interloper, an observation that the skew-sighted Kelli was able to confirm, he queried Oelefse about their apparent absence.

·"Tjapu is here, and works to protect his people. By reputation he is a good man, a strong defender. He keeps his territory cleansed. Do not worry about these rock faces and precipices we walk between. He will already have dealt with them. In the local Kija language, Kuwarra means 'cliffs you can't climb.' "

Cody was heartened, until several tries at the door of the last house produced no response. Though it was unlocked, Oelefse chose not to enter. Instead, they walked around to the back, where they were surprised to find a modest, neatly laid-out garden composed of carefully nurtured desert plants. Several were in bloom and boasted unexpectedly brilliant flowers.

At the far end of the garden path they came upon a small, narrow pool; a place where still water had gathered as if for protection beneath a slightly undercut, overhanging cliff. A single large log rested at the edge of the water. It had been trimmed and groomed to form a kind of bench. Seated on the log and facing the water were three locals; all male, all aged, almost identically clad in shorts, short-sleeved shirts, and battered sandals.

The first had a neatly trimmed white beard and wisps of a darker gray peeking out from beneath his hat. Cody guessed him to be about seventy. His neighbor's whiskers were as long and full as those of a department store Santa, above which eyes were set deep in ebon skin. His face was as convoluted and tormented as the surrounding geology. He might have been eighty, or ninety, or over a hundred; the archaeologist could not tell. Seated to *his* right was a similarly bearded elder who was the perfect image of an aboriginal Methuselah.

None of them looked up at the newcomers' approach. None turned from contemplating rock and water to offer query or greeting. Silently, Oelefse took up a seat at the near end of the log, put his briefcase down on a flat red stone, and proceeded to stare fixedly into the placid desert pool. After whispering a description of the scene to his wife, Cody led her forward and together they assumed similar positions.

They all remained just so for at least an hour, all six of them staring quietly at water that did not respond. In that hushed canyon, nothing moved. The other houses were likewise silent, their younger men away tending to sheep and cattle on nearby stations or working at the distant diamond mine.

Terminating the brief eternity, the youngest of the three elders finally turned to Oelefse and asked, as if no time at all had passed, "Where you from?"

"Germany. My friends are from America." Leaning forward slightly, the old man gestured. "I am a friend of Tjapu Kuwarra."

The speaker nodded once. Without another word, he and his neighbor rose, turned, and departed. Again, no goodbyes were offered. They were leaving, and that was farewell enough. The action being self-explanatory, there was no need for superfluous declarations. In the country of the Kimberley, even language was scrupulously conserved.

Rising from his seat at the far end of the log, the oldest of the contemplative trio came approached the visitors. His astonishingly advanced age did not appear to have much of an impact on his movements, which were fluid if slightly shaky. Smiling through his white monument of a beard, he reached out to embrace Oelefse.

"Long time since I had a visit from the Society. Welcome!"

In the presence of so much hoary sagacity, Cody felt like a stammering child. Having nothing wise to say, he demonstrated wisdom by saying nothing. After introducing his companions, Oelefse proceeded to explain the reason for their visit.

Tjapu listened solemnly, every now and again nodding as much to himself as to his visitors. When Oelefse finished, their venerable host turned and headed back toward the house, moving with easy, rapid strides.

About to burst from anxiety, Cody did not wait for Oelefse to explain. "My wife—can you help her? Can you do anything to alleviate her condition?"

"Oh sure, mate." Looking back, the ancient one smiled. "We fix her right up. The doing of it might be a little dangerous, but we for sure got to give a try, you know? If everything works, she'll be right. No worries."

"And if everything doesn't?"

Kuwarra shrugged. "Then maybe we be dead. But in the long run, we all dead, fair dinkum." Opening the back door, he led them inside.

Though it did not boast the wonderful forced air-conditioning of the store, the interior of the concrete-block house was far cooler than the sweltering conditions outside. Amid a wealth of astonishingly detailed paintings done in traditional style, they sat and stared while their host served them lukewarm tea, chocolate biscuits, and chicken sandwiches. All the while, Kuwarra was studying Kelli, searching every inch of her face, gazing into eyes that could not look back.

"S'truth, she got the Sight, but not sight. We fix that."

"How?" Cody sipped at his cup, marveling at the absence of ice in such a climate. "Oelefse has tried rattles, and chants, and tea brewed from the blue leaves of the *ilecc*."

"*Ilecc* leaves!" their host exclaimed. He turned to Oelefse. "You blokes been doing some serious traveling."

Holding his cup as delicately as if he were at court, the German replied genially. "We had a few awkward moments, yes." He indicated Kelli. "She was very ill. The *ilecc* restored her health, but left her vision turned inside out. Thanks to his research, our friend Cody is Sighted. It is because of that research, which is important and inimical to Those Who Abide, that he and his wife were singled out by them for special attention."

"If not for him," Cody added as he nodded in Oelefse's direction, "I don't think Kelli and I would be here now. Or anywhere else."

Kuwarra nodded sagely. "The Society is glad to help. I am honored in my turn." Rising, he turned and started for a back room. "Got to get some things together. You finish eating. Spend the night here."

"Is there a motel?" Kelli asked hopefully.

That brought forth a burst of laughter so bright and refreshing it seemed to cool the room ten degrees. "A motel! In Warmun! That's a good one, sheila. A motel." Still chuckling to himself, he vanished into the back.

"We will sleep here tonight." Finishing the last of his tea, Oelefse discreetly set his cup aside. They had not been provided with saucers. "Tomorrow we will go into Purnululu."

"What's in there?" Cody was wary of the answer.

His friend would only smile. "This is Tjapu's country, not mine. You will have to ask him. Not *ilecc* bushes, I promise you."

"Something else," the archaeologist murmured.

"Something different. As different as this land is from Austria, I suspect." Reaching out, he patted Kelli's hand. "Whatever it is, we can rely on Tjapu to make good use of it."

"If it doesn't kill us first," Cody felt compelled to point out.

•   •   •

After the comparative cruising comfort of the paved highway, the fifty off-road miles into Purnululu came as more
than a slight shock. In places they were reduced to bouncing and banging along dry creek beds, following signs
that had been battered and weathered almost beyond
recognition. With the Jackaroo grinding over rocks and
stumbling across mini-gorges, by the time the fabled, isolated range itself finally came into view, the two Americans were sore and tired. In contrast, neither of their
elderly companions seemed to have been affected by the
difficult ride.

Ahead loomed the most remarkable collection of hills
Cody had ever seen. He did his best to describe them to
Kelli.

More than anything else, the Bungle Bungles resembled a collection of giant beehives. Horizontally striped
in red, yellow, ochre, and every shade in between, the
domes rose up out of the surrounding rubble like a vision from Bosch. Trees clung to the shady places between
the sandstone cupolas while Livistonia palms hid in cracks
and chasms in the highly eroded rock. As the abused
Jackaroo trundled forward along the dirt and gravel track,
a nail-tailed wallaby burst from a bush to rocket past in
front of them. The spectacular array of mineral-inspired
colors was enhanced by a backdrop of cloudless blue sky.

Turning right, they followed the track until they eventually left it entirely. Behind the wheel, Oelefse paid careful attention to Kuwarra's directions. Cody was acutely
aware that they were leaving behind any semblance of
civilization or development. On the eastern half of the
escarpment were no tourist facilities, no roads, nothing
but beehived sandstone, heat, and the maddening, Dante-
esque flies. To the south lay the empty vastness of the
Great Sandy Desert, thousands of square miles of waste-

land uninhabited save for a few marginal sheep stations and isolated aboriginal communities.

On the rim of the range the terrain was relatively flat and negotiable in the Jackaroo. Peering at the jumble of resplendently striped domes and spires, Cody wondered aloud how they were going to coax the four-wheel drive more than a short distance inward.

"We're not," was Kuwarra's answer. "Got to walk. There's a creek we'll follow. Can't drive on these hills anyway. That pretty banding you see is a crust over the underlying sandstone. Just walk on it wrong and it flakes away."

The archaeologist eyed the hills with new respect. They didn't look half so fragile. "Okay. So we go up a creek. To find what?"

"These hills," Kuwarra asked him, "what they look like to you?"

"Beehives." Cody responded without hesitation. "Big beehives."

"How about eggs?" The Warmun elder was grinning. "They look a little like eggs to you?"

"Maybe a little. Awfully garish for eggs. Easter eggs, maybe."

"S'truth, mate." Kuwarra pointed and Oelefse responded with a sharp turn of the wheel, heading the vehicle into the looming, multicolored hillocks. "Sandstone here, sandstone there, but every now and then you find an egg. That's what we looking for. That's what we got to find to help your woman. Bonzers from the city, they just see rock, rock, everywhere. Walk right past an egg without seeing what it is. Don't matter to the egg 'cause they don't try to break it open. We do different."

Watching the rounded hills, some of them hundreds of feet high, draw near, Cody frowned. "You're saying that some of these domes aren't stone, but eggs?"

"Too right, mate. Bunyip eggs. That's what we gonna do: crack open ourselves a bunyip egg."

Bouncing on the padded bench seat next to her husband, Kelli spoke up. "What do we do then? Make an omelet?"

Roaring with laughter, the aged aborigine slapped his leg. "Bunyip omelet! That's a good one, woman! No, no omelet. We do something else." He nudged Oelefse, who was concentrating on the gorge they were approaching. "You hear that, mate? Feed a lot of folk, that omelet would!"

"All of your community?" Cody asked curiously.

"Maybe. Depend on the bunyip. Maybe feed Warmun, sure." Turning, the white-haired elder met the archaeologist's gaze. "Maybe feed Perth."

Cody was left with that image to ponder as they entered the shallow creek that had eaten a cleft in the rock, allowing them to penetrate the range. Curving, sheer-sided walls closed in on both sides. Even in the shade, it was hot, but nothing like the searing semidesert they had left behind. When the chasm grew too narrow for the Jackaroo, they parked it in a little side canyon. Kuwarra passed out small day packs. Cody and Kelli's contained only food and water. In addition to his pack, the elder carried in one hand a three-foot long wooden tube, a piece of tree that had been decorated with many symbols and dots in white and dark red. Kuwarra defined them as best he could, tracing paths and stopping-places in the Dreamtime, highly stylized animals, and creatures few people would recognize. Cody was one of the few, having seen Interlopers before.

They advanced in silence, following the overachieving trickle of a creek until the water vanished into the sand. Kelli held tight to her husband's guiding arm. Above them the sky was reduced to a narrow, winding blue streak that followed the line of the gorge. Everyone kept a careful eye out for Interlopers, but despite the profusion of native stone, they saw none. Their absence in such a potentially hospitable place struck Cody as peculiar. He said as much to the two old men who were leading them onward.

"The reason is simple enough." Kuwarra explained as though it was the most obvious thing in the world. "They keep away from this place 'cause they scared."

"Scared?" In all his many conversations with Oelefse, Cody could not recall the German mentioning anything that could frighten an Interloper. Enrage them, yes. Through his research the archaeologist had succeeded in doing that himself. But scare?

"What could frighten an Interloper?"

Kuwarra's laughing smile vanished and for once he was wholly serious. "You never seen a bunyip, mate. When you see one, you have your answer."

He did not elaborate. Nor, Cody decided abruptly, did he want him to.

•

Seventeen

Eggs.

Observing the domes and spires through which they were hiking, Cody could not banish the image from his mind: something a hundred feet high, or maybe two, having the appearance of solid, banded sandstone, suddenly rumbling and cracking and splitting wide open to release—what? Every image his brain unwillingly conjured to fill the void was more disturbing than the next.

Kelli helped to calm him. If the danger was that great, she argued, then surely Kuwarra would not have brought them here. There had to be a reason why their actual presence was required. If it was simply a matter of finding and gathering something, some special ingredient for a potion or pill, the elder could have come by himself, or in company with Oelefse, or Oelefse and Cody, just as her husband and his European friend had gone to fetch the blue leaves of the *ilecc* to bring her out of her coma.

Her rationale, Cody realized, was sound. But while he approved of the logic that led to an inarguable conclusion, he didn't like it.

Kookaburras and galahs guffawed in the Livistonia

palms that filled the chasm. Where fast-flowing runoff
from the Wet had scooped depressions in the sand of the
creek bed, dark pools had collected, their depths as still
and shadowed as the dust-free surface of black pearls.
Even in the near perpetual shade, it was incredibly hot.
Sweat poured down everyone's face except Kuwarra's,
staining collars and sleeves. Tjapu Kuwarra did not sweat.
In any event he had nothing to stain, having left everything in the way of clothing back in the Jackaroo but for
a skimpy pair of briefs.

The chasm widened out into a bowl-shaped pit. The
far side was dominated by a vast undercut ledge, a smooth-
ceilinged cavern large enough to hold a thousand people.
Splashing through ankle-deep water, they halted beneath
the ceiling of the impressive natural amphitheater. Even
a whisper was clearly audible, reflected and magnified by
the superb natural acoustics of their red earth surroundings.

Slipping his pack off his back, Kuwarra brought out
an incongruously powder-blue, cheap plastic lady's
makeup kit. From its contents he extracted glutinous paints
and natural resins with which he proceeded to paint his
body from face to feet, not neglecting to dab some bright
reds and yellows in his remarkable beard. Cody looked
on in quiet fascination, doing his best to describe the simple but bold patterns to Kelli. Working in silence, Oelefse
stripped off his own clothes and proceeded to emulate his
friend and colleague. The designs with which he streaked
his pale skin were utterly different from those that decorated the nearly nude form of the aged aborigine.

When both elders turned to face Cody, he wondered
if he would also be expected to offer up his torso for
duty as a canvas. Or worse, Kelli's. Noting the look of
concern on the archaeologist's face, Oelefse hastened to
reassure him.

"You are perceptive, Coschocton Westcott, but you are not a member of the Society. There is work to be done here, and it is for my friend Tjapu and me to do."

Cody nodded understandingly. "What about Kelli and me? What do you want us to do?"

"Stay out of the way." Kuwarra's eyes were roaming the sheer stone walls that enclosed them. "Stand. Watch. And be ready."

"We can do that," Kelli told him. "Where do you have to go next?"

"Where?" Kuwarra gestured expansively. "We are there, miss."

Turning in a slow circle, Cody examined the handsomely banded, wind- and water-washed sandstone. It contained every earth tone imaginable, from deep magenta to bright yellow. He saw nothing but gravel, boulders, weathered stone domes, and sand. Since entering the range they had not seen a single Interloper. They were afraid of this place, their guide had explained. Of the bunyip. What in hell was a bunyip?

Did he want to find out?

Settling himself down on a cool patch of sand by the water's edge, Kuwarra passed something to Oelefse. It was a half-foot long piece of wood, smooth on both sides, shaped something like a squashed banana. Intricate painted patterns decorated both flattened sides. At one of the two pointed ends, a stout knotted string passed through a hand-drilled hole. Oelefse held the string loosely, letting the piece of wood dangle near his ankle.

Taking up the hollow tube he had been carrying, Kuwarra put one open end to his mouth. Beeswax formed a smooth seal between lips and wood. When he blew into it the resultant drone, enhanced by the acoustics of the sandstone amphitheater, spooked every bird from its midday roost for half a mile around. Wings briefly filled the sky overhead before disappearing in all directions.

What the aborigine patriarch played could not be called a tune, but it was surely music, Cody knew. As an archaeologist, he had heard didgeridoo before, though it had been nothing like this. Instead of a hypnotic, barely modulated drone, Kuwarra punctuated his playing with as weird an assortment of whoops, squawks, squeals, and moans as could be found in a haunted house on Allhallows Eve. In his hands the didgeridoo became a living thing, an imprisoned orchestra, an insistent long-distance call to an atavistic past that went beyond music to penetrate to the heart of whatever it was that made its listeners human. It was mesmerizing, enthralling, all-embracing, and the Kija elder played without pausing to breathe, utilizing the traditional cycle breathing that had been developed for use simultaneously with the instrument itself.

Within a banded beehive dome of a hill across the shallow water, something stirred.

As soon as Cody saw the sheer rock face begin to quiver, he put an arm around Kelli and drew her back, instinctively putting room between them and the two elders. Bits and pieces of the highly colored sandstone crust began to flake away from underlying stone, tumbling to the sandy creek bed below. Kuwarra never broke off playing. If anything, his playing grew more insistent, more convoluted, evolving into the didgeridoo equivalent of a fugue. Cody paid less attention to the panoply of sounds than he did to the shuddering stone.

Kelli took an unexpected step forward and pointed. "I can see it!"

The archaeologist squinted, scanning the exfoliating rock. He had to raise his voice to make himself heard above the wail of the ancient musical instrument and the now rapidly peeling cliff face.

"Where? I don't see anything."

"There—it's right there!" She was gesturing emphatically. "Can't you see it?"

Between a band of yellow and a band of mauve, the rock was parting, cracking open, widening to reveal a dark hollow place in the solid stone. To Cody it looked like a mouth opening wide as a pair of colossal lips parted. But that was all he could see.

"Oh—it's coming out!" Kelli took several steps backward, compelling her husband to retreat with her.

"What? What's coming out?" Anxious and frustrated, Cody stared so intently at the widening maw in the cliff that the backs of his eyes began to throb. "I don't see any . . ."

There was a crack of thunder. A crack of thunder in a cloudless, clear blue sky. The two-hundred-foot-high dome split vertically, like a mound of rainbow sherbet cleaved down the middle by a hot butcher knife. From depths within emerged a bluish silhouette, grotesque and malformed beyond imagining. Shimmering and glittering with malevolent fire, it turned a thousand luminescent fangs the length of a man in the direction of the four tiny figures on the sand below. Without warning, preamble, or hesitation, it struck, a descending synthesis of all that was sharp and lethal.

Just before it attacked, Oelefse had begun to whirl the banana-shaped piece of wood over his head, like a loop on the end of a lariat. With each revolution the brightly painted wood thrummed through the air, generating a deep-throated humming like the whir of a colossal, contemplative bumblebee. As the mad aggregate of blue-tinged razors lunged at Kuwarra, the wooden bullroarer struck. Fangs exploded, bursting on contact with the ancient device in a shower of azure sparks that flamed briefly blue before sinking into the sand. Outraged and thwarted, the horrific visage withdrew preparatory to striking again.

"It's an outline!" Clinging tightly to his beloved, Cody tried to shield her as best he could. "Just an electric blue outline. There's nothing else there."

Within the tenuous safety of his arms, Kelli struggled to swallow, and failed. "No, Cody. It's more than that. I—I can see *all* of it."

"But how . . ." As he turned slightly to meet her blank gaze, the rest of the archaeologist's question died in his throat. All he could see was a silhouette, a suggestion, a roiling hint of what the flickering blue enclosed. Damaged, altered, her perception transfigured, Kelli could not see him. But her clouded eyes could see—other things. The truth was right there, blatant as the stone that surrounded them. In spite of himself, despite his fear for his wife's safety and his overriding desire to shield her, he pulled away from what he saw. He could not be blamed for doing so. No one could have withstood the horror he saw then—not even Oelefse.

The bunyip was reflected in her eyes.

As it drew back, gathering itself to strike again, Oelefse whirled to face the two archaeologists. His painted countenance was no longer that of the urbane European gentleman. Like the rest of him, his expression seemed to have slipped back ten thousand years in time. Even as he shouted, he continued to whip the bullroarer over his head while Tjapu Kuwarra sustained the steady drone of the didgeridoo.

"Kelli Westcott! *Inhale!* Take a deep breath. Now, as deep as you can! *Do it!*"

Questions flared like matchheads in Cody's mind, but there was no time for thinking. Reacting to Oelefse's command, a startled Kelli sucked in as much of the ozone-tinged air as she thought she could. Beneath her shirt her

chest expanded with the effort. It coincided with the bunyip's second attack.

Once again the strike was deflected by the disk of
power generated by Oelefse's bullroarer. But this time the
frightful apparition was not hammered backwards. Instead,
reflecting the angle at which it had impacted the bullroarer's circle of influence, it was shunted sideways,
knocked askew. Something caught hold of it, drawing it
forward instead of casting it away. Though it struggled
mightily, twisting and writhing like a runaway dynamo
with awful insensate life, it could not resist.

Cody felt as if he had been struck by a pillow filled
with pudding. The force of it knocked him down, breaking his grip on Kelli's shoulders, then picked him up and
threw him six feet away so that he landed flat on his back
on the soft sand. Looking on in helpless horror and fascination, he watched as a single flash of condensed blue
lightning vanished down his wife's smooth-skinned,
tanned throat.

Kelli sat down hard, her hands at her sides bracing
herself in a sitting position. Startled, dazed, she blinked
several times, as if she had swallowed nothing more than
an errant bug. Putting aside didgeridoo and bullroarer, the
two elders instantly rushed to her aid. As they started to
help her up, a furious Cody brushed them aside.

"What happened?" Trembling with rage, he stared
down at his stunned wife. *"What did you do to her?"*

Oelefse replied gently—more gently than Cody had
ever heard him speak. "Ask her if she can see you, my
friend." The old man nodded encouragingly. "Ask."

The archaeologist did not have to. Her eyes welling
up with tears, Kelli had reached up and was running her
fingers over her husband's features; touching, caressing,
loving. The answer to Oelefse's query was evident in the
way her face moved, the way her smile widened.

"I can see you, Cody. I can see again. Everything."

The fury went right out of him. Whatever hideous marvel he had just witnessed, it had restored her sight. Except for some initial, momentary shock, she seemed none the worse for the experience.

"Most people," he muttered falteringly, "can get by with swallowing a lousy pill to cure what ails them." Then he was bending toward her, his face inclining toward her own, his mouth and lips reaching for the warmth that was so familiar, staring into . . .

With a cry he fell back, stumbling away from her startled face, his trauma greater than hers. *It was still there.* The bunyip was still there—in her newly restored eyes. He had seen it—and it had seen him, staring murderously but impotently back from within the depths of his lover's self and soul.

It wanted out.

Yet, as he gathered himself and struggled to deal with the shock of what he had just seen, it struck him that she seemed to be suffering no ill effects. What had happened, was happening? Did the bunyip now possess her—or she it?

Her expression was one of frightened bewilderment. "Cody, honey—what is it? What's wrong?" She was oblivious to that which was now dwelling within her.

Slowly he walked back to her, putting a hand on each shoulder. "How do you feel? Anything unusual or irregular? What about your eyes?"

"They feel fine. I can see again. They ache a little, and I'm kind of nauseous, but it's nothing I can't handle." In her voice, confusion was paramount. "What's the matter? You look so strange, Cody. Almost as if you're frightened of me."

Still holding her, his expression grim, he turned to confront the other members of the little party. They were observing in silence. "Well? What just happened here? *Should* I be frightened of her? Should we all?"

The two elders exchanged a glance. Oelefse left it to their guide to explain. "It was the only way, mate. The part of her mind that sees right was all cocked sideways, you see. Had to be knocked back into place. Need a big shock to do that, too right!" He gestured at his colleague. "Without me and Ole here, the bunyip maybe come out of its egg and eat you for sure." He ventured an encouraging smile. "Instead, we make a little music, a little magic, and *she* eat *it*. Suck it straight down, your sheila did! Knock her eyeball stuff right back into line."

Cody and Kelli struggled to make sense of the unfathomable. Kuwarra's words were clear enough, but the antediluvian meaning behind them was not.

"Then it hasn't gone away, this bunyip thing? It's still inside her?" Summoning a great effort of will, the archaeologist made himself gaze once more into his wife's eyes. What he saw there would have made a strong man blanch or a weaker love turn away. "I can see it."

Oelefse nodded. "All surgeries have side effects, my young friend."

"Side effects! What are we supposed to do now? Go home and go back to work? Resume a normal life while Kelli walks around with some irate eldritch horror fuming inside her? The idea behind all of this was to keep Those Who Abide *away* from us. Not make them part of the family."

"The bunyip is not an Interloper." Oelefse explained patiently. "It is something else."

"I'll say it is!" Cody's angry voice reverberated off the burnished, buckled sandstone walls of the amphitheater. "It makes the worst Interloper I've seen look like a stuffed toy handout from a fast-food chain."

"Of course we will exorcise it from her." The elderly

German's tone was soothing. "But if you are willing, not here. There is a better place."

"Better place?" Frowning, Cody looked from one composed, impassive elder to the other. Kelli's expression reflected similar uncertainty. "What do you mean, a better place?"

Kuwarra took up the explanation. "Something is on the verge of happening, mate. Something real very bad for the very real world. It got to be stopped, don't you know." He spread his hands wide. "To prevent something real bad you got to use something real bad. Nothing around that's badder than a bunyip." Straining to see, he tried to peer speculatively into Kelli Westcott's eyes. "Especially an angry one."

"So you need this bunyip to—" Breaking off, Cody stared open-mouthed at the two old men. Despite the heat, an all-encompassing coldness ran down his spine, penetrating him to the core. Gracious, concerned, kindly, the two elders gazed back, waiting for him to speak—a pair of evenly matched, compassionate cobras.

"How long?" he finally found the wherewithal to whisper. Realization had stunned him beyond anger. Deeply confused, Kelli started to say something, only to be hushed by her husband. The gesture alone was enough to quiet her. Cody never tried to silence her. Few people did. Of those few, rarely did anyone succeed. The look on her life-mate's face was enough to kill any words aborning.

Oelefse sighed heavily. "From before the beginning, my friend."

"Don't call me that!" Cody was beyond irate.

"Your call for help was not the only one considered, you know." Picking his briefcase off the sand, the old man opened it and withdrew a small towel from its depths. As he spoke, he wiped paint and stain from his face and body. "But because of your backgrounds it was decided that you two would be the least vulnerable to the revelations that were bound to follow."

"You used us." A still disbelieving Cody was shaking his head slowly from side to side. "You helped us because you needed a vessel. Just like an Interloper needs a human vector. You needed someone to serve as a bottle for a bunyip."

Oelefse's voice was still firm, but he was beginning to look more than a little uncomfortable. "It could have been anyone, but your wife's condition was serious. Saving her was our first priority."

"Was it? Was it really? Tell me something." Letting go of Kelli, he took a belligerent step forward. "Could you have cured her, brought her out of her comatose state, without adversely impacting her vision? Without leaving her unable to see her world? The real world?" He did not let the ensuing silence linger before raising his voice. *"Could you?"*

With obvious reluctance, Oelefse nodded. "I could lie to you, my friend, but that is not the way of the Society—usually. *Ja*, it could have been done that way—but then she would not have been able to serve as a suitable alembic for the bunyip. And we need such an alembic, Cody Westcott. We need it very badly. Time was—time is, short." He nodded toward the solemn-visaged Tjapu Kuwarra. "As you have just heard, something very bad is on the verge of transpiring. Something that must be prevented at any cost."

" 'Any cost'." Cody's tone was mocking. "You mean *our* cost. Kelli's cost. Not yours."

"We are all at risk," Oelefse said adamantly. "You remember the *ilecc*?"

"As I recall, I was busy with other things while you were picking leaves."

"A tea brewed from the stems of the *ilecc* would have

been enough to restore your wife's sight to normal. In contrast, the tea of the blue leaves left her vision altered and her self open. Open and able to receive and store almost anything. Such is the power of the *ilecc* shrub. Now she has her sight back, and additionally from now on will be able to perceive Those Who Abide as well as you or I. Only one small thing has been added."

"Small thing?" Kelli had started the conversation far, far behind everyone else, but was catching up quickly. "If that same ghastly specter that I saw is what's inside me now, it was as big as an airport terminal!" She swallowed. "No wonder I'm feeling nauseous."

"It is only temporary," Oelefse assured her. "Tjapu and I can coax it out at any time."

"Then bring it out now. Right now!" a furious Cody demanded.

"This not the best place, mate." Kuwarra's response was as resolute as his smile. "Not the time, either." His gaze drifted northward. "Soon. Where we can maybe stop this thing that's otherwise going to happen. No, not maybe. Got to stop it. It falls to us four here. It been put in our hands."

"Well, Kelli and I don't want any part of it! You hear me?" The distraught archaeologist's hands fluttered in his wife's direction. "Get it out of her! Make it go away. Now!"

"Maybe first you have a listen." Kuwarra's smile shrank but did not disappear entirely. "What we done here today we don't do lightly, mate. It really really is important. Nobody toys with a bunyip for fun."

"That's real reassuring," Cody replied bitterly. "I suppose there's no risk to Kelli involved in waiting, either?" He did not include himself in the equation because he did not care about himself.

"Nobody say that." The aborigine elder continued. "No

lies now, mate. There's risk to us all. Anytime you got to deal with something this big and bad, there's always risk."

Turning away from the patriarch, Cody murmured solicitously to his wife. "How are you feeling, love? You still okay? How about the nausea?"

"It's still there, but it's not getting any worse." She hesitated. "At least, not so far."

Biting back the sarcasm that rushed to his lips, but that he knew would have been wasted on the stolid pair of elders, the archaeologist had to content himself with glaring at them. They waited with maddening repose for his response. "Okay—we'll listen. But if we decline to get involved in your 'real bad thing,' whatever it is, then you have to promise, to swear to me, to drive this monstrosity out of my wife. Is that understood?"

"Unequivocally." Pivoting so that he faced westward, Oelefse raised a hand and pointed. "Do you know what lies over there, that way?"

Kelli replied before her husband. "I remember you talking about it. The town of Hall's Creek."

"Beyond that." The elderly German waved, trying to stretch his fingers to encompass more space. At this point, Cody would not have been surprised if those manicured digits had actually grown a foot or two. But they remained their normal, natural length as Oelefse spoke.

"The town of Broome. The Pacific Ocean." Kelli responded absently, her restored vision constantly distracting her with a view of an interesting rock or intriguing insect.

"Farther still." The tired old man turned back to them. "I will tell you. India lies there. And next to India, Pakistan."

It was a struggle for Cody to remain focused on Kelli's tribulation and not to show interest in Oelefse's words.

"So what? They're big, all right, and I guess sometimes they're bad, but what's that got to do with us? Or with your Society, for that matter?"

Having removed the last vestiges of paint from his face, Oelefse moved on with the cleansing rag to his chest and arms. "They do not like one another, these two countries. They are favorite habitats for Those Who Abide. So much misery concentrated in one area provides them with an ideal feeding ground. Any large city in either country contains more healthy, rapacious Interlopers than any state in America, or Germany. They are among the most heavily infested places in the world."

"That makes senses," the archaeologist conceded grudgingly.

"It is not enough for them, my young friend. Those Who Abide are never satisfied. They are always hungry for more. More suffering, more despair, more wretchedness. They grow and multiply, and as they do so, they demand more nourishment; the provender of woe. To create opportunities for feeding, they will do whatever is within their power to increase it. Pitiful incidents may be sparked by several Interlopers working together."

Thinking back, Cody remembered the bicyclists at the university who had nearly entrapped him: collision and collusion. "I know. I've seen them at work."

"The greater the number of Interlopers toiling together, the more extensive the grief they can induce. In the subcontinent they have had great success. Even as we stand here, in this isolated place, they are planning another tragedy. Have been planning it for some time. Have you forgotten that I once spoke to you about such momentous malignant events? When first I came to your house to offer my help in curing your wife?"

Cody thought back, remembering. With a shock he recalled that the scholarly German had even mentioned India at the time. "So this is what you were talking about? Something that's going to happen in India or Pakistan?"

"It will take place in neither country, and in both. You have heard of Kashmir?"

"The northern province that both countries claim? Sure; we follow the news," Kelli said, finding herself distracted from her inspection of a school of small gray-white fish that were swimming just beneath the surface of the shaded desert pool. Joining in the conversation also helped to take her mind off the nightmarish phantasm that was now abiding somewhere within her unsettled self. "They've been arguing over dominion of the place for decades."

"Not just arguing." Nearly free of paint, Oelefse dropped the busy towel to his legs. "They have fought several wars over the territory. People die there all the time. One man's terrorist is another man's freedom fighter." His voice fell slightly. "In the past years, something has changed. Something that raises the specter of violence and destruction on a scale that reduces everything that has gone before it to a tantrum between overgrown children. Both sides, both countries, are now in possession of nuclear weapons and the means to deliver them."

"We know that." Cody found himself becoming engaged despite his protests. "Kelli just told you—we follow the news." All of a sudden he did not like the tack the older man's conversation was taking. Given his wife's present unhappy condition, there were very, very few phrases powerful enough to divert him from her situation. In the liturgy of distractions, the wholly unexpected mention of "nuclear weapons" was one of the few that would qualify.

"Their existence must please the Interlopers," Kelli presumed.

"It does not just please them." Wiping the last of the

paint from his calves, Oelefse neatly folded the now deeply stained towel and slipped it back into his seemingly bottomless briefcase. "It excites them. It tempts them, it draws them together, it sets them to the most malicious scheming and planning. They have been conspiring for some time now."

"To what end?" Cody couldn't help himself. He had been drawn into Oelefse's recital as neatly as dirt down a drain.

The older man took a deep breath. "If nothing is done, some time within the next couple of weeks, a large mechanized Indian invasion force that has been assembling in secret north of Rajput will make a dash for the Kalkuma Pass. The only road suitable for tanks, armored personnel carriers, and heavy mobile artillery is presently clear of snow and obstructions. They will attempt to take possession of and secure all of Kashmir. Once through the pass, they will split up to eliminate any local or Pakistani resistance. Designated elements will drive all the way to the border with Pakistan and dig in, ready to repel any counterattack. All this will come about because extremist elements of the Bharatiya Janata, the Hindu nationalist party, have seen their strength slowly slipping away due to the failure of their economic policies. They hope that by thrusting a jingoistic diversion before the masses, they will be able to shore up their flagging popularity.

"Much the weaker country, but with a highly trained and well-equipped military, the Pakistanis will respond immediately. They will be driven off by the entrenched Indians. Extremist Muslim elements within the government and the army will then demand that the 'honor' of the nation be upheld." His gaze unwavering, Oelefse was staring hard at the archaeologist. "You can guess what will happen next. The Pakistanis will employ tactical nuclear weapons in the field against their Indian adversaries.

The Indians will be driven back from the border into Kashmir, but they will not be driven out.

"They will then respond with their own—devices. The conflict will escalate until one side or the other attempts to trump its opponent through the use of nuclear blackmail. When this bluff is called, as it inevitably will be, a small bomb will be fired at a large city." He let his words linger in the dry, desiccated air. "After that, the limited nuclear arsenals of both sides will be brought into full play. Millions will die. Many millions more will be horribly scarred and mutilated. Cancer and radiation poisoning will doom additional millions, as well as untold numbers of children yet unborn."

"Those Who Abide," Kuwarra added as he lazily stirred the sand with the end of his didgeridoo, "will get stuck right into this people barbecue. The poor folk won't even know what is happening to them."

"But that is not the worst of it." Oelefse waited patiently for a response.

"There's worse than that?" Kelli had momentarily forgotten her nausea.

"Once the full might of arms of both countries is involved, they will call upon their erstwhile allies for help. Linked by religious and cultural ties, the entire Middle East Gulf region may throw its economic and military muscle onto the side of the Pakistanis. This will have the ancillary effect of driving world oil and therefore energy prices higher than the steeples at Cologne, consequently sending the world economy spinning into chaos. Seeing a grand opportunity to defeat a hereditary enemy with which it has fought similar border wars in the past, the Chinese will open a second front in northeastern India. Assailed from two sides, the Indians will then swallow their pride and ask for outside help." Oelefse nodded at the stunned archaeologist.

"That may bring your country, and mine, and the rest of the developed world into the conflict. At that point no one can predict what might happen, except to say that Those Who Abide will grow sleek and contented. It is not the Black Plague, or perhaps even the Second World War—but it could be very, very bad. All of this, of course, from the military buildup in northern India to its projected conclusions, has been aided and abetted by those humans infested with Those Who Abide. Without their incitement, such a confrontation would be unlikely, if not outright impossible."

"You say 'may' and 'could.' " Cody's earlier anger had fled and he was much subdued.

"The Society's predictors cannot see much beyond the initial clash between the subcontinent's dominant countries. Subsequent to that, all is hazy speculation. But as to the course of the initial hostilities, they are confident."

"How can they be?" Kelli's expression was anguished. "How can they know all this is going to happen? Can some of your Society people see into the future?"

"No, not exactly." The old man smiled gently. "Several thousand years of knowing one's opponent and striving to outthink it leads to specific techniques useful in forecasting certain trends. Also, we have people in all countries, those of the subcontinent included. We have been tracking this secret military buildup on the part of India ever since it was initiated. We know their plans and have recorded their stratagems. From there, extrapolation can be made with a reasonable degree of accuracy."

"And you," Cody had already realized, "you and the Society, you plan to try and prevent this from happening."

Both elders nodded simultaneously. "We must."

"And for that you need something like a bunyip. What

for—to frighten the troops and keep them from advancing?"

"That would not work." Oelefse explained patiently. "Its appearance would trouble only a few soldiers, and would be explained away as a clever Pakistani deception by the fanatics in their ranks. The assault would proceed with little or no delay. Our predictors note that the Indian advance has been carefully timed. If it cannot be carried out this year, before winter snows in the Karakorams close the Pass, then support for it within the ranks of the Indian military will fade. By spring, the political power of the Bharatiya Janata is forecast to be much reduced. The threat of military action to divert people's attention from the state of the economy will evaporate, and a new, less extreme coalition government will take power."

"If you're not going to use it to try and scare soldiers, then what do you need a bunyip for?" Cody pressed him.

"You already know that, mate." Using his didgeridoo, a grinning Kuwarra blew a soft honk at a galah winging its way over the chasm. "To frighten away Interlopers."

Husband and wife exchanged a confused glance. "What Interlopers?" Kelli asked. "The ones in India? Is that where we're going next?"

"Not at all." Turning slightly, Oelefse pointed northward. "We need the bunyip to frighten them away from the Hook. There are several that can be utilized. This one, having the strongest association, will be defended. After the guardians are driven off, we can yoke the bunyip and make it pull. It will not take much of a tug to do what must be done."

Yoke the bunyip. Cody found himself yearning for the comforts of home and the warm, enshrouding predictability of staid academia. "If we're not going to India, then where? Pakistan? And what the hell kind of a 'hook' are you talking about?"

Oelefse smiled cheerfully. "You will see, when we get to Hoskins."

"Hoskins?" Kelli made a face. "Is that near Perth? Or Darwin?"

"Somewhat farther north," the German told her. "On the island of New Britain, which is part of northern Papua New Guinea."

"New Guinea!" Overwhelmed by seemingly unrelated places, persons, and events, Cody was too exhausted to object. "I thought the danger was in Kashmir?"

"So it is, mate." A relaxed Tjapu Kuwarra casually slung his didg over a shoulder and started back down the narrow rock-walled gash in the Earth that led toward their waiting four-by-four. "But the Hook ain't."

Eighteen

Lost in individual contemplation, neither of the West‐cotts sought to press their elderly guides for details during the long ride back to Kununurra. The specter of looming nuclear war on the Indian subcontinent was more than enough to keep their thoughts occupied. Unspoken between husband and wife was any thought of abandoning the two elderly men to return home to America. If they were telling the truth, then millions of lives were at stake. In that context, their own minor personal problems receded to insignificance.

Besides which, Kelli could hardly return to a normal life of housekeeping and teaching while carrying around a condensed bunyip in her belly. Somehow Cody doubted even a prescription purgative would be strong enough to alleviate the condition. And if by some chance it did, it might well result in consequences far worse than their present situation. In essence, then, they had no choice but to "volunteer" their support.

From Kununurra they flew to Darwin, and then by small plane to Port Moresby. As they were crossing the coral-encrusted Arafura Sea that separated the island of

New Guinea from continental Australia, Cody jokingly asked the ever upbeat Kuwarra if his passport was in order, mimicking the admonition the archaeologist had heard on more than one occasion from Oelefse. By way of response, the aborigine elder brought forth the document in question and handed it to Cody for inspection. Upon opening the small booklet, the younger man was confronted with a bewildering mass of official stamps and impressions that covered every available square inch of every page. Reading the names was like skimming a worldwide travel agency's main brochure. Kelli's eyes widened as she looked over her husband's shoulder at the battered pages.

Abashed, he handed it back to its owner. "I owe you an apology. When we first met you I never would have supposed you were a world traveler like . . ." His words trailed away as he became even more embarrassed by the implications of his comment.

Kuwarra was not offended. "Like my good mate and colleague Oelefse? Why would you think that? Because I live in a small house in a tiny community in the outback?" His grin was, as always, infectious. "The Society got members everywhere. It has to, mate, or we'd all of us be bloody walking birdhouses for Those Who Abide." He slipped the thoroughly astonishing passport back into his shirt pocket. "You being archaeologists, you and your woman got to visit Heidelberg some day. See the scrolls saved from the library at Alexandria, that sort of thing. Very cool stuff." The plane banked to starboard and he leaned his face against the window. Ahead and below, ravine-cut green-clad mountains towered above a dusty coastal plain and turquoise sea.

From Port Moresby they flew across the lofty spine of the world's second largest island, until the pilot announced their imminent arrival at Hoskins. Looking out the window, Cody and Kelli saw a smaller replica of New Guinea itself emerge beneath the plane. Though not as large, New Britain was a huge island in its own right; an impressive, mountainous crescent more than three hundred miles from end to end that averaged some forty often impenetrable miles across.

"A difficult place to get around," Oelefse informed them as the Fokker began its final descent. "There is no road from north to south and no road across. Only a little potholed pavement here and there on the west coast, then tracks. Lots of tracks. And the Hook."

Having made the discovery at the beginning of the interisland flight that a Fokker F-28 has less leg room than the average baby carriage, Cody struggled to massage some feeling back into his long, cramped legs. "How do you know so much about such an obscure place?"

"When one joins the Society, the first thing one is taught is the location of those places on the Earth that possess distinctive characteristics unfamiliar to contemporary science. But I am also familiar with this part of the world from ordinary secondary school. For many decades, this was a German colony. We are presently flying over the Bismarck Sea, you know."

"What happened to the German presence here?" Kelli's expression reflected her internal discomfort. Despite the best efforts of her husband and friend, she had been suffering from recurrent nausea all the way from Australia. Dramamine, they had discovered, did not work on bunyips.

"The Australians happened," Oelefse told her, "followed by the First World War. But reminders of the early colonial presence are still scattered across these islands."

Hoskins was a ramshackle collection of westward facing buildings on the shores of Kimbe Bay. The commercial hub of the central and southern half of the island, it was being dragged kicking and screaming into the twenty-first century. Aspects of the old South Seas clung to it like lost adjectives from a novel by Conrad: wisps of clapboard buildings on posts and smiling dark-skinned women hauling fruit and chickens and children in the brightly colored woven string bags known as *bilums*.

There was no road across the ragged, emerald-draped spine of the island, but there were a number of well-used trails. Crossing on horseback, they arranged for final supplies in the town of Pomio before proceeding inland once more. The main trail terminated at Ora, a tightly knit knot of wood-and-thatch houses little changed from those built in the previous century. Naked children gawked at them out of wide eyes while suspicious village elders sat with their arms wrapped around their knees and stared solemnly at the outsiders. Ora saw perhaps a handful of visitors a year, and that only in a good year.

Dismounting, Oelefse began transferring supplies from saddlebags into a backpack. As always, the ubiquitous briefcase never left his side. Draped in a long cotton cloak decorated with intricate symbols and animal designs, Kuwarra was gazing deep into the mist-swathed jungle that enclosed them on all sides.

"From here we walk," the elderly German was telling them. "This is a place where the world stumbles. The local people will go no farther." He gestured inland. "North of here lies a mountain called The Father, that the locals know as Ulawun. It is over seven thousand feet high and cloaked in impenetrable rain forest." Listening to him declaim on what lay ahead, watching him prepare for a conflict whose parameters remained unknown, Karl Heinrich Oelefsenten von Eichstatt struck Cody as a cross between Rambo and Geppetto, with a pinch of Merlin thrown in.

Retching sounds made him look elsewhere. Poor Kelli

was standing at the edge of the forest wall, throwing up again. She had done so at least once every day since leaving Purnululu. She would continue to do so, an apologetic Oelefse explained, until the time came to void the bunyip. Every upchuck was tinged, however delicately, a light blue. The locals observed the sick white woman stolidly. Once informed of the visitors' intended destination, any hint of sympathy had fled from the village. They were not hostile, but neither did they offer any help. Sensible folk did not seek the slopes of Mount Ulawun. Truly dangerous *raskol* bands used that country to hide from the law, and it had forever been the abode of malicious spirits.

Bidding farewell to their guides and horses, the four travelers struck out into the jungle, following the faintest of paths through the turgid, cloud-blanketed rain forest. Rustling sounds in the bush hinted at the hesitant passage of tree kangaroos and giant rats, while the spasmodic hollering of unseen birds-of-paradise echoed their progress.

They spent the night by the side of a megapode nest, a huge mound of decomposing leaves and forest-floor litter that the peculiar bird used to incubate its eggs. Volcanic heat rising from the ground aided the parent birds in maintaining a comfortable temperature for their offspring. It also warded off the dampness that rapidly descended on the travelers.

Bidding them draw near, Oelefse unfolded a map alongside the fluorescent lantern as Kuwarra used a shirt to ward off entranced moths the size of dinner plates.

"See here," he told them, tracing lines and locales on the wrinkled paper, "out here in the western Bismarck Sea near little Aua Island the point of the Hook lies embedded deep in the ocean floor. It then runs in a perfect, unbroken curve through the Ninigo and Hermit Islands, on through the much larger island of Manus, before rising out of the sea at New Hanover." He drew his finger across the map in a slow downward arc. "The curve of the Hook continues through New Ireland and becomes the northern tip of New Britain. Here near Mount Ulawun lies its easternmost point. At this place it begins to disrupt the crust of the Earth. The heat you feel beneath you tonight is of volcanic origin, as are all these larger islands. The Hook then bends back toward the mainland of New Guinea, giving rise to volcanic islands all along the way. Karkar, Manam, Kairiru—all active, and very dangerous, volcanoes." Folding the map, he brought out another. A world map this time, Cody noted.

"You can see clearly where the line attached to the Hook goes, running perfectly straight down into the crust of the planet." His finger moved as he spoke. "The line ends here, where it is secured to the mantle."

Cody could have laid out the path with a ruler. Unbending, unvarying, never deviating, the line ran from the north coast of New Guinea, across southeast Asia, to terminate under . . .

Kashmir.

"Fortunate coincidence." Kelli stared at the map.

"Not at all." Oelefse proceeded to refold the map. "Other hooks are tied to other localities. We are fortunate only in that the one we require lies near to Tjapu's homeland. It has saved us some traveling. The effort will be the same."

"About that effort," Cody wondered aloud. "Just what is it we're supposed to do here?"

"Use the Hook, of course." Oelefse smiled at him. "To do so we must get to its easternmost point. Then you will see."

It took them several days of tramping through the sodden undergrowth to reach a ridge that was dominated by eroded needles of limestone. Surrounded by innumerable other, smaller versions of itself, the spire a triumphant Oelefse singled out was not especially distinctive. In a karst landscape, Cody knew, such spectacular rock formations were the geologic norm. To him and his wife the whitish stone monolith, festooned with ferns and epiphytes and clinging bushes, did not stand out among its disinte grating brethren.

"We will set ourselves up at its base." Thumbs tucked under the straps of his backpack, the elderly German led them forward. "If all goes well, we will be on our way back to Ora Village by nightfall."

All might indeed have gone as well as Oelefse hoped, and his prediction come true, had it not been for one complication.

They were not alone on the ridge.

There were fifteen or twenty of them, Cody estimated hastily. Certainly too many to fight. Having no experience with the notorious *raskol* gangs of Papua New Guinea, he could not tell if these were more or less scruffy and threatening than the average band of local miscreants. What surprised him most was their stature. Perhaps half hailed from the highlands of the main island; typical of their tribes, they averaged less than five and a half feet in height. The ferocity of their appearance made them appear considerably taller.

Most were armed with traditional weapons: stone axes, spears, bush knives, or bows and arrows fashioned from the flexible stalks of the black palm. Half a dozen carried firearms, including a trio of homemade shotguns made of iron plumbing pipe, with nails for hammers. Two of the grim-faced men wielded AK-47's while the apparent leader wore an army-issue Glock pistol at his waist.

They emerged from their hiding places behind the monolith and its cousins, spreading out to form a semicircle in front of the travelers. Either it had not occurred to them to encircle the visitors to prevent their escape, or more likely, they knew they could easily run down the swiftest of the intruders. After a brief exchange among themselves in Melanesian trade pidgin, the leader stepped forward and addressed them in broken English. His eyes lingered entirely too long on Kelli Westcott for Cody's liking. But neither their hostile stares nor their eclectic collection of weapons was what worried the archaeologist the most.

Every last one of them, as near as Cody could tell, was host to an Interloper.

"We not get many tourists up here. You want to see Mount Ulawun, you will need guides." The pistol-toting leader wore a broad, confident smirk. "You hire us."

Oelefse, who could perceive the roiling, shifting shapes of the abiding Interlopers as clearly as his younger companions, nodded tersely. "We are willing to do that. How much do you charge?"

The headman glanced at his men. A few chuckled softly, whispering among themselves. "First we take you to see Mount Ulawun. Then you give us everything you got, including your clothes. Then maybe we don't kill you. That fair, is it not?"

"You can have my clothes now." Kuwarra began to undo his colorful cloak, a masterpiece of traditional aboriginal art.

The chief *raskol* gestured sharply. "Maybe we let you keep yours, brother. Maybe we even let you share a little bit." His eyes had roamed back to Kelli, who was standing as close to her husband as possible.

"We can share right now, mate." Having removed his cloak, Kuwarra flung it in the direction of the leader. Startled, the other man reached up to ward it off. Wrapping itself around his upper body, the cloak continued to flutter and pulsate. The way it moved reminded Cody of the flapping wings of a bat. The analogy drew strength from the prominence on the back of the cloak of a beautifully rendered flying fox. Perhaps the cloak drew some kind of strength from the exquisitely rendered icon as well.

Cursing and flailing at the confining cloth, the *raskol* struggled with the cloak. As he did so, the cloak fought back. The nearest members of the band rushed to aid their chief. Momentarily flustered, their heavily armed colleagues could only look on in bewilderment. As they did so, Kuwarra unslung his didgeridoo from his back, his movements as swift and precise as those of a samurai unsheathing his sword. The notes he proceeded to blow were unlike anything Cody had heard before, even at Purnululu.

Attention shifted away from the lurching, cloak-enveloped *raskol* to the elderly aborigine and his braying instrument. A couple of the highlanders started in his direction. As they did so, Kelli abruptly staggered several steps backward and clutched at her lower abdomen with both hands. Traveling from her ears, the eerie drone had finally reached her stomach.

Something was emerging from between her lips. Something dark blue, noxious—and angry.

"Quickly, my friend—come with me! *Schnell, schnell!*" Pulling on Cody's wrist, Oelefse was dragging him toward the monolith with one hand. In the other he held his stained, somewhat battered, but still intact briefcase.

"But Kelli—!" Cody struggled to resist the old man's surprisingly powerful pull.

"She is safe with Tjapu. Hurry, while there is time!"

Against his will, Cody felt himself hauled, reluctant and stumbling, toward the looming limestone tower. Its peak submerged in fog, it looked no different from the others nearby. He wondered what unseen features distinguished it in Oelefse's eyes.

Behind them, chaos had broken out. Drawn forth by
the bawling drone of the didgeridoo, the enraged bunyip
erupted from the prison of Kelli Westcott's belly to find
itself confronted by an ancient enemy. A couple of bursts
from the Kalashnikovs passed through it as if through air.
Massive, tenebrous blue tentacles lashed like whips. They
caused only a shudder in the dense human matter of the
raskols as they passed through their fleshy bodies, but
upon contact, the Interlopers so struck shriveled and died
in frightful convulsions. Echoes of elsewhere, their eerie,
otherworldly screams lingered in the air long after their
passing.

Standing protectively over Kelli's gasping, retching
form, the aborigine elder continued to blow the didgeridoo as the *raskols* staggered and fell. Driven mad, one
sprinted right off a nearby cliff, spinning and tumbling
to the rain forest below. Others clutched at their heads
and screamed or moaned as the unsuspected unearthly en-
tities they hosted were flayed from within. By the time
Cody and Oelefse reached the base of the Hook, all but
two of the band had been laid flat on the damp earth,
weeping and wailing and twitching helplessly.

Having swept the ridge of its archenemies, the mad-
dened bunyip sought new foes. Outlines of multiple eyes
settled immediately on the two humans who were exerting themselves at the base of the monolith. With a cry
like a bad wind rising, it flowed down the slight slope
toward them, tentacles lashing, multiple mouths agape.

From the briefcase Oelefse had drawn forth a rolled-
up net of glistening twine that shone like spider silk. He
tossed one end to the archaeologist and began to back
away. Only when the twine was fully extended did the
old man point at the limestone pinnacle and shout.

"Now, my young friend! Cast it up, over the top!"

A disbelieving Cody frowned at the hundred-foot-high

spire. "What, this—fishing net? What good will that do?"
The twine was light as air in his fingers, which meant
that while its weight presented no problems, having no
mass would make it next to impossible to throw any distance.

"Just throw!" Oelefse was watching the bunyip, slough-
ing downslope toward them. Thus far it had slaughtered
only Interlopers. The more its azure tint deepened, the
longer it lingered, the denser it became. Another minute
or two would see it sufficiently solidified in this reality
to where it could begin to impact humans. They had very
little time. "On three! *Ein, zwei . . . !*"

Given no time to think, Cody did as he was told. To
his considerable surprise, the net soared up into the mist
as if of its own volition, easily cresting the point of rock
and floating down the other side. On either side of the
spire, the loose ends hung trailing in the air.

Something slammed into the ground nearby. Eyes wide,
Cody saw the incensed bunyip swiftly bearing down on
them. Its rapidly curdling footsteps began to have an impact on the earth. Upslope, Kelli was sitting up and
screaming. The drone of the didgeridoo had drifted, swallowed by distance. Dimly, he heard Oelefse shouting at
him.

"Now—*run!*"

Stumbling backwards, Cody fought for balance and did
as he was told, his long legs carrying him downslope as
he ducked beneath the bottom flap of the glistening net.
Limestone boulders protruding from the rich, loamy soil
threatened to trip him up, and the steepness of the grade
promised a serious, possibly fatal fall if he lost his footing. Behind him, the bunyip howled insanely, tentacles
reaching for the two humans still standing.

It crashed into the net that lay draped over the apex
of the monolith. Instantaneously entangled, it flailed and

struck out wildly. The impact of its headlong rush generated a rumbling sound Cody immediately recognized
from the time he had spent in South America. It was at
once familiar and terrifying.

Earthquake.

Expending every iota of the unimaginable energy to
which it was heir, the bunyip fought to free itself from
the increasingly restrictive netting. As it did so, it yanked
the entire limestone pillar infinitesimally forward. Yanked
the Hook, Cody realized as he was thrown to the ground
and found himself rolling downhill.

Deep within the Earth's crust, the effect of the bunyip's sudden, violent lunge was disproportionately magnified with increasing distance. The quake thus generated
rolled up through the outer islands of New Guinea and
down through the mainland. Karkar and Manam volcanoes erupted simultaneously, spewing hot ash and fiery
lava into a pristine sea. From the Gazelle Peninsula to
the mountains of the north, the ground trembled and
heaved. There was fear, but no panic. The inhabitants of
one of the most seismically active parts of the world were
used to such tremors.

Its kinetic energy growing by orders of magnitude, the
tectonic oscillation raced down the length of the Hook,
rattling every city and village in Irian Jaya as it raced
northwestward beneath the Celebes Sea. Passing deep
under Indochina, it did no more than shake teacups in Da
Nang and disturb priests' prayers in Mandalay. To anyone able to track its progress it would have seemed that
its strength had been lost, dissipated in the depths of the
continental crust. In reality, the exact opposite was true,
but the effects did not become apparent until the traveling fluctuation reached the end of the Hook—sunk securely into the fabric of the planet deep beneath the Deosai
Range.

In a part of the world where a mountain must rise above twenty-five thousand feet simply to be considered high, twenty-one thousand-foot Muat Kangri drew little notice. Ignored by international climbers and locals alike, its comparatively moderate slopes overlooked the pass between the villages of Kargil and Marul, between Indian held and Pakistani-controlled Kashmir. Through that pass ran the only paved road between the two disputed territories. It was through this defile that the massive Indian force that had been assembling in secret in the city of Srinagar planned to roll.

Muat Kangri, however, possessed one characteristic the taller, more impressive mountains that surrounded it lacked: Its base, buried deep within the Earth, was the northernmost terminus of the Hook.

Striking with incalculable force, the ascending oscillation that had traveled unseen and largely unfelt beneath the Earth's surface all the way from east New Britain wrenched at the root of the mountain like a dentist tugging on a rotten tooth. Had anyone been present to document the aftermath, it would have been noted that the entire bulk of the mountain actually shifted to the northwest some two and a half inches. The result was a powerful but deep earthquake whose effects were devastating but highly localized.

The most immediate and noticeable effect was the colossal avalanche and accompanying landslide that roared down the southern slopes of Muat Kangri, completely obliterating the road through the pass. It would take, declared the engineers who arrived on the scene days later, months to clear away enough rubble to allow even one-lane, one-way traffic to inch its way through the entombed pass.

No military buildup the size of the one at Srinagar could go unnoticed for so long. Quietly, as unobtrusively

as possible, it was disbanded, tanks and troop carriers and
mechanized artillery dispersing to their accustomed bases
throughout the northern portion of the subcontinent. No
one knew how close the two countries had come to war
and possible nuclear catastrophe. Subsequently weakened
at the polls and in the elections that followed, the radi-
cal Bharatiya Janata party was never again in a position
to contemplate so extreme a mobilization of aggressive
forces in the vicinity of Kashmir-Jammu.

Drawing the bullroarer from his briefcase, a perspiring Oelefse began to whirl it over his head. The deep-
throated drone rose above the hum of the forest and the
muted shriek of the entangled bunyip. With his free hand
he extracted something else from the open case and tossed
it toward his younger companion. Cody caught the ob-
long object reflexively. The shape of it was vaguely familiar.

"What the hell am I supposed to do with this?" Shouting to be heard above the moan of the bullroarer and the
wailing of the bunyip, he held high a solid-gold, intricately inscribed kazoo.

"Blow on it! When I give you the word, blow with all
your strength!" Oelefse was spinning the bullroarer faster
and faster. It was an indistinguishable blur now, its basso
groan an abrasive howl that sounded like whole mountains grinding past one another.

"But," the archaeologist began, "I don't know how to
pl—!"

"NOW!" Matching velocity to direction, Oelefse let go
of the string, sending the whistling bullroarer flying toward the bunyip just as the cerulean monstrosity finally
broke free of its bonds and came hurtling down the slope
toward them. Immediately, the old man threw himself to
the ground, face down, and covered his head with his
hands.

Vacating every alveolus in his lungs, Cody blew what sounded to him like an extremely sour but very loud note on the kazoo, whereupon he did his best to imitate his mentor's actions. As he hit the ground, he felt the wind of a razor-edged blue tentacle descending toward him and smelled the fetid, otherworldly breath of the bunyip on his neck.

Then it exploded.

Cobalt light suffused the surrounded atmosphere, tingeing the air with an actinic aroma of ozone and scorched flesh. Daring to raise his eyes ever so slightly, the archaeologist's jaw dropped as he observed the graceful, lazy fall of blue snow. Twinkling brightly as they struck the ground, the fragments of detonated bunyip left little black streaks where they seared the earth. Several struck him and he leaped unbidden to his feet, slapping and flailing at the hot spots on his clothing. Nearby, Oelefse was performing the same energetic dance, albeit in a more dignified and reserved Teutonic manner.

When he was reasonably certain he was no longer on fire, a panting Cody fought his way back up the slope. A sobbing Kelli met him halfway, near the base of the limestone spire. Tjapu Kuwarra had recovered his cloak from the indisposed leader of the *raskols* and had wrapped it around her. Clutching his didgeridoo, he stood in shorts and shirt, his eyes alive with delight, his white beard streaked with blue as if he had pushed his face deep into a brightly colored birthday cake.

"Quite a bang the bunyip makes, s'truth. She'll be right now." Glancing over at the dazed, sluggishly recovering *raskols*, he made a face and raised his didg as if to blow in their direction. Yelping and moaning, the thoroughly intimidated would-be assailants staggered for the cover of the forest. Much to their surprise, they found that despite their horrific, mysterious encounter on the mountain, to a man they felt healthier and happier than any of them had in quite some time.

"The explosive situation in Kashmir?" Cody thought to ask when he and Kelli at last eased their tight embrace.

Kuwarra and Oelefse exchanged a glance before the elderly German replied. "If everything there happened akin to everything here, then it should by now have been alleviated, we believe."

Kelli was shaking her head in disbelief. "How do you know that? How can you tell?"

"Everything work here," a grinning Kuwarra told her. "No reason why everything should not work there." Taking a deep breath, he surveyed the now tranquil, fog-shrouded mountainside. "Beaut country, this. Good place for sheep, maybe." He affected an exaggerated shiver. "Too cold for old Tjapu, though."

"And too uncultured for me." Turning, Oelefse extended an open hand. Wordlessly, Cody passed him the golden kazoo. The spider-silky net and his friend's bull-roarer had been vaporized along with the bunyip. "I need a slice of good torte, with lots of chocolate, and a decent cup of cappuccino."

"Might as well look for that in another dimension, mate." Chuckling to himself, Kuwarra turned back to the two younger members of the quartet that had just saved the world—or a significant segment of it, anyway. "How about you blokes? What you want now? Go back to your teaching, I guess."

Standing on the steep flank of the green mountain, enveloped by mist and rain forest, Cody's gaze met that of his wife in a long, contemplative stare. When he finally responded to Kuwarra's query, he knew he was doing so for the both of them.

"If you don't mind, I think Kelli and I would like to learn a little more about this Society you and Oelefse belong to. It does dovetail somewhat with our work, you know."

"And maybe," Kelli added hesitantly as she clung to her husband, "sometime in the future, if conditions were right and we absorbed the necessary precepts, we could even join? Just for reasons of self-defense, of course."

"Of course." Tjapu Kuwarra's expression turned uncharacteristically solemn. "The Interlopers are ever active, and always hungry. They have always been with us, holding mankind back, impeding our progress, feeding off our misery and despair. It is the job of those of us who belong to the Society to do our best to see that they starve." Extending his hands, he took one of Kelli's and one of Cody's in each of his. His long fingers grasped theirs powerfully, his firm grip belying his age. Deeply felt emotion seemed to flow from the old man into them, raising their spirits and warming their souls. "The help of those who have learned to perceive is always welcome."

"Good." Wincing suddenly, Kelli reached down to grab at her stomach. Cody reacted with alarm.

"What, what is it? Something else the matter?"

"Yeah." As she turned to look up at him, her grimace was replaced by a smile, radiant and gloriously free of the multiple torments from which she had suffered for far too many weeks. "It's strange, but for the first time since I can remember, I think I'm actually hungry. My stomach's so empty it's growling."

"That's okay," her relieved husband managed to reply, "so long as you're not feeling blue."